Dubai Wives

A Novel

Zvezdana Rashkovich

authorHOUSE®

AuthorHouse™
1663 Liberty Drive
Bloomington, IN 47403
www.authorhouse.com
Phone: 1-800-839-8640

First published by AuthorHouse   1/14/2011

ISBN: 978-1-4567-7232-1 (sc)

Printed in the United States of America

Chapter 1

Jewel

*I*magine *a world of superfluous wealth and extravagance. Then imagine a sun-drenched, glittering city in the middle of the desert. Visualize towering skyscrapers, golden beaches, rolling sand dunes.*

Here, many say, everything is possible.

It is a world of clashes, of contrasts. Incredible wealth and beauty coexist with unexpected poverty and heart wrenching wickedness. Like the elusive, luminous pearl, this world too has to be pried open to reveal itself. Graceful palm trees cast their shadows over wide, serene streets. Lush foliage spills into the neighborhoods in a tumble of lively colors.

Spectacular palaces hide within, surrounded by their flawlessly landscaped gardens, shining domes and dancing fountains. Possessively tucked away and watched over by grim security guards, their abundance is obvious. They lurk behind high walls and ornately engraved iron gates.

These walls are necessary because they covetously guard their occupants'
secrets.

******

Jewel Al Gaafari lived in one such palace. The white and gold mansion overlooked the sea, nestled cozily in a quiet back road.

Here she reigned supreme. She was the queen of this castle. Jewel loved the mansion. Designed for a true Arabian princess, she thought sarcastically. This morning she woke up early, with a familiar, unsettling feeling weighing like a lead cloak over her shoulders. Her husband Jassim was not in bed next to her. He had not come home last night.

Jewel looked quizzically into the ornate mirror hanging above her dresser. A shadow passed over her impassive face, a flash of anger. Then just as quickly, it was gone. Leaning forward she examined her makeup, checking for something she might have missed. The black eyeliner formed a perfect line, due to many years of practice. Her powdered skin looked fresh, almost dewy, belying her age. Perfect, arched eyebrows furrowed in displeasure. Today was going to be a long day. She stepped back into her dressing room, pulling down a long, black Abaya from a rack overflowing with dozens of them. This one was new. She admired the feel of the silky material between her fingers, the elegant cut, and the sudden burst of light reflecting off the Swarovski crystals. They made her think of the black desert sky, dusted with stars. Her eyes fell on Jassim's white *Gotra* thrown carelessly across a chair, the brilliant white of his *kandoora*; a startling contrast to the black of her *Abaya*. Jassim had changed his head cover and long traditional robe in a hurry last night. He must have been preoccupied with other matters; he could hardly wait to get dressed. She knew he was with that dancer, the Romanian girl. This affair had gone on longer than his previous conquests, and Jewel was losing her patience. All of a sudden, she felt anger well up in her chest. He needed to end it…if he does not do it soon; she will find a way to put a stop to it herself.

Jewel slipped the *Abaya* on, snapped the small buttons securely, and stepped into her favorite sandals. Shaking her head at how much the world had changed, and how much the garment had evolved since her youth she snapped the sandal clasps into place. The first time she had tried wearing an *Abaya*, when she was fifteen, her stepmother had laid it on the bed, waiting for Jewel's response.

"What do you think?" she had asked. She was a somber woman, not prone to expressing her emotions, and stood there with arms on her hips, waiting. A yelp of surprise had escaped the young, bright eyed Jewel, and she had put the ladylike garment on, giggling, twirling, excited that she was finally a grown up. Since that day, the *Abaya* had been her faithful companion, welcome on every venture out of the house. Quickly she had learnt that in her world, a woman's status was clear from the *Abaya* and the *Sheila*, she wore, and additionally by the decadent amount of expensive traditional perfume, the *Oud*, she used. Half Emirati half American Jewel felt at home with her Arab heritage. She went back to her closet, this time opening the chest of drawers and pulling out a long piece of cool, black silk...a veil.

The *Sheila* covered Jewel's luxuriant and lovingly tended to hair, shiny from years of dedicated oiling and brushing. Usually, she wore her waist long, light brown hair coiffed into a large bun and kept in place by elaborate hair clips. An image of Jassim flickered in her mind, the way he had loosened her hair, the times he had stared at it in awe, and twirled a lock in his fingers. Irritably, she twisted the mass of curls onto the back of her head and searched for a clip in the drawer. She found a perfect match, and clipped it firmly on.

The early, translucent sunlight streamed in through the windows, sweeping across the room, bathing it in soft warmth. Her maid Viola, had brought in the tea, and Jewel took a satisfying sip. She walked to the window, cradling the cup in her hands, took in the blue vista in front of her, as always in wonder at the majesty of the sea. She thought of Jassim.

She could still recall every detail of the day he had told her about her best friend Mozza. The day he had confessed. The day he had murdered her just as if he had cut out her heart and pulled it out of her writhing body. The pain he had caused with his previous infidelities paled in comparison. It had been a few days after one of his uncles died. Wracked by illogical guilt for quarrelling with the gravely ill old man before his death, Jassim had turned to her for comfort...for absolution.

"So sorry... *Allah yerhamu*," she had said...may Allah have mercy on him. Jassim was sprawled on the bed in his *Kandoora*, a hand thrown over his somber face. He appeared to have been crying. In spite of his infidelities, his arrogance, she felt sorry for him. "How was the funeral?" she had asked, because according to local custom women did not go to the cemetery, but stayed behind mourning at home.

"Hard," was all he said. She stroked his hair, sympathetically. He removed his hand and looked at her. Their eyes met. Jewel felt the familiar pull, his magnetism in her blood, as it started to swirl, to swell softly in her veins. The swirling, fiery russet in his eyes never ceased to work its magic. There was something else in his eyes today. She looked closely. "What is it Jassim, are you all right?"

Could it really be? Was she imagining it? A flicker of guilt in his deep set eyes, a promise of an apology.

"Jewel, I want to tell you something," his voice scraped across her skin. She looked down at her hands and the small henna flowers and dots zigzagging across her palms and fingers. They trembled. *No do not tell me, stop.*

"Once when we had a fight," he paused, "I went to see Mozza." Looking uncomfortable, yet for reasons she never could understand, he pressed on. "I wanted to ask her advice...I thought she could talk to you about us."

Jewel pulled away from him...waiting. Jassim kept his red-rimmed eyes on hers, but hesitated, almost retreated, "I don't know how or why, but something happened between us that day." There was no need to spell it out. She knew what they had done.

Jewel had heard others speak of a moment in their lives when their entire worlds had changed irreversibly. She knew this one was hers. Her childhood friend had betrayed her more that Jassim ever could. The confession had left Jewel paralyzed, unable to draw a full breath, repulsed at the slightest thought of Jassim and Mozza together. She had been unable to eat or sleep, skulking around the house likes a deranged woman while her insides burned a raging, continuous fire. It had been months since she had seen her best friend. Mozza's odd, guilty behavior, the frequent trips outside the country, made sense.

In those torturous days and nights, Jewel had metamorphosed into someone else. The fire that had blazed before, currently only smoldered. The children were Jewel's whole life now, they were the reason she stayed on, the reason she got up in the morning, dressed, and attended to her duties. The reason she started her own business. She wanted to congratulate herself for being strong, patient and for putting up with the degradation that Jassim had caused to her sense of worth.

That unpleasant sense that she needed to do something, that she had to deal with something, fluttered in her stomach, making her ill. She wrestled with an ongoing feeling of dread, waking up terrified in the middle of the night, sometimes feeling as if she was going insane.

In the back of her tormented psyche, which she kept concealed from all but herself, when all had been said and done, she knew who she was. What she had averted her eyes from in order to live this life, to wear the expensive jewelry she was wearing…to socialize with a certain privileged group of people, to sail on that forty-foot yacht. She was a spineless, feeble woman who had settled for less, who shared his bed even after she knew it all. Maybe she did so out of fear, out of denial, but the truth remained, she had sold herself out.

Jewel carried that certainty around with her. She tried to ignore it, but it gnawed at her daily, like a vicious, deadly cancer. The uncomfortable truth was that she was totally and hopelessly in love with her arrogant, lying, adulterous husband.

She picked up the veil and wound it effortlessly around her face and hair, creating a dramatic looking headdress. Her green eyes, outlined in thick black eyeliner, stared back from the mirror defiantly. She took a deep breath. Now, she was ready.

******

Jewel stepped out into another searing, humid day, greeted her driver Raj, and settled into the back seat of the pleasantly smelling car. She inhaled deeply, the scent of Magnolia brought back loving memories of her mother.

Surreptitiously, as she did every day, she glanced at the driver's profile. He was new. He drove well, kept to the speed limit, and had a pleasant disposition with the children. Sometimes she even looked forward to their trips to the supermarket or the tailor. With Raj, she did not feel alone on these mundane errands. She noticed his strong jaw line, black hair curling at the nape of his neck, and muscular hands on the wheel. She really should not be checking her Indian driver out. Flustered, she fumbled for her phone. She needed to call her housekeeper. Jewel had been busy sending the kids off to school this morning, and forgot to discuss the evening plans.

Jassim was having a dinner party for some friends at the house tonight, and she had planned it to perfection. She doubted that Jassim would appreciate her efforts.

"The catering company is arriving at noon and you can coordinate with them. They will deliver the flowers sometime before two pm. What else…" She paused, distracted by the vivid slip of blue in the distance, the sea.

"Umm, I'm sure you will do fine until I return this afternoon, I should be home by three, in time to have lunch with the children." Then in a softer tone, she thanked her, "*Shukran* Amnah."

5

Jewel closed her diamond-encrusted Vertu mobile phone and sighed. The wiry energetic Ethiopian handled most of the intricacies of their huge household. Jewel had started delegating more of her duties to Amnah. The children adored the kind and loyal housekeeper, making her indispensible to the family.

It was liberating not to have to worry about all the dozens of humdrum details of running a twelve-bedroom mansion and monitoring her full time staff of fifteen whose cultural and religious diversity made things even more complicated. There were South African nannies, Filipino maids, Indian drivers, Egyptian cooks, Afghani gardeners, Nigerian and Emirati security guards.

Sometimes she thought of those Victorian era movies of European courts and all that intrigue that went on reminded Jewel of theirs. Brewing like a bowl of fermenting yeast, their household was constantly riddled with scheming, drama, jealousy, and catfights among the housemaids, drivers, cooks, and everyone else.

She looked out of the window again, fascinated by the heat reflecting off the roads, like a mirage. She decided to ignore Jassim and the Romanian girl at this time. She wished her cousin Najla had never seen them on that plane to Bangkok. Jewel had kept Najla's awkward revelation to herself. After the opening of her new boutique, she will have more time to deal with it.

They had passed the *Madinat Jumeirah*, a sprawling indoor Arabic style market, slowing down at the intersection. There was an accident. Jewel settled in for a long wait, glancing into the rearview mirror, catching the driver staring at her again. She ignored him.

There it was…that haunting, vague feeling of foreboding once again. She had always been highly sensitized to some invisible undercurrent, one only she seemed to feel. If only she knew what these messages of the subconscious meant…instead, she was left frustrated, unable to decipher them.

Outside the tinted window of her new Bentley, swaying tall palms, and newly planted flowers bordered the road. The car had been a gift from Jassim. He had led her outside to the driveway a few months ago, surprising her in his typical generous manner.

Seeing the new car, she had been so happy, thinking that at last he will allow her to drive on her own, for whenever she had asked for her own car, Jassim had discouraged her.

"Jewel you are aware it is not appropriate for a woman like you to drive herself. My position in the Emirate would not allow it," he explained in his annoyingly sensible way. She had heard this line many times, before, *his* position, *his* family, *his* honor, *his* company.

"My beloved, *habibti,* why do you want to drive when you can be comfortable," he took a deep drag from his cigarette, and exhaled, "don't you know the traffic in this crazy city?" His eyes did not waver away from her face as he went on confidently, self assuredly, as usual. It infuriated her that he felt no regret, no hesitation about squashing her hopes.

"No, it is much better, more decent for you to have a driver and not worry about such things." This had been his final verdict about her driving.

"*Zein*, all right," she had said, expressionless. "Thank you for the car, it's really nice."

He had grinned and changed the subject to avoid further arguing. She did not want to argue either. She had decided years ago that it did not make any difference whether she complained or not. She had kept quiet, biding her time.

Jassim came from a powerful, prominent, and wealthy family involved in real estate, hospitality, and luxury retail. They socialized with other distinguished families of the region. They married into and from those families. They took their children on vacations in dream villas on the French Riviera, Vienna, and Los Angeles. They owned luxury apartments in London, Cairo, and Kuala Lumpur. They learnt to ski in St. Moritz and Aspen. The pampered, easily bored family island hopped all over the Mediterranean in their hundred-foot yachts, mingled with celebrities from a dozen countries and they 'shopped until they dropped'. In other words, they were the crème-de-la-crème of society. Good-looking, rich and educated, they had the best money could buy and expected the best from life. Jassim and his family had no niggling self-doubts of their entitlement from life. They just were, the *Gaafari.*

Roused from her thoughts by the approaching view of the Palm, Jewel looked eagerly out at the 'Palm Jumeirah' the biggest residential manmade island in the world, built in the shape of a palm tree.

Jewel felt pride rise in her...how incredible her country was. How strong and proud her people were. They had done amazing, impossible things in a generation. Those generations who roamed the desert confidently, the valiant and hospitable Bedouin.

She was anxious for the drive to end. She fiddled with her *Abaya* and *Sheila*, which kept slipping off her smooth hair. One more look at the gold plated compact mirror to ensure her make-up was perfect. Satisfied, she stepped out as Raj opened the door. She could feel his downcast eyes on her. Immediately, a clammy layer of moisture soaked her body and face, the D&G sunglasses fogged up so that she could barely see her way into the huge foyer of the building.

"Raj wait for me in the drivers' room, I should be done in a few hours," she told him over her shoulder, speaking quickly and a breathlessly...eager to get out of the heat.

Chapter 2

Liliana

*S*omewhere from the back roads of *Deira,* exotic Arabic music wafted into the warm night. A dismal haze clung heavily above the downtown. The rundown hotel building seemed to rise out of a thick cloud.

Inside the building the beat of drums and cymbals was getting faster, more frenzied, climbing to a feverish climax. Complete darkness enveloped the stage with only a single candle gracing each table, casting ghoulish shadows over the occupants. The air in the crowded nightclub was thick with the smoke of dozens of cigars and cigarettes, the cloying sweet smell of *shisha* the most prevalent. That ever-popular water pipe, that both men and women had puffed on for centuries in the Middle East.

The aroma of apple, strawberry, vanilla, and mint flavored tobacco permeated the space. The more adventurous opted for watermelon, caramel; mocha…the list was endless. Such was the Middle East's love story with the beloved Shisha that these days a special menu existed which presented previously unheard of exotic flavors. More than the welcome smell of smoke and *shisha,* another, more animalistic, intensely primal scent persisted…the scent of lust.

Abruptly the music stopped. The interior of a gaudily decorated and furnished interior emerged from the darkness. Slowly, a ceiling covered in blinking lights appeared above the spectators and in their weak glow; they were able to see a female form.

The audience held its breath in anticipation. There, on a small-elevated podium, lit by the blush of red spotlights, a woman kneeled, her head bowed. A curtain of long, jet-black hair hid her face. She stayed motionless for a torturous moment, as if teasing the impatient oglers, until the stirring sound of music begun once again. Theatrically choreographed smoke started to rise slowly from the floor, obscuring the woman slightly, adding to her allure.

Middle-aged men watched her, intently. They sat at tables of two or four, in the dim interior of the nightclub. Some were accompanied by their girlfriends or mistresses, a pathetic crowd of hangers on…multicultural in appearance but identical in nature. Mostly though, the men came alone or with others who wanted the same. Their faces eager, some noticeably excited, not taking their eyes of the still shape, they waited in hope of more pleasures. For watching Liliana dance was undeniably a pleasure for any man, and many women.

The young woman started to move, rising slowly from the fog…like a siren would from the froth of the sea, or a gypsy from the mist of the woods. Her clothing made a soft tinkling noise. Still, she moved slowly, effortlessly, until the atmosphere in the room seemed ready to explode from this curious affliction.

. The red bejeweled bustier swayed generously, to the beat, heavy with the weight of her tanned breasts. Her voluptuous hips, minimally covered with a red skirt of the same design, swung back and forth in a sensuous circle, the silver tassels on the hem barely skimming her golden thighs. They could see her face now, enraptured by the music, eyes closed. The shimmering hoop earrings she wore, emitted minute sparkles onto her skin, causing it to shine luminously. A sharp intake of breath arose from the crowd. They could not take their eyes of her angelic face. She was young, only twenty-five. Exquisitely sculpted cheekbones, nose, and mouth, adorned her flawless face. Her eyes…now open, were an impossible violet blue. Heavily lined with kohl and startlingly catlike they stared into space defiantly.

Soulful music started to play next. Skillfully, the woman begun to shimmy her hips, then raised her milky arms above her slightly tilted head, and gracefully twirled them in a fluid circle. She turned, one, two... then tiptoed on her toes across the stage...keeping her eyes focused on the spectators, a smile playing on her lips. As she swung her hair from side to side, a small, delicately tattooed butterfly on her left shoulder peeked timidly at the crowded room. Its wings were widespread, poised to take off it seemed...to escape the drunk and lusty looks that welcomed it nightly.

Finally, the music stopped. Liliana spun around wildly, coming to an abrupt, perfectly choreographed stop, and then bowed, a sincere smile on her flushed face.

Some of the younger men whistled and cheered loudly, the older ones, suddenly embarrassed by their own evident intensity, clapped feebly. Their girlfriends were either too drunk or simply did not care, as long as it was not them up there every night, having to ward of the advances of an inexhaustible source of red blooded men. A few wives however, cast envious looks her way, and shot warning ones at their husbands. Liliana walked off the stage gracefully, politely nodding at the appreciative applause, before heading to her changing room, followed by the club security guard, Habib.

"Nice show Lila," Habib called her by her childhood nickname, reserved for those closest to her. Liliana looked up at the kindly giant. He was a massive man, with bulging biceps that strained against its sleeves. Sinewy veins climbed up his thick neck, and she often wondered whether his tightly buttoned collar choked him. His shirt buttons threatened to burst at the chest. The olive skinned face gracing this aggressive body perplexed in its furthermost opposite. Smooth skin, slim nose, a benevolent look in the small, close set eyes, seemed as if placed there by mistake from the body of some studious professor.

"You must be tired, right?" he put his arm around her shoulder protectively as he escorted her back to the changing room. "Mr.Iliya is too much bad. Sometimes I want to punch his face."

"Thank you Habib, you are always kind to me," she smiled sadly. He loved her accent...the almost imperceptible lilt in sound, right at the last syllable.

"Some of the stupid men were drunk tonight and were make so many noises," he said in his best attempt at English. "I have to take one fat one, out...kick him out." He was angry, menacing.

"Don't be mad, Habib, they are here for fun...it doesn't bother me,"

Liliana was lying and both of them knew it. She had been dancing at 'The Gypsy' nightclub for almost two years and spent a lot of her time there with Habib. He had comforted her when she cried sometimes after the show, when men accosted her, with lewd propositions and more.

Habib told her stories about the men who visited the club, of what he had seen and heard in his years here, and it revolted her. Hordes of men frequenting the 'Gypsy' went to great trouble to visit this playground for grown men, making up endlessly creative reasons for spending any amount of time in Dubai.

After all, they had told Habib in a drunken surge of intimacy; where else could a man walk into a nightclub or bar and be instantly surrounded by ravishing women from all ethnic backgrounds. Where else could a man lounge in inconceivable opulence and at the same time feast his eyes on a procession of spectacular women from over a hundred countries? Liliana knew that a few honest souls came for knowledge and understanding. Thousands came for all the wrong reasons. Habib had listened to these slurred conversations, spoken in the late hours, in the dimness of the club, the calculating, and the planning they thought no one would hear.

Liliana listened to Habib's stories carefully. Over the years, she learned enough from him to know that thousands came to the city with the promise of easy get -rich-quick schemes, shady investment deals, and expectations of an 'erotic' fantasyland. Just as many were disappointed when these alluded to promises failed to materialize, and regretted their decision of coming here for the rest of their lives. Wishing they had not… And cursed the city, for making them trust her as they would a beautiful, deceitful woman.

******

When she was a little girl growing up in Romania, Liliana dreamt of being a famous dancer. Her parents were common, hard-working, and practical people. Her father was a gas station manager and her mother a supermarket sales clerk. Their life was uneventful, their home tidy and peaceful. Nothing in their previous lives had prepared them for the excitement and the drama of Liliana for she was a passionate and headstrong child.

When she was three, Liliana's mom took her to ballet and gymnastics lessons at the Youth Academy in Bucharest. Straight away, her coaches realized that she was gifted and incredibly determined. She had practiced four days a week at first, and by the time she was in high school, she had competed in many national gymnastics championships and won one silver, and two bronze medals. She was well on her way to the European semi-finals and a celebrity in her hometown. She was particularly popular with the boys. Liliana's dreams vanished forever when she broke her ankle while doing a double somersault on the balancing beam.

Ten years later, her dreams forgotten, Liliana walked into the dressing room of the sleazy hotel. The room was small and dark, hidden away at the back of the club. Its shabby interior, lit only by spotlights revealed a hodge-podge of designs. Five girls shared this space...for changing... sleeping...eating and everything in between. One of them lay huddled on a low couch, a disheveled knot of long hair, thin limbs, and streaky make-up. She was sobbing loudly, tears and saliva spilling and drenching the pink embroidered cushion that she cradled.

Liliana hurried to the girls' side and knelt on the floor, scooping her in her arms, "Sheri...Sheri...what happened?" The room was dim, with a single shaded lamp in the corner casting its modest glow onto the girl's face. Sheri was one of the newer girls and extremely young. She was Thai and petite, with a fragile face and a childish nature.

Dread rose in Liliana. She looked at Habib, nodding at him to bring her the tissue box from the console. She used the tissues liberally, wiping Sheri's face and the layered globs of streaming makeup. All this time she stroked the long black hair and tried to hush the gut-wrenching sobs.

Habib stood by the girls' side wordlessly...a giant with a heart of gold and the disposition of a child. He stared at the two girls, immobilized by intense feelings, rooted in the spot with a grimace on his face. Liliana thought it looked like he was grinning, when in fact she knew he was not.

Pain stamped itself on his face for the drama unfolding in front of him, and his inability to do anything about it, except smash something frustrated him. He looked around desperately, but knew he would be in trouble for breaking anything at all inside the room.

"Lila," he tried to speak, "I will wait outside," he managed feebly and rushed out. In the narrow hall was an assortment of unused club paranphelia, old plastic chairs, used props, costume hangers, cases of empty liquor bottles...out of commission band gear...waiting to be somehow disposed of.

Liliana followed him, and watched as Habib grabbed the gear and methodically started to throw it at the wall, huffing and sweating in the process. She stayed, watching, unafraid of this outburst of rage. She knew that he needed to vent his anger and this was the only way he knew how.

After a few minutes of wild throwing and hushed swearing he stopped. In a daze, he looked at the terrible mess in front of him. Words escaped through his clenched teeth, "For sure I'm going to get in trouble with Mr. Iliya for this right?"

Liliana smiled and nodded. She stroked his repentant face, "don't worry. I will explain it to him, just put it all back the best you can ok?" She left him to it and hurried back to the room.

Liliana listened to the sobs, waiting patiently until the girl calmed down enough to talk. "Did someone do something to you, Sheri?" Liliana handed her another tissue during a brief lull in crying. This time the girl blew her nose and wiped the tears with no help. Sniffling, she finally spoke in a small voice more befitting a little girl. "Mr. Iliya told me I had to sit with that man...the businessman, remember him?" Sheri slurred a lethargic answer in her singsong English.

Yes, Liliana remembered that fat sadistic *porcule*, that lecherous pig, because on his previous visit to Dubai, he had almost raped her in this same room. Thankfully Habib was never far and had grabbed the sweaty, greasy man by the collar and flung him outside the room. Mr. Iliya was not pleased because the businessman happened to be extravagantly wealthy and well connected.

"When I refuse to go with him to his hotel he get angry…he start to swear at me and slap me," her English became garbled, her words entwined with sobs and whimpers. Leaning closer Liliana noticed red welts on the girls' thin wrists. She got up and turned the overhead light on...and drew her breath in, startled by the previously unseen clues of a battered face.

Holding her tears, at these undeniable signs of abuse, Liliana swallowed hard and forced herself to look for the first aid kit. She grabbed it from the overflowing drawers. Quickly she got a bottle of water out of the fridge and sat next to Sheri. She offered her a sip. Words lodged in her throat.

So many times Liliana had wanted to leave Dubai because of the wrong she witnessed at the club. Yet here she was going into a third year in this cesspit of dishonesty and immorality. She was not sure what it was that she was lingering for, waiting for. She could not help the girls who arrived daily to the promised city, lured by promises of high salaries and perpetual fun in the sun. They came wide-eyed and star struck, with assurances of modeling jobs, the possibility of rich husbands. Incidences of suicides due to disillusionment were common and heartbreaking, for the pure, desperate folly of those who committed them.

Going back to Romania was not an option for Liliana, not yet. She could not face her parents and relatives without first achieving something. Then there was Jassim to consider. Liliana felt her pulse accelerate, but then frowned. She turned to Sheri.

"Sheri, listen you have to tell Mr. Iliya that you will not accept this treatment. Do you hear me, if you keep quiet and keep it to yourself that pig will continue to abuse you each time he happens to be in town?"

Liliana dabbed the antibacterial cream on Sheri's wrists and face in case of infection from the barbaric man. The yellow dots in her violet eyes glinted in outrage. There was not much she could give her other than a couple of extra strength panadols and maybe a shot of vodka to calm her nerves. "Actually I will have one as well," she said as she got two small glasses and the half-empty bottle of Russian vodka Mr. Iliya had brought from his last trip to Moscow.

"Do you really want to work here Sheri," Liliana handed the girl a glass, "maybe this is not the job for you," she smiled at the young girl who was calmer, and sipping her vodka daintily. "This is a hard life my dear," she felt an intense compassion for the young girl.

Sheri looked at Liliana with a wide childlike gaze, eagerly paying attention to Liliana's words.

"Things happen to girls when they are in this kind of work, sometimes good things, but also bad things Sheri," Liliana's face clouded. "You have got to toughen up and take care of yourself, or you could get hurt." Sheri continued to stare at her with clouded eyes. Liliana doubted that the young girl realized how much trouble she could get from working in a nightclub, in any city in the world. She knew Sheri was a novice at this job, and terribly innocent. It broke her heart. Sheri looked funny sipping the vodka. Like a kid.

Liliana laughed. "This is how you drink it, you silly." She titled her head back and gulped the hot liquid in one go. It burnt her throat and she coughed slightly. Right away, she felt warm and relaxed. "This Russian vodka is a powerful one." She winked at Sheri and indicated for her to do the same. Closing her eyes and wrinkling her nose, the girl finally gulped it, choking, and spluttering in the process.

"Drinking vodka this strong is a skill that takes years to acquire my little one." Liliana laughed again heartily and went to find Habib and her cigarettes. She found him in the hall, muttering angrily to himself in Arabic, and repentantly sorting the mess, which he had created. He looked comical with his huge body bent over and his clothes groaning to stay on the colossal muscles…an exasperated look on his face.

He looked like a big boy ordered to clean the mess in his room. Liliana could not suppress an escaping giggle. The entire terrible incident played like a scene from a movie, maybe one of those cheap Egyptian or Hindi larger-than-life dramas.

She could see the mockery in the situation, all the elements of a thriller…the shady boss, the attractive but helpless dancer, and the lovable, giant protector. At the moment, their protector was in need of comforting. Liliana patted him on the back sympathetically and he grunted, ashamed at what he had done. "Habib, it's okay, she will be fine, she needs to sleep, and I will talk to Iliya," she smiled affectionately at his worried expression. "Don't worry my friend." She knew how much he cared about the girls at the club.

Habib clenched his fists, "Believe me Lila, you are like my sister," he looked at her with tenderness in his eyes. "I want to punish these sons of dogs for doing this to her, to all of you," she heard his teeth grind together. "I don't know how to help you."

Liliana smiled at this dear man. What was he doing working as a bouncer in this horrible place? What were any of them doing here? Both of them were unsuited for this world, for these kinds of men.

Unfortunately, those men were many and often Habib felt powerless in the face of so much malevolence.

Chapter 3

Tara

Tara and Dr.Ghassan embraced silently, in a dim corner of his office. She leaned against the desk as he touched her face, slowly. A ray of sunset sneaked in through the curtains, peeping in at the hidden couple like a curious child, and sliding over her features, for just an instant. Then it was gone, and they were safe in the hushed, moist warmth of the room.

Whenever he saw her, he was in awe of her mocha colored skin, the golden aura that emanated from it when exposed to the subtle, concealed light in his office.

He removed her *Hijab*, the long piece of cloth that wound around her head, like a gift, gradually, deferentially. He was always patient, relishing these moments when she gave herself over…grateful that she allowed him to unveil her, piece by piece. The Hijab came off and her wiry black hair sprung loose. She shook it out and looked into his eyes. She was offering herself to him, and he realized the solemnity of the act. He had felt this way each time they have been together these past months.

The first time was unavoidable, both could not deny the pull, the attraction that threatened to consume them. After each appointment, Ghassan had felt physically drained, unable to receive his next patient until he had calmed down, regained control of his body. Thoughts of eternal damnation passed through his head, and he cringed at first, terrified. Slowly, stealthily, this feeling had evaporated into thin air. Suddenly nothing seemed more important than being with her, nothing more crucial to his survival.

Now as she unbuttoned his shirt, he closed his eyes and waited for more, eagerly...trembling as a teenager would on a first date.

They were the same height, the male, and female, both voluptuously built and strong. The man was older, silver grey strands visible in his thick hair, in his neatly trimmed moustache. He had the look of someone distinguished, respectable, exactly as a psychiatrist should. Her curls tickled his bare chest and he sighed. He pulled her closer into him. The woman submitted, deeply, trustingly. She seemed virginal and pure. He felt flattered that she had chosen him with whom to share her ultimate surrender.

For months, Tara had suffered from guilt, wrestled with her faith and her conscience. Then on one of those exceptional days in Dubai when rain hammered down on the city, she arrived into his office, crying, and helpless. His feelings overcame him, his professional code of conduct flung aside in order to soothe her. He had held her hands in his for a long time while she cried and talked. He listened, trying to stop the voracious feelings of his dishonest heart.

While she cried, his eyes had roamed over her body, the long skirt skimming the tips of her sensible flat shoes, over the long sleeved blouse, still slightly damp from the rain; clinging against the straining buttons on her chest. He panicked, pulled his hands out of hers, worried that he would not be able to control himself. She had looked up at him confused, with those moist brown eyes, eyelashes clumped together and eyeliner smeared on her cheeks. She looked like a mystical being.

His eyes drifted to a small spot of exposed flesh where her *Hijab* had slipped aside. He focused his eyes on a golden sliver of brown skin, a pulsating vein in her neck, both of which stroked his senses. He could not take his eyes of that tantalizing, throbbing, vein. Her eyes met his and they stared at each other speechlessly, riveted. He could not identify which one of them moved first. It did not matter because they were together that day…for the first time.

Many times since, they had met in his office, where behind the locked door in the deserted clinic they found relief for their loneliness. They also found passion.

He pulled her closer and kissed her mouth. Tara lifted her face up to him, closed her eyes. She savored it and smiled. She did not dwell on the reasons that had brought him into her life, into her heart, or the reasons why she had given him her previously sacrosanct body.

Oh yes, she fought him in the beginning. Even stopped coming to the therapy sessions for a couple of months. However, he was always close, like little paper cuts that throbbed hotly, even though invisible to the eye. He was there, enticing, coaxing in every drop of water as she watched it drain from the bath, in the glance at a passersby silver hair, lurking in all the corners, every nook and cranny. There was no escaping this ultimate test.

"Are you sure no one will disturb us today?" she continued to undress as she spoke, and as he kept his eyes on her unwaveringly, she unbuttoned the modest long sleeved white shirt, let the cool silk garment slide to the floor, and then slipped out of her demure floor length skirt. Then, Tara removed her silk slip. A night lamp cast a devilish glow over her body. Soon she stood in front of him… unashamed, smiling confidently, invitingly.

He had pulled the heavy brown curtains tightly closed and personally locked all the doors into the clinic. They were safe here.

"I only have forty minutes…the girls' ballet lesson finishes at six." She whispered, suddenly shy, aware of her bareness.

"Don't worry, you will be there on time," there was an urgency in his barely audible voice as he approached her, as he hugged her. Tara pushed Qays and her girls out of her mind. She closed her eyes and thought of nothing else but these incessant waves of joy sweeping over her unfaithful, sinning body.

******

At home the next morning Tara tripped, almost falling in her rush to get out the door. "Miriam, Aisha, let's go… now!"

The twins' ballet and gymnastics outfits were scattered over the floor in the hallway. She looked at the jumble of little girls' belongings, breathing in deeply, and stubbornly refusing to let herself get angry.

"Every morning there is a mad rush and we are late. I'm going to be stuck in traffic, then I will not find parking space, and then…" she fumed under her breath, all the time picking up the pink, purple, and white leotards, tights, and tutus off the floor.

Flustered because of her energetic sweep through the house, she was unaware of two pairs of eyes following her intently. The twins were standing by the door dressed in their blue and white uniforms, little puffy sleeved blouses, pleated navy skirts, white bobby socks, and black Mary Jane shoes. Their hair was pulled back into tight ponytails and they looked clean, eager.

"Mommy, we're ready," Aisha and Miriam, said in unison. Tara turned and a grin crept on her face. She wanted to be mad at the girls but she could not. She spoilt them too darn much. Of course, they knew. Tara knew it as well.

"Okay come here you little monkeys. Give mommy a big, juicy kiss and a huge bear hug and let's go!" she smiled at her girls and they ran into her open arms, giggling, hugging, and covering their mom's face with those 'juicy' kisses. Mommy was a big softie, they knew it, and they knew that this bad mood usually disappeared as soon as they gave her their 'puppy look'. This, of course was a look that had the power to melt the toughest mom into puddles of goo. They had that look fine tuned to perfection.

Tara and the girls made it to school on time after all. She was pleasantly bewildered that traffic on the legendarily congested Sheikh Zayed Road was moving along nicely this morning.

She hurried with the girls down into the school and walked them to their class. The morning was sunny as usual, gearing up to be hot later in the day. The building was pleasantly cool though, and Tara marveled once again at the school facilities. They were lucky to have the girls in this private school. It was impeccably clean and boasted an Olympic size pool, state of the art computers, and a well-stocked library, and highly qualified American staff.

The twins waved a hasty *"Bye Mommy"* and immediately became engrossed with the other children. Tara sighed. She missed her babies while they attended school, but became overwhelmed by their intense personalities once they were at home.

On her way out, she ran into a couple of hyperactive moms and chatted dutifully, parents usually took a few minutes to catch up before leaving the school each morning. 'International day' was coming up at the school and she had agreed to be on the organizing committee.

"So Tara, did you manage to get all the items on your list?" teased a chubby, new to the school mother.

"We were talking about how much you have taken on, it isn't fair to you," a petite mom from New York, stood alert on hearing this. This was the first time Tara heard of such concern for her.

"Listen guys its fine, really." Tara smiled modestly, "plus all of you have tons to do as well."

A couple of moms passing by started another topic and thankfully, Tara was able to escape. Dozens of little issues needed her attention in the coming days and she dreaded them all. There was a meeting with the school administration and other committee moms. In addition, it was Tara's duty to double check about the rental tables for the displays and the decorations.

She had to collect banners, flags, and any other items from the donating parents. There was a list of articles, and it was a yard long, which she had to check on. Cowboy hats and Native American headdress, mini replicas of the Statue of Liberty, maps of United States; someone even had a carved bronze eagle for them to use. Her American mom's group had collected hundreds of small flags for each student to receive as a token.

Tara had a grand, ambitious vision of her culinary contribution to the popular school event...she was going to bake three pies, apple, pumpkin and pecan, make two dozen candy apples, a tray of rice crispies, and a colossal bag of caramel popcorn.

She contemplated baking some cupcakes and having Miriam and Aisha spend an afternoon frosting them with red, white, and blue icing for fun...

However, as the day approached she was starting to have some serious doubts about her own abilities. It was hot and she was tired...the list of 'things to do' was getting longer by the day and the other moms were becoming irritating with their annoying boundless energy and their daily changes and constant additions to their original plan.

"Hey, Tara...wait up," a short woman hurried towards her, waving her arms gleefully.

"*Salam Alaikum*"...Tara greeted politely.

"How are you?" the woman spoke in short staccato sentences, "Good... yes," she answered instead of Tara. "How are the costumes coming along...?" she sucked a breath in quickly. "I'm still making mine...it has been crazy busy, right?" incredibly the lively Jordanian managed to walk, talk, and gesticulate simultaneously, and with remarkable speed.

"Well, I already finished the twins' costumes... how...," rudely interrupted by the Jordanian as she waved to another mom in delight then gushed, "I will talk to you again Tara…Ok? …bye," and she was gone.

Tara had come to anticipate all kinds of quirky characters since living in Dubai. The city had its share of the good, the bad, and the nutty…this was for sure. After the initiation period into the lifestyle of Dubaians, Tara had ceased to get upset. She got into the van and joined the procession of other leaving parents. Many of the moms were heading to the gym at the various health clubs in the city. A few were getting together to have breakfast or coffee. Proponents of walking headed to the Safa Park or the Jumeirah Beach, where dozens of women attended to their morning walks industriously. Others went home to do housework and cook lunches before picking up the kids in the afternoon. She went to see her Psychiatrist, Dr.Ghassan. A guilty blush crept into her face as she remembered their last session. What would the other moms think if they knew what she did while her girls were in school or at their ballet lessons? Tara, the selfless brownie baking, costume making, devoted mom…Tara, the Hijab wearing wife of a religious man.

She drove past the park and could not help but smile at the diversity of walkers and joggers jostling on the track. A skimpily clad female walked briskly right next to a fully veiled one with the hint of a funky Adidas outfit showing under her Abaya. Hobbling Arab grandmothers and muscled fitness fanatics ran or walked next to obese, out of breath young women. Others opted for more liberating attire, some bordering perilously close to unlawful. As she waited for the traffic light to change, a group of women in an assortment of contradicting forms of dress walked across.

Her thoughts turned to the costumes. She was pleased with her effort. Miriam was going to wear the Native American outfit and Aisha, was set on being a Pilgrim. Tara had bought the material and the trims and designed the outfits herself. A local tailor on *Satwa* road had done the big job of putting them together but she did most of the details herself. The outfits looked adorable.

She joined the freeway and the hundreds of whizzing cars, undoubtedly all on their way to somewhere terribly important. In spite of her guilt, she looked forward to seeing Ghassan again this morning, last evening in her rush to pick up the girls she had forgotten to get her prescription. Qays had already left for his office, where he had started to go earlier every day. She decided not to think about him today at all. It made her sad.

"Oh, my God," Tara screamed as a huge Land cruiser drove at her aggressively, appearing out of nowhere, forcing her to evade by driving kamikaze style into the impending traffic. At the last minute, she was able to turn her car into the right lane, to escape the furiously approaching, horn-beeping drivers.

"You crazy idiot!" trembling from shock and enraged, Tara pressed her foot down on the accelerator and found herself chasing after the getaway Land Cruiser at breakneck speed. Running her white Toyota minivan into his rear end was her one thought. On the other hand, if that attempt proved unsuccessful at least she was going to wave her fist at the anonymous maniac behind the wheel.

Must be another one of those arrogant drivers who thinks rules do not apply to him, driving one hundred and forty miles per hour down Sheikh Zayed Road. Those pompously proud of the fact that they can cope with the crazy daily changing map of Dubai, the constant construction and shifting road structure. They imagine themselves a breed of 'road warriors' and behave accordingly. Driving petrifies all newcomers to Dubai.

The long-term residents will snort at these novices haughtily, and make no effort whatsoever to help them. If they happen to make a mistake while getting off the freeway by taking a wrong exit and attempt to do a u-turn, God help them. Hot, tired, hungry, and half-delusional from sitting in traffic for the past three hours these haughty Dubaians will ignore these petrified weaklings.

This might take some time, as they stand there stopping traffic behind for a mile until some poor soft hearted sod, probably new to the city like them, finally lets them in. Most will be so relieved to get out of everyone's way without getting hurt and will feel like crying with relief.

So there was Tara speeding like a demon in the traffic, when she realized that there was little hope of catching the speeding car in her slower minivan. What on earth was she doing? Tara braked, and in the process almost had another collision. She felt weak all of a sudden and had to get off the road at once. She pulled on to the emergency ramp and pushed the hazard lights on. A cold sweat covered her face and she rubbed it with her hand. Giant pliers threatened to compress her heart. She felt like she was going to pass out...

Laying her head down on to the steering wheel, she fought the queasiness, the unexplainable fear that tried to swathe her in a spiraling darkness. She felt disconnected from herself, this strange and in some way funny sight. Funny yes, here she thought she was an avenger in the style of Charles Bronson or Clint Eastwood movies. *Oh, she was going to bring the offending driver to justice was she?*

How pathetic…She thought as she sat there fighting to breathe, to stay conscious. The driver of that Land Cruiser probably had an emergency, there had to be a reason to drive like that, she told herself. *An emergency, definitely an emergency*…she repeated trying to calm the mad dashing of her heart.

Her breathing was slowing down and the rush of nausea subsiding as she talked herself through it, as Dr.Ghassan had coached her to do. The thought of him made her feel better. She had started seeing him six months ago after a particularly bad anxiety attack. Her swinging moods and unpredictable bouts of depression were making her life a living hell. As Qays withdrew from reality into another special world of his own, the world of silence, prayer, and daydreaming, Tara found herself pulled towards the man she knew would not condemn her, a man she could tell anything.

He was not shocked with her outbursts of anger or personal revelations. In fact, the more she told him the more interested he became. She struggled to behave normal in front of the girls but her relationship with Qays was seriously troubled.

Dr. Ghassan was a highly respected psychiatrist in Dubai. She had liked him from their first appointment. A calm, soft-spoken man, he had a soothing aura of self-assurance about him. Born and educated in the United States, Dr. Ghassan Ahmed was first generation Iraqi-American. A widower in his early fifties he was devoted to his practice. Tara saw him once a week at first, and then monthly. Each time she eagerly anticipated that hour spent with him. It was not as if she had sought to feel this way about him, rather it had crept up on her like a cunning thief in the night. Stunned, thrilled, and terrified by this revelation she could barely contain herself during their sessions.

Tara had wanted to tell him he was her best friend. Time spent in that clinic; was her only refuge from the hectic, intimidating world outside. Over the course of her treatment, their conversations had become more personal…warm discussions about people, life, and family. Thoughtful and kind, he always had some sensible words for her at the end of the hour.

"Tara, you must make some changes," his voice was soothing. "You have to take care of your needs, face them…otherwise the therapy will not work."

Every time she left the clinic, Tara felt like she had the potential to becoming a better and healthier person. She emerged from the hour, her head buzzing with ideas, hopeful, invigorated. She felt able to face the world again, and especially her husband, Qays.

Tara realized that she felt calmer and was able to breathe normally again. In a hurry to get away from the emergency parking spot she was in, she checked her face in the rearview mirror, appalled at her frightened eyes and somber face. Quickly she adjusted the brown headscarf, which threatened to slide off her unruly hair.

You are fine, keep positive, and think of the girls. She drove slowly, still shaken by what had happened. Today was one of those times the medication failed to cushion the impact of the world on her.

If only she had the courage to face it all…

Chapter 4

Ameera

It was a few months after the girls' parents died when they had an unexpected visitor. The three sisters had just finished their chores. Ameera, the oldest had helped Grandma Balqis with lunch, a hot *tagine,* made with a small piece of lamb on a bed of *couscous.* Samar had swept the two rooms and the courtyard, fighting the blowing wind, banging around with the frayed straw broom like a girl on a mission. Raya fed the chickens, exclaiming proudly at her discovery of five whole eggs.

"*Banat*…Girls…!" shouted grandma Balqis, fussing over the important caller. Little Raya, only six years old, hid behind Ameera's *Jelbab*, a long, loose Moroccan garment with a pointy hood. Eyes as big as saucers peeked out, sun kissed, bouncy curls bobbing with each frightened step. The three sisters stood in the middle of the dusty courtyard, their long hair fluttering madly in the hot summer wind. Raya was holding a lollipop, which the strange guest had handed her with a smile on arrival.

Strangers were rare in their village, a haphazard collection of small, rundown dwellings, clinging to each other precariously on a windy plateau in the Atlas Mountains, high above the sprawling metropolis, Marrakech. Lollipops were even rarer.

Samar, twelve, was feisty and robust. She carried proof of their Berber legacy in her almond shaped, hazel eyes. She glared at the stranger with unabashed disapproval. "This is *our* Aunt Kareema?" she scoffed and without another word walked off indignantly into the dilapidated room, which served as the girls' bedroom. Samar was wearing Ameera's handed down jeans, and Ameera noticed how they were already too small.

Ameera sighed, her younger sister had always been willful, but since *mama* and *baba* died, she had become extremely aggressive and angry at the world. Ameera's heart clutched sickeningly from sadness and despair at their situation.

All three had stopped going to school since the accident, because grandma had no money to send them, to clothe them or to buy their books. This had devastated their world even further. All relatives disappeared after the first three days of obligatory mourning, leaving them to grandma Balqis, a nervous and frightened woman.

"Girls, come over immediately and kiss your aunt…she has come from Dubai especially for you," Grandma talked quickly, ushering their guest inside their ramshackle living room. She kept asking the woman whether she was comfortable. The visitor looked out of place in their humble home. She perched on the edge of the wooden chair, picking up her long skirt off the dusty floor, clutching her glossy black bag in her lap as if afraid someone would snatch it from her. The girls watched with curiosity as the woman piled her frizzy red hair in a nest on top of her head. She proceeded to dig out a piece of paper out of the bag, and fan her face with it. Ameera marveled at the color of her hair. It was dry, like the straw they fed their two goats. She marveled even more at the rainbow of colors on the woman's fleshy face, red lipstick blue eye shadow, pink blusher…so much makeup.

Ameera approached the expensively dressed guest slowly; holding tightly onto Raya's little hand lest she too tried to take off. Grandma Balqis would be very angry if that happened.

"Come here child…come," their aunt had a deep gravelly voice. It made Ameera uneasy. Raya hid behind her sister.

The older girl shook Aunt Kareema's extended hand warily, gasping, when suddenly propelled forward into a generous bosom.

"Oooh, my daughters, my poor, poor daughters, how sorry I'm for you and how unbelievably sad I'm for what happened to your parents," Kareema hugged the girl tightly and dabbed at her heavily made up eyes, but Ameera could not see any tears. She finally disentangled herself from the unwelcome embrace. She thought of her mother and father, of the day they died.

Grandma Balqis proceeded to wail, retelling the tragic events of her only son's and her daughter in law's death. "They had been to work in the city, he as a janitor, and she, an assistant cook in a hospital. *"Allah yerhamhum,"* she paused, blew her nose into a crumpled tissue, "they were on the bus heading for home after a hard day's work…a truck overturned in front of them on the highway. They were the first to die." The old woman wiped her eyes, "they had been good parents to their three daughters."

"Ya Allah…God, I cannot bear it…it has been too painful." The old woman slapped her hands in distress and her plump face seemed to crumple upon itself from grief. Her dull white scarf slipped off her grey hair and she forgot to pull it back on, in her usual jittery, birdlike way.

"Allah you are merciful, please, absolve their souls, and bestow upon them forgiveness and *Rahma*…mercy," their grandmother sobbed quietly, occasionally blowing her nose into a soggy paper tissue. Ameera felt sad for grandmother. It had to be difficult for an old person like her, she thought. That is why she did not complain, cry, nor ask grandmother for anything. She could feel Raya's thin body shaking behind her and knew the little girl was crying.

She held the tiny palm even tighter, squeezing it slightly, teasing. The shaking seemed to slow down. Ameera thanked *Allah*. She stood wordlessly waiting for grandma to settle down. Then she asked, "Auntie would you like some *na'na*, mint tea or some water?"

"Yes, Ameera do bring our guest some *chai* and some water, she must be thirsty after the long trip." Grandma seemed to calm down, suddenly remembering her manners again. She turned to her cousin's youngest daughter. She had not seen her for more than fifteen years but had heard all sorts of rumor about her. They said she had divorced a wealthy man and had her own business. The nature of this business was unclear…probably a recruitment agency. By the gold shining on Kareema's hands, it appeared whatever business it was it must have been doing well.

Grandma Balqis eyed her mysterious relative surreptitiously while she talked. Balqis was an old and simple woman, her relatives' obvious success in the alluring world of the Persian Gulf impressed her.

"Tell me auntie, what are these girls going to do now, after their mother and father are gone...how will you manage?" Kareema put her manicured hand on the old woman's shoulder gently. "I know the girls have no family left except you and an uncle in jail."

Balqis did not like to think of her daughter-in-law's family, one that they have never met. She avoided looking at the younger woman when she said, "Yes Kareema...we have been relying on the insurance money but it is not much, and I'm old...we have no other income." Ameera brought in a small tray with a plastic flask of hot *na'na* and two tumblers.

"I was thinking of a way to help you and the girls, auntie...if you agree," Kareema looked into her aunt's eyes and smiled. Her gold bangles jingled as she raised the teacup to her lips daintily. "As you might have heard I have a highly successful business in Dubai...I'm sure I can find some work for your granddaughter." She smacked her lips, enjoying the sugary tea.

"*Walla,*" Balqis was astonished. "Really...you would do this for us?"

"Of course *Khalty*...I came as soon as I heard, we are a family auntie," Kareema smiled, her full lips curving into a glossy arc.

"You will be blessed *binty*, my daughter...*Inshallah Allah* blesses you and rewards you....did you hear Ameera?" the old woman was bustling, excited at the possibility. Yes, it would be a great favor if Kareema took her granddaughter to Dubai. Ameera pretended to be arranging the tea tray, frightened by the conversation. *Surely, grandma Balqis will not go along with this.*

Balqis felt her mind work feverishly. *Many of the young people who went to the Gulf countries found good jobs and sent money and gifts back home to their families.* Balqis made up her decision. "Well then, I better talk to the girls about this, and tell you in a few days," her voice trembled at the possibility.

Kareema cut her off, "Sorry auntie, I need to know today, you see the visa I have has to be used within a day or two," she looked disappointed. She waited, unmoving, for the old woman to make the final choice.

"So you want Ameera to leave now...today?" Balqis blinked her eyes rapidly, looking for an escape. The situation seemed to be getting out of her control. Her plump face once again shook as she looked back and forth fearfully from Kareema to the girls. Samar had joined her sisters and now they huddled together, stunned at the developments taking place in their lives, the uncontrollable forces pulling their small family apart. All of them waited fearfully for the old woman's decision.

The rest of their lives hung in this one pronouncement, and Ameera prayed that for all their sakes, it would be the right one.

Chapter 5

Ginni

The thin Chinese model sashayed down the ramp expertly. She flashed a smile, turned, and then, for more effect, looked over her shoulder coquettishly as the guests applauded wildly. Pulsating rap music drowned the applause as the last model did her thing and it was time for the designer to take a bow. Revolving strobes of light flashed incessantly, and thousands of pink satin ribbons and clear balloons fell from the ceiling, covering the guests' and the models' hair. They looked like pink haired mermaids.

Ginni held her breath and despite herself smiled. It felt good. It felt good being the star of this show. Her designs looked fabulous, the models were excellent this year, and the theme of the show unusual and unique. She walked out onto the ramp, amid more applause, flashing light bulbs and media frenzy.

"Ms.Karisma…this way," that nasty photographer from a local fashion magazine was calling out nervously. Other reporters and photographers were all over the hotel, and earlier she had given a couple of interviews to Marie-Claire and Emirates Woman magazines respectively. She flashed her expensive smile at the photographer, waved at the crowd and bowed, all with complete self-assurance. They were in the ballroom of the luxurious Burj Al Arab Hotel. Months before Fashion week came to town, her employees had scouted for a venue for the party. Mercy had insisted that this location had all the right ingredients, and sent the right message to the foreign companies looking to buy their designs or develop further business projects with Ginni. It said class, power and was an iconic display of the affluence of Dubai.

"Ms. Karisma, Celebrity TV is here to talk to you," her chubby assistant Mercy was gesticulating frantically, and looking ridiculous as she did. Ginni furrowed her dark brows in exasperation. Mercy tried to keep up with Ginni's long strides. It was comical seeing this short Filipino girl scamper, trying to keep up with her boss's demands. '*What Ginni wanted; Ginni got'* was her mantra, and she expected her staff to abide by it.

Ginni had wanted to fire Mercy plenty times, because of her cloying friendliness, but the girl had excellent contacts in the public relations and events industry as well as a docile character, so she let her stay.

Mercy answered her mobile, frenetically adjusting her earpiece and hurrying off to the corner of the room speaking in a deferential tone. *One of the many Sheikhas who wanted to buy my designs,* Ginni thought with satisfaction. She caught sight of a filming in another part of the ballroom.

"Ginni Karisma Fashions…has an impressive clientele list in the United Arab Emirates consisting of most of the royal families and local billionaires as well as prominent politicians, renowned doctors, and oil and gas executives who were the movers and shakers of this wealthy country." A young, impressionable reporter was yelling into her microphone animatedly, waving her arms at the stylish, conceited crowd behind her. The camera operator followed her faithfully, swinging his equipment left and right like a torero in a bullfight.

Ginni stopped again when she saw Clara, a well-known Lebanese socialite approaching, a purposeful smile on her flawless face. In her late forties, Clara favored the scantily clad fashions worn by teenage girls, and strutted around in them, completely oblivious to the snickering stares of her fellow discerning Dubaians."What an amazing show Ginni," Clara's breath smelled of cigarettes.

They kissed the air around each other's face, gushing with fake affection. "Thank you so much *ya habibti,* my love," she smiled, tilting her head in true Indian fashion.

"I want you to meet my friend Fares Dracolakis." Clara was hanging on to the arm of a gorgeous and stylishly dressed man who looked as if he had stepped of the pages of GQ magazine. "He is an interior designer from Lebanon," she bragged. Clara liked to show off her most recent collection of men-friends.

"Enchante," Fares bowed slightly at the waist as he took Ginni's hand in his and kissed it lightly. "Fabulous designs mademoiselle Ginni– *mabrouk,"* he had a thick French accent with an odd lilt to it. The Lebanese-French inflection, so musical and provocative, sounded even more captivating when he spoke. She had heard it spoken thousands of times in the years she had lived in Dubai. She could speak Arabic and French fluently. However, it was the first time the accent had this impact.

Fares spoke slowly, magnetically, rolling his letters across his tongue while looking right into her eyes. He was still holding her hand, far longer than necessary for sure. Ginni held his gaze and managed to say in a dignified way, feigning indifference to his obvious charm, "A pleasure to meet you, and thank you for coming to my show." Then in rapid succession she blurted, "I hope you will stay for the party," sounding *as if, she was... what...desperate?* Telling herself that she was a famous designer and should not behave like an awestruck girl, Ginni graciously led the way through the crowded room. There will be time for Mr.Dracolakis later she thought to herself. He was too fascinating and attractive and she was not going to let him off without at least one more encounter. Clara was still chatting with yet another fake blonde-haired woman, who obviously had way too much cosmetic surgery done.

Fares walked with Ginni slowly. She tried to get a waiters' attention. She needed a glass of champagne badly; it was time to celebrate all the months of hard work. A cute Serbian cocktail waitress passed by with a tray of champagne glasses and Ginni nodded in her direction. The girl offered the tall flutes of the outrageously expensive champagne. They looked lusciously cold and bubbly. Fares took one, handed it to Ginni, and then took his own. The server kept her eyes on him all the time. Ginni did not miss that.

Sipping 'Crystal' from her glass she looked at him covertly, her eyes half closed, and her black eyelashes thick and long. He was tall. Under the Armani suit, she could see he worked out, his body fit in the right way. He turned to look at the rest of the party revelers, and she glimpsed the back of his hair, light brown, curling on the nape of his neck. "You have a nice party here," the voice again. His English was not good.

"We were lucky to get one of the best DJs in the world. She came to Dubai from Sweden for another event and my assistant Mercy pulled some strings to get her for us." It was Ginni's turn to show off. Fares nodded, apparently impressed.

The ballroom smelled of scented candles and cigarette smoke and expensive fragrances. The open glass doors leading to the balcony brought in the fresh and fishy smell of the Arabian Sea. In the distance, she could see the periodic lights of the tanker ships entering the Port of Rashid, the lifeline of Dubai populace. She took another sip when she actually felt like draining the glass.

Nearby, a tall African woman with a fuzz of platinum hair tittered by on skyscraper stilettos, giggling and hanging onto the arm of a beefy, older man. He leaned and whispered in the woman's ear, and she threw her head back and laughed…showing perfectly white, straight teeth, her long crystal earrings sparkling in a million slivers of light. They hugged and groped unabashedly and continued on their way, apparently oblivious to the many amused stares following them. A couple of photographers took note and started to follow the intoxicated couple. It must have occurred to them that it would be a great photo op for tomorrows' society pages.

"Extra, extra…read all about it! Saudi Billionaire so and so snapped carousing with Dubai model!" thereby, were setting the tongues wagging for a few days.

However, the capacity to shock was short lived in this town. Dubai jet setters and socialites had seen it all, tried it all…and had an inexhaustible gift for understanding and forgiveness. Perhaps that was so because they expected it for themselves as well, one day.

"The *Burj Al Arab*…the only hotel in the world that is rated seven stars," Fares was talking, craning his neck to take in the sweeping ceilings, the high windowpanes, and the lavish interior décor. "I worked on many hotels in Lebanon, Qatar, and Saudi Arabia, but this is my favorite."

"Wow, you must be really good," she shot him another covert glance and a broad smile. He laughed aloud. His laugh was deep and masculine, "Oh yes, I'm very good."

Ginni took a deep breath and put her arm lightheartedly on his shoulder, moving her hand up and down, once. She continued to look into his eyes and smile demurely, but her eyes glowed with a fire that was evident to him. Yes, definitely, she would have to arrange it with Clara of course. This will not be the first of such encounters, and Clara knew to be discreet. Her reputation in certain Dubai circles depended on it.

"What kind of name is Dracolakis anyway?" she inquired turning to wave at a group of society wives in their well preserved fifties. Wherever she looked people motioned for her to come over waved, or smiled, some imitated applause, clapping their adorned hands lightly, nodding their heads in approval. *I really must mingle* she thought. *This will not do...I need to network and thank my supporters*, she told herself. Somehow, she did not feel like it yet. She needed to get away for a moment from all these well-fed, well-traveled, and well-dressed people.

"....my grandfather was Greek and my mom, is half-Jordanian half Lebanese. Therefore, I'm a third Greek, third Lebanese, and a third Jordanian. I have lived in Canada most of my life and recently moved to Lebanon," Fares was gushing on about his roots.

She had missed the first part of his speech. It was typical that he was a mix of many ethnic backgrounds. How utterly disappointing it was when someone happened to be *just* plain old French, Spanish or Japanese! Ginni twisted her lips contemptuously thinking of the baseless theories of many of her fellow Dubaians. Their false notions that multi ethnicity was somehow exotic and intriguing compelled most to dissect their ancestry into minute fractions. Nowadays there were your Global Nomads and Third Culture Kids, your half-caste, and a six part of this and twelve parts of that.

Her excitement was not only for the handsome decorator, but also for her success and the opulence surrounding her, the authority, and the wealth. Suddenly feeling indestructible Ginni wanted to scream, laugh, and gyrate in front of her conceited guests...but instead she sipped her champagne, smiled politely, and played the role of the gentle and accomplished designer. Drinking steadily throughout the evening had made her feel hot and weak. Her thoughts seemed like an incoherent muddle. Ginni walked by a famous Bollywood action star and he smiled and waved, beckoning her to come. A dozen swooning women and girls surrounded him, and she waved back, forcing a smile. She would rather talk to him later when he was alone.

"Ginni, halloo!" a statuesque American called out to her, waving her arm in the air.

"Oh no," Ginni pretended not to have seen her, but it was too late. Fares seemed bemused, and continued to sip his champagne calmly. His composure impressed her.

"Oh *dahling* there you are." The woman was from Georgia and had retained her Southern Belle charm and accent…*a fabulous creature really*, Ginni noticed, admiring the woman in front of her.

Married recently into a prominent family the American came across high competition in the glamour and beauty department from them. Groomed to perfection, dripping in diamond jewelry and an exquisite *Abaya*, her perfect blond fringe left uncovered by the silk *Sheila*, her feet clad in Manolo's, she portrayed a picture of opulent perfection. Now she kissed Ginni warmly on both cheeks.

"Ginni, what a fabulous show, really," she dazzled them with a hundred watt bleached smile, silencing Ginni's protests. "I have to buy your entire collection," she gushed on, "honey it is just to die for."

"Well, thank you so much." Ginni looked into the blue eyes, the perfectly drawn blue eyeliner above the eyelids, and could not believe this was happening. She was enjoying herself, all the adulation, and people vying for a few words with her…the famous designer. All and sundry at the party wanted to be seen and photographed with her. However, she could not help but feel a nudge of disappointment. They only liked her for her fame and wealth. No one liked her just for her.

That old feeling of trepidation and shame descended on her. One minute she was on top of the world and the next she felt like she was drowning into a bottomless vortex of faces. They appeared to spin around her like fiendish apparitions in a terrifying collage of sneers, grins, and smirks. She started to fall…Fares was faster, and held her up before she hit the sparkling marble floor. Deftly, he grabbed her around the waist and ushered her through the crowd of gathering people, tickled by the drama in front of them, dying to know the scoop.

"You know Ginni Karisma, that famous designer?" They will say tomorrow to the unfortunate friends who had not been important enough in this shallow world of nonsense, and therefore ungraced by an invitation to the party of the century.

"Well, she collapsed last night, and this unidentified man had to half carry her out of the party."

"No way, really?" they would say. Gasps of shock, then feigned sympathy and beneath it, snickers of delight for being the first to know the juicy gossip. In the privacy of their homes, they would say what they really thought of her. "She always was bizarre…all those parties…the drinking and the men…and who knows what else…"

"They say she is actually the daughter of one of the sheikhs…"

"Oh, I heard from a friend of a friend that she was involved in a dreadful incident..."

"In India, yes!"

"Her father had apparently worked for someone famous...I heard it from Ginni's assistant directly."

"Really...I heard she grew up in a slum...was terribly abused."

It would go on like this for months, until she reappeared again, resurrected, elegant, and glorious, infuriatingly unapologetic. When she finally joined the mainstream Dubai society again, most of them would fall silent, indignantly speechless when confronted by her arrogance and her deliberate contempt for their approval, her disdain for the rules of their little cosmos of society.

Ginni never allowed 'those people' to dictate her behavior. On the contrary, it brought out the unbridled stubbornness of a wild Arabian stallion in her. She had oodles of talent, powerful contacts in the city, plenty of her own money and could play their game.

This assured tightly sealed lips from those who had previously gloated in her failures. There were many indescribable incidents, shocking scandals, and abounding rumors. Ginni attracted attention of the worst and best kind wherever she went. For the time being however, everything would go on as it always has...

After all, this was Dubai.

Chapter 6

Parisa

On a hazy warm Monday morning, Parisa Agamirzebaj woke up in a buoyant mood. The mural above her bed met her eyes first.

She had painted it herself, a spectacular design of the Persian countryside where she was born, complete with glistening stallions, their thick manes cascading like dark waterfalls as they galloped across the grassland. Parisa smiled with last night's memory.

Her husband Luca had taken her out to a lovely, romantic evening at the new and swanky Atlantis hotel. They feasted on an elegant dinner, veal, and salmon respectively, served gracefully by a certain world-renowned chef. Later they had drinks on the patio overlooking the Persian Gulf waters…dark and precarious. To the left, another sea of twinkling lights beckoned.

Dubai.

Later at home, they continued their evening in the bedroom, a perfect ending to an extraordinary day. Sometimes she wanted to pinch herself... to make sure she was not dreaming it all, the gorgeous doting husband, success as an artist, this fantastic home...

How could it be? She would ask herself repeatedly. *Was it going to last?* Her eyes flicked open again and she stretched languorously on the bed.

Luca came into the room, drying himself from the shower. The scent of expensive bath oil and body lotion trailed after him as steam escaped from the open bath door. She looked at him with pride. He was the most handsome man she had ever seen. Above average height, tanned, rippled muscles running over his athletic body...due to the many sports he played devotedly, polo, golf, tennis. He skied well and occasionally surfed. Sky diving and competing in desert motor cross races were also on his list of achievements. It was an impressive list.

Luca's wavy black hair fell into his eyes, and he ran his hand through it impatiently. He was young. In fact, he was twelve years younger than she was.

"Buonguirno amore," Luca murmured as he snuggled next to her in the soft bed. He smelled of something manly and animalistic...something that tickled her nose and made her weak and pliable in his arms. Black satin sheets crumpled under their embrace and they spent the rest of the hour that way. Parisa was in a trance of surrender. She gave herself up completely and totally, to Luca...he could do as he wished. He was the master...and, she...his obedient slave...

She heard the door slam and the clicking sound of heels on the marble floor. *Zoya must be coming to see if I'm ready*, she thought realizing that they had not locked the door of their bedroom... and regretfully untangled herself from Luca. She put her finger to her lips conspiratorially and grabbed her silk robe just in time as the door swung open. A flurry of white bounced on their bed.

"Missy, get down." Parisa attempted to regain her dignity, fumbling with her robe, distractedly stroking the poodle her daughter had let in.

"Mother!" the seventeen year old exclaimed in a shrill voice. Like a petulant little girl, she marched into the room and plopped her slim body on the red chaise lounge.

She rolled her eyes at her stepfather. Parisa smiled sheepishly and slowly moved away from the bed and Luca who was glaring at her reproachfully with his indigo blue eyes. *"Ciao* Zoya," Luca winked at the girl, eliciting a contemptuous sneer.

"Zoya, honey what were you thinking simply coming in without knocking?" Parisa regained her composure, giving the two of them a weary look. Their constant bickering was driving her mad. Sometimes she wished Luca would behave more maturely. Like two rivaling siblings, they vied for her attention and love.

"I think I told you this many times before, you need to respect my privacy , like I respect yours, sweetie," she fumbled with the cigarette lighter and turned away from both pairs of angry eyes.

Walking towards the French doors overlooking the private beach of their villa she could not but admire the view. In spite of the embarrassing situation in the room, the artist in her stood in appreciation in front of the calm beige beauty of the desert superimposed against the bright blue exuberance of the sea. Tall imported palm trees swayed in front of the window. Parisa remembered how much they had cost her and shuddered.

"Well Mother I'm in my own house and don't agree that I always have to knock," Zoya glared at Luca, not bothering to hide her contempt.

"Anyway, I was coming to tell you that I need to be on time for school today," she gave her mother a sarcastic glance, "that is if you can manage to take me on time." She stood up and walked out of the room slamming the door as hard as she could. The door vibrated in its hinges. Parisa sighed. She continued looking outside at the manmade islands and a lagoon, unhurriedly exhaling the smoke from her drug of choice, Virginia slims. She felt Luca approach her from behind, and then his arms wrapped around her.

"Sorry about that *cara*," he kissed her cheek and she leaned back into him.

"I know this is bad, that she saw us together, we will be more careful with the door next time okay?"

"Now smile...come on give me big smile...baby," he pulled her by the arms and twirled her around him. Parisa laughed. He was so fun, so young, and happy. Sometimes she felt worn-out by the entire bustle he had brought into her life. She needed the quiet and contemplative time she cherished as a painter. She craved that time in order to regroup. In order to do that she needed frequent time in solitude, she liked being alone. Luca was like an explosion in her life...colorful, loud, Italian macho Fiesta! He was a breath of much needed fresh air in the stifling and lonely life she had in Dubai, yet sometimes she worried if she had not been hasty getting married to him.

They had met at a nightclub. Parisa was celebrating her forty-sixth birthday with a group of close and dear friends. Luca had sauntered over confidently and asked her to dance. Somehow, the reasons for their ill matched union evaporated as time went on, as he pursued her with a tenderness and fervor she had no strength to battle.

Luca had injected the much-needed fun into her life, bringing a contented smile and a fresh glow to her face. Unfortunately, he also brought an enormous drain on her expenses. Luca dabbled in various projects. Most had to do with the film and music industry.

Somehow, his projects never took off. In his perpetual distress, he spent huge sums of her money pursuing expensive sport hobbies and indulging in the best that Dubai had to offer.

He loved to eat at the scandalously expensive five star restaurants where Michelin chefs cooked for an exclusive, spoilt clientele. Luca loved to travel, and a weekend jaunt to the many plush spa resorts in close proximity to Dubai was the norm, not requiring a special circumstance.

Once those close to home getaways became dull, they ventured further away. "*Amore*, how about a few days on Phuket?" he asked lazily sliding a finger along her thigh as she read in bed. Four or five hours on Emirates first class took them to the exotic island.

She bought him a Hummer for his thirty- fourth birthday this year. Then she threw a generous party, catered by the five stars Lebanese restaurant 'Hummus,' one of Luca's favorite. She hired an event company to organize the entertainment....with the theme of 'Arabian nights'.

The party was a huge success and the hundred plus invitees danced the night away on the private beach lit by tall torches. They gorged on mouth-watering Arabic *mezze*, grilled *kebabs,* and cheered the belly dancers and fire-eaters, hired for their enjoyment. The party cost an obscene amount, but she could afford it.

"Parisa, halo," her friend Jane had hugged her, followed by two kisses on the cheek. She looked around approvingly, "the party looks great." There was a long pause and then she mumbled, "You really spoil that husband of yours my dear."

Jane had laughed loudly, and others had joined in. "Yes, she does but who can blame her...did you see that man?" another artist commented nodding towards Luca. He was gorgeous, she thought. An attractive model was completely engrossed in conversation with Luca in a corner of the garden, and he laughed merrily now, throwing his head upwards and arching his back.

"When is his family going to come and visit?" Jane persisted. Parisa sighed. Nobody seemed to like Luca. Her daughter despised him and her friends mistrusted him. Parisa was yet to meet any member of her new husband's family, his background remaining a titillating subject for hearsay amongst her circle of friends.

Parisa earned tens of thousands of dirhams selling her art because her paintings hung on the walls in palaces of most art collectors in the Gulf. Many admirers of her work from across the world, as far away as Argentina, commissioned her paintings. She missed her first husband Babek, Zoya's father who was her rock of support in all matters. A legendary real estate investor and fifteen years her senior he had died eight years ago, leaving Parisa and Zoya set for life with a small fortune in the bank.

Parisa put out her cigarette and sighed. Stripping her robe, she walked naked to the rain shower and opened the massage jets on full blast. The hot water slammed her skin and a million tiny needles pierced it. She closed her eyes, enjoying the incessant pounding and the effect it had on her aching shoulders. Too many hours of concentrating on a painting did that. Finished, she wrapped a fluffy white towel around herself and peeked into the room to see Luca, asleep, sprawled on the bed, blissfully unaware of her troubling thoughts.

She was meeting with a gallery owner from New York interested in displaying her paintings and she was looking forward to a few hours away from the house. Later that day she was supposed to have lunch with her friends Jane and Jewel. It was the first time they were getting together after Jane's last surgery, and lunch at their favorite sushi restaurant in the Old Town sounded great after the morning's events. She dressed elegantly, a linen beige pants suit, a black silk shell blouse, and black pumps. A swipe of lip-gloss, subtle eyeliner, air-dried hair and she was ready to go.

As she walked out, she saw the new housemaid, flirting with the gardener. The girl was a nuisance...she will have to talk to her when she gets back. Right now, she was not in the mood for more drama.

She hurried to her car as Zoya arrived too, her face twisted into an angry scowl. Her curly hair, identical to Parisa's except for its attention grabbing shade, bounced as she fiddled with the seat belt, avoiding her mothers' pleading eyes. Parisa glanced over at the thin limbs poking under the too short uniform, the bright pink nail polish. Her heart ached in tenderness for her child. Zoya was so young, so lonely. She sensed her daughter's pain but felt unable to reach out to her. Luca's presence in their lives created a barrier as real as if he had erected an impenetrable wall.

Parisa sighed as she watched her daughter settle in the seat. "Ready?"

she inquired softly. She wanted peace. Zoya shot her a contemptuous look and ignored the question. Parisa realized it would be better to leave this discussion for another time. They were already running late as it is. She sped onto the road, hoping the traffic would not be too bad today.

The large iron wrought gate swung open slowly, and Zoya made irritated, snorting sounds in disapproval. Parisa wondered when Luca was going to wake up. She forgot to ask him whether he was going to work today. She felt annoyed with him all of a sudden.

As she turned to click the gate closed with the remote control, she saw no one. The chubby housemaid and the gardener were no longer there, she noted...hopefully both were back at work.

Chapter 7

Jane

There was a phrase coined in Dubai that was perfectly fitting for Jane Andrews. The phrase was, 'Jumeirah Jane', the precise name needed to go with this native to Dubai expression, homegrown in the exclusive neighborhood, by God knows whom. Here was a city where a simple English girl could recreate herself into a gorgeous, skinny, tanned goddess in a matter of months. Of course with the help of a bundle of her husband's money and the expert hands of Dubai's best known surgeons, beauticians, hairdressers and stylists, to name a few. As much as Jane wanted to act as if the moniker disturbed her, she could not. There was something totally delicious and decadent about being a 'Jumeirah Jane'... how perfect! All the Susans and Elizabeths, Donnas, Margarets and Kates, and thousands of other English names, and here she was a *plain* Jane.

Back home in Brighton Jane was a clandestine slob. She hid it well, but it was obvious to those closest to her, like her husband David. Jane loved David and their son Jake and their Scottish terrier, Kibbles.

However, Jane was always a tad too busy with her many projects to take her appearance seriously. She would rather be volunteering at the old people's home or talking to her sister for hours on the phone than getting a haircut or having a manicure. She would rather be walking the dog, reading Agatha Christie, or watching the news. Anything else but shopping for clothes. She did not notice that her teeth were a tad yellow, her hair graying, and her face graced with a couple of jowls. It did not worry her that her body was marked with the passage of time in the form of wobbly bits and pieces. However, after moving to Dubai two years ago, an amazing transformation took place in the Andrews' household. A deeper, darker need had begun to lurk inside Jane's chubby body. This craving had suddenly burst loose from its confines by the sight of the undulating sand dunes and by the unpredictably stirring whiff of the Arabian Sea.

"Karen how do you manage to stay so fit and groomed?" She had admired loudly, stunned by her new friend's spotless, wrinkle free face and gravity defying breasts. Karen only laughed, embarrassed. The two of them were lounging by the pool, and as Jane admired her friends' shiny hair and taut stomach, she noticed her own-chipped nails and hid them under the towel.

She tried to revive previous closeness with David a couple of times. He traveled extensively and frequently because of his job. Jake settled in comfortably in a prestigious Dubai English school, making new friends and quickly adapting to the Dubai teen scene. Jane went about her usual way for the first four months. She hovered above her life, lonely, and confused. Something was coming to surface inside her and she was not yet sure what it was.

On her fortieth birthday, as she was sipping a glass of wine in front of the TV set with images of the glamorously decked out women of Dubai society, with the ostentatious fashion shows and charity ball attendees parading in front of her eyes, she had a revelation. She wanted to attend the same shows and smile off the pages of society magazines like these attractive women. She wanted to be dressed in a fabulous designer gown, her neck, ears, and arms adorned with sparkling jewelry, laughing confidently at the camera.

She wanted to be pampered and massaged and rubbed by exotic oils, she wanted her body slim and firm again. What was so wrong with wanting to be well dressed, perfectly coiffed and manicured!

It felt bloody liberating realizing this truth. For years, she had told herself that women who followed the media and society in their search of beauty were traitors of all womankind and set bad examples for the younger generations of girls. She had been proud of her refusal to conform to the mainstream. It felt like a definite victory on a personal level. After arriving in Dubai, she had felt even more defiant, contemptuous of these empty headed, shallow Dubaians, forever in pursuit of the next set of fake silk nails, the next facial, the latest miracle moisturizer. Watching and observing her fellow English girls who morphed into Hollywood 'glamazons' as soon as they stepped foot on this hot desert soil.

However, things changed over time for Jane. The more she had observed this tanned, trim, manicured and happily lunching Jumeirah crowd, the more she longed to be a part of it.

******

"Mrs. Andrews...Mrs. Andrews can you hear me?"

A Filipino nurse was hovering above her and smiling gently. "How are you feeling Mrs. Andrews? Your surgery went well," a cute nurse in a veil bent over her. "Dr.Dia will be around to see you in a short while... try to rest."

Her voice drifted away and Jane managed a mere mumble through the bandages on her face, chin, and neck. The taste of anesthesia was making her gag. He body throbbed; she squirmed from the vile pain. She had expected soreness, of course with such an extensive surgery, but not like this. *This was excruciating*, she thought to herself fighting sleep and pain at the same time...*I have to tell these idiots to give me painkillers.*

A light was shining directly into her eyes now. She struggled to come out of the nauseating and drugged state. She wanted to complain about the pain. Dr. Dia was chatting cheerfully and giving orders to the nurses, checking her vital signs. Rumor had it that he had operated on numerous prominent Emirati and Arab celebrities and many wealthy wives and girlfriends from around the world. In any case, Jane was confident of the outcome of her surgery because this was the third time Dr. Dia had worked his magic for her and she was not worried. She knew he would have achieved exactly what she envisioned for her face. The only thing was this pain...it...it was making her teary and scared. She mumbled again and gestured with her hand.

"I know dear, there is some pain...I know," Dr. Dia was shaking his head sympathetically and turned to give an order for more painkillers. He was in his sixties and looked like a kindly professor. Short and podgy with round spectacles perched on his nose and a fine moustache speckled with grey...he appeared to be a jovial fellow.

"Jane dear, your operation was a success...I know you will be pleased with the results," his face crinkled up in a smile. "We will take the bandages off in a week but you will be bruised and feel sore for a few weeks," he smiled again kindly. After her first surgical procedure, Jane kept coming back. First, she had the face rejuvenation package, which comprised of a mini facelift, neck liposuction and eyebrow lift, as well as an acid peel."Jane, are you sure this is what you want?" Dr.Dia asked repeatedly, looking worried.

"Why of course Dr. Dia, absolutely sure," she had an infectious optimism in those days.

"You look lovely Jane, the surgery went great." Dr. Dia had been extremely pleased with the outcome, in awe at what he could do. "I think we are done here don't you?" he had asked her pointedly after he took the stitches out. Jane was adamant to go on with a combination tummy tuck and breast augmentation surgery. Confident in her new body and garnering tremendous admiration for the first time in her life, Jane did not want to stop. This time she wanted her nose shortened and she wanted cheek implants.

"Jane, are you sure about this?" the doctors' increasing concern irritated her. Sometimes everybody irritated her. The constant pain from surgeries, the adjustment to her new body, and her full social calendar put tremendous pressure on her already.

"I'm positive," she had said adamantly, her already changed face set stubbornly.

Jane had experimented with fillers and Botox injected into her cheeks and forehead as well as silicone injected in her lips. She had expensive dental work and bleaching done on her teeth. Her smile competed with the best of Hollywood celebrity smiles. She had minor procedures done at other clinics too. Things like electric facials and Hypoxi body manipulations, salon and spa treatments that she could not keep track of anymore, hair treatments, like the waist long hair extensions...all of which had had cost David a small fortune. There was a compulsion, a craving, in Jane, which neither her husband nor the surgeon would ever understand.

Dr. Dia was doing the rounds, slowly making his way through the ward. He was checking in on his other patients, filling forms, when a nurse approached him "Dr. Dia…please could you have another look at Mrs. Andrews? She is insisting to speak with you again."

The doctor hurried to Jane's curtained off bedside, "Jane, are you all right?"

He drew back, and Jane realized she had startled him when she grabbed his hand, and whispered fiercely, "Please stop this pain." She whimpered, "I cannot stand it," grinding her teeth in agony.

Chapter 8

Raj

The uniformed Indian driver opened the door of the gold colored Bentley and waited respectfully. His young, handsome face strained with effort as he repeatedly tucked his oiled hair back into place under the snappy gold-rimmed cap. The polished gold epaulets on his jacket shone brilliantly in the morning sun. He did not need to lift his big brown eyes to look at the woman walking towards him but he could smell her familiar, exciting perfume. He did not need to see her face to know she was beautiful. He kept his eyes lowered, yet was intensely aware of everything.

"Good morning Raj," Jewel said in mellifluous, slightly accented English. Her voice sent a slight shiver through his body. He had been driving her around this city for two months and since the first day; he knew he was in love with her.

"Good morning Madam," he said, frantically swallowing the lump caught in his throat. He felt as though he could not breathe, his heart starting to jump around in his chest rapidly. He had read somewhere that these were the symptoms of a looming anxiety attack. Quickly and with great deference, he closed the door after she climbed into the car and then sprinted around to the driver's seat. The car was already cool and pleasingly perfumed with her favorite scent…magnolia. Soft music was playing. Of course, the music had to be her choice, the crooning of that American, Lionel Richie.

He detested Lionel Richie. Some lively Indian *Bhangra* music would suit him much more thank you very much.

He turned his attention to the smooth feel of the new car, as the Bentley pulled out of the winding, palm tree lined driveway soundlessly, and Raj steered it onto Jumeirah Beach Road, heading to the club. It was going to be another hot and humid day, with a familiar shroud of grey haze hanging over the city. "Raj, I'm not going to the club today," she said gently form the back. Raj nodded quickly, startled from his reverie by her soft voice.

"I will be visiting a friend of mine, she lives on the Palm. Could you please drive there and I will give you directions as you go." Already busy talking on her phone she had sunk back into the comfortable leather seat of the car. Raj adjusted the rearview mirror, but kept his eyes on the road and his ears on the conversation in the back. It seemed she was talking to the housekeeper. He settled in for a long drive, drifting back to the last few months in his life.

Almost every morning, except for Friday, which was his day off, he would take the Madam to the exclusive Ladies Club for her exercise routine, then to the spa, where she indulged in a multitude of puzzling beauty treatments. The forgotten brochures and leaflets discarded on the back seat assuaged his curiosity about her activities. He had flipped through them, while he waited, unbearably bored, as she went about her busy life.

These brief, forbidden forays into the glossy pages of her fancy magazines opened a door for him into her perfect world. Flawless faces and bodies, breathtaking hotels, white beaches, page after page of sinfully expensive clothes…cars…food.

Frequently he would drop her off at one of the lavish, glittery shopping malls where she went shopping with her rich friends. Sometimes she would ask him to follow her, and carry her purchases.

"Raj, could you get those?" she would ask softly, politely, gesturing towards the bulging, shiny shopping bags. She would never look at him directly, appearing composed. He was alarmed that she was aware of his stolen glances.

He would carry the bags self-importantly, walking with the proud gait of a peacock, conscious of the other shoppers' eyes following her as she moved around the mall. Everybody paid attention when Madam walked by, because of her beauty and because of that unmistakable aura of affluence surrounding her.

Those shopping trips were his favorite times, when he could study her stealthily from behind as she swayed gracefully in her high-heeled pumps, the silk black *Abaya* trailing behind her. The garment was dramatically beautiful in its simplicity. Made out of supple, sensuous fabric and floor length, it tempted him, made him curious about the concealed, the out of sight.

It appeared to him the majority of women favored the black *Abaya*, even though some, seeking to break with tradition and possibly make a fashion statement, experimented with different colors. Raj had become a keen student of these intriguing, out of reach creatures, spending inordinate amounts of time perusing the women's magazines, in search of answers. These graceful, fascinating women took his breath away, parading in their magnificent attire; some studded with outrageously costly Swarovski crystals and patterned using gold or silver threadwork. Like graceful swans, they appeared both feminine and fragile, safely cocooned in this time-honored garment. It seemed each woman was on a quest for the most jaw dropping *Abaya* of all. A cloud of sinful, heady fragrance, and a lavish *Abaya*, both equally alluring, trailed proudly behind them.

Raj's favorite was the one with the tiger print design on the back, so as he followed the Madam, struggling with the dozen or so shopping bags in his hands, he could slyly stare at the tiger and the black eyes which gleamed back at him, mocking him in his agony of hopeless and wretchedly impossible love. His Madam had designed her *Abayas* personally, and had him drive her to her Indian tailor in Bur Dubai, who would then sew the garments meticulously. "The best tailor in Dubai," she had said proudly once, in a rare deviation from her usually reserved character.

"Sir's grandmother used to have her *Abaya* tailored at this same place, it is a tradition." Amnah, the Ethiopian housekeeper was an affable elderly lady, and always had some special treat for him, left over from dinner parties. Gladly, she inducted Raj into the ways of the rich locals, and of his employers.

On one such trip to the tailor, he had observed a group of local women in the shops' waiting area, arguing feverishly, in rapid Arabic, incapable of making a decision about their designs. He sat on a plastic chair, in the shadows, watching them with interest. "Salome, see this one!" a short young woman produced a long piece of lace, waving it for all to see. The group inspected it, their thick brows burrowed, sounds of *tsk, tsk* escaping their glossy, petulant lips in disapproval.

Finally, their choice made, Raj watched as they picked out the most extraordinary ornaments with which to decorate the precious garments; bags of mad looking feathers, faux fur, rock chic leather, meters of exquisite lace, shining gold and silver thread, handfuls of genuine sparkling Swarovski crystals; mother of pearl…bunches of vividly embroidered satin flowers. The list was only as limited, it seemed, as their imagination and resourcefulness.

He had eavesdropped on their urgent phone calls from a hysterical relative, assuming they were regarding the latest *Abaya* drama. "*Esh akhti…* what happened sister…did the tailor delay your *Abaya* again?" came the concerned questions, then the attempts to calm the fretful cousin, sister, friend. His presence did not seem to perturb them, and he remained anonymous, never venturing into the inner sanctum, the changing and measuring areas, which were off limits to males. Sometimes Raj went outside, even though it was unbearably humid, in order to escape the incessant chattering and to have a cigarette. What was new, he grumbled irritably, it was always hot, humid, and hazy in Dubai. It was October, and he had been here all of August and September, therefore, only experiencing the cruel weather of the Gulf.

When the job offer came through a local agent, some hardened veterans of the Gulf had warned him about the rich Arab employers. What they should have warned him about was the legendary Gulf humidity and the *Shimal* sandstorms.

"Listen *Bacha*, child, be careful over there," his uncle had said in hushed tones, as if afraid to be overheard.

"The ways of the Arabs are strange and different from ours," he paused to spit out a used lump of dark tobacco out of his mouth.

"If you work hard, keep your head low and your eyes on the ground, you'll be fine," he proceeded to roll a ball of the damp, fresh tobacco then stuff it into the front pocket of his lower lip, creating a pregnant lump. Hailing from Rajasthan with its gorgeous snow-capped mountain landscape and profuse forests, abundant flowers and clean air, the assaulting heat in his new country had shocked Raj more than anything else. However, he made ten times more money here as a driver, than he would in India, and his living conditions were better than back home. Something had to give, he thought to himself philosophically after he arrived at Dubai airport.

As soon as he stepped off the plane, he had felt indignantly violated by the fifty-degree heat. It had knocked the air out of him at first but then he inhaled, in shock, blinking.

Madame was talking to him again, guiltily he lowered the music, pretending he did not hear. He cut off Lionel Richie in the middle off *"Hallo, is it me you're looking for?"* perversely thrilled by this act. She was telling him to pull over into the date tree lined driveway of a palatial villa. He admired the neighborhood of custom designed houses, the fact that the sea bordered them on three sides.

"Yes, stop here," she seemed eager to get out. It was a long drive and she had to be anxious to get on with her day. Raj stood respectfully, keeping his eyes lowered while holding the door open for her.

However, this seeming politeness was just a Machiavellian ploy, because as he looked down he could watch out of the corner of his eyes. He could see her high, strappy stilettos as she stepped out of the car and wrapped the black *Abaya* modestly around her body. A slim white ankle showed... then a dark henna design, small squiggly flowers intricately painted on the smooth skin, glossy black nail polish making it all the more provocative. He tried not to stare as she hurried into the villa.

He knew that one of these days he will be in huge trouble for looking at her, albeit sneakily. Once in a spur of desperation he had confided in his friend, the security guard called Zachariah. "But I love her," he had said defiantly, as only a young fool could."Who can stop anyone from love?"

The tall muscled Nigerian had almost hit him, his coal black eyes gleaming dangerously, whispering in his characteristic African accent, *to stop tinking foolish tings.* They were stealing a cigarette break behind the drivers' accommodation. "This is not like in your Indian movies my poor man." Zachariah looked around nervously. "People have gone to jail for things like this here, and worse things have happened to them," he kicked at an invisible stone on the ground.

"You can never, ever tell anyone," he growled threateningly. His dark face turned stormy, "you'll get us all killed man. Quit this mad talking and stick with your job or I'll personally beat the crap out of *ya.*"

Since then Raj had kept all his dark, sinful, and hopeless thoughts to himself. His fantasies about the unattainable 'Madam' kept him energized. He looked forward to his boring job each morning...driving in this sweltering, traffic congested city with nothing much to look forward to except a glimpse or two of the 'other' side of the proverbial fence.

That elusive world where apparently everybody had superior looks, made infinite amounts of money, and smelled of magnolia. It was a world where people did not worry about taking care of their ailing, elderly parents. A place where no one agonized about coming up with a way of paying shamelessly large wedding dowries for their sisters, who waited patiently in some mountaintop Rajasthan village. These demi-gods existed in a weird and wonderful place. A fortunate group, who did not have to worry about doing any of this, as well as sustaining themselves, entirely on one measly salary.

Raj saw a titillating foretaste of a way of life where people took what they wanted without waiting for it for years… decades…maybe forever…

Chapter 9

Cora

*C*ora looked up from the soapy dishwater. She finished rinsing the dishes and started to dry and stack them on the kitchen counter. Her movements were slow and dejected, like someone in a deep sleep with no intention to wake up. Her brown eyes wandered sluggishly to the big kitchen window above the sink. Tall palms and exotic yellow flowers swayed in the balmy breeze. She could see the gardener hard at work plucking the weeds out of the immaculate flowerbeds and then spraying the wide leafed shrubs in the luxuriant garden.

The new housemaid approached the gardener and appeared to flirt with him. He stood up and leaned on a tree trunk, all the while looking anxiously around him. Apparently he was not comfortable with flirting in broad daylight and while the owners were still at home.

Cora smiled sadly, how fun that was…to be flirting harmlessly in a garden and laughing with someone who is young and free. Sighing heavily she took the stack of hand painted plates and stashed them into the oak cabinets carefully. She hated to break anything. It was so awkward and Madam Parisa was always unhappy when it happened. She was a kind woman not prone to outbursts, but got rightfully upset when Cora carelessly handled the costly dishware and glassware.

The new housemaid, Dalisai, had recently arrived from the Philippines and was hired to take care of madam's daughter's needs. To clean her bedroom suite, wash and iron the clothes and keep track of the shoes and accessories, the makeup drawers teeming with stuff and shelves bulging with clutter. Dalisai was here to cater to Zoya's complex teenage needs.

Now she entered the kitchen, shuffling her plastic slippers, wearing the same uniform Cora had on, a beige housedress with a white trim around the sleeves and collar. Madam Parisa liked the clean crisp look of light colors. Dalisai swung her long ponytail and gave Cora a sly look under her eyelashes. She was young and extremely uncouth, sadly not fitting any even remotely civilized household. Her capacity for rude and slovenly behavior was boundless. Flirting with all able-bodied men who showed up at the villa, going through her employer's things when they were away, trying on Zoya's makeup and clothes. Eating anything and everything she wanted including the expensive cheeses and caviar that madam brought from her trips to Europe, as well as once consuming a whole box of indecently expensive *Bateel* chocolates and even a half bottle of good wine. Cora had to admonish her daily. *"Kumain mo'to?"* she would demand horrified, "did you eat this?"

"Why should I care?" was the insolent answer, as Dalisai continued stuffing her mouth with Zoya's favorite gourmet chips. "They have so much, they don't even notice what I take...look at the clothes and the shoes in the closet." She took a swig from a can of coke and let out a burp to make a point. "I work all day, I deserve to eat." She grabbed a box of biscuits from the shelf and sat down at the kitchen counter again, shooting Cora dirty looks.

"Listen Dalisai, you have to stop behaving like this...you are paid well and fed well."

"No I'm not, the British family next door pay their Ethiopian maid more and let her go out in the evenings," was the mulish reply.

"That family does not sponsor the maid...so she gets to do what she wants most of the time."

"Well I still don't see what the trouble is and how it's a problem for you Cora," Dalisai got off the kitchen stool and marched to the fridge.

She rattled through the containers and then pulled out a packet of muffins and proceeded to munch on two of those, all the while glaring defiantly at Cora.

"You should not be picking on me this much…you are not so innocent yourself," she mumbled with her mouth full.

"What do you mean by that?" A cold sweat broke out on Cora's face and she turned away, reaching for the broom. She started sweeping the kitchen marble floor with gusto, not looking directly at Dalisai's deviously smirking face.

"I'm not just a stupid village girl my dear Cora," she walked over the crumbs that Cora had swept into a pile and looked at her triumphantly.

"I have noticed that you are sick in the mornings and that you are tired all the time. I have also noticed that you do not come with the other girls when we go to church on Saturday." Cora continued attacking the floor silently.

"Why is that Cora… ha?" Dalisai swung her legs onto the high kitchen stool belligerently. Her uniform rode up on her chubby thighs and she pulled at it. Cora stopped sweeping and waited to hear the rest. "If you have a boyfriend you should let your husband back in Manila know at least…but maybe he will take your baby then…what's his name again… what do you think?" the plump features tilted sideways mockingly. Cora felt her face drain of blood. Dalisai made a show of leaving the kitchen, aware of Cora's terrified expression. She was gloating in her victory over the snobbish Cora.

Who was that Cora to tell her to behave, anyway? She should take care of herself first then be the one to have fancy manners and an attitude. *She was another Mindanao island girl after all….* "Pfft," Dalisai made a disdainful noise, and proceeded to the laundry room, loath to do any work but realizing that she will eventually have to get to it anyway.

Cora put away the broom and slipped out of the kitchen hastily. She had seen Madame Parisa leave the house in her black Mercedes with Zoya in the front seat, sulking.

She climbed the stairs noiselessly to the master bedroom and knocked on the door twice. Without waiting for an answer, she went in and turned the key in the lock. Tiptoeing she approached the big bed…stopping for a moment to admire Luca, rosy in the morning light, his back and shoulders shimmering like a large sleek reptile.

Mahal kita, I love you, she whispered softly. He must have been awake the sly man, because he suddenly grabbed her hand and pulled her on top of him. "*Ciao Cara mia,*" he said, blowing morning breath on her face. She struggled against him at first, fought to get up, but then returned his passionate embrace. After a few minutes she wriggled out of his arms "Luca, no!" she jumped up, terrified. *How could she continue to do this... what a stupid girl she is...oh my God, what if someone came and found them like this? Wasn't she in enough trouble already?*

With disgust at herself, she smoothed her uniform and fixed her long ponytail. Luca was still on the bed, arms behind his head, his biceps bulging, grinning at her, mocking her again. *What a handsome and yet wicked man. Oh yes, she knew the power he wielded over women. Look at poor madam Parisa. Like an old fool, she did everything for him...if she ever found out what they have done...*her thoughts rushed frantically. She felt al little dizzy and incredibly nauseous.

"What is wrong *Bella*...why are you afraid?" his accent made him sound even more charming. She took a deep breath. She had to tell him, she could not keep it to herself anymore. She was worried and scared all the time and had no idea what to do about their situation.

When it all started, she had regrettable fantasies of running away with Luca and getting married, of living a life of romance and wild passion in his native Italy. She hoped against hope that she was right, that he will come through with his promises. He swore he would protect her if needed. Well, this was the time, right now.

She should have been more careful. Steeling herself for what was to come she blurted out the toxic words. They tumbled out desperately, "I have to tell you something." Her entire body swayed like a grass blade in the desert wind. He still had a playful smile on his full lips, not a shred of worry. He had no idea that his life would change forever with her next sentence.

"I'm pregnant," she spilled the words right out afraid to stop, "it is already four months old...I'm sorry," tears rolled down her pretty round face, "I didn't tell you before ," her eyes implored him, pleaded with him and getting more distressed by his narrowing eyes, and his darkening face.

He sprung out of the bed angrily, walked naked to the bathroom, and banged the door with force. She stood in the middle of the room astonished and confused. Luca had a habit of behaving childishly at times. That was a part of his charisma, his charm.

He was still in the bathroom ignoring her, while she waited, hopefully, knowing that he had feelings for her. She was sure they would figure out a way out of this unfortunate situation, rather she knew they would. After all, he couldn't deny it, could he? After all these months of passionate feelings and of the sweet, gentle words he had spoken to her he had to accept it. After ten minutes of waiting patiently for him to exit his juvenile hideout, she was wringing her hands, still standing, unwilling to leave but worried someone will come and find her here.

"Luca, Luca," she tapped on the door furtively, listening for a sound coming from the bathroom. With her sleeve, she wiped the tears. He did not stir from behind the door or answer. As she was about to turn around and leave, the door opened as fiercely as it had closed before, and he emerged, fully dressed, his hair combed slickly over his head. In spite of herself, her heart skipped a few beats as she steeled herself for a battle.

"Cora, did we not agree that this couldn't happen?" he walked to the dresser and seemed to be searching for something on it, his back turned. "Was I not completely clear about that?" He turned around and she was startled to see his eyes, the way he looked at her with hatred and impossible, contempt! A shiver went through her body.

"I wanted to tell you as soon as I found out Luca I swear...I did not know either," her voice pleading, apologizing.

His sharp reply cut the tense air in the room like a gunshot. "Well, Cora what do you want from me now?"

*What a fool she had been...*she could see him now for what he was. She realized with a sick feeling that his disarming crooked smile, the playfulness, and the teasing, all seductively revolting, all of it had been amusement for him. Desperately she hoped he would come around, he would embrace her, say he is sorry and that he is only teasing, that she could have the baby in Italy, while he arranged for them to be together as soon as possible. However, he continued to glare at her, his hands pushed deep into the pockets of his jeans...grim, silent, and waiting.

She stared at him, unprepared for this reaction. She had expected that he would be angry; she had expected that he would blame her entirely for the pregnancy...but it happened, and he was as involved as much as she was. *Oh, my God,* she thought of her little boy back home with her mother. Her husband was a drunk and she felt no remorse for cheating on him, he had it coming for a long time. "What should I do Luca?" he stared. "Tell me what you want me to do?" she could not continue, because her throat refused to move, struck by fear.

He spoke now, slowly, coldly. "You should have never let it happen, what did you think I would do?" The world was surely coming to an end she thought, disbelieving as he went on, "I never made you any promises, I thought that was clear, it was nothing but fun for both of us."

But it is not fun for me, she wanted to scream. She would love to scratch his handsome, untrustworthy face and make him take his words back. She did no such thing. She stood there, like a criminal waiting for the judge to pass his verdict.

What will happen to her baby boy? He was only two. Her elderly mother desperately needed the salary Cora had been sending monthly in order to take care of him. During the months spent with Luca, he had substantially contributed to that salary. After this, it was clear that Luca did not intend to help her.

"I can give you some money, go take care of it," he buttoned his jacket... he needed to leave. She was holding him back from all the important things he wanted to do.

"You Filipinos know how to take care of these things, "he gave her a withering look, "and make sure my wife never finds out, *Capisci?*"

Yes, she understood. She understood she was on her own from now. The enormity of what was happening hit her like a semi truck and her body crumbled.

All of a sudden feeling faint, she sat on the edge of the bed. Her head spun, in rapid, uncontrollable circles. She heard a swooshing sound in her ears, like the sound of that waterfall by her village where she used to bathe as a child. She felt herself sliding slowly onto the floor, unable to stay upright. Last thing she saw before she passed out was Luca's cold, emotionless face, still staring at her with those piercing eyes, ripping her soul...and then marvelous relief as the room went black and she slid into the depths of the blue water, into its turbulent, whirling bottom.

Chapter 10

Tara

Qays looked to the right nodding his head in a gesture of greeting and then to his left. *"Al Salam Alaykum,"* he repeated each time, softly. This was the fourth prayer of the day, the *Maghreb*, sunset prayer.

The large congregation mirrored him, in perfect unison. It was an uplifting sight, over two hundred men, united in devotion, in comforting prayer. The golden glow of the setting sun filled the quiet mosque. Its high-multicolored windows shone as if on fire, casting an incandescent aura over the praying men. The mosque was one of the finest in the Middle East. It resembled a vast, gold encrusted palace with its eighteen-carat gold plated columns and soaring, intricately ornamented ceilings. The ceilings had been carved painstakingly by the best of Indian and Pakistani stonemasons…commissioned for a full year to do the work.

The main prayer hall consisted of separate, splendidly decorated quarters for the women as well. On Fridays, as the congregation prayed

61

and the *Imam* led the faithful in the most important prayer of the week it was transmitted directly on massive screens to the female worshippers, gathered on the upper level of the structure.

Praying in the huge foyer caused awe in a Muslim and in many of the visiting Christian tourists as well. The tourists came on 'Mosque tours', inspiring to many, creating a sense of appreciation for the often-misunderstood faith.

Qays got up from the prayer carpet and walked unhurriedly towards the exit of the prayer hall, bowing his head heavily, as if it was too much for him to hold up. His normally energetic gait was slow, uncertain. He put on his brown leather slippers and returned a greeting to the other exiting worshippers."*Al Salam Alaikum WA Rahmat Allah WA Barakatu,*"his head still bent, and deeply in thought, he approached his car. The white Toyota waited in the far end of the parking lot. He stood still for a minute in the post prayer silence. Calm descended on the neighborhoods immediately after the call to prayer, a tranquility that assured him of the power of his faith.

It was as if the approaching night and the air stood at attention as well, listening to the Imam's haunting voice, the potent words , feeling the benevolence wash over like a wave.

He turned his car slowly onto the main road. Deep in thought, he drove on some subconscious autopilot. He thought about what the Imam was saying this evening. He talked about how the mosque tours brought in many tourists, many non-Muslims, who came curious, hoping to understand. Local tour guides took pride in explaining their religion and way of life. Qays knew well that some boundaries were not crossed. They talked about the cultural integration but in reality, many preferred to mix with their own compatriots. He knew that it was so because it was easier than venturing out into the potential minefield of cultural and religious faux pas.

Qays could not remember getting home, but here he was being hugged by his little girls who giggled and hung from his neck shouting, "Daddy, daddy did you bring us something?" excitedly like two little kittens, cute and lovable and yet so shrewd.

"*Ya habibti,* wait …let daddy take his prayer clothes off and then I will talk to you," he entangled himself from the lanky arms and legs and giggles and escaped into the bathroom locking the door. He looked into the mirror hanging over the sink. Bleary, tired eyes stared back. A handsome brown face graced with a generous beard and moustache hovered in the reflection.

His hair felt damp and his palms were clammy. He needed a shower, a long hot shower.

His thoughts whirled around in his head and he attempted to calm them, form a coherent sequence, but could not. The only time he would feel calm and peace was when at the mosque…praying.

He removed his white *Jelbab* and *sirwal* and threw them in the hamper. The old showerhead rattled at first but finally managed to perform and it poured abundant, cold water. The maintenance in their Umm Suqeim Villa was disgracefully slipshod.

He stayed under the water until banging on the door startled him. His wife Tara demanded his time, his presence, "Qays?" a panicked question in her voice. Then irritably, "are you okay in there?" A longish pause, filled with anger, followed by, "we are waiting for you in the living room. The girls are going to bed and want to see you," then again shrilly, "Qays did you hear me?"

He ignored the voice, letting the water run. He could sense her on the other side of the door…both angry and scared expressions clashing on her face, maybe even that contemptuous look that he had caught recently. Her angry footsteps indicated she had stomped off, probably to put the twins to bed and apologize on his behalf.

"Daddy is so tired girls, he will see you in the morning…he is so tired from work you know he loves you guys," she would lie, hating him for it.

After another twenty minutes, Qays emerged, his skin wrinkled and scrubbed raw with the loofah. He liked using it on his skin. The rough material felt good, the repetitive strokes relaxed him. Made him feel cleansed, untainted.

Tara was in the kitchen making the girls' next day lunches. He could see that she was making a cheese sandwich on brown toast for Zeinab and lunchmeat in a long bun for Miriyam. From her jerky and irritable movements it was obvious she was furious. The smell of baked chicken and fresh salad hung in the air. Tara was a great cook; he wished he had eaten dinner with the girls. He stood there looking at her, remembering how they met.

They had been attending the same university in Ohio. Tara was majoring in Middle Eastern Studies and he was an ill-adjusted Engineering student from Yemen. The American girl in a Hijab, a recent convert to the faith, who attended Friday prayers with other members of the student Muslim association and who cast shy looks his way, had intrigued the lonely young

Arab from the start. Because of her dark skin and her Hijab, Qays was convinced at first that she was from an Arab or African country.

The group held regular meetings and social functions, which they both attended. Gradually, they started talking. His calm demeanor, his exoticism piqued Tara's curiosity and Qays felt drawn to her kindness. She reminded him of his own mother in many ways, of home. When Tara graduated, they got married at that same mosque. For a few years, they struggled while he worked for a drug company and she worked on a Masters in Education.

Eventually things turned around for them and he was offered a position in the Middle East, one that provided an incredible financial opportunity, as well as proximity to the Arab and Islamic society they so craved.

"Tara," whispering, Qays approached her.

Her body stiffened but she continued slapping together the sandwiches and chopping orange slices silently as if he had not spoken. A tight lock of black hair escaped her ponytail and she pushed it back nervously. Her slim hands and fingers trembled, her chin quivered hopelessly. He knew he was hurting her. She was a good woman, a *salha* woman, and a good Muslim. She fulfilled all the duties that her faith asked of her...yet he continued pushing her away. He wanted to keep this distance for her own sake; he knew she would not understand.

"The girls are sleeping, you should have come out sooner," she said coldly.

"I know...I'm sorry I have some problems at work...feel so tired."

"You always have problems Qays," an angry bang of the cupboard, "we can't live like this. You are never around and you are not involved with either the girls or me." She leaned against the sink, facing him. A look of complete anguish on her face startled him into silence. "I feel like I'm not even married to you," tears welled up in her eyes. She brushed them off and started washing the dishes left over from the girls' dinner.

He was silent. He did not know what to say. It was all for the best that she and the girls grew detached from him. Slowly he went into the living room and clicked open the TV to *Al Arabiya* channel.

******

Tara hated it when Qays watched the Arabic channel. She did not understand the language well. She was capable of following the Quran and saying her prayers in Arabic, but the fast-paced news reports were beyond her. Sighing heavily she went into the bathroom. From the medicine cabinet she took out the pills Dr.Ghassan had prescribed and swallowed one without water. She glared at her image in the still steamy mirror.

What was she going to do? Tara closed her eyes. She saw herself with Dr. Ghassan, in his office, and thought of the things he did. Of the things she did. Her face felt like it was on fire. Shame and delight flooded her, at the same time. She retched into the sink, bringing up white bile.

Tara was weary of trying to reach Qays and bring him out of the ominous, gloomy disposition he had for almost a year. She was tired of struggling to keep it all together, the girls, the house, her wavering faith in her religion, in this marriage, which she now saw as a mistake. She went into it earnestly, imagining an idyllic Islamic union. When she converted to Islam, Tara had hoped to find the man who would live up to all the high values and teachings of Islam. Sadly, it was not to be.

Back in the kitchen, Tara rinsed the last of the dinner dishes and started to wipe the counters with a wet cloth. Then she put away the girl's lunch bags, homework folders, and gymnastics gear next to the door on a chair.

She could hear the TV in the other room and that Syrian newscaster's well-known voice reading the news in rapid Arabic. Tara thought of her life before Dubai. She thought how disillusioned she had been with the western requirements of beauty and sensuality as a means of acquiring a man. Her mother had moved on from man to man since her parents divorced when she was eight. Whenever a new man came into her life Tara's mother swore he was the one. Months later, she would take those words back and start all over again in her relentless search for happiness. Watching her mother struggle Tara felt rebellion bubble up inside her. She began to see her family and people around her with different eyes.

Her quest for knowledge, for wisdom started first with a scholarship. University life then led to dabbling in various spiritual beliefs including Buddhism, Sufism, and Baha'ism.

She knew they were all not right for her. Her relationship soured with her mother even further and she moved out. The only unexplored religion left was Islam. Through the student community, other American converts to Islam, she learnt all she needed to make her decision. She knew that this was the faith for her. The modesty of Islamic woman, the protection of the *Hijab* had appealed to her own sense of rebellion against the vulgarity of her own life.

She cast a critical look at Qays, the television still blaring. Without a word, she climbed the stairs to her room, feeling bone tired. She stripped her clothes and got into a comfortable cotton nightgown.

She felt incredibly alone. Her open eyes stared into the darkness of the quiet room. Still, she could not relax and kept drifting back and forth about her failing marriage. *How did she do all that she had done? What was she thinking of?* She had no answers. *Maybe she was simply born bad…like her mother, unable to control her urges.* Tara turned onto her back, tried not to think. She waited for the pill to work, impatient for it to wash over her worn out body.

Her and Qays had big hopes, big expectations when they moved to the Middle East. After years of hoping to live in an Islamic country, it was finally happening. They would be able to visit Qays's family in Yemen and to familiarize their children with their father's culture.

After having the twins, Tara had devoted her time and attention to them. She had a circle of friends from the convert community, women in similar circumstances, and they were her rock of support during this period. Dubai was an active city with loads of activities for children of all ages. As the girls grew, their interests changed and so did Tara's. The circle of friends changed too, as many left the country and others arrived.

Dubai was in constant state of flux. Tara's good friends moved away due to jobs, and new faces arrived with endless possibilities in their eyes. Sometimes that made it difficult to keep friendships intact. However, all this movement brought new ideas and experiences into their midst along with its newcomers.

For eight years, they had lived here. Some of it was challenging but she would not say it was disagreeable. They lived in a pleasant exclusive neighborhood where the girls had access to a large cool pool and a palm tree shaded bike path. They had friends to play with during the long afternoons and she had other moms to socialize with.

In fact, her social life was thriving with a whirl of coffee mornings, school activities, and attending Islamic lessons. She volunteered at a shelter set up to support local victims of domestic abuse. Her group of friends came from different parts of the globe. Many had married wealthy locals and had the means to contribute benevolently to as many causes as they wanted.

Such gatherings led her to meet some of the most prominent women in Dubai. Some of who broke the expected local traditions by pursuing unusual paths…by becoming university graduates in their fifties or working in industries typically only open to men. Like the sixty-year-old successful businessperson and mother of seven, or a wealthy divorcee, philanthropist and founder of the Women's Society...or the young, intelligent film director. She particularly liked Jewel Al Gaafari, the half-American wife of a local billionaire entrepreneur, and one of the most controversial men in Dubai.

Tara and Jewel hit it off at a local charity luncheon last year, and spent an hour in an avid conversation, about fashion and all things in between.

"What an exquisite *Abaya*," Tara had admired the craftwork openly. She was waiting for her tea at the buffet table and could not stop staring at the elegant woman next to her in line dressed in a lavish outfit. They struck an immediate cord with each other and moved to a quiet table to drink tea and talk.

Jewel radiated compassion and intelligence and as they talked, the two women found many shared interests. Motherhood, Islam, and their zeal for charitable causes drew them closer. Aside from being a mother and wife and a well-known philanthropist, Jewel pursued many different interests. One of her favorite was fashion and how it could be a source of uniqueness to the Arab, Muslim 'Fashionistas'.

She had told Tara while they sipped the sweet Arabic beverage, "I'm so excited about my new boutique because it's an entirely new concept in this part of the world," Jewel said self-effacingly.

"Yes I have heard about it, there is quite a buzz in town about it," Tara agreed, nodding.

"Certainly, it is not for the commercial value I'm interested in... since a large percentage of the boutiques profits will go to charity," Jewel continued. Tara had heard of the woman's immense personal fortune and her generosity, it would have been hard to miss her numerous photos in local magazines.

"I'm interested in developing a designer brand on a global scale for the Arab women, especially the veil wearing women." Jewel greeted a few women, kissing their cheeks, hugging. Then she sat down again next to Tara.

Soaking up each word, already admiring Jewel immensely Tara said, "Coming from the States I know how the general public feels about Islamic dress, not positively I'm afraid."

"It is vital that our daughters and future generations of girls in this part of the world identify correctly with their heritage, culture, and religion.

Up until recently there was no Islamic fashion to speak off," Jewel seemed upset at this, arching those amazing eyebrows again.

Tara shook her head in complete understanding, "You are so right, I have two girls myself and know what you mean."

Jewel flipped her fabulous Swarovski embroidered *Sheila* over her hair and continued passionately. Tara could see that this was a topic close to her heart.

"I want my daughters to be able to wear designer clothes that won't clash with their traditions. I want them to be proudly wearing an Emirati, Kuwaiti, or Egyptian label...one that would become recognized across the globe," her face lit up when she smiled. "So yes...my boutique is an attempt to provide a special place for special women but all women will be able to shop there and find fantastic clothes to wear...whether they were going to wear them in Dubai or London."

They had chatted amicably throughout that afternoon and parted promising to see each other again.

What a nice woman, Tara thought afterwards...telling Qays about the meeting. "Her husband is a known philanderer," he scoffed, "the man is like the devil himself...he just takes from this world...his loose morals are the talk of the town," he said dismissively, while watching the news channel.

Tara wished she had not mentioned the encounter. Recently any topic got Qays into a dark, spiteful rage. She kept her subsequent contacts with Jewel to herself. Jewel and the other Arab women fascinated Tara. Tara found them empowered and self-assured which was more than she could say about herself.

Here she was, an American, born and bred in the land of the free, yet intensely fearful and confused by the uncontrollable events in her life.

Chapter 11

Jewel

Jewel flipped the *Sheila* off her head and all but ripped the expensive *Abaya* in her hurry to get it off her hot and sweaty body. She was sweating more these days. Her doctor had told her it was a symptom of menopause. Jewel was not having it though. *The doctor was surely mistaken.*

As she shook her head upon entering the villa, her thick hair tumbled down to her waist, finally released from its confinement. The glorious locks bounced wildly, as if deliriously happy to be free. She was wearing her favorite jeans and a bright yellow Channel blouse.

*"Halla, Halla Ya Jewel…*you look lovely today!" Mozza, the woman who used to be her best friend, who betrayed her in the ugliest way possible now greeted her in her typical loud, boisterous fashion. They kissed, thrice on the cheeks and hugged affectionately. Mozza's round face and big brown eyes looked at Jewel admiringly.

"Walla, you lost weight, *ya habibti…*my love…what have you been

doing while I was away," she teased sheepishly. Both women had decided not to reveal their true feelings.

Mozza put an arm around her friend's taller form and they walked together through the large foyer. Mozza was much shorter and they presented a funny lopsided duo. Oblivious to this, they chattered away about their respective news. Mozza had been away for a long time. Months spent in self-imposed exile. Jewel knew the reason was her betrayal with Jassim.

The foyer was grandiose, smooth colored marble and soaring, engraved columns, a wide, majestic staircase winding above them.

They walked into the *majlis*, the formal living room. Jewel had been here many times, but the villa never ceased to astound her anew. She was accustomed to palatial and luxurious homes, yet Mozza had outdone herself with this one. It conjured feelings of being in a five star hotel, somewhere in the tropics, with tall potted palms, and sweeping French doors lining one long wall of the room as breathtaking Swarovski crystal chandeliers dazzled above them. Imported handmade Italian furniture in neutral tones invited seating....dotted with jewel colored, embroidered cushions. Jewel admired the glass topped and crystal studded coffee tables, which shone like disco balls in the sunshine, which poured in through the tall windows.

As they walked left through the room and towards the beckoning garden and beach beyond it Jewel admired the paintings and art tastefully displayed. Most of the art was by local artists but a few creative Pakistani and Iranian painters' work featured as well.

"How are the children?" Mozza asked her friend as they walked through the house, towards the sound of female voices.

"*Alhamdulillah,* they are well, and yours?" Jewel raised a brow. Mozza seemed distracted today.

"Oh, they are good, good," she smiled. Jewel felt a sudden twinge in her belly, a flutter of wings. She bit her lips. She was not going to say anything. It will be as if her friend was still loyal and had not done a terrible thing. They continued on their way, both of them subdued as if an unseen current had passed between them. Nothing seemed to have transpired to make it so. However, everything had changed.

They circled an indoor fountain, where tinkling water splashed the palm-sized goldfish. The fish swam on unperturbed, languid, and fat. "They are all already here, they came early," Mozza attempted a smile. Jewel looked at the petite woman sadly.

They had been friends since grade four, when Jewel moved to Dubai from California. Her parents had amicably divorced soon after she was born. Jewel saw her father in the summer when he visited and lavished her with presents. She could see him looking at her sadly sometimes, and as she grew, he wanted to share more of her life.

After her mother died following a sudden, short battle with cancer, her father, a respected businessman by that time, had married his cousin, and had two children. Once in Dubai, Jewel felt abandoned and lonely in her new environment. She missed her friends and the familiar life in America. Mostly she missed her mom.

Mozza was the youngest daughter of elderly parents and accustomed to getting her way, a bossy little thing from a young age. Under her guidance and protection, Jewel learnt the traditions and customs of her new society. Mozza spent countless hours teaching Jewel how to wear the *Abaya* and the *Sheila,* to speak Arabic, and to dance the traditional hair dance.

Mozza had introduced her to Jassim...a good friend of her older brother. She was at the forefront of all Jewel's major life decisions for the last thirty years. Jewel loved her unconditionally until her friend had committed the ultimate betrayal. The two friends exchanged knowing, sad looks. Fifteen pairs of eyes settled on them as they walked in into the sunny 'ladies' sitting room.

A tall woman with startling green eyes, a mane of golden brown hair and the lithe, graceful body of a dancer, next to a petite curvy one, less glamorous but stylishly dressed. A harmony of sounds, laughter, shouts and teasing ensued as they all kissed and hugged and greeted in the elaborate, warm manner of Arabs.

Jewel was delighted to see the familiar faces. Her cousins, their sister-in-laws, were here and oh, her youngest cousin....all dear faces.

The villa was equipped with central stereo speakers and rousing Arabic music by a prominent local singer wafted through them, eliciting cheers from the women. Apparently, it was a favorite Emirati song for some.

"*Yanni* Jewel, so you disappear until Mozza comes back from England" her friend Fatin was saying admonishingly, raising her well threaded eyebrows. Jewel now understood the subtle ways of Arabic etiquette and good manners, and took no offence.

On the contrary, she knew that Fatin had missed her and felt overlooked and this was her way of saying so without losing face. If she had not cared about Jewel, she would not have blamed her.

"I'm sorry, *asfa,* really I was busy with the children and the boutique,

71

and you know I do not mean to ignore you," she gave her pouting friend a big hug and settled into the plush pink sofa next to her.

It was so deep and soft that she struggled to stay up and thankfully, her legs were long enough to keep her stable. A few of the shorter women were perched on the edge of the pink monstrosities fearfully, worried that the mass of fuchsia cushions might devour them.

Fatin seemed appeased by the hug...basking in the attention she received from Jewel. Jewel sensed that she was the best friend they all loved to hate. They wanted to be a part of her glamorous and exciting life yet were a little envious as well. Jewel was half-American and by that fact alone branded an outsider in some of the tightly knit local circles. The fact that she was also gorgeous and married to a prominent and handsome Emirati made it even harder to like her. Behind closed doors, in the privacy of the women's *majlis,* most of these women would find fault with her marriage.

"Ladies, please, *itfadallu,* the breakfast is ready." Mozza ushered them into the sunny dining room. This was the ladies dining area, one of three in the villa. A feminine room, decorated in white French country furniture, masses of silk flower arrangements, in shades of rose, bursting out of white wicker baskets, and hanging pots of flourishing ivy swinging happily from the ceiling. A table set for a buffet breakfast displayed baskets of Arabic pastries and warm breads, cheese and spinach croissants, freshly baked by Mozza's resident Syrian chef.

An enormous centerpiece of artistically displayed fruit, carved into bite size flower and leaf shapes, and then presented in a pink bone china bowl, took center stage at the table.

More pink platters creatively presented a variety of cheeses, olives, cold meats, stuffed grape leaves, *hummus,* and *tabbouleh* salads. Exclamations of glee and approval arose from all the women as they complimented Mozza on the food and creative presentation.

Cherry pink roses and carnations in crystal vases dotted the table, and other pieces of furniture, in a cornucopia of vibrant fragrance and color. A fabulous mélange of scents inundated the air...warm bread, freshly chopped parsley and cucumber, blooming flowers, and a heady mix of sandalwood oil, which the women used liberally.

Four neatly dressed Filipino housemaids politely served coffee and tea from a tea trolley, presenting long stemmed glasses of multicolored, freshly squeezed fruit juices on shining silver trays. Sunlight yellow of the orange...thick, crimson strawberry and light green melon, competed for attention on the tray. Jewel reached for the deep gold mango juice.

The maids' uniforms caught Jewels eye. Their black and white housedresses looked professional, and starkly different from the usual pinks and mint greens. For some reason she thought of Raj sitting outside, smoking, waiting for her while she drank cold juice.

"Tell me Jewel, how is the boutique coming along?" Mozza asked after they had filled their plates and were sitting down to eat. Jewel took a spoonful of the delicious parsley and mint salad. It had a zesty, refreshing effect.

"Actually I was going to invite you all to the opening in one month," Jewel had no chance to finish her sentence. Gasps of surprise startled her. Immediately the women erupted in excited congratulations, shrieks of *Mabrouk*, congratulations, and call outs of *Mashallah*, Praise be to Allah. Dubai was the hub of legendary shopping, and a mention of a boutique opening by one's friends is never taken lightly.

"Did you decide on a name yet Jewel?" one of her cousins asked, her curiosity piqued.

"Yes, I called it *Jawahir.....Jewels;* Jewel was pleased by their reaction.

"Ahhh, good, I will be the first shopping there," her cousin promised cheekily.

"I think your husband will not let you near a boutique anymore, you are ruining him already," squealed a large, pretty girl wearing the traditional *Jelbab*, a long silk kaftan, embroidered lavishly with silver thread around the neckline and sleeves.

Her target was small and thin, no match for her much larger cousin, so she wrinkled her nose in that direction ignoring the troublemaker. It was certainly embarrassing to mention a husband's unwillingness to supply his wife with vast amounts of Dirhams in pursuit of the latest collection from Jimmy Choo or Prada. All of the women in the room quivered in horror at the possibility of such a thing happening to her.

Most of them were serious shopaholics, including Jewel. She always admitted sheepishly that she cared dutifully for her four children...her home and husband, and therefore deserved at least one weakness. Finally, she had put this vice to profitable use by opening a boutique, catering to the chic and modern Emirati woman.

"Bravo Jewel...really, *Wallahi,* this is what all of us should do...take care of ourselves instead on relying on the husbands or fathers or brothers," a dark skinned energetic woman was protesting from a plush pink armchair. A few more women joined in with approvals and calls for mutiny.

Their hair clips bobbed like agitated parrots as they shook their heads in vigorous consent. These hair clips brought out a mad display of chintzy artistic effort in the women. Ornamented with sequins, ribbons, crystals, huge bouquets of silk flowers, a copious bunch of feathers …these vital decorative pieces were flashy, flamboyant creations. They were the source for an infinite release of creativity.

The arguments stopped abruptly when the dessert rolled in on the trolley!

Jewel giggled. She loved these women. She had missed their regular breakfast get togethers, their carefree smiling faces.

They were strong and funny, they were fighters. You had to be, to live in this barren desert, in households sometimes numbering a dozen or more family members and extended relatives. Many of her friends wore the veil and others, a face cover, which accentuated their striking eyes. Jewel knew from experience that many a man could not prevent himself staring at those mysterious eyes, curious about their owner, imagining extraordinary treasures beneath the obstacle of the notorious face cover, the '*Burqa*'.

Yet enviously, these women were treasured, sheltered, and honored as only women in the Arab world were. Jewel was sure others would welcome a horde of protective and helpful male relatives, brothers, uncles, and cousins, standing by, ready to jump in to assist, to defend when needed. *What kind of female would not need and value a multitude of relatives always by her side… grandmothers, aunts, cousins, and sisters advising, supporting, and being there through marriages, births, celebrations, as well as sickness and death,* she wondered.

Jewel was not oblivious to her friends' petty competitiveness and jealousies…of their occasional venture into speculations on her marriage. She knew of it, but accepted it and understood it on some level. She took a bite of the warm pastry, flavored with *Zaata*r, a delicious oregano and olive oil paste, savoring the tangy, nutty taste. Tuning out the happy chattering, her eyes felt drawn to the outside, to the stretch of perfectly manicured grass leading to the private beach, an artificial waterfall and a pagoda, and further, the sweeping view of the cerulean waters of the Persian Gulf. A wooden pier extended into the lagoon. A couple of jet skis and a speedboat rocked gently in the shimmering morning light. It was still early.

Despite the fun company, Jewel's mind drifted to Jassim. After his last trip to Hong Kong, he had seemed tense. More absent minded than usual. He worked a lot, she knew that, and wrestled with the numerous social functions and family duties. Jewel's jaw tightened and her brow shot up in an angry arc. *Whom was she kidding? He was probably busy with his latest conquest…that dancer.*

Jewel had her ways of finding out all she needed to know about her husband's mistresses. Employees in his company for example, friends, her cousins. It was hard to hide infidelities when you were Jassim Al Gaafari. That unsettling, confused feeling she got whenever she thought of him crawled in again, casting an ugly shadow over the morning. She had fallen in love with Jassim quite young. She had been twenty and he was a brazen and confident twenty-eight. He courted her the conventional way, polite, charming, and gentle. It had all been traditionally proper and their families had arranged the whole thing, as was custom.

From the first time, they had met at Mozza's house while visiting, Jassim had literally knocked the air out of her. His dark, intense eyes belied his apparent politeness while in the presence of others. She could see it all in those eyes; could sense his enigmatic power even while she moved around the room that day, talking to other people. Pleasantly conscious of him and his hooded, furtive looks, her heart galloped in her chest, her laugh suddenly wedged in her throat. Unfocused, she pretended to converse nonchalantly with other friends of the family.

Jassim was present after a prolonged absence, studying in America. They had never met previously, even though they moved in the same circles and their wealthy families knew each other. Jewel was certain that he was the one man she would love. The one she will readily obey and follow to the ends of world. Those first cautious and surreptitious feelings led to an engagement, and one year later, they were married in a glitzy, traditional Emirati ceremony, attended by the elite of Dubai. Dubai society magazines proclaimed it the wedding of the year. For a long time afterwards, Jewel was insanely happy, living a fascinating, extravagant life, the newlywed couple jetting around the world, and Jassim lavishing her with attention and expensive gifts.

"You are my queen, *malikati*", he would whisper into her ear, his embrace tight and possessive. She swooned whenever he touched her, allowing him to take over, gladly drowning in those delicious feelings. Later, as his infidelities became obvious, she despised that feeling, and she loathed herself for loving him in spite of his betrayal. Twenty years and four children later, following numerous reasons for disappointment in Jassim and their supposedly grand love, Jewel treaded carefully. In several ways, she knew he still cared for her, in his twisted manner. She feared him in many ways…he had the power to make her tremendously happy and the same power to destroy her.

Too vain, too proud, he would never accept it if she tried to leave him, even though he knew she was aware of his 'other women'. Unbearable as it seemed, with half the females of the city envying her marriage, envying her the man who broke her heart and then proceeded to trample it in the desert sand.

"What's wrong Jewel?" Mozza was by her side again. She had a concerned look on her face this time. "You look so sad, cheer up!" she pinched Jewel's arm lightly. Jewel realized that her face had given her away.

"Oh, I was thinking about the opening of the boutique," she lied. "Actually, your good friend Ginni Karisma has been working with me on the collection." She was never going to tell Mozza she knew the truth about her and Jassim. She will remain silent and patient as always.

"Really, fantastic," Mozza was pleased. Ginni's father had been a loyal employee for many years in their household and had finally brought his daughter to live with him after many years of separation. Ginni had arrived into Mozza's life at the age of fourteen and remained in their home as Mozza's companion. After Ginni's graduation from a design college, her father died from tuberculosis but Ginni remained in Dubai and never returned to India. "I miss her, she has not been coming around lately," Mozza sounded wistful. "Do you remember all the crazy things the three of us used to do back then?' she looked at Jewel with nostalgia clearly etched in her eyes.

"Yes, those years were the most fun I ever had in my life." Jewel felt a profound sadness for the past, when life was how it should be and the world had called out to them, full of fabulous promises and dreams. Both women fell silent for a long pensive moment, certain that those innocent days were gone forever and life was never going to be as they had wished it would. Then abruptly Mozza turned to one of the maids and requested more tea in her cup. The girl poured the hot liquid carefully, but a few drops escaped her trembling hand and landed on Mozza's silk skirt.

"Akhh!" Mozza screamed, when the hot liquid touched her skin. "What is wrong with you?" she stood up, shaking her skirt frantically, a storm on her previously smiling face. "Such a stupid girl, go get me a cold cloth or something," she waved the terrified girl away.

"Sorry, madam, sorry," an older woman approached with a wet towel, apologizing for her younger, less experienced coworker. The other guests got closer, hovering over Mozza, alarmed.

"It will be all right," Jewel said calmly, "here let me take a look, just calm down ok."

This was not the Mozza she knew, the Mozza she loved. Both women had changed, the decades of friendship and sisterhood gone like the capricious, shifting sands of the desert. She patted Mozza's arm and said, "It looks fine, slightly red."

Mozza smiled feebly, leaning against the pink cushions, looking guilty. "Thank you Jewel," her eyes looked wet, as if she was going to cry, "You are always so nice to me."

A look passed between the two women. It was as if they were alone in the room. The thickening smoke from the burning incense threatened to stifle. Jewel held her friends' gaze steadily. Mozza gasped, looked down, shamed. *Mozza must be aware that I have found out her betrayal. Jassim probably told her. Now the guilt is eating her inside.* Jewel could sense a looming climax in the leisurely unraveling story of her life. She would welcome it.

She looked around her. At the smiling faces, the flowers, the steaming cups of coffee and tea. Even the carefree giggles of her friends could not disperse the hidden grey cloud of foreboding, hanging over the pink room, the heady scent of the gardenia and the soulful *Oud* melody wafting tearfully through the air...

Chapter 12

Liliana

The sun was already setting behind the soaring *Burj Khalifa* when Liliana finally managed to leave the club. Outside, a heavy blanket of fine sand particles obscured the world.

Weather alerts were sent out over the news...a massive sandstorm was raging somewhere over Iraq, and its potent strength pushed it down south once again. Due to that, most of the Arab Gulf countries had been almost entirely immobilized. Kuwait, Qatar, Dubai, Abu Dhabi...all felt the impact of this terrifying force from the desert.

Covering her mouth and nose with a scarf, she ran to her car in the eerie silence of the parking garage. After spending hours with Sheri comforting her, Liliana hoped the frail girl was going to be at least somewhat all right. Then she had a quarrel with Iliya. He was a small, greasy, and vile man. Green eyed and mean as the monster by the same name. His rages were legendary, and Liliana rued the day she had agreed to work for him.

Backing out of the darkened garage in her little Mini Cooper and fiddling with her cell phone, checking for messages she almost backed into an oncoming car. Startled, she whipped her head around to look at it. It seemed to have appeared out of thin air. The car windows were tinted black and she could not see the driver, but he did not budge as she gestured for him to move out of her way. Liliana squinted, trying to see through the dimness and the dust. Suddenly, she felt the hair on her neck stand up. There was something menacing about the way the car stood there... with someone inside, staring at her silently. She quickly pushed the auto lock on and looked around the dismal garage uneasily. The garage was getting darker now and the neon overhead lights had not come on yet. She regretted not having Habib escort her to her car. He wanted to, but she insisted he stay with Sheri, who needed him more.

Remembering her cell phone, Liliana started to dial Habib's number but at that moment, the car revved its engine and sped off. Angrily, it seemed to her. It took her a minute to compose herself, stop her hands from shaking.

How ridiculous...why was she scared, she admonished herself, annoyed, and embarrassed that she had overreacted. She decided to call her flat mate Vikki, and ask her to go out tonight. They could go watch that new John Travolta movie at the Mall of the Emirates and maybe get some Thai or Chinese for dinner.

Traffic was moving at a snail's pace on all roads. Petrified drivers huddled over their steering wheels, hazard lights on, visibility almost nil. On days like these Liliana thought of her native Romania, and the snowstorms she witnessed while growing up in its mountains. The stillness after the snow had fallen, the feeling that it was not over, was the same here in the desert, during a sandstorm. Except the sand was much worse, and she always felt claustrophobic, unable to breathe, grateful to escape into the relative safety of an indoor area.

Scolding herself internally for being such a baby, she turned on the radio and joined the inching traffic. A niggling memory at the back of her mind was bothering her though. With a jolt, she remembered what it was. She had seen that car before!

One evening last week, on the way home, she had stopped to get groceries from Spinney's on Wasl Road. As she walked to the car with her cart of shopping, she noticed the same white Toyota, and the same tinted windows. It was parked a few spaces from her black Mini Cooper, its engine running, and had pulled out behind her as she was leaving the parking lot. For some reason its presence had made her feel nervous. Later, she was on the phone in the car and did not remember the unsettling incident until now.

For same incredible reason a few cars whizzed past her on the dusty sixteen lane freeway at outrageous speeds. She wondered how these drivers could see their way in the haze blanketing the city. They behaved like *Kamikaze* drivers on a suicide mission.

She grabbed the wheel and prayed that the monstrously huge GMCs', Land Cruisers, and Hummers will not mow her down in her almost indiscernible little car. Run-on thoughts swirled through her head. She was shaking from staying awake for almost twenty-four hours straight, the need for food, and the incident with that car.

Even though she tried to disregard and chalk it to coincidence, she was still worried about the sinister Toyota and its mysterious occupant or occupants. *Maybe it was one of the clients from last nights' show.* She signaled to turn into her familiar but strangely deserted street in.

Must be the sandstorm, everyone is in hiding. The gloomy sand blanketed street, the anxiety of the day, the ominous, threatening meeting with the white Toyota put her in a brooding, fearful mood. For a split second, a flash of her former, carefree, adventurous self popped up, and then vanished. For a moment, Jassim's eyes appeared taunting her, mocking her, caressing her with his eyes. Then that too was gone.

She approached their building, a thirty-storey apartment high-rise, with modest apartments but with much coveted, ample views of the Arabian Gulf.

Last night while she was on stage, Habib had to escort a few rowdy young Pakistanis out of the club.

It was inevitable that men would follow her and approach her quite often and she rather expected it…being a dancer she was used to propositions of all kinds. However, the incident tonight was rather unusual and she had a disquieting feeling in her gut about the entire episode.

To many men, her chosen profession falsely signaled that she welcomed their lewd propositions. Sadly, for some of the girls that she worked with and associated with that *was* the main intention. Not for her though. Liliana was genuinely interested in dancing.

Vikki did not answer her cell phone. Liliana finally gave up after the third try. Her friend was probably cozying with her new sugar daddy for the evening. Vikki's latest fascination was a wealthy Syrian businessman, recently divorced from his wife of twenty something years and the father to two teenagers. Adam was on a journey of self-discovery, unabashedly dating girls half his age and frequenting all the hottest Dubai nightspots. Vikki was his third girlfriend in the last few months and apparently, they were still on their honeymoon stage…he had Vikki convinced she was the 'One'.

Liliana let out a frustrated sigh. Many of the girls she worked with sought to marry a rich Arab man, and live happily ever after. She was ashamed to say that she too had fallen victim to this age-old delusion.

From all over the world, from the four corners of the globe girls came to Dubai. These girls arrived in hordes, positive that they would make it big in Dubai, the last land of opportunity. Competition was fierce, because the city was home to a multitude of gorgeous, exotic women, all looking for the same things.

Being tall, blonde, and thin did not guarantee and easy life here. Girls like that were dime a dozen in Dubai. All of them sought the attention from that special elite group of bachelors, but for that to happen you had to be more than blonde-haired, and have perfect proportions. There had to be something else, something unspecified but vital, in order to make a girl unique.

Young, rich, and handsome men, spoilt for choice, played the field. Until that special, something caught their eye. Fairy tales did happen of course. She knew a few girls who met their Arab prince and got to live in their own castle.

She put out the last of her cigarette in the car ashtray and swung the little car into her parking spot. It was completely dark now and the muggy, fishy air greeted her as she got out. Looking around she saw her neighbor, Amrou, getting ready to leave for a night out. He was from Egypt, a sweet man. She waved to him. He grinned and stopped, rolling down his window.

"Hey, *ya* Liliyaana," he dragged her name out in a typical Arabic fashion.

She liked the way he said her name, in that singsong Egyptian accent. "Hey *ya* Amrouu," she teased back swinging her bag over her shoulder and grabbing a hanger with costumes from the back seat.

"What are you doing tonight? You want to go out with us?" Amrou did not waste time as usual. She knew he liked her and she liked him back.

He shared a flat with a friend, and she shared hers with Vikki. Sometimes they all went to the coffee shop downstairs, sat at one of the tables on the Jumeirah Beach Walk by the sea, people watched, had muffins, and laughed like crazy. During times like these, she felt like a normal young woman. Going out and doing normal things, away from 'The Gypsy', the sleazy customers, and Iliya. More importantly, it kept her from thinking about Jassim, her Arab prince…the one who was supposed to whisk her away from all her troubles. Yes, wretchedly, she too had been guilty of dreaming of that special someone who will sweep her off to his palace on a fabulous Arabian stallion.

Suddenly overcome with fatigue she declined, the thought of laughter and coffee sounding too exhausting. Last night was a long one and this mornings' unpleasant situation with Sheri and subsequent argument with Iliya made her feel angry and powerless. She felt her blood start to boil in her veins. She was tired of being mad and used all the time. *She needed to do something about it, but what?*

"Sorry Amrou, how about another time…I'm tired tonight. Ok?" she winked at him. He winked back happily, "promise?"

He was already reversing and waved again as he sped off into the dusty street. She stood in the street holding the plastic shopping bags and looked at the departing jeep, swallowed immediately by the night.

✶✶✶✶✶✶

The next morning, feeling bleary and tired Liliana ran into Vikki on the way to the kitchen.

"Oh, hey, good morning sweets," the petite girl stood on tiptoes and gave Liliana a cheerful peck on the cheek.

Vikki was Australian, with an accent and attitude to match. Big blue eyes looked at Liliana pryingly. Vikki looked like a fragile ceramic doll, all porcelain skin, blond curls, and rosy cheeks.

"Did you see Adam or what?" Liliana poured the already boiling water over the instant Nescafe coffee in her *I love Dubai* mug and took a quick sip. It burned her tongue but felt delicious after the horrid night she spent. She could not get the car episode out of her mind and Sheri, Iliya and Jassim showed up in strange detailed dreams that seemed nightmarish but which she could not recall in the light of day.

Vikki grinned, "well, yes I did see Adam thank you very much, miss grumpy…what's wrong with you girl?"

They carried their mugs of hot coffee to the small kitchen table by the window. Their flat was on the twenty-seventh floor of a new cluster of high rises. The view of the Persian Gulf was spectacular this morning. A haze free, cloudless, bright blue sky greeted the day…no trace of last nights' dust storm in sight, apart from a layer of fine dust on their furniture. Both girls sat for a few minutes, silenced by the incredible vista. "Wow look at that, the storm is over!" exclaimed Vikki, beaming.

"Ever since you met Adam you have become nauseatingly cheerful," Liliana grumbled lighting a cigarette. "What have you done with Vikki you impostor," she blew the smoke in her friend's face and smiled forlornly. She was glad Vikki was happy, yet she feared that it would be short lived.

Vikki grinned and took a deep drag of her cigarette too, "how are you doing babe?" She gave Liliana a shrewd look over the rising circle of smoke.

"I feel strange Vikki...like I'm on the edge of something but don't know what yet," she looked at Vikki, wondering if the girl will understand what she herself did not. "You understand what I mean, right?" Liliana took a cautious sip of the coffee.

******

Vikki was a smart girl. She had observed her friends' relationship with Jassim with concern and felt immense relief when it ended about a month ago. She realized that Liliana was in love with the man who frankly did not deserve anything except contempt. Alluring, handsome, and incredibly wealthy, Jassim Al Gaafari had swept Liliana off her feet almost effortlessly.

At first, he told her that he was in a loveless marriage, arranged by his family and that he might get divorced. Liliana believed him.

As perceptive and confident as she had previously been with men and as skeptic of relationships, she had been all her life...Jassim managed to alter that. What ensued was an affair of incredible passion and romance. Weekends spent in secluded private beach villas throughout the country, accompanying Jassim on his business trips, occasionally spending three of four precious days at a time in cities all over Europe and Asia.

Once he took her to Bangkok and they stayed for a week at a secluded villa by the sea. They hardly ever ventured outside, content with their time alone. Liliana did not care. She was completely in love and took what he could offer her of himself.

Liliana asked cautiously, "so how are things with you and Adam?'

Vikki grinned. "I know you won't believe me Liliana, but he is so nice...really sweet you know?"

"Well, I'm worried; you were so hurt after Luca left you," Liliana explained.

Vikki shifted in her seat and held up her hand. "No way, it is not like with Luca. I'm glad he is out of my life, seriously…what a looser," she shook her hair adamantly. "Adam is so mature and intelligent, not into showing off like all the other freaks in this city."

Liliana rolled her eyes, "yeah, yeah, yeah…and he is also ten meters tall and as handsome as a Greek god and he can fly…I've been there I know the feeling sweetie." Vikki giggled and lit her second cigarette.

"Give me one; I'm out of my Marlboros," Liliana lit another of Vikki's Menthols even though she hated the taste. She made a face to demonstrate. "Ugh, how do you smoke this stuff? Either smoke or not…will you please! These things are like weenie cigarettes." She blew smoke at the ceiling. "So, what about his wife and kids," Liliana hated to bring that up.

Vikki leaned across the table, a pleading expression on her face, "he told me he will deal with it, I believe him, and it's been such a short time… but I'm sure he loves me." She reached out across the table and held her friends' hand, "really Liliana I wish you could believe he is not a bad guy."

"I hope so too Vikki," Liliana gave her friend an affectionate smile. "You deserve someone good. I mean it. I would really hate to see you get hurt again, that is all. Same way you don't like to see me get hurt, right?" They looked at each other over the little kitchen table, smiling.

The two had been through a lot together ever since they met at the nightclub the first night Liliana performed. Previously working as a dancer in a Sydney nightclub, Vikki had been in Dubai for four years. She had been in a relationship with an Italian model and had followed him here from Sydney, hoping to make it into something permanent. It was clear to all that her boyfriend, Luca had other plans for his future in Dubai, none of which included Vikki. He pursued a glamorous party lifestyle, hung out with all the 'in' people in Dubai, and Vikki soon became 'just a dancer' to him.

The rich and glamorous loved to party with girls like Vikki but did not take them home to their parent's wedding anniversary dinner or to the Emirates Golf club for lunch. Vikki was gorgeous, kind, and loyal but that made no difference. She was still a dancing girl and therefore *persona non grata* in some circles. Luca fervently wanted to move in those circles. Eventually she left his apartment leaving him a note…he did not pursue her. She moved in with Liliana and the two girls quickly became close.

A few months later, she heard he had gotten married to a much older woman. Rumor had it that, she was a wealthy Iranian widow as well as a famous artist. Luca had finally found someone who was sure to open those coveted gilded doors, to the greener pastures of high society.

Vikki had called him once to congratulate him, regretting it later, as he had been unbelievably rude and asked her straight out not to call him again. Disappointed that he was the man she left home for, a man she had been smitten with, Vikki spiraled into a self-loathing depression. Liliana was there to coax her slowly out of it, to listen and to comfort. Slowly but surely, the tough Aussie spirit won and Vikki shed off the self-pity and bitterness to emerge her old, bubbly self again.

Frequently, Liliana would buy a bucket of Marble Slab coffee ice cream and they gorged on it…talking, laughing, and crying late into the night.

"Hey listen, something really creepy happened last night on my way home." Vikki got up to get a slice of toast that had popped up from the toaster. She handed one to Liliana before biting into her own. Liliana had enough of the foul tasting menthol and put the cigarette out. She could not believe she had forgotten to buy her cigarettes last night.

"What did you say?" Vikki's eyebrows shot up in alarm. The girls were always vigilant and kept their eyes open. Working in a nightclub had its sinister side. Last year a jealous boyfriend attacked one of the dancers, right in the parking garage in the basement. He beat her up so badly that she was in the hospital for weeks and never returned to work after the incident. Later she left the country, went back home to Brazil.

In the last year, lone girls walking on the street at night have reported persistent and frightening encounters with strange men…sometimes followed home. Typically, it was an overzealous admirer, but there were some freaky people out there and that is why they had Habib and a couple of other people for protection. However, when they went home they were on their own. It was a rule that all the dancers report any strange or suspicious incidents to Habib as well as to each other.

"Well, I don't know if it means anything but…" she told Vikki about the Toyota.

"Jeez Liliana, you should have told me at once, and called someone. You know what happened to that poor girl last year," Vikki's baby blue eyes bulged from the shock. She stood up, to get the phone from the living room. "I'm calling Habib and Iliya and all the other morons at the club, right now, the least they can do is guarantee us some safety, what are they waiting for?" she was visibly nervous. "I can't believe it Liliana, I'm so sick of those guys," she spat out. " I'm so close to picking up, and running out on them, you know," her hands shook as she tried to dial on her mobile, "they treat us like their possessions, or worse."

"Listen Vikki...don't call him, Iliya and I had an argument." Liliana proceeded to fill Vikki in on the details.

"Oh God...this is even worse than I thought...things are getting seriously wacked out at this club," Vikki's face darkened when she heard of what had happened to Sherri. She pulled her feet up on the chair, "I'm telling you Lila we have to do something...we are not protected at all... that shmuck Iliya better do something about security or else..."

Liliana laughed "Whatya gonna do, ha?" she teased her diminutive friend. Vikki looked adorable...elfin, her face pink from anger, wearing baby doll pajamas. She resembled a petulant little girl. "Listen, calm down, I told Iliya all this already," Liliana tried to calm her feisty girlfriend. "He promised he would deal with it." Vikki did not look appeased by her friends' assurances. "Besides what's the worst that could happen girl?" Liliana pulled out the cushion she had been sitting on and threw it at Vikki playfully.

Chapter 13

Ameera

"Ameera means princess in Arabic right?" he was close to her face, his revolting breath smelling of cigars and vodka. He was not a bad man only lecherous, she thought. He was middle aged, well groomed, and well dressed.

She was able to shut down like that. She could see herself through a rose-colored haze, as if she was above, watching a movie, floating carelessly, callously dissecting the familiar scene below.

"Yes it does, it means princess," she turned her face away from him, continued staring at the ceiling. The man had dimmed the light as soon as they had entered this room at the back of a nightclub. A yellowish glow came only from the night lamp by the bed. It shone off his oiled, bald spot.

She tried to tell herself that he was probably the best customer she had been with so far. He was polite and had offered her a drink...he had touched her lightly. He took his time with her, seemed keen to talk first. Nevertheless, she wanted it to be over with so she could leave and wash his smell off her skin.

"How old are you princess?" he whispered in her ear again…this time his voice sounded husky. Then, before she could answer, his face contorted and he abruptly grabbed her long hair and yanked it back, hard. She gasped in shock, biting her lip to stifle the scream wanting to come out. He smiled at her, a thin, leery expression. She understood. He wanted to play games.

It does not matter. Nobody will come anyway…let him get what he wants from me. Still, she felt sad that he turned out the same, like the other men she slept with for money. She felt sad that she had been wrong…

The man was not big, but seemed huge to her. Ameera was petite, and curvaceous in build. He forced her on her stomach roughly and she did not fight him. She struggled for breath as he pushed her face into the pillow, her saliva soaking it…

"Seventeen," she managed to whisper, "I'm seventeen years old."

Floating…Flying…she watched calmly as the man continued, unrelenting in his grip of obvious pleasure and frenzy. He groped her with his cold thin hands, roaming, pulling, and pinching at will.

"Yes, yes you are a princess, so pretty," his words became barely audible, his panting hot in her ear. Ameera lay motionless, not struggling at all. Then, she found a pocket of air, and twisted her face towards it. Finally, she could breathe.

She was still hovering, not concerned, it did not concern her…she was not here…*How many times had this happened to her?* She could not recall. *Ten…twenty?…*She truly had no idea.

It had become one big blur of faces and bodies and pain and nasty words and unbearable demands. She had stopped counting after the first time. A fifty-year-old, potbellied client, on vacation in Dubai had injured her so badly that she could not walk for a week. Kareema had remained unmoved when Ameera showed her the bruises. She gave her painkillers, shrugged her shoulders, and then muttered, "It comes with the job." Ameera looked at the woman's face searching for something, anything that indicated humanity. There was nothing to see.

She had taken a long shower and slathered Vaseline on the scratches on her arms and legs. She cradled her body, pulling up her knees to her tender stomach, her burning navel, and her raw, aching thighs. She stopped feeling the pain. It was gone, absorbed as if by magic by her body. She did not feel anything at all.

Plum colored bruises had covered Ameera's skin a week later, when Kareema applied heavy makeup over her body and sent her on a 'dancing' assignment. She said that one week was more than enough time to get well. That particular client had expressly asked for Ameera.

"I cannot refuse a request from one of the most generous patrons we have," Kareema had spewed. "He always pays more."

Ameera looked at the monster unwaveringly, "I want those pills," she had said matter of factly. *It was the only way to go through with this.* Kareema nodded. This time she made no witty, cruel remarks. She had handed Ameera the pills silently and looked on as the girl swallowed them greedily.

The man above her was silent now…he had stopped pressing down on her neck…his breathing was rapid. She could feel his heart beating rapidly against her chest, for a moment deliberated what she would do if he had a stroke while with her. *Would she leave him to die in agony alone or would she call for help?* Whenever she took those small white pills that Kareema doled out liberally, like candy, Ameera's mind would think up the strangest things.

What if she looked on while he died in agony, watched as he begged her for help, as his eyes rolled back and he took his last breath…what if that happened?

It's ok…everything will be fine…I'm untouchable, pure and peaceful. She felt a calm spread over her body, in spite of what was happening to it. She thought of her parents up in heaven because that is where they surely must be…she hoped they could not see her.

Nothing could hurt her now, she was not even here, and she was soaring above…and watching…watching…

******

Iliya closed the door to his private room, and hastily adjusted his shirt and tie. He smoothed the few, wisps of graying hair with his damp palms and glanced quickly at the Persian mirror hanging in the hallway. He liked what he saw in the reflection. The expensive Armani suit, shirt, and the gold Rolex on his wrist filled him with pride.

Not so bad for a poor boy from the old Soviet bloc, he felt the need to tell himself often. He shuddered, regretfully summoning up scenes from his childhood, the poverty, drabness, the perpetual cold, and most of all, his father's drunken abuse. He felt lucky that he had escaped that hellhole a long time ago. He thought of the girl…he needed to get rid of her as soon as possible. Better to let Lazar deal with her. She had been fun for the past hour but he sensed an unnerving strangeness about her. Her complete lack of emotion frightened him.

"*Lazar sto delas?*" he called out to the scruffy looking man lurking in the corner of the hall, leaning on the wall indifferently, and smoking. In the dim interior of the hall he looked sinister, and *rightfully so*, thought Iliya, since Lazar was his 'strongman'…a cold and remorseless *sadista*. Iliya would never admit it but he feared him slightly. He had known Lazar for decades; ever since their years back in Moscow working any kind of job they could get their hands on. In fact, he knew Lazar so well that sometimes he wished he could erase those memories. The things the two of them have been through, the things they had done…he felt suddenly chilly as if a gust of freezing Siberian air brushed by him.

He took out his box of cigars and let Lazar light one for him, lazily looking at the taller, lighter skinned man through the glow of the lit match. Lazar barely mumbled an incoherent answer.

He was rarely in a mood to talk. "Waiting," Lazar finally answered, as he blew a circle of smoke towards the ceiling and continued to stare into the dimness of the busy club.

Lazar was one ugly Siberian, Iliya thought to himself, he was the kind that gave the wrong impression about the rest of them to the world, *typical Russian underground henchman*. The kind you saw in Hollywood movies all the time.

Iliya sucked on his expensive Cuban cigar petulantly…*what did they know about Russia? Pfft! Those Americans.*

If only some of his compatriots would do like Iliya and clean themselves up a notch, it would help portray a more civilized face of their country, one that was sophisticated, affluent, cultured, and modern.

Why, just look at him, Iliya Tarasov. Look at what he had accomplished, how he had transformed himself. He was the talk of town back home and people feared him now. Finally, he was in charge, he was ready to cut loose from those baboons back in Moscow and be his own boss.

"Keep an eye on that girl in my room," he said, getting ready to join the crowd. Over his shoulder he added, "she should be leaving soon…she is in the bathroom…make sure she is paid and does not make any trouble…. *ponimaete?*"

"*Da*", Lazar nodded imperceptibly. He understood. Once again, Iliya patted his silk Italian tie and with a well-rehearsed smirk, he entered the grand room of the 'Gypsy'.

To his delight, he could see that the night was in full swing already. Loud dance music vibrated throughout the nightclub, tipsy patrons seemed to be enjoying themselves.

Some ate their five course dinners, some smoked their water pipes, and some talked...laughed loudly. Others tried to impress their friends by telling anecdotes of their financial successes in the booming property market, something that in the past Dubai had been famous for. Many more seemed to be waiting for something. They smoked or drank quietly, anticipation on their faces.

Iliya went around the large and luxurious interior of the club, amicably greeting regular customers...checking on others who were first-timers, and speaking to the waiters and the live five-man band on the stage.

He felt electrified by this evening. He felt powerful. A couple of pills he had consumed earlier contributed to this euphoric feeling. The hour he had spent with the girl compounded with the stimulating atmosphere filled him with a manic excitement. He loved to see the club full and the customers happy and drinking. 'The Gypsy' had become an icon of Dubai's nightlife. Everybody who was anybody in the city wanted to be here, to see what all the fuss was.

He made his way to the elevator. He had an important meeting in the basement. His thin lips lifted slyly. If only these rich, fattened, pampered and spoilt people knew what he knew. The shock that would rattle the city would be of such tremendous proportions, of such irreversible damage, even Iliya Tarasov could not recover after such a scandal. He cringed at the thought of what these arrogant and famous people would think of him and his posh nightclub if they only knew what he had been doing the last hour. If they knew, what he was arranging to do. Involuntarily, the Russian felt a shiver wash over his skin.

Unbelievably, it appeared that even Iliya Tarasov had a conscience, however infrequently it visited him.

Chapter 14

Ginni

Ginni thought of her dead mother as she crouched, huddling under the leaking verandah roof. Some water dribbled on her forehead and down her frowning, brown face. She wiped it off, staring at the courtyard where some of the children jumped in the slushy puddles. The ground was gummy from the water, since it had been raining for ages it seemed to her. 'New Delhi Primary School' was anything but new. Decrepit buildings, peeling paint and rusty squeaking metal doors and window shutters, indicated a school in dire needs of injecting some 'New' in its misleading name.

A sad looking swing and corroded seesaw were the two equipments of choice at break time, when the excited children poured out in their hundreds onto the muddy, slippery courtyard. *Maa would say its 'raining cats and dogs', Maa* had loved to watch American movies on the rare visits to the city theatres.

"Look at that Ginni," her friend Anjuli turned the older girl's face, cupping it gently between her small hands, "do you see that strange boy looking up at the sky?"

Anjuli was pointing a thin finger at a large, older looking boy standing in the center of the playground, his face tilted, his eyes open, and staring at the cascade of rain. Anjuli was even poorer than Ginni. What's more, she had no *Maa or Baap; at least I have a dad*...reasoned Ginni, feeling sorry for her skinny little friend.

"That boy is 'cuckoo in the head' you know," Anjuli continued bragging about the insider information she had, "I heard Mrs.Padukone talking to the new helper in the teachers' room about him."

Ginni shivered, pulling the thin cotton sweater tighter around her body. She glanced at Anjuli. The girl was shaking like a banana tree leaf in her damp school uniform. "You should not have gone to play in the rain Anjuli, look how cold you are...Come here, come."

She unbuttoned her worn out blue sweater and drew the little girl inside as much as she could, stretching the flimsy fabric so it would fit both of them. The warmth of her body helped and Anjuli stopped shaking.

"In any case it is better than nothing, right?"

******

"Ms.Karisma, are you finished with the sketch?" The voice transported her back to the present clumsily. Mercy was peering at her face. Ginni tore her eyes away from the refreshingly grey Dubai sky. Sometimes they got lucky and had completely unexpected cloudy days in the desert state. It looked like rain had finally arrived and as always brought her recollections of things best left forgotten and hidden in the pockets of her mind.

Her office on the second floor of a villa had a full view of the busy *'al Wasl Road'* running in front of it. An intricate cast iron staircase led the way downstairs, to the showroom, boutique, and various quarters for her assistant designers, cutters, and tailors. A large open studio where she designed, sketched, and created her outfits, opened into the back of the villa and overlooked a small, but blooming garden. There, heavenly smelling jasmine and bougainvillea bushes vied for admiration with the fragrant gardenia and the chunky dwarf palm trees. The studio had plenty of light, which inundated it from the windows and skylights.

Ginni oversaw all aspects of the interior design in the villa. Richly colored rugs and an assortment of cushions of different textures scattered throughout theatrically. Indian vases and Buddha statues, ornately carved

Persian mirrors and Arabian art pieces, created a mysteriously alluring and eccentric home and work area. Intrigued and undeniably influenced by her Indian culture, Ginni's designs and ingenious ideas portrayed an eclectic mix of the finest of Arab, Persian and Indian traditional style and art. The result was an extraordinary, individual vision.

"Ms.Karisma, the sketch for Mrs. Gaafari...sorry, but did you finish it? They are waiting for it in the cutting room." Mercy was clearly terrified but insistent in getting her boss's attention. A tiny thing, not more than five feet tall, but endowed with guts and brains, which Ginni admired as much as she loved to terrorize the girl. Finally, Ginni faced her, swinging her tall body in the leather chair and leaning back.

She was not traditionally good-looking, but her classic Indian features, beautiful skin, and glossy hair together with her height, created a remarkably attractive woman. She was religious about regularly attending to her appearance.

Frequent visits to the best spas and hair salons in Dubai, or whichever country she was in at the time, and a few quiet trips to a dermatology clinic ensured she always looked her best. Ginni considered looking immaculate necessary, otherwise her insecurities got the best of her, and she reverted to that helpless little girl again, a girl she wanted so badly to forget. Ginni planted her extension lashed eyes on Mercy. To the younger girl's delight, she did not try to bite her head off or pour acid from her tongue as usual.

"Yes. All the sketches are finished for Mrs.Gaafari's collection. Tell Pierre that we will need them all by the weekend. Mrs.Gaafari is coming by today to have a look at what we have done so far." Pierre, the perpetually groomed, frustrated Frenchman, who was in chronic distress over what he alleged were his 'unworthy' clientele in Dubai. "These people..." he would begin his usual rant sauntering around the design studio in a huff, pins in his mouth, and a measuring tape around his short neck, a picture of French indignation. "...Are unaware of the great art that is created by us, fashion designers," he would click his tongue scornfully. "They are ingrates...*cretins.*"

Pierre had a falling out with a 'certain' famous label in Europe and ended up moving to Dubai to start afresh. He had joined Ginni in a collaborative attempt at a partnership but down the road, she decided to break away and create her own brand. Five years later, he was still with Ginni and cursing the unfairness of the world, his stilted career, fussing and swearing over the slightest incident of imperfection in the studio. His passion for fashion and persistent need to prove he was the best, benefited Ginni, and he was the only person in the company she humored and coddled.

Ginni turned her attention back to the desk with the drawing board and resumed working, ignoring Mercy, clearly indicating that the conversation was over.

"Ms. Karisma?" Mercy cleared her throat. Regardless of her boss's dreadful temper and wacky behavior, Mercy appeared to have a baffling sense of sympathy and compassion for Ginni.

Instead of an answer, Mercy watched stunned, as a tear slid down Ginni's cheek, unchecked, and landed on the pile of sketches. Mercy had seen Ginni drunk, hysterical and wild, but never sad. She had witnessed Ginni cavorting with men on the dance floor at many a party; she had withstood the worst of temper tantrums over numerous breakups and lovers quarrels. She had been in the thick of countless fights and arguments with staff, and occasional meltdowns.

Yet, she had never, in all of the three years that she had worked with the moody designer, seen her cry, silently, sincerely, at her desk, in full view of her assistant, as the typically rainless Dubai sky opened up, pouring warm, unexpected rain.

******

Ginni sat at a rickety plastic table trying to do the math homework. She kept thinking though, about her dead mother and her absent father. Only a year ago, they were all together. *Maa* was her best friend. *How she missed her.*

A dim-witted moth got too close to the oil lamp, and she watched as it incinerated quickly, in what must have been a painful moth death.

The window was open to let in some fresh air into this stifling, smelly room. It smelled of cheap tobacco and home brewed alcohol, which her uncle drank without fail, every night.

Her aunt, watched silently, never arguing with him. In the eighteen years, they had been married, she did not give him a child, and due to that single life-changing event, she continued to allow all sort of degradation to herself by her spiteful drunk of a husband. In time, she stopped talking and went about her household duties quietly, like a shadow, but somehow still living, ambivalent as to where she belonged, appalled at the curve her life had taken, yet frozen into passive silence by centuries of tradition. It was easy to overlook her aunt's presence in the house. She crept about noiselessly in plastic slippers, only speaking to Ginni to ask her if she had eaten or done her homework.

Tonight, after a meal of spicy *dal,* and warm *naan* bread they sat together for a few minutes. Her aunt sat on the floor mat, silently and what seemed to Ginni contentedly, sewing a ripped sari. She was always mending pieces of clothing; new clothes were a complete luxury in their neighborhood, an ocean of corrugated steel shack dwellings on the outskirts of Delhi.

Theirs was a neighborhood of poor people. Men went to work as laborers, masons, carpenters, bricklayers and a special lucky few who held the desirable and important position of supervisor or laborer overseer. They worked all day for a pittance, making enough only for the basic survival, two maybe three meals a day, a leaky roof over their head and their children attending the charity school run by local nuns.

Still, this life was many times better than that of unfortunate millions all over the country who begged or committed unspeakable crimes in order to survive. Ginni knew well the many nasty things that happened to people who were alone and helpless. She knew what happened to young girls with dead mothers, and absent fathers to guard them from the malice of the world.

"Aunty did my father send for me yet?" she spoke softly, afraid of the answer, that usual disappointing answer.

The woman looked at her for an exceptionally long time, her sewing suspended in midair, her eyes glazed at first as if she did not understand the girls' question. Then she bent over her stitching again and muttered almost inaudibly, "no, not yet *bachcha*", not yet child, her voice flat and detached as usual.

Ginni looked at the bent head, the long thick braid resting on the floor by her aunts' bare feet, twisted and poised as a snake ready to spring. She felt tears burning her eyes, urgently trying to escape, but she would not let them. Tears brought no mercy in this house, not for any of its inhabitants.

"But *Baap* said he will send for me last month aunty. What happened to him? Why is he not sending for me?" her voice trembled as she clenched her fists, hoping uncle would not get back yet. Not before, she got Aunty to talk about father.

"Please *Chach*i, please talk to me…when will I leave to see father? When will I go to Dubai?" her words tumbling out fast now, before she lost her nerve. Previous inquiries like this have produced no results and even worse, her repeated mentioning of her father seemed to infuriate uncle and drive him into a drunken rage.

"I have fed you and clothed you and took care of you all these years," he would bellow, spittle showering everyone in his vicinity.

"This is how you repay me?" his bloodshot eyes had bulged at her. "By asking to leave with that man?" he had slapped his hands together in mock disbelief. His eyes reddened and menacing, his dirty t-shirt hanging over his belly, he continued to bemoan his condition and called her an ungrateful child, and what else could one expect from the daughter of a man like her father.

To hear uncle speak, it sounded as if her father was a man of lower class, someone who was useless and despised. He was 'a bloody dog', who abandoned his wife and child to disease and poverty and went on to live a life of comfort, of freedom from his responsibilities, choosing the easy life in a prosperous Gulf country. After all, he was the kind of man who left his wife to die alone, and now he has left his *ladki*…his girl, behind too.

Chapter 15

Qays

The seven men had been debating, arguing, and planning for hours. They sat on the floor, on supple cowhide cushions; knees crossed, their bodies leaning forward, tense with animated conversation. The carpet they sat on was richly textured and skillfully woven, the work of Afghan masters, who had toiled painstakingly for months, over masterpieces like this one, for a mere pittance in pay. The same rugs later sold for exorbitant prices to men who had no difficulty paying such sums, in order to possess a work of art as exceptional as this.

Above them, a colorful Persian chandelier hung, yet another amazing display of ancient and delicate traditional artistry…containing two dozen swirling light bulbs that cast soft yellow and gold light onto the men's faces. Shadows danced across the large *Majlis*, deceitfully portraying a mood more suitable for an intimate romantic dinner than a religious meeting. Thimbles of tea were passed around by the man they called Abu

Salem. He was a giant of a man, his long beard, and swarthy skin tone giving an immediate impression of authority. He got up gathering his *thobe* around him, the expensive white fabric rustling loudly in the silence of the room.

Abu Salem offered traditional Arabic tea, light in color and flavored with a few mint leaves that swirled limply in the diminutive teacups. The men inhaled deeply, the delightful aroma of fresh tea, mint, and cardamom.

"Shukran ya akhi," thank you brother, they said humbly, in turn, respectfully accepting their steaming sweet beverage. Qays took his glass and muttered the same. Then he withdrew from the circle, away from the light, sipping the tea, staring off silently into the distance. The men enjoyed their tea in silence for a few moments. Abu Salem passed around a glass bowl brimming with ripe dates, plump and golden. They accepted again, chewing on the sticky, delicious fruit in harmony. Some of them had furrowed brows, obviously deep in contemplation; others had serene, passive expressions on their bearded faces.

A chubby African man spoke, "Abu Salem...did you get to speak with our leader in Cairo?" His plump legs contorted on the pillow...he was obviously finding it uncomfortable to sit in this position due to his ample weight, and struggling to stay upright.

He looked comic, and Qays noticed a shadow of a smile crossed Abu Salem's lips before he spoke. "Yes, brother Omer...our brothers in Cairo are ready for us anytime." He continued to sip his tea; exhausted it seemed, from the long meeting that had concluded."

This was their fourth round of tea and dates and he was tired.

Long gone were the days when Abu Salem could expound the infinite wisdom and wonder of their religion, sometimes if required of him, for days at a time, with only short breaks for prayer and partaking of food. He looked fondly at some of the younger brothers, still full of passion and zest for the truth.

A tall, thin man was speaking to the group in a despondent tone. He kept positioning his dazzlingly white *Gotra* repeatedly, unsuccessfully trying to get it to settle on his head just so. "Yes, many have strayed wishing to please the world Even true believers are now weakened by these pressures of society and vice," he said.

Qays interrupted, speaking in a low voice from his shadowy corner of the room, "But brother, those on the wrong path are those who must be led." His face detached until now, it suddenly clouded with an agitated fervor, and he continued. "They are weak in flesh and in their spirit, afraid to stand up and face the masses, with their true feelings," the other men murmured an unidentifiable comment, startled by the sudden outbreak.

Qays continued. His voice rose into a shrill pitch. "There are many who are not able to pronounce their convictions in a loud and proud voice." A silence fell over the room. All eyes were riveted on Qays. He went on, "I have tried to understand those who do not crave to lead a decent life, a clean life…for many years I have watched them and studied them." Qays's voice trembled, shook like the foundation of an old building, one that was ready to collapse. "I still can't understand," he carried on, one side of his lip twitching unchecked, the color of his usually tan face darker, sallow, apparently unaware of his companions, of their frightened, embarrassed looks.

Slowly, Abu Salem raised his eyes from the lifeless mint leaves in his cooling tea. What Qays did not know until today was that for weeks the group had been disturbed by his negative, almost violent attitude. It had slipped brother Omer's lips inadvertently that Abu Salem had tried coaxing information about the reason for this change. Omer explained that their elder had done it privately with each brother, fearful of embarrassing Qays.

Abu Salem's clear voice rang across the room, "*Ya akhi, Estahda Billah*, calm down brother," his eyes twinkled dangerously. "You have been plagued by this concern, incessantly. It is not a failure if you do not understand the logic of those who do not fear God, who do not wish to praise his glory… and those souls who lead an immoral and wasted life."

A few of the men nodded their heads in agreement and whispered amongst themselves animatedly. Oblivious to Abu Salem's warning look, Qays replied immediately. "They are, cowardly, averting their eyes from the impropriety in the streets." He pulled on his beard distractedly, "*Walla*, by God, did you not notice the loose morals, and fallen women, who are arrogantly walking amongst our children?"

Murmur of understanding and sympathy arose from the congregated men. Abu Salem raised his hand and a hush fell over them. Unwelcome, persistent, scantily dressed 'women of the night' thronged the malls, the beaches, and main streets of the city. All the men in the room wrestled with this reality, struggled to live with it.

"Brothers, let us not get excited over issues of morality, when bigger and more important matters await our energy and focus. Let us not forget the reason we are here." The tall man looked sternly at each of his visitors.

Some shifted uncomfortably under his gaze. Qays however, continued to scowl, unappeased and unconvinced.

Even Abu Salem's authoritative position and seniority in years did not seem to deter him from his stubbornness, "*Ya Akhi* Qays, my brother, I'm telling you again, do not scatter your energy on the misled and the wicked. It is not our place or job to judge them." He attempted a smile, "the all powerful one in the heavens above knows what is in each of our hearts, and he alone can be the judge."

"*Subhanallah*...yes you are wise Abu Salem," one of the group announced excitedly, glad that the tense moment had passed. "Leave them to their creator, that is the right thing to do," he looked relieved.

The other men started to confer amongst themselves again, and Abu Salem used that opportunity to address Qays, who had not moved from his place on the carpet.

"Brother, calm in the name of Allah, this is a peaceful meeting, a way to focus on issues of importance to the community." He clicked the sandalwood prayer beads in his hand rhythmically, like wheels on a train, "It is not a meeting for angry and volatile speeches like yours which focus on that which is not for us." His face was stormy but his voice calm. He had moved closer to the dismal looking man, leaning towards him slightly. He had looked closely at Qays's resolute face.

Qays did not speak. Abu Salem tried to persuade him further, "You will bring great misfortune on yourself and your family if you persist like this. Pray to our all knowing and all forgiving *Allah* so he will lead you to the right path..." His words were passionate, pleading. With that, he gathered his flowing white robe and got up. He approached the animated group of men who were laughing, and sat down amongst them. Thankfully, they seemed to have forgotten the incident.

Qays sat on the floor for a while longer, his legs crossed, his eyes set in narrow slits, his mouth set decisively. His agitated mind spun in circles. He found no relief, no comfort in Abu Salem's wise words. There was no relief for sinners...for adulterers.

If only they knew. If only they knew, what he had done. If only they could see into his hypocritical soul. If only they knew...it was himself he was talking about.

Then he got up and walked out of the *Majlis*, all the while followed by the kind, concerned eyes of Abu Salem.

Chapter 16

Jane

The *'Maydan* racecourse was home to the richest horse race in the world. The grand prize was five million dollars and riders from all over the world flocked to the city in the hopes of hitting the jackpot. Sheiks, politicians, ambassadors, and celebrities attended. Some flew in private helicopters to the VIP lounges in order to watch in relative anonymity.

Others did the opposite. They craved recognition and meant to leave their mark on the Dubai social scene. Wearing the right clothes to this event was of the ultimate importance. Dubai socialites spent months in preparation, getting their dresses and headwear ordered from overseas or handmade by designer milliners to assure its uniqueness. Jane had been looking forward to this event for months. David had looked on with amusement as she had fussed over her outfit, her hat, everything. Finally, today was the day. David felt a sense of relief that it would soon be over.

"Jane, are you ready dear?" David spoke with a slight lisp. He looked at his Rolex worriedly. He fidgeted with his pink tie and tried to keep calm. Jane was late as usual. Ever since they moved to Dubai, she had morphed into a different woman. Someone he no longer recognized. He blamed this city. It brought out the worst in both of them. At the same time, Dubai had spun its alluring web around him, rendering him her obedient servant. Sometimes he missed their simple life in England, the long walks with the dogs and the Sunday lunches at the modest local restaurant. No pretenses and no demands to behave the way one did not really feel or want to.

Jake was a pleasant boy then, willing to join in their plans and weekend trips to the beach and such. Nowadays he was always away with his friends going to clubs, or the beach or wherever it was these Dubai kids hung out. David ran his hand through his pale, thinning hair dejectedly. What had he done wrong? He blamed himself for his family's current predicament and tried to fix it the one way he knew how. Without complaint, he provided them with more money whenever they demanded, money for Jane's surgeries, treatments, and vacations, money for Jakes' private school and expensive school trips.

Why, he recalled, last month he paid for a ridiculously pricey ski trip to Switzerland. Before that, there was a weeklong hiking trip to Malaysia and prior to that a quick jaunt to London for a must see rock concert.

"I'm ready dear, we can go now!" Jane looked cheerful and confidently strode towards the waiting limo. Her last surgery had not gone well and she had become quite fond of painkillers. Externally Jane seemed perfect, but inside her, an anxious drug addicted woman teetered around.

They were riding with another couple to the races, and only a limo would do, Jane had insisted. "This is a once in a lifetime event David dear, something we will remember forever, why not do it right?" she had giggled like a girl and evidently was excited at the prospect, so David had agreed. More than anything, he loved to make Jane happy.

"You do know that our lively Mexican friends are taking the helicopter don't you?" Jane had informed him about that fact three times during the past week. Moreover, yes he did know that pretentious couple. They were the kind of people who looked down their noses at anyone not rich enough to take the helicopter for a spin.

Jane's surgeon was a wizard it seemed. He had created a subtly younger, lovelier Jane. David winced remembering at what price this beauty came. He had tried to reason with her repeatedly. "Jane, don't you think the medication is too much?" He was tired of her terrible mood swings, the crying, and the drinking. "Darling if you are in pain, you need to see the doctor," he had begged his resolute wife. "You can't keep taking the pills like this."

Jane had rolled her eyes, "David, the doctor is the one who gave them to me."

He looked up, brought back to the present moment by the smell of her perfume. David looked at his wife in admiration. She looked incredible! Dressed in a white, perfectly fitted creation by a local designer, Ginni Karisma, her long blonde hair pinned tastefully in a Romanesque hairstyle, she appeared ethereally delicate. Her body and face looked radiant due to a perfect tan, and the custom-made wide brimmed hat, in soft cream color that graced her head and cast soft shadows over her perfect cheeks. She represented the exact embodiment of a truly pampered and high maintenance corporate wife.

"You look gorgeous," he muttered, as she waited for him to give her a kiss on the cheek. In spite of it all he still loved this woman. This was their first outing since her last surgery and he was seeing the full results of the dreadful, pain wracked weeks she had endured. His eyes swept over her body resting on her recently much larger bosom. *Oh yes Jane had really changed.* He tried to hide a silly boy grin and suddenly felt like a teenager on a first date.

Recently he had been feeling inadequate somehow when around his wife. Her sudden attractiveness and self-assurance and her growing circle of male friends made him feel of no consequence. The stronger he performed at work and the more accolades he received in his career the less important he felt at home.

"Thank you dear, are you coming?" she was looking at him inquisitively, waiting by the door. He hurried, following her sheepishly and climbed into the waiting white Hummer limo.

"You look nice too," she patted his arm as he sat down next to her.

Karen and Peter were already there, breaking out the bubbly, set on their promise of 'getting smashed' at this party. Karen was a tennis-playing brunette with long legs and large teeth, a wide, clueless smile constantly pasted on her face.

Today she wore some kind of contraption on her head that resembled a tray of fruit. Peter was vice president of marketing at 'Gaafari Enterprises International' a jolly fellow from Dublin who loved a good laugh and drink.

"Karen, what an entirely wicked hat," Jane exclaimed as she fondled the pineapple, then the strawberries perched on Karen's head. David felt like bursting out with laughter.

"Yes absolutely divine, where did you get it from if I may ask," David said with a straight face. Jane shot him an annoyed look. She still knew him, he thought, suddenly content.

"Jane darling girl, you look fabulous if I can say so myself," Peter did a half bow in front of Jane. The couple was fun to have around, most of the time.

"David my fellow, come and have a glass, this is really good stuff!" he attempted to stand up as the limo took off suddenly, causing the slightly tipsy Irishman to shoot backwards into his seat comically, with a perplexed look on his face, eliciting uncontrollable laughter from the other three.

******

The limo sped through the notorious Dubai traffic heading towards the 'Maydan' racetrack. The famous race was the social event of the year for many Dubai socialites but also for those who arrived from Europe, America, and Australia to attend this glittering occasion. Among the multitude of those were true equestrian lovers and enthusiasts who enjoyed every moment of the race.

"Look, over there," Jane gesticulated frantically as they approached the convoy of limos at the gate waiting to disembark. A famous American actor was posing for photos at the entrance. "Unbelievable, this could never have happened to us in England. We would never be doing this over there," she looked out of the window, her face flushed, and her blue eyes wide and shiny. She was happy, excited. She always was when they went to parties. David sunk against the leather seat of the Hummer, "I'm glad you are happy my dear," he murmured.

Once ushered through the security gates, they headed to the 'Gold Room', a private, overpriced thousand dollar per head tent, offering a five-course dinner, and unlimited beverages. Here they could rub shoulders with the movers and shakers of Dubai society and live to tell about it. A couple of hundred people were in that tent, all of whom chose to splurge on the hefty ticket. Many of the women Jane already knew. They air-kissed, shook hands, hugged warmly.

Tanned and fit, expensively dressed and flawlessly primped and prepped by the best beauticians and hairstylists in town, this group flashed their bleached teeth in self-assured, tipsy smiles. Many of the men came over to say hi too, mostly for Jane's sake. She glowed, basking in the special moment...

She laughed loudly, happy, confident, and entirely unaware of her husbands' lingering, disappointed gaze following her around. Then the moment passed, and David was laughing again, tearing his eyes away purposefully, and making his way towards the American CEO of a Dutch Oil company. *"Alsalamualaikum,"* he first greeted a young Arab billionaire who was deeply engrossed in conversation with the lanky American. All three men shook hands amidst much laughter and shoulder slapping.

"How are things over at my friends company?" the billionaire asked David cordially. David smiled, "Good, you know how Jassim is. Successful at everything he touches."

"Well, I must say that they have it going well over there. He is a lucky son of a gun that Jassim," the American laughed loudly, sending spittle David's way."On the other hand I heard that there could be trouble brewing, since he had called the auditors in eh?" David's hands felt cold. *Auditors?* This was the first time he heard these unsettling news.

"Yes, I guess he is lucky," David took a tentative sip from his champagne flute. He felt tired. The loud music and voices grated on his ears, the pleasantries rung untrue. He thought of the numerous parties and gatherings he had attended since arriving in Dubai. One thing he knew for sure was that he was becoming quite fed up with the familiar, superficial scene. All three men turned their attention to the dance floor. Peter was making a spectacle of himself on the dance floor, gyrating with a busty Lebanese wife of a prominent executive.

Jane and Karen had gone out to catch some of the race action...*and no doubt to be photographed for the magazines,* David pursed his lips in disapproval. Jane had gotten it into her head that most of the women, and men, attending the race should have their picture appear in the local society magazines. People queued up patiently, in their fancy hats and coordinating outfits, sweating under the mocking Dubai sun.

David on the other hand, had matters of a more serious nature on his mind.

Chapter 17

Tara

Tara kept Miriam and Aisha busy with private ballet and gymnastics lessons and after school activities. Her hope was for them to grow up citizens of the world, tolerant, compassionate, and honest. She tried to expose them to as much cultural diversity as she could.

One of Tara's friends was a gutsy Chicago girl called Wendy, married to a man of Arab origin as well. He was not the practicing kind and Wendy had not converted to Islam after marriage. They struck a special friendship over their monthly playgroup. At Christmas, Wendy would have a party for the kids and Tara and the girls always went, along with a crowd of moms dragging their kids in tow. It was an inspiring thing to see, because no two moms were from the same country or married to men from their native countries. The result was a miniature gathering of the United Nations.

When it was time for Easter egg hunting they were there too…hunting for the painstakingly colored eggs on the lawn of Wendy's big villa in

Jumeirah Islands, wearing pretty hand decorated Easter bonnets and frilly dresses. About a year ago, Qays had started insisting that Wendy was a bad influence on Tara and the girls, and that she should not see her anymore.

"Why?" She had persisted. He had looked at her over his laptop screen. There was never a smile on his face lately. She could not understand the reason for his visible unhappiness.

"Because, I think it is best for us," was the curt answer.

She gasped at the coldness in his voice, "I still don't think that is a good enough reason, she is my friend, and I will continue to see her," Tara started to walk off, dismayed with this strange man sitting in her husband's chair, sleeping in her bed.

"Did you know that he drinks?" Qays slammed the cover of the laptop and stared at her, ready to pounce on her answer.

"You knew and yet you never told me?" the girls were playing in their room, and the house was quiet, except for the rattle of the construction drill outside. They were working on a new freeway next to their compound. Tara could hear the accusation in his voice; see it in his heavily lidded eyes. They stood silently, weighing their options. Tara remembered Dr. Ghassan, his soothing voice coaching her. *"You deserve all good, you deserve love, and you deserve respect."* After that argument, their Friday afternoon lunches and picnics with Wendy dwindled to nothing, and whenever Tara mentioned the subject, even though knowing it was hopeless and that Qays would not associate with them anymore, he would go into a rage and lecture her on the sins of unbelievers and their forthcoming retribution. His eyes, the color of untainted honey, would get that odd look as he expounded how the wrath of God is going to catch up with sinners and consumers of alcohol. He terrified her.

"Don't you know what they are?" he would almost spit out the words. His face trembled with rage, "Why do you want me to know people like that?"

Tara was afraid that her husband had gone quite insane, feeling relieved when he stormed off to read and listen to the news in the living room.

Over the course of the next few months, their relationship soured even more. She observed him wordlessly, not arguing or demanding explanations for his bizarre behavior. She went around her life wearing a fake attitude of contentment, devoting her time and energy to the girls, and the charity work. Many months passed with no discernible change in their lives.

However, unknown to Tara, the wheels of that ever-watchful force in the sky were already turning, already spinning, bringing into the world that which should have remained nameless.

Chapter 18

David

David looked around the oval conference table. His calm blue eyes swept over the men and women facing him. They all wore dark designer suits and ties, their respective wrists, necks or ears adorned by expensive watches and jewelry. Their lavish lifestyle extended beyond that. The cars driven by the group assembled included a Mercedes, two Hummers, and a Porsche.

The only female in the assembly, and the youngest, Alexandra, a curvaceous, fair-haired PA from Barcelona, sped around Dubai recklessly in her convertible Aston Martin, accumulating thousands of dirhams worth of speeding fines, for which the company paid. Among the group, Jassim stood out in his choice of vehicle, for he alone drove a stunning white Maybach.

David himself was the proud owner of a black Land cruiser. Driving over the sand dunes in the powerful vehicle, he felt like the king of the world. He leaned back in the supple leather conference chair, rocking in it slightly. The voices in the room faded into the background.

He could see the sprawling city around him from his place at the table. The company's conference room was huge in proportion, spanned on two sides by floor to ceiling tinted glass panes; giant pieces of custom designed tempered glass, making it possible to appreciate the expansion of the city beneath them. In the distance, were the giant developments and feats of architectural engineering...the three Palms and the World. Engineering and construction projects, astonishing in ingenuity and massive in design, visions really, of a remarkable people.

The Bedouins had a plan for their desert city he realized with respect. They wanted a wealthy, abundant oasis, surrounded by soothing cool water, brought to the desert nation tirelessly, stubbornly, by impressive endeavors of engineering. This fascination with water and things aquatic was most surely born out of its obvious and painful lack in the desert nature of the land. The Bedouin tribes struggled for centuries with this essential life giving force, or rather the lack of it.

Thankfully, in the present world, water came more easily to the desert and to its inhabitants, to those thirsty for it for many centuries.

To the immediate right, the world renowned 'Burj Khalifa' tower stood proudly erect...glimmering in all its slim silver glory...a familiar and kindly giant. This towering wonder pathetically dwarfed the other skyscrapers along Sheikh Zayed Road. Whether a manmade island or a mall the size of a small city or the first self-driven monorail system in the Middle East, David could not help but admire the city's spunk and stubbornness. Jassim Al Gaafari the CEO, addressed him abruptly, bringing David's attention back to the meeting, "David, did you attend the meeting with the Canadian subcontractors for the 'Dubai Discovery' project?"

"Er, yes, yes I did, in fact I have another meeting scheduled on Thursday with the director." He shuffled the notes in front of him, obviously not prepared for the question. He cursed. *Where was the damn report?*

"I have heard from the building Authority," Jassim leaned back in his chair before continuing. "There are incorrectly submitted construction permits from our people," he looked around the table. David felt singled out somehow, threatened. "Please make sure that your staff is thorough in this regard David. Correct protocol of government policies is crucial for smooth operation within the company."

David felt his face redden. He shifted in his seat. Jassim was not done,

"I do not need to remind all of you at this table, of what happened to one of our good friends due to a similar oversight a couple of years ago". He looked at David suggestively for a moment from his position at the head of the table. Even though David had not been working for the 'Gaafari Group' at the time, he was aware of the alluded to incident.

A well-known saga in the real estate development and construction business, it had all the elements of a good thriller. Conspiracy, fraud, misappropriation of millions of dollars, and high profile international mix of executives involved, resulted in a scandalous and highly public debacle that followed for many months afterwards. Seasoned peers retold this tale as a cautionary lesson to the recently arrived in the country or the industry, effectively scaring the living daylights out of them.

Jassim continued, slightly adjusting his *Gotra,* or headdress…a long white material hanging onto the shoulders from the head kept in place by the circular black rope, the *Agal.* Both were worn in combination with the long sleeved white cloak, the *Kandoora* a traditional outfit worn by the local men of the region, "We need to schedule a meeting with the rest of the senior management from the Japanese company," he shuffled some papers. "And I can see that we are making good headway with the commission on labor rights, which is excellent news," he looked up, smiled at the group. Praise from Jassim was rare and cherished like the sun when received. "We need to assure them of the quality of our human resource department, do make sure they get a tour of our labor camps," he was reading from the diary, efficiently organized by his assistant, perusing it quickly, obviously in some urgency to wrap up what had already stretched into an all day meeting.

Jassim exuded charisma and power, his manner firm and unyielding… the same principle, he applied to rearing his children and his relationship with his wife. If there were any shortcomings to his character, he kept them well hidden out of public scrutiny. Few dared question Jassim Al Gaafari's decisions.

Because he was not the sort of man who took rebuke and embarrassment easily, his reputation in business circles stayed above reproach, and was necessary for the success of his respected group of companies.

"Alexandra, I'm surprised that you have not briefed me on that last meeting with Dubai Property and Land Group…it is extremely important I meet with you about that."

"I tried to see you yesterday Mr. Gaafari…you were not in the office," Alexandra fiddled with her pen and kept her eyes on the pad in front of her, then swung her perfectly blow dried hair. "In any case I will make sure I do that."

Jassim gave the assistant a look that was obvious to all present at the table. "Well, if we are done with agendas I will call this meeting finished and we will meet on Sunday again. Hopefully by that time all the points we have covered today would be dealt with."

David and the others around the table hid their knowing smirks and grins well. Jassim might try hard to hide his real weakness, but it was clear to everyone else around him. Jassim had more than a reputation in business. He had a reputation for women...for torrid, frequent affairs. His strange relationship with Alexandra was the best-kept secret in the company.

Rumor had it that allegedly the fiery tempered PA used to work for a Spanish company that was doing business with the Gaafari Group. Soon after, Jassim had offered Alexandra a job in Dubai. She had accepted immediately. It was an offer she could definitely not refuse. She was young, unattached, and hungry for success in all its forms. After only a year at the company, she sat at the most important meetings in the firm, and accompanied him frequently on 'Business' trips. Recently however, he seemed distracted and did not call her as often as before. Alexandra knew he saw other women...he had made it clear from the beginning that he was not interested in leaving his wife or any other woman for her. In fact, he had no plans to alter his lifestyle for any of the women in his life.

He was quite happy pulling the many strings in the game he played. Powerful business deals, as well as intense, controlling relationships. They made him feel alive and challenged. He loved the chase much more than the final victory. In the business world, he was a risk taker and some said reckless in his company's investments.

Many in his close family circle had voiced their concern over his vision and direction, sometimes not compatible with the rest of the family...

A couple of uncles, his father's brothers, were not ready to hand over their stake or their say in a company that had been in the family for decades. Arguments erupted frequently. The family frowned upon his brazen dalliance with women. Every one of his relatives abhorred the immoral pursuits of this troublesome yet successful heir to the hard-earned family fortune...

David knew all this because he had access to a lot of personal information about his boss that he should not have been privy to. The company teemed with jealousy and backstabbing, and information was available for the right price. He studied the man and listened attentively to all the chat in the office, and at social functions. Sometimes, a member of staff publicly shamed by Jassim, or a vengeful ex-employee gladly parted with inside information when asked the right questions. David knew which questions to ask.

People liked to tell juicy stories about the rich and famous. The delicious, scandalous, often times tall tales equally thrilled and petrified the sensibilities of mere mortals. Stories of the local privileged Arab billionaires and celebrities were the most popular...due to their inaccessibility to the mainstream public, to the ordinary folk of the city; their mystifying and elusive lifestyle became a breeding ground for exaggerated and repeatedly bogus information.

Back in his office after the meeting, David closed the door and called Jane. "David darling, how are you?" her voice sounded winded. She was probably on the treadmill, David thought.

"So far, today, I'm all right. Jassim is keeping everyone busy," David swiveled in his big leather chair, "You know how he is," he looked outside his large windows to the city buzzing below.

He was fascinated by the view and by his expensively furnished, office. At times he could not believe that he was actually here...working for one of the prime multinational group of companies in the world...associating with millionaires, investors, playboys and celebrities. When he remembered his respectable but far from lavish office in London, it seemed like a dream, somebody else's dream.

His answer seemed to have annoyed Jane, "What do you mean so far you are all right?" she asked.

Last night over dinner, David had complained about the highhanded way Jassim treated him. He thought she would remember the conversation. "Ah, it's nothing, I simply meant I'm fine, because of the new project," *liar, coward,* he told himself. Jane accepted this explanation.

David knew he was boring Jane with his woes of Jassim. She did not see anything wrong with the courteous and attractive man when they met at various social events. His boss was always the ultimate charmer, the perfect gentleman with the ladies.

"Well darling do not forget we are expected at that anniversary barbeque this evening," she sounded like a mother admonishing her forgetful son. Her tart answer felt like an icy shower to this reverie. Nevertheless, he was instantly apologetic

"No, darling I did not forget of course, I have a lot to worry these days, you know with the new assignment and," he tried to elaborate but she cut him off.

"Sorry to hear that. I'm sure you can handle it though." Jane was cheerful all of a sudden, did not want to be bothered with his business problems.

"Well of course, I hope I can leave in time for the party," he said.

"Seriously David," her voice rose a note. Jane did not have the so-called emotional episodes that most women supposedly had. However, Dubai had changed her. She had become different in countless ways. It seemed as if her personality deteriorated in exact ratio to her physical enhancement. She sighed into the phone, "Sometimes I feel like I'm all alone in this city David."

David gripped the phone handle. Her suddenly softening voice piqued his interest, "What do you mean darling, I'm here with you, and so is Jake."

She was silent for a moment, and he wondered whether she had heard him. "I know, I know you are here, but I feel so lonely, so terribly alone sometimes." The voice that had risen in anger now sounded like that of a young, frightened girl. David felt his heart go out to her. He had observed her struggle to fit into their new lifestyle, into the exhausting competitiveness of her new group of friends. Often she seemed like a woman bent on self-destruction.

"I'm sorry love, I wish I could be there for you more," he really meant it. "Please try to stop the medicine, please," his voice quivered. Overwhelmed with emotion, the long stressful meeting, and a sense of crumbling desperation he felt his eyes fill with tears. He wanted to fix everything for her, for Jake, for himself. However, David worried that he might already be too late.

Her transformation was not merely physical due to surgeries. She had become demanding, self-absorbed, and constantly agitated. She had become either unwilling…he thought to himself regretfully…or unable to listen to him, as she used to, back in England. David worried of the effect her weight loss medication and painkillers were having on her.

Flashes of their life before moving to Dubai rushed through his mind. The 'normal' life they shared prior to coming here…to this legendarily lavish and excessive place, where wealth and power waited in abundance for those special persons who had a plan, and then the nerve to follow through. He missed his good old Jane, her devotion, her patience and understanding of his many faults. However, it was too late. They were both too deeply involved, had too much invested in Dubai. They were both willing prisoners of the intoxicating city.

He had meant to bring up the issue of her maxed out credit cards, but kept postponing, dreading the unavoidable confrontation. He knew they might have a big argument and therefore kept putting it off. Jane was apparently oblivious of any financial limitations and spent freely on a daily basis.

"You need to be at this party on time. There should be no excuse. It is their twenty fifth wedding anniversary after all," Jane's change of tone startled him, and David sat stock still listening to the once again cold and distant voice. She had withdrawn again and he wondered what he had said to offend her.

He could visualize her face…her bee-stung, plump lips, freshly accentuated by collagen injections, pursing sensually in exasperation. He wiped his wet face with a tissue and blew his nose.

"I also need you to call the bank about that deposit I told you about, last night. Did you remember to do that?"

His throat was parched and he looked at his cooling cup of tea longingly, "Jane I meant to talk to you about that dear…"

"Yes David we should talk about *that*. I'm not pleased with this arrangement. I hate to have to ask you for money all the time. I think we need to talk about that as soon as possible."

David couldn't believe it. Jane had really gone around the bend. She was spending tens of thousands of dirhams every month and had unrestricted access to their account. He gave generously, never complaining.

They did well and he loved to see her happy, he saw no reason to hold back from her. The comments made him realize she was completely delusional about the extent of her spending.

"You know David; I truly believe you are not aware of our expenses at all," Jane insisted. David truly wanted her to stop. She went on, exasperation in her voice, "I paid the maid, and the gardener, the pool company, and the club membership was due this month. In addition, we had attended all these charity functions and your work related functions in the last few months".

The list of caretakers, needed to attend to their every whim, was apparently endless. Ridiculously, there were twice as many staff members than family members in their household. Their seemingly worry free, exciting whirlwind social life had its drawbacks. Expensive clothing and accessories, all so essential trips to beauty salons and debates of what to wear, preceded every single such event, making it a very costly as well as being an emotionally arduous affair.

Jane did do her share of charity work. She was a member of a local expat women's group where she volunteered regularly and donated charitably to its many diverse causes. However, she saw no reason to deny the maintenance of her appearance any expense.

"Jack's school skiing trip payment was due and I took care of that as well," she was irritated. "I did not expect you to question my spending David."

David's forehead crumpled in puzzlement. He had barely managed to say anything, and here she was…rambling on and suddenly they were in the middle off a fight in the middle of the day. *How did this happen in a span of ten minutes?* He really did not understand women.

"Listen Jane darling, I don't want to argue. I really have to go…of course I will call the bank…how much should I deposit in the account?"

******

After the tense conversation with David on the phone, Jane felt exasperated. *David used to be such a dear, dear man.* She stormed off to the pool for a quick swim, ashamed of her momentary weakness in front of him. Quickly changing out of her workout clothes and into a gold colored bikini, Jane hurried to the garden where a large, refreshingly chilled pool waited for her. She dove in expertly, resentment fuelling her brisk half hour swim.

Later as she relaxed, on the lounge chair by the pool, exhausted by the argument and the vigorous exercise, she thought of David again. Of course, she knew that she had changed. It was intentional after all. She was weary of being the mousy goody two shoes Jane, the undemanding and martyr like wife of a successful man.

She loved David but the change was inevitable. Moving to Dubai had been the incentive and opportunity she needed, the catalyst that preceded extremely stressful adjustments in all of their lives. She was well aware that David had changed as well. What is more, his transformation was not one she approved of.

Her mobile rang, "Hello Tara how are you…yes of course I will come… just had a swim and then am going to get ready…okay then, see you there," she had to hurry and get ready for her weekly belly dance class at the Dance Center. The Egyptian instructor was strict about being on time.

She had been attending the lessons for the last few months. Jane loved it, and after the initial inflexibility revealed a formerly buried, daring side to herself. Maybe it was the electrifying atmosphere in this city, she thought...as she stood in front of the huge mirrored closet, wondering which outfit to wear today.

Maybe that black slinky skirt and the tight fitting embroidered tank top that she had bought on their weekend jaunt to Oman. ...*She could tie the gold belly dance belt around her hips today.* Yes, it was her favorite, and the little coins hanging from the material tinkled to the beat, as she playfully sashayed to the music.

If someone had told her one year ago that she would be wearing these kind of clothes, and confidently, sensually, moving to the previously alien beat of exotic Arabic music, she would have told them they had another thing coming!

It seemed that this desert metropolis with its long, hot days, the luxurious hotels and spas, the glittery dinner parties and fashion shows, and the endless pampering, was responsible for rousing some unexpectedly addictive behavior in her. The Middle East had enamored Jane almost overnight.

What was once the mysterious and bizarre world of the Arabs, the previously unfamiliar delights of Arabic music, cuisine, and *shisha* or water pipe developed into cherished, frequently enjoyed activities. She loved driving out to the desert on the weekends, for wild rides in their four-wheel land cruiser, called dune bashing or for sand buggy races with Jack, and all night camping in Bedouin tents, going to sleep under the endless sea of stars.

On one such trip to a desert camp...she had attended a belly dance show where she had watched a stunning dark haired belly dancer for the first time.

"They said she is from Romania." A tipsy looking woman by her side volunteered." Jane listened politely.

The woman was persistent about sharing the information, "I heard the men talking about her...did you know that a big majority of Romanians are actually gypsies?"

*Well, in that case it explains everything...*thought Jane, curving her lips distastefully at the woman's snobbery. The dancer had been gorgeous, with catlike blue eyes, and wild, waist long hair. Jane had been awe struck, and promised herself to try the dance, no matter how silly it sounded.

Jane had watched the rest of the show in disbelief, as the contingent of men present at that camp that night, morphed into a sorry sight of giggling fools, by that simple vision of a desert genie, as she had undulated tantalizingly through the hazy flames of the campfire.

As they left the camp that night, slightly dizzy from the desert air, the food and the music…Jane heard someone call out to the dancer. The wind had carried the words her way and she only heard her name "…Liliana."

Chapter 19

Liliana

Another long day, Liliana thought grumpily as she entered the club. I am back to where I started…no money, no man, and no luck. She lit another Marlboro. Sometimes it all seemed so pointless. All the running around, trying to find love and be happy…*Really, just how many people got everything they hoped for in Dubai?*

"*Sabah el kheir, ya* Lila," Habib was there leaning on the doorway greeting her in Arabic. His lips lifted in a kind smile.

"*Sabah el kheir…good morning,*" Liliana answered in a nearly perfect Algerian dialect. "How are you… *kayfek,*" she spoke Arabic well enough to get by, and Habib was insistent on making her practice as often as possible.

"Where is the *Roosy*… the Russian man?" That is what they called Iliya on a good day.

"He with Lazar…they fight…loudly," Habib smirked, looking secretly pleased. Liliana hugged the big Algerian and grinned. Everyone hated Iliya but even more, they loathed Lazar, his assistant and right hand man. That man was the nastiest human being she had ever met. Liliana shuddered at the thought of his icy blue eyes, boring into her, nightly, as she danced. Even Iliya with his sleazy looks and crooked ways seemed decent compared to the malevolent Siberian.

"Well we can hope that they will kill each other one of these days, and then we can all be free," the words were out of her mouth before she knew it, shocking her for their nastiness. She was becoming as vile as those whom she detested. "I should not have said that Habib…it's not right."

Habib nodded his head, understandingly. He opened the door for her and she stepped into the inner sanctum…the nucleus of the nightclub.

Iliya had spent a large amount of his suspiciously earned monies on hiring a decorating company and using imported materials. Decorated in lavish semi-Arabesque style, it aimed at depicting an air of tantalizing exoticism, failing miserably and only succeeding in looking like a first class brothel.

The girls were here. This was a group of thirteen gorgeous female species, handpicked by Iliya and Lazar for the job. Each woman represented a dream…a lurid male fantasy. Each one arrived from a different part of the world, each a skilled and talented dancer and entertainer, each well educated in the fine art of performing and make-believe, each devoted to her particular artistic type. They were like luxurious treats in a man's fantasy playground.

Liliana's gaze swept the enormous hall, it flickered with candlelight. The smell of stale smoke and food from the kitchen drifted into her nostrils. She kissed and hugged her coworkers in turn. Some of the kisses were warmer, some hugs tighter and more genuine. Still, the girls all stuck together in tough times.

"Liliana, are you going to do that modeling show for that Indian designer next month?" a girl wearing a seductive skintight black evening gown addressed her. She glanced at the exotic looking Colombian.

"I think I am, the agency told me I'm on for that night." Liliana looked forward to the extra money. Iliya permitted the girls to work outside the club, on the condition that they shared a percentage of their earnings with him and that their outside freelancing did not interfere with their schedule at the club.

"The man from the tour agency was asking for you again today," the Colombian beauty looked at her piercingly. All of them made extra money dancing at private parties or modeling and Liliana could not refuse that opportunity.

"That must be the guy from that desert party I danced at a few months ago. He was a real sleaze ball and tried to talk me into making a visit to 'his lonely friend' in a private flat." Liliana shuddered at the memory. She brushed away the thought of that encounter. Being mistaken for a sex worker was one of many unpleasant aspects of their job.

Liliana sat down at the bar, and took her compact and lipstick out. She checked her makeup and then lit a cigarette. The money she had made freelancing she sent back home to her parents. They struggled with the small pension check and Liliana could not stand to see them in need. Silently, she had been wiring five hundred dollars each month to their account. Her father was too proud to acknowledge it, but her mother called every month in tears to thank her. Liliana stubbed out the cigarette angrily. It had burnt her finger. She considered a drink before the evening program started, before the ogling regulars arrived, dreading that one day soon she would become like them, spoiled and cruel.

She waved at Girlie, a vivacious and temperamental Filipino. Lately, a rumor abounded about Girlie's certain supplementary activities. Liliana brushed the thought aside. *She was not going to believe all this malicious gossip.*

"Hey Liliana girl…how are things with you?" A tall, buxom Nigerian greeted her warmly. Liliana was certain the girl had something going on with Iliya. It was hard not to believe that after she had caught them in a compromising position once. Liliana shuddered at the thought of the two of them together. White hot pants and a yellow tank top accentuated the girls' oiled, glistening skin.

"Good my dear, how about you, haven't seen you for a while …been busy or what?" Liliana gave her a quick hug. *What could drive a girl to want to be with Iliya?* The answer sprung to her head instantly. *He had threatened her, of course.*

"Well, a little, I was working with those events people; they needed me for a few modeling and hostessing gigs." She blew smoke towards the ceiling. Her manner was relaxed. Liliana liked her.

Sherri hugged Liliana again, pressing her skinny body into hers. Since Liliana helped her after that incident with the plump pervert, the elfin like Thai girl had looked up to her as a mentor.

"Hi Lila…are you okay?" Sherri managed to say before Iliya entered the hall. He clapped his hands pompously to get their attention. Lazar stood by his side, hands in pockets, brow furrowed, a brooding look on his pale, thin face.

"Ladies, my queens," Iliya bowed deeply...*zdrastvye, hallo.*" He looked at each of them dramatically. "Every week we meet here and I'm always pleased to see all of you. It is a great pleasure to watch such fantastic, lovely ladies dance for me every night." He gesticulated grandiosely, with his customary theatrics.

Liliana heard a hushed "humph" from behind her and chuckled inwardly. The girls were weary of his weekly 'prep talks' barely understood due to his poor English.

There was a phony clearing of the throat from Vikki, and a pretentious cough from the feisty Jamila. They were like a bunch of naughty schoolchildren and Iliya was their detested headmaster.

Iliya deserved every impertinent, hostile reaction he got. "Okay, Okay...I know you are fed up with this talking, but believe me it is important for our group to talk and be friendly every day, to keep our finger on each other's...how they say...pulse."

Liliana wanted to throw up. The only thing Iliya Tarasov wanted was to keep the girls in his control so they could make him more money.

It was going to be yet another entirely too long night. She wished she were in the Maldives with Jassim right now. She got goose bumps while thinking of their trip a few months ago to the magical resort on the lush island in the Indian Ocean. Everything seemed possible then, even the unbelievable dreams of an infatuated Romanian dancer.

Chapter 20

Cora

"*B*ur Dubai please," the pretty Filipino girl in the back of his taxi looked weary, Zohour thought, as Cora settled in on the back seat with a heavy sigh.

"Okay," he replied and swung his mint colored taxi head-over-heels into the psycho traffic.

Zohour glanced in the rearview mirror furtively. He was a keen observer of people. In this city, he was seldom out of intriguing and speculative material for his observational talents. "Taxi drivers should get certificates in sociology or psychology," he complained to his fellow taxi men.

"We are on the forefront of this society, observing every crisis and development firsthand...why, I could write books about some of the things I have witnessed in my taxi...*Subhanallah.*"

He campaigned loudly about the rights of taxi drivers, claiming the populace abused them. The newspapers were screaming with allegations of taxi drivers' erratic driving and outright insolence. "Often they refuse to stop," claimed many.

"I had to stand in fifty degree heat for two hours and not a single taxi would stop," they whined.

"Once a taxi driver yelled at me and refused to take me to my location," complained yet another.

"I almost got killed riding in a Dubai taxi, these guys should be arrested!" and on they went.

The ungrateful residents of this great city. Zohour and his cabbie friends spent endless hours discussing the average Dubaians. They were ungrateful, spoilt, and impolite. Did they not see how wonderful their life was? Did they forget where they came from? At first thrilled and grateful to move to this city of opportunity and perpetual sunshine, they quickly forgot those feelings. They became like those conceited thousands before them. Zohour prayed for these lost souls, making *dua...* plea, every evening for the city and its many citizens.

"*Subhanallah,*" wondered Zohour many times. It was as if these wretched newcomers became very important, simply by shifting their geographical location. They might not admit it publicly, but secretively they felt just a little bit special because they happened to live in Dubai.

This girl is in a lot of trouble, he thought with certainty as Cora pointed to a dilapidated building. It was an old three storey residential building in a busy street. Filipinos and Somalians, Egyptians and Kenyans favored the neighborhood, for its low rents and sense of community. The streets of this area bustled with people of every ethnic race and color...a storm of languages assaulted the passerby.

Little shops battled for the most prominent space...displaying goods from all over the world. A Filipino market specialized in providing staple Filipino groceries and Tagalog magazines.

Further down the street a group of handsome young men in dark blue uniforms run back and forth to the waiting cars lined up for orders in front of the Egyptian *foul* and *tamiya* cafeteria, 'Al Pasha'. The Egyptian fava bean dish remained celebrated throughout the Middle East for its taste. It came accompanied with the little garbanzo bean patties called *tamiya*, staple food of Egyptian peasants.

"Yes here...stop."

"How much?" she handed him the correct amount wordlessly and got out of the car slowly, hesitant. Her sad eyes swept over the street and the building, taking it in. She had an old, black duffel bag with her, and due to its uneven outline, apparently packed in a hurry, he deducted, pleased with his detective like ability.

The girl stood on the sidewalk for a few minutes, as if not sure why she was here. Then, as she finally turned to walk into the grimy building, a gust of warm wind blew against her thin body and Zohour saw her distended belly, which until this moment the loose fitting blouse had skillfully concealed.

He watched her intently for a few more minutes, until she disappeared through the door. An old man rapping on his window startled him. It was the neighborhood beggar, toothless, bent, and swathed in layers of white clothing. His long beard was completely white and the hand he extended in a gesture of pleading, sunburned and terribly gnarled from age and hard labor.

Zohour immediately handed him the loose change he kept in the unused ashtray. The old man showered him with blessings in Pashtu, the language of Afghanistan. He had done so previously a few months ago when Zohour had been in the same street dropping off Australian tourists at the Ethiopian restaurant.

The beggar seemed to remember Zohour and nodded affably at him before continuing on his route, knocking on other car windows, hoping those passengers too will show the same generosity as the kind taxi driver.

Sighing heavily Zohour turned his taxi around, back towards the glittering lights of Sheikh Zayed Road, lined with posh hotels and exclusive shopping boutiques. Skyscrapers…each one more beautiful than the next, lined the twelve lane freeway, basking in the sunshine and the awe of all those who admired them. Satisfied that his skills of deduction were as strong as ever, Zohour thought of his first impression of his troubled customer.

The minute she had stepped into his taxi, he had sensed her desperation. It was like a thick veil about her, a cloak of blatant fear.

*A housemaid on the run, absconding from her employer…*he felt pretty sure about these deductions, based on his many years of scrutiny. Throughout the long commute, he deliberated about what kind of predicament would drive her to flee her employer's house.

Zohour shook his head in a delightfully characteristic Asian manner. A strong gust of wind had solved this mystery and now he knew exactly what kind of trouble she had found.

******

Loud Malayalam music blared from the taxi CD player, apparently a necessary attribute of any self respecting Dubai cabbie. Cora felt annoyed by it. Overwhelming developments in the last few months have rendered her physically fatigued and emotionally numb.

The pregnancy had continued unhindered, and still she had hoped for Luca would realize his mistake, came back to her, contrite. She did not quite know what she expected of him at this point but certainly, it was not this. He had shunned her abruptly and completely, he did not speak to her or look at her. She had repulsed him as soon as he had found out about the baby.

For these last few weeks, as the sacred life grew in her womb for the second time in her young life, she remained suspended, faltering... humiliated. Terrified of discovery, yet wanting to shout it from the rooftops.

She had stayed on at the villa, keeping a low profile in the hope that her cruel and uncaring lover would love her and accept her again.

"Yes that is the road; take this roundabout then first street right," startled she realized they were drawing close to her destination. Her pulse beat rapidly; she was dreading what was to come. She had visited this neighborhood before. Her distant cousin Girlie lived here. Cora looked at the bustling noise infused street with curiosity; it was entirely more vivid than the one she had left behind. They drove by the ethnic Ethiopian restaurant, modestly decorated but busy, serving the famous *zigne* dish, a devilishly spicy concoction of chicken, onions, and a mix of traditional spices, eaten by using spongy traditional bread. On the corner, a Chinese family operated the 'Mandarin 'restaurant, famous all over the city for its succulent noodle dishes. Cora had asked her cousin for help a few days ago.

"Cora you can come, I'm not home much anyway, I'm either working or staying with my boyfriend," Girlie had giggled suggestively. Cora drew out a long, tired sigh. She hoped her relative would make better choices than she has. She felt much older than her years, like an old woman with many heavy troubles on her shoulders. The taxi stopped in front of Cora's building. The elderly taxi driver gave her a curious look filled with sympathy. He smiled kindly and nodded as she exited the cab. The duffel bag felt heavy. Inside it, all she managed to take with her in her hurry to leave Luca, unable to stand one more day of his chilly, unapproachable stare. All she could think of was to go somewhere and plan her next step.

And so, here she was. Alone, except for a photo of her little boy in the bag, and another growing life inside her belly.

Chapter 21

Jane

"Ladies it's ...one...two...three...then, left...one, two, and three." Jamila shimmied her voluptuous hips ridiculously fast, in beat to the popular Egyptian song.

Tara struggled to keep up with the energetic Belly dance instructor. The woman was a dance demon! A rumor that Jamila worked as a dancer in some nightclub in the city, coursed through the center. Someone had seen her, but as with all rumors, no one knew who that was for sure, and it remained a tickly uncertainty among the aspiring belly dancers, elevating Jamila to unprecedented, although secret fame among the students. There was a quality of danger around the belly dance teacher that the women basked in. Unable to lead their own swashbuckling, devil may care, passionate lives, the one who did could at least train them. The studio was nestled snuggly in a small villa, part of a larger multifaceted dance centre, one that was 'all the rage' in upper class circles of Dubai.

Tara did the shake and the shimmy in fast succession, following Jamila's instructions…looking over to her side she giggled.

Jane grimaced back, her body ridiculously contorted as well, doing her best impression of Jamila, and somehow always not getting it quite right.

The floor to ceiling mirror covered the four sides of the room and only served to amplify their wretched attempts. Nevertheless, the women pushed on, seemingly unmindful of their bodies' shortcomings as well as their uncooperative genetic dispositions. A soft limber body and an ear for the eastern rhythm were preferable. Only a blessed few however, had the essential qualities of an innate belly dancer.

"Faster, faster…ladies this is not yoga," Jamila did a sashay to the right all the while swinging her hips spasmodically, the little metal coins on her hips jingling maniacally as she did so.

"Another time…*Yalla!*"

"One more, yes…now back side…"

"Push your hips down…like this…"

"Good, now twirl your hands above your head…similar to what we did last lesson."

"Very good…."

"Let's bend….down and up and circle…*Sirkle.*"

Whenever Jamila got excited, her charming Arabic accent grew more obvious, causing hilariously sounding outbursts such as 'sirkle' for circle. Now she led her exhausted class into a final set of moves…'the circular hip swing'.

Legs apart, body slightly bent at an angle Jane moved quickly downwards in a sensual loop, coming back up and facing the mirror. She repeated this impossible maneuver six times, to the beat of a fast Turkish melody, until Jamila was finally satisfied with their performance.

She encouraged, advised and prodded, physically arranging stubborn body parts into position as she went around the studio, resolutely coaching her students. Jamila was not giving up on this bunch however hopeless and stiff they seemed.

I will make belly dancers out of them yet, so help me God! "Now ladies…the best part…the freestyle…do anything you like…let us see you move!"

"*Yalla, Yalla*…lets go…"

Jane, Tara and the rest of the eclectic group of students labored hard to give their best. Some of the attempts looked more like fantastical dances from 'One thousand and one nights' or rather their interpretations of it. Apparently, a few of the ladies envisioned themselves as reincarnations of Scheherazade and their freestyle dancing was theoretically supposed to depict that remarkable era. Unfortunately, the dancing came across as lumbering...all that exaggerated swinging of arms, and out of pace gyrating of the hips would have been funny if they had not been so terrible. A few hardened veterans twirled and jiggled self-importantly in their own corner, lest the stiff, talentless mortals taint them. Some did their best 'dirty dancing' moves.

Her forehead moist from exertion, but deliriously free and weightless, Tara moved around the room, sometimes closing her eyes, enjoying the music. These belly dance classes have been pure therapy for her these last few months. Qays had become even more withdrawn and preoccupied lately. She had been unable to reach him, to get him to open up. All her attempts ended in violent arguments and his denial that anything was wrong.

"How are you?" Jane had asked while they waited for the last few stragglers at the beginning of the class.

Tara smiled, "I'm fine, and you look amazing, younger every day."

Jane appeared pleased by the compliment. "How are things with your husband...better?" she asked. Tara had confided in her English friend months ago after a particularly bad fight with Qays. In a moment of weakness, over tears and coffee in the neighboring mall, Tara's clandestine business with the kind doctor had poured out. More such meetings followed.

Her girls, volunteer work, and this dancing class have helped her pull through. She was going to see Ghassan this week because she had decided it was time to stop her dependence on medication and even more so...on him.

Jane sashayed by, noisily. Something caught Tara's eye. *Was that a new belt?*

The music reached its final crescendo and the women all tried to give their best finish...some more successfully and in less pain than others. The group had a few older British women who attended regularly and giggled like crazy throughout the class, obviously having the time of their lives. A young and slight Chinese girl twirled gleefully, and a Brazilian grandmother swayed self assuredly to the beat. Jane looked over to where Tara was doing the cool down stretch, "You seem better today."

Tara nodded, smiled sadly. She thought back to the time her and Jane's arms kept colliding mid air due to lack of space...that is how they met actually. It seemed, at first glance, that, the pair had nothing in common.

However, over the year, they got together regularly at the class and then lunch or coffee before Tara had to rush off to pick up the girls from school. Jane continued, "So are you going to tell me about it or not?"

The group exhaled together. Tara sighed. "I do feel better, I made a decision you know. I decided to stop seeing him," she explained.

Jane's eyes widened, "Well, good for you, what made you decide that?" Then quickly, "did you tell him already?" She was on the floor, bent over, reaching for her toes. Her friend continued to amaze her. Who would have believed that this simple looking convert, minivan-driving mom of two could be hiding a secret like this? Jane understood her. Tara was lonely, and Jane understood loneliness.

Tara shook her head, "No, he doesn't know, I will tell him at the next appointment, tomorrow."

"I am happy that you made your decision, I know it's been hard for you, struggling with this," Jane's eyes filled with tears for some inexplicable reason. She had grown to love this conflicted but good woman. "I want you to know that I appreciate your trust. I don't take it lightly, and if you need anything I will support you okay?" she hugged Tara. The class was over and they were the last ones left in the quiet studio.

Tara hugged her back, "I know Jane, thank you for listening. I appreciate you being there for me more than you know." She closed her eyes, "I think I might cry, I better be off." She laughed uneasily.

"Yes, off you go, and I will call you, we need to have coffee soon." Jane felt Tara's discomfort. Sometimes she wondered why Tara had confided in her. It felt good being useful; it forced her out of her own self-involved world. What a pair they were, Jane mused while driving home. *How was it that they could be friends?* Tara was certainly a divergence from her usual group of wealthy corporate wives. Yet, here they were, a coddled Englishwoman, with a penchant for a glass of wine and plastic surgery. The other, an American scarf-wearing convert, who was secretly having a torrid affair with her shrink. Their worlds seemed ridiculously apart...and yet they had hit it off immediately.

Human beings were funny that way...sometimes just when you think you got them all figured out and then, when you least expect it...they surprise you.

Chapter 22

Parisa

One had to unwrap dozens of levels and sublevels to figure out Dubai. Countless people never attempted to do so. They came and they left, blissfully unaware of the inner workings of the city, its many sub layers of lifestyles. Their entire time spent within their own little clique. Many never ventured past their own cozy enclaves to discover others. Downtown neighborhoods of *Deira* and *Bur Dubai* were dynamic, milling with a large Indian population. Huge, new villas popped up overnight in the new suburb of *Al Barsha*, usually inhabited by wealthy residents.

After a few years, most came to expect the lifestyle, forgetting their humble beginnings back home, in their various native parts of the world, where achieving any of this was laughably impossible.

Many dived headlong into the verve and bustle of social life of the busy city. Many took longer to find their place under the sizzling Dubai sun. One of the better-known clusters of this upscale life was in Jumeirah…an affluent suburb, populated mainly by western expatriates. As usual, the sun was shining over a bright; pleasantly dust free sky this afternoon. Three attractive, expensively dressed women in their early forties sat at one of the tables in a chic French restaurant. They were here for their monthly lunch meeting.

"This is really lovely isn't it?" Parisa looked around, smiling.

"Beautiful, and look at the menu?" Jane exclaimed in her bubbly, happy way holding it up.

Jewel broke out in a giggle, "Jane you are the only one who notices these things, but it is a very nice menu indeed. Now do they have something on it with no calories at all?" peals of laughter follow that question. Jewel's eyes wandered to the promenade, and then the endless blue sea behind it, which always called out to her wherever she was near. A surreal world existed in Jumeirah, one that seemed far removed from the reality of an Arab country.

In spite of it being one of the oldest residential areas in Dubai, this beachfront neighborhood of clean white beaches, well-watered parks, and ridiculously expensive private schools, remained the darling of Dubaians.

The jogging tracks, the numerous coffee shops, countless 'Starbucks' and 'Costas.' Shopping at supermarkets like 'Choitram' and 'Spinney's', both groaning with loaded and bulging shelves of products from England and America was a must for any self respecting expat.

"Ladies isn't Tara going to join us today?" Jane asked looking at her gold Rolex.

"She did say she would be late, she had to see her psychiatrist before lunch," Jewel smiled and stirred her tall glass of ice tea. Jane gave her a warning look. The two had become close even though Jewel was the 'boss's wife. They had met frequently at company events and parties as well as their regular charity work. Jane had told Jewel strictly in confidence about Tara's 'situation' with her therapist, regretting it later. Sometimes the pills and wine combination made her mouth run amok. Tara would be terribly distressed if she found out about this.

"Tara seemed like a really kind person, when I met her at Jewel's last dinner party," Parisa looked eagerly at her friends. "She is quite intelligent," Jane nodded her head. Jewel talked about how much she liked Tara.

"Look at the table next to ours," Jane nudged Parisa, pointing in the direction.

A group of tanned, cosmetically enhanced, attractive women had arrived and sat down at a table next to them. They jostled their massive

Birkin bags, Swarovski covered mobile phones and designer sunglasses while saying their hellos. Their manicured hands displayed sparkling jewelry and their pedicured feet, the latest Jimmy Choos.

"Jumeirah Janes," whispered Parisa, winking at Jewel.

"Are you trying to tell me something?" Jane laughed and took a long sip of her champagne. She gave her friends a fake pleading look, "Guys give me a break, and I'm not like that."

Jewel and Parisa stared at her speechless. She was the epitome of a Jumeirah Jane and the woman had no clue. She looked the part.

"Where did you just come from?" Parisa asked her and raised her brows.

"What do you mean... the salon of course," Jane answered, disdainfully.

"Which one?" Parisa persisted, a twinkle in her eyes.

Jane looked like dumbstruck, and then she admitted grudgingly, "Sally's."

Parisa almost fell of her chair laughing. "Point made," she said, patting Jane on her shoulder. "But I love you anyway my Jumeirah Jane."

"Well enough of that," Parisa declared. "Should we order?"

The women ordered salads, and then Parisa looked at Jewel inquisitively. "Are you okay, you seem quiet?"

Jewel did look odd, quieter than usual, different somehow. Parisa could not put her finger on what it was exactly.

Jewel shook her head "Oh, I'm fine, just having this migraine again." *She is such a good liar; I can see it in her eyes.*

Tara's arrival interrupted their conversation. She arrived, apologizing for her tardiness. After they all kissed and greeted her and she had ordered from the menu they turned to her with curiosity.

"So Tara, do you recommend this psychiatrist that you are seeing? I was thinking of maybe taking my daughter Zoya to see a therapist," Parisa leaned across the table, eager for information.

Tara looked up from her juice, "Er, yeah he is really nice, you should try him," she blurted, her eyes flicking around the table nervously.

Jane jumped up from the table and mumbled how she needed the toilet, almost breaking out in spasm of laughter on the way. Parisa was flabbergasted. *What had gotten into her friends today? They were both acting strange.* Jane was back within minutes and with a straight face, resumed conversation as if nothing had occurred. Tara seemed self-conscious, and kept shooting inquiring looks at Jane.

"Too bad Ginni could not make it today?" Jane said sadly. She loved Ginni and her fashion line. "What a talented girl, but such a sad life," she said between bites of her greens.

"I have to agree with you, she is definitely a complicated person. She has had a hard life," Jewel was playing with her food, moving a cherry tomato around in her plate.

"Ginni Karisma the designer right...I have met her at your house once," Tara interjected.

"Well you have to come to my opening night and meet her again then," Jewel said, graciously, "I have sent the invitations anyway, so you should be getting them any day now."

Their salads tasted delicious and the warm sunshine felt pleasantly relaxing on their skin. Finally, all four were eating their lunches.

Then Jewel's driver Raj walked in. He was here to pick up the madam he said. Parisa and Jane stared openmouthed at him. This is Jewel's other driver? They had not seen him before. He was a strikingly good-looking man. Other women from nearby tables turned to look at his ruggedly chiseled face and athletic body.

He ran his hand through his thick black hair. It rippled through his fingers. "I'm sorry madam, but my phone, there was no signal," the driver kept his eyes of the women as he explained, apologetically. He should not have entered the hotel's premises, he knew the rules, but his phone had no signal and he got worried that madam was looking for him.

"It's okay Raj, thank you, I will be finished in half an hour," Jewel dabbed her lips, played with her fork, looked at her mobile, but she never looked at Raj directly. Jane watched this exchange and smiled. Parisa looked at Raj, then Jewel. Tara sat stock still, grabbing the napkin in her lap. They were stunned. What had happened?

Raj left, followed by the eyes of most women in the restaurant.

"He is a really handsome driver," Jane stabbed at her lettuce, shoved a bunch into her mouth, and then looked Jewel in her eyes.

Jewel pulled on her *Sheila*; it kept slipping and making her nervous. "Really, I haven't noticed," she said and looked at her friend. Their eyes met. Jewel averted her gaze first because her phone was ringing and she answered, thankful for the intrusion. Parisa and Tara had finished their salads; Jane finished her glass of champagne.

"Well it was so nice to meet you again, Tara," Parisa was smiling warmly at the American.

"Same here Parisa, it has been an honor. I really admire your work," Tara meant it. Parisa's art was breathtakingly beautiful.

Jane felt sad. She was suddenly overwhelmed with how fragile all this was. She was aware that this moment was precious, the sunshine, these women, the sea…it could all be gone in a moment.

"Jane, you should stop with the champagne darling, you know you always get sad after you have had some." Parisa hugged her warmly, reassuringly. She helped their slightly tipsy friend up. "I think I'm going to take Jane home." Tara and Jewel nodded. The women exchanged promises of meeting again soon…very soon.

Jane waved her finger at Jewel, "I need to talk to you soon my love," she giggled.

As Jewel drove off in her car, driven by the mysterious new driver, Parisa's eyes lingered on the stately woman's disappearing form. It was an inquisitive look, deep and wise. Later, after she had dropped Jane home, on the long drive back, Parisa asked herself repeatedly, what *was Jewel Al Gaafari up to?*

Chapter 23

A Castle

*J*ewel looked out of her bedroom window. She could hear her children's laughter and their squeals of glee. The precious sounds were coming in through the slightly open, Persian style glass panes. Now that the pleasant weather had arrived again, the children were out most evenings in the blossoming, cool garden, playing with their respective 'toys' of choice. Michal, fifteen, slim and with a newly growing mustache, sped around on his custom-made sand buggy. Two years younger and the spitting image of his father, Faisal loved the mini quad bike and Nora, seventeen and green eyed like her mother roller bladed like a pro on the smooth paths surrounding the spacious compound. Ten year-old Layal monopolized the large, fenced trampoline where she showed off her jumping tricks. Her children lacked nothing in manner of material possessions. Jewel sighed and called out to her personal maid. "Viola, please bring the tea to my sitting room…"

She had given birth to all of her children while living in this house. Here she had experienced extreme passion and extreme love, and here she had felt her deepest disappointments, the worst betrayals.

Lavishly decorated, the four-room suite invoked the feeling of being in an ancient Persian castle. Elegantly painted murals adorned the ceilings, climbing ivy and white clouds in a blue sky.

Flawlessly hand carved furniture, a four-poster canopy bed, sumptuous velvet cushions in deep purple, pomegranate red, and regal gold, silk and cashmere sheets and bed covers, and soft Persian carpets...all equally tempted the visitor and the owner to lounge lazily. Billowing silk curtains hung over dome shaped Arabic doors leading to the terrace.

Jewel sniffed the air and it delighted her with the scent of a dozen frangipani-scented candles. Fresh cut white orchids graced Lalique vases throughout the suite. The bedroom led off into the dressing room, bathroom, and her personal spa. Jewel appeared unearthly as she floated noiselessly through her quarters, the gold silk robe trailing behind her. A melancholy smile played on her lips.

Jewel had been missing her mother's family dreadfully after she moved to Dubai to live with her father. Her cousin and Aunt came to visit after she got married to Jassim and were stunned the first time they saw the mansion.

They had heard of people living like this in California...but those were movie stars. What her two relatives did not understand yet was that Dubai was Hollywood, Vegas and Miami all rolled into one. After spending a few summers with Jewel and her in laws the young American girl understood.

Picnics on their private island off the coast of Dubai, and shopping sprees in any capital of the world when the boredom bug bit...these were the kind of activities the Gaafari family took for granted. Jewel did not like to flaunt their wealth, it frightened her. She feared for her children, but it would have been hard to hide.

Last year, many local and regional business magazines had interviewed Jassim. His face was on the cover of a major financial magazine as one of ten wealthiest people in Asia. It would have been odd trying to act as if they were your average upper class folks, when in fact they were among the wealthiest families in the country.

Jassim liked to brag about his tribe, "You know, the Al Gaafari family can trace their ancestors to the very first bedouins of the legendary clans," he told her repeatedly over the years. She had stopped listening to him a long time ago. Unfazed by this, he had the children now as a fresh, easily impressed audience.

He went on, "...a tribe renowned for its chivalry, for its military prowess. The children and great-grandchildren of our tribe still practice their famous generosity in their daily life."

Jewel smiled at the rapt faces of the children. They were their father's children no doubt; they loved stories of the family glory. A Bedouin's home was always open for any unexpected visitors who would without doubt be welcomed with unmatched kindness." Jassim had hugged his children in turn, kissed them three times.

The girl brought in the tea tray.

"Thank you," Jewel smiled at her, "Set it on the small table please... and Viola...tell the children to come up and see me when they finish with their baths, all right?" She shook her head, ridding herself of the abrupt memory of the Romanian girl, as she would of an annoying fly. Jewel had seen a photo of her in a magazine. It was an advertisement for the sleazy nightclub where girls of her kind performed. Jewel shuddered at the thought of Jassim at such a place.

"Yes madam," Viola nodded her head and left quietly. Jewel poured herself some mint tea from the pot and sat at her handmade mahogany desk to go over the boutique opening invitations again. She still could not believe that it was so soon and that she had pulled it off.

For years, she had dreamt of having her own income, an independent business, but Jassim always disapproved. He did not think there was any need for her to worry about all the aspects of the 'nasty' business world.

"You are well taken care of," he always insisted, offended at the prospect, and need not look further for accomplishments. They were right here in this house with her. She had her lovely children, her beautiful home, and him.

"If you are bored, why not attend some art classes at the 'Ladies club?" He suggested benevolently. "On the other hand, maybe a trip up to Lebanon and spending time in the villa in the mountains would help. Yes, a change of scenery always helped," he would say, pleased for being the generous understanding husband.

Jewel shook her head; she had to stop thinking about him. Then, after a moment of deliberation she called Viola again, "Viola, please call the driver, Raj, tell him I need to talk to him.

"The girl looked surprised, "Here mam?" she asked.

"Yes here Viola, is there a problem?" Jewel raised her brows questioningly.

******

Jassim's chest swelled with pride when he looked at his wife. She was beautiful, dignified, the mother of his children. She came from an exceptionally esteemed family, a long line of judges and lawyers. He did not want anything to jeopardize that element of his life. A wife, children, and home were a matter of great pride for every Arab man. He was a protective husband and a great provider to his four children.

Jassim took great precautions in keeping his two lives separate so as not to disrupt the status quo. His success and reputation depended on it. The first time he had been unfaithful to Jewel he had felt guilty. His culture and religion forbid it strongly. He went through a period of introspection and remorse.

Eventually however, the many lengthy business trips he took alone and the availability of attractive young women everywhere shook that resolve. It was not that he did not love Jewel. It was more exciting when the chase was on.

He loved the thrill of the unknown, the exhilaration of the hunt and finally, winning. Eventually that conquest would weary him too, and he moved on to the next beautiful girl or woman who would be desperate to please him, to keep him. He had never felt the inclination to stay faithful to any of them, until Liliana walked into his world.

When he saw her the first time at a gala party for a movie premiere, she was wearing a long, tight red dress. Her black hair cascaded like a wet waterfall down her bare back. She was hired for the celebrity-studded event to act as a hostess and usher people around the huge premises, to provide information and assistance.

Jassim had literally skipped a step. Warmth radiated upwards throughout his body...finally suffusing his face, causing a shocking feeling of pleasant breathlessness, as if he had been running.

Flustered and embarrassed by his obvious excitement he tried to escape his boring companion, the company's chief financial executive, David, a dull Englishman who Jassim had never felt an affinity to.

The man was a genius with numbers though, and came highly recommended from Jassim's London office. His wife, Jane, a beautiful and smart woman had become close friends with his Jewel. Jassim however, felt a vague feeling of duplicity emanating from the stocky Englishman.

Since that evening, Jassim had pursued the raven-haired, blue-eyed Romanian dancer with unrelenting passion. The more often she said no to his expensive flower arrangements and ignored his persistent phone calls, the more he grew frustrated. In disbelief that she had the nerve to rebuff him. Bewildered, rejected he fumed, *"Why is she doing this? Doesn't she know who I am?"* He could not see that his new love interest had an uncanny resemblance to his wife, Jewel. In another world, they could have been sisters, because Liliana looked like a younger version of Jewel. Sadly, Jassim was the only person unaware of this.

******

Diminutive physically, Mozza had been a giant in Jewel's eyes. Mozza had introduced her to the local privileged society and the subsequent activities of rich Arab girls.

After a few years, Jewel started to enjoy these activities, most of which were similar to those of American teenage girls. Shopping, parties, appointments for manicures and sleepovers, and of course flirting, the worldwide-preferred 'activities of choice' of teenage girls. Slowly Jewel accepted that her life in America was in the past, and that her new life in Dubai was not as dreadful as she had expected it to be.

Her relationship with her father improved and gradually as time passed so did her relationship with her younger siblings and her father's extensive family. As the years passed, she allowed her bitterness over her mother's premature death to develop into something else. To become a tribute to her mom by the way she would live her life, to honor her mother's memory in front of the world. Unfortunately, she always felt like the half-caste daughter of the dead American wife...

"That is not true dear daughter," her father had reassured her many times. Still, she did not feel complete. Throughout all this, Mozza stood by her side, encouraging, listening, forever the trusted friend. That is why when the deception occurred it was a shock of unbearable magnitude.

Jassim had seemed to understand Jewel's internal struggle at first. He was caring, kind, incredibly protective. It took only until Michal was born, and then that sparkly bubble, had collapsed. It had created a surge of astonishing pain and shame. She remembered the first time intensely even after all these years.

"Where have you been Jassim?" she had asked, alarmed at the late hour. It had been a month after Faisal was born, and she was surprised by Jassim's frequent late nights.

He had looked at her for a long time, an eternity it had seemed to her. A bored, almost triumphant look flashed across his face.

"I have been at a meeting, where else."

He walked into the bedroom, without kissing her. Jewel blinked her eyes. She was exhausted from the birth and the lack of sleep. Was Jassim as cold as he seemed or were this her hormones wreaking havoc, she had wondered at the time.

"But Jassim I was alone, and you did not answer your phone," she walked up to him, tried to kiss him on the cheek. *Oud* perfume accosted her like a repulsive animal, like a monster that had finally shown its face. She recoiled. He smelled of another woman.

It could be any number of women from his family, she told herself. After all, even his elderly aunties use *Oud*. Maybe he had visited and they must have hugged him and kissed him as they usually do. *Yes, that is what it is, nothing less, nothing more.* For Allah's sake she had just delivered his firstborn son, he could never...

"I need to know Jassim, where were you exactly?" her voice cracked. *Did she really want to know? Why was she going down this path? Khalas, enough, he said he was in a meeting...forget it, believe him.*

Then it happened again...and again. At first, she had yelled, pleaded, and cried. He had denied it all. Laughed at her, and then became angry. "Who do you think I'm?" he screamed enraged. "You think I sleep with any woman I come across?" he stormed out of the house, revving the engine of his Porsche, creating a dramatic scene in front of the staff, not to return for hours.

Jewel had finally gone to sleep, her face itching from the river of salt, her body aching as if someone had beaten her all over with a stick. It was close to dawn when she heard him come in, quietly. She smelled his sweat, mixed with his masculine, raw odor. *Only Jassim smelled like the desert and the sea at the same time.* The trouble causing scent of *Oud* had disappeared, making her think she had made it up, and exaggerated everything.

He did not go to the bathroom or switch on the light. Jewel heard rustling of clothes, knew he was removing his *Gotra*, then his *Agal, and* finally his *Kandoora.* The soft materials made a swishing sound as they fell rapidly to the floor. She pretended to be asleep but Jassim crawled into bed with her anyway. He inched nearer, then placed his arms around her waist and pulled her close. She could not move, could not object, and could not breathe. She did not wish to move. She did not want him to stop. Her entire body dissolved under his touch. The desire to be united with him again was stronger than her anger, than the loathing she felt with herself.

"Only tonight, just this once," she had told him, weakly, in his ear. He did not reply, but continued, on his silent mapping of her body.

As the years passed and her children arrived, in rapid progression, she accepted this fate, steeled herself in public and forced herself to bide her time. Outwardly, they were, if not happy, then content. Their children were healthy and they had every comfort imaginable. Jewel devoted herself to the children.

Chapter 24

Parisa

*P*arisa stepped back and looked at the unfinished painting on the easel in front of her. One dark, perfectly threaded eyebrow lifted worriedly. Her lips pursed in frustration.

There was something wrong with it, she thought while dabbing her brush at the canvas dejectedly. Her heart was not set on painting today. This morning Zoya had one of her famous tantrums again and stormed out of the house with her boyfriend Jake, screeching away in a friends' red Ferrari.

"How dare you talk to me like that?" Parisa had insisted during the row. Zoya wanted to attend an all night party on an island off the coast of Dubai and Parisa was not having it.

"What am I doing mama?" her daughter puckered her lips and rolled her eyes. Zoya had developed a sassy, careless attitude over the last year.

Her sweet little girl was gone forever it seemed. In her place was this… this…stranger.

Zoya continued to tap a message on her mobile phone with her newly done gel nails. Her hair spread around in a wavy mass of black and purple. A newly acquired diamond stud sparkled on her nose.

Parisa had always instilled a sense of individualism in her daughter, in fact had insisted on it, but this had backfired in the form of this atrocious purple hair. Parisa hoped the nose piercing would be the last of that sort of experimenting.

She felt sad by their souring relationship. Her marriage to Luca was turning out to be a huge mistake after all. He had failed her repeatedly, his absences, his spending, his flirting. Sighing, she scrutinized the face staring back at her.

It was a woman's face, an exquisite face. The woman wore an *Abaya* sprinkled with crystals. The crystals shone like stars on the black background. She sat somewhere in the desert on a sand dune, her legs curled under her slim body gracefully. She stared thoughtfully into the distance, the wind making her long sleeves flutter, while honey colored; waist long hair billowed sensually in the air. A dark and moody sky hovered above the woman's form. Dramatic eyes the color of foaming sea bore into Parisa's soul.

Jewel Al Gaafari was an outstandingly beautiful woman. Parisa reached for her cigarettes.

This painting was her gift for her friend Jewel. She wanted to do something special for her. It captured Jewel in an alluring way…and yet Parisa was not pleased.

It had been a testing week for Parisa. Sudden and baffling issues had cropped up while she was under pressure to organize her biggest exhibition to date.

The week had started with her favorite housemaid Cora running off. To Parisa's dismay, the girl had simply walked out one morning. The new maid Dalisai told her that apparently Cora had packed a small bag and got onto a bus stop right by the house, without explaining anything. Dalisai swore that she had no inkling about the reason.

Parisa disliked the younger girl. She had an attitude of disdain and haughtiness about her and her very presence in the house irked Parisa. However, she managed her chores well, and was at Zoya's disposal whenever needed so Parisa did not feel justified in letting her go. Inevitably, another housemaid would arrive with her own set of quirky habits and might be even more eccentric.

After a week, they had not received news off Cora and Parisa hoped that the girl was not in some trouble. Numerous maids ran off from their sponsored employers only to find that they have made a terrible mistake and were in even worse circumstances. Sometimes they ended up forced into prostitution: illegally residing in the country and unable to approach the authorities for fear of prosecution. She would have to go in and file an absconding maid report at the station. She felt Luca before she saw him.

"*Ciao, amore*," Luca whispered into her ear.

He snuggled up to her from behind. She did not turn but leaned into him. Luca had that power over her; his presence filled her with a torrent of surging desire and inescapable weakness. *What a foolish woman I have been...*she thought to herself as he nuzzled her neck and they rocked silently together.

"I like it," he said finally.

"I still have a few touches...I'm not sure about it," Parisa turned around and looked up into his blue eyes. His eyelashes were ridiculously long... sinfully so for a man. He was fascinating to look at.

Parisa knew she was not a beautiful woman. She had a nice figure and kept herself healthy, dressed well and used all means necessary to keep her appearance youthful and attractive for him, but she had never resorted to surgery. It seemed desperate to her somehow. The artist in her had hoped Luca could see the beauty that was not skin-deep.

Her nose was somewhat hooked...her lips a tad too thin...her jaw too square. Her eyes and hair had always been her best feature. Unruly and wild her hair seemed to rebel against the elements of nature and nothing she did to it could bring it under control. Finally, she let it be. It reminded her of her paintings, which were wild, unpredictable...temperamental.

Her eyes were an extraordinary color. They were a rare blend of green, yellow, and brown that her grandmother swore only lucky people are born with. Like rare jewels, they sparkled, vestiges of her Armenian lineage, doe shaped and thick lashed. Now they looked at Luca with sadness and curiosity.

"Why did you marry me Luca?"

He blinked a few times, taken by surprise. Luca Finelli had always thought he had it all figured out. Since his young days as a struggling model in Europe, he had created this alternate persona, Luca the Italian stud, Luca the successful model, entrepreneur and socialite. His ascent to fame and fortune had not been easy or pretty. In his hurried climb to the top, the handsome son of an angler from Bari had to step on some feelings, even cause grief for many. For a second he thought of Cora, then Vikki, and numerous others, who were now a blur, faces that he could hardly recall. Most had been used to his advantage and discarded when he saw it necessary.

"What do you mean *bella?*" his Italian inflection was very musical, always soothing. "I love you that's why. I loved you since the first time I saw you," he smiled.

Parisa moved away from him. "You are out all the time," she lit another of her slim dark menthols and turned to face him.

"You know I have to do that, I'm always at this event and that event… you know it's for my work." Luca tried to put his hands on her shoulders again. "Come on, what's wrong with you today? Are you worried about Zoya?"

"Yes I'm worried about my daughter, Luca," she put emphasis on the word 'my'. During the time they had been married Luca and Zoya had never seen eye to eye. Their relationship had been rocky from the start. Parisa saw that regretfully, Luca had made very little effort to become a father figure to Zoya. She had hoped that the three of them could create a happy little family unit…in spite of the obstacles their age gap and incompatible backgrounds created. Here she had been a forty something widow, acclaimed artist, educated and smart. Then there was Luca, a young model, adventurer and chaser of schemes, a chaser of status. Somehow, all the effort had been hers. She coached, guided, and financed Luca in all his endeavors. In the beginning she had trusted him, she believed him when he said he loved her maturity and her unbridled talent.

"Young women are stupid *bella*…I'm tired of them," he had purred into her ear, nibbling, teasing. "I desire a woman who is not afraid to say no to me," he gazed deep into her sad eyes, giving her his famous 'look'.

He went on that night, and she had believed him, wanted to believe him.

"I want a woman who opens a door to a whole new, fantastic world for me."

Somehow, his reassuring words did not ring true anymore. A sickening sensation deep in her gut told her that it would soon be all over. Terrified by this probability, she almost felt relief as well. That was the advantage of middle age. Knowing when to give up and move on and accepting that this too, shall pass.

Chapter 25

Ameera

They kept Ameera in a small, stifling room, infested with scurrying, brown cockroaches, in a flat on the outskirts of the city. She had not seen much of the great city of Dubai after she arrived except when they drove her to the so-called 'parties'.

Turned out 'aunty' Kareema did not care about Grandma and her three little granddaughter's after all. Just as Ameera had feared, the kind and sympathetic act in front of grandma was a ruse, a cunning strategy in order to lure Ameera to Dubai.

Those first weeks were a hellish nightmare from which Ameera had still not woken up. Every day brought her further humiliation on the hands of her jailers, a callous woman called Samiya who worked for Kareema and an Iraqi man. The short bearded man was in charge of driving Ameera to her 'assignments' as well as making sure, in Kareema's own words "that the girl does not attempt anything stupid…"

'Anything' stayed suspended, hanging in the air.

"Today you have to go to a party Ameera." Kareema sat on an old brown couch in the flat, wearing her customary heavy makeup and kitschy clothes. Ameera could see a new item of gold around the woman's neck that she had not seen before. A round coin shaped pendant swung heavily on a thick necklace.

Ameera had been very lucrative for Kareema's business.

*Bringing the girl here was a stroke of genius...*the Moroccan thought as she inhaled deeply from the *shisha* pipe next to her...all the time appraising the young, chaste girl favorably, like a cat would a bowl of fresh cream.

How pretty she was. 'Mashallah'...If I had a daughter I would want her to look like that. Her gold bracelets clinked as she picked up her coffee cup and took a sip, never taking her eyes of Ameera.

"Samiya, give her those clothes that she used last time at that beach house party," she crossed her legs, leaning back into the sofa and then waved her hand expansively at her 'Assistant'. Her long purple nails flailed around like the talons of a bird of prey. She cleared her gravelly voice, coughing up phlegm. Ameera looked away. She felt nauseous.

"The purple one, with the silver stars right?" Samiya had a misleadingly timid air about her, deceptively hiding her true character. She spoke softly, unlike Kareema who was, despite her external carefully groomed image, coarse and loud.

"Yes that one...and listen...wash her hair and oil it, it looked nice with that Indian oil last time." Her lips turned up into a sly grin before continuing, "The clients were really impressed with our Ameera last time."

Ameera bowed her head in shame at the memory. A few days after she had arrived in the city, Kareema sat her down on the same dirty sofa and told her.

In explicit detail, snickering slyly, she explained to the young girl what they expected of her. Ameera had recoiled in horror.

"*La, ya Khalty*" no aunty, she pleaded. They had ignored her tears, pleas, and sobs. Kareema and Samiya remained unmoved and uninterested. When she did not stop crying and beseeching, they had hit her, slapping her face until it was an angry red, until she begged them to stop.

Afterwards, they had locked her in the dark stifling room for days, bringing her a plate of cold rice and some water once a day. She ate and drank greedily. The lone window in the room had been boarded with plywood and heavy draperies pulled over it. After five more days came the final, crippling threat.

"You know Ameera…" a tormenting pause and then, "I can make many problems for your grandma back in Morocco."

Ameera froze. Exhausted and weak, delirious from fear and loneliness, she gave in, agreeing to the woman's wicked orders.

"But I will not because you have finally gotten sense into that pretty head of yours and everything will be fine from now on." Kareema flicked her tongue around her crimson mouth, reminding Ameera of a snake.

" Don't worry I will take care of your sisters," she smiled lazily. "Listen to your aunty Kareema *habibti.*"

She had attempted to embrace the frail girl but Ameera wriggled out, sickened by the vile breath and heavy body odor.

Allah must be punishing her already, Ameera thought to herself many times since that day, because even with all that money Kareema remained a crude, uncouth woman, and worst of all, an unbeliever. For sure, both Kareema and her partners in this revolting crime would suffer the worst of the burning fire of hell, she thought vengefully. She was positive that God would avenge this horrible thing happening to her. After all, she was a *yateema,* an orphan, and they were under special protection in all the teachings of the holy book. Meanwhile she prayed.

Please forgive me, and pass mercy on me…I'm your obedient slave. I know you are merciful and all knowing and you can see into my soul…you can see my 'niya', my intentions, are honest…oh God.

Ameera had recited fervently to herself while being dressed and coiffed, while Samiya applied heavy makeup to her face. She had continued her silent prayer while the fat older woman rubbed a copious amount of glitter lotion all over her bare body and while she finally applied two shiny silver stars to her small breasts, smiling lasciviously, enjoying herself.

Ameera recited it passionately while being driven to the desert in the four-wheel vehicle with the dark tinted windows. She recited her plea fervently while dancing half-naked for the group of drunken and lecherous men, pretending not to hear their lewd suggestions…their direct comments about her body, her exposed breasts, and her rear, which Samiya had dressed in skimpy purple shorts. It was nightmarish, and it occurred repeatedly since that first time. This was only a prelude however, to the real nightmare awaiting her. One morning a month after she had started dancing Kareema called her again.

"I want to talk to you about something," she started.

Ameera knew that whatever Kareema had to say would only bring her more anguish. The loathing she felt for the woman filled her with the raw rage of a dishonored, tormented soul.

"The time has come for you to do all the things that are asked from you," her face was as unmoving as a stone.

A blazing fire burnt in Ameera's hazel eyes. She continued to stare fiercely at this hideous woman. At closer look, a tempest of feelings, brewing silently, could be detected in them.

"So far you have only been dancing...you see, the other girls do," meaningful pause, "much more than that..." The woman did not take her eyes off Ameera.

Other girls? There are more like her? Ameera's head was spinning. She understood the full meaning of Kareema's words...had hoped that by some divine intervention she might escape her venomous demands.

Now it was all over. She knew that she had no way out and nobody will rescue her. There 'was' no body to rescue her. She was truly all alone in the world. Her head started to throb and the room lurched out of control. Kareema's face floated in front of her looking grotesquely malformed...evil.

She heard the older woman ask her if she was all right, saw the alarm in her sly eyes, and felt a wave of pleasure for causing her distress.

Oh how she wished to be back home. How she missed the soft arms of her little sister around her neck...how she missed the scent of her grandmothers' cooking ...especially the delicious *Bastiya*...sweet and rich in her mouth, its flaky layers crumbling in her hands. She missed her parents...

Then suddenly, she relaxed. It seemed like all her worries and fears had evaporated...simply, floated away. Ameera looked down at her arm, stunned by a sudden sharp sting. Then she rolled over and slid to the dirty floor.

Kareema was leaning over her, shouting obscenities at Samiya. The obese woman was holding a needle in her hand and watching Ameera's reaction like a hawk. Her dark, nugget like eyes burned all the way through to the young girls' soul. Ameera lay there on the faded old linoleum, collapsed like a brittle, crystal figurine, barely breathing. The potent drug spread through her veins quickly. Its effect on her emaciated, feeble body was almost instantaneous. The pain was gone.

The fears were gone too. There was only the warmth and the soft, cotton like fog enveloping her now…if she could just curl up and sleep awhile she would be okay. She would think about all this tomorrow.

Yes, tomorrow everything would be all right.

Chapter 26

Ginni

"These designs are lovely Pierre," Ginni said. She contemplated the short Frenchman affectionately. Pierre was in a flurry of activity... measuring, yelling out orders, and fluffing the creations displayed in front of Ginni for final approval. He reminded her of a wrinkled old turkey... his gait pompous, visibly basking in pleasure from all her flattery.

The designs for Jewel Al Gaafari's boutique were ready. Lovely chiffons and soft silks, flowing dreamy beiges and neutrals, foam like azure blues and mint greens. Touches of burnished gold on belts and in needlework represented the sunshine of the desert. The entire collection was the perfect match for Jewel's vision. The garments astounded Ginni. She had worked tirelessly for months to bring Jewel's idea to life. Pierre and the rest of the team exceeded themselves as well, working throughout the night many times in order to get everything ready for the opening.

The final product was even more extraordinary than they had expected.

The long, modestly cut gowns and dresses recreated the sensation of undulating sand dunes and the calm of the sea.

Genuine pearls in all their shades and sizes were included into most designs as a tribute to the local pearl diving history.

Ginni remembered the early days when she had started out by designing the local *Abaya*. In those days, the designs had been conservative, plain. She smiled inwardly at the progression of the garment. Young women these days wore daring, bold designs, inserting individually eccentric details in vivacious colors, not shying away from childish pom-poms or multihued buttons, placed at strategic locations across the garment. The long sleeves came in a variety of shapes, flared, slim, wide, and crazily embellished with funky hanging bits and pieces, which swished gleefully every time the arms moved.

Those rebels, who really wanted to distress their relatives would wear outrageously attention seeking, scandalously see through, tight fitting, body-accentuating *Abayas*. This kind of behavior unsurprisingly caused fits of offended outrage from the older, more conventionally inclined family members.

"*Ya bint!*" you girl, wizened grandmothers in black *Burqas* shrieked at the sight of their granddaughters in such a shocking state of dress.

"*Walla*, you will shame us, what will the neighbors think?" bristled their spinster aunts in indignation.

However, those deviants from tradition went out to the malls anyway, clicking their sky high Jimmy Choos, swinging their Birkin bags and pouting their glossy lips in defiance, their doe like black eyes fluttering with the weight of the heavy lashes and the thickly applied *Kohl*. Worn in tandem with a black, and elegantly wrapped hair-veil, called the *Sheila*... the outfit held enough allure to hold back even the staunchest critics of Islamic dress.

Bizarrely, many members of 'Islamic dress' opposition groups, became keenly impressed, when themselves offered an opportunity to try the garment on...delightfully basking in the pure femininity of the moment, because like some little girls, even grown women loved a chance of looking like an Arab princess on occasion.

Mercy stood behind Ginni, her hands clasped, awed at the sight of dozens of these visions. "I would love to wear one of them," she said with a wistful look on her face.

"Well people let's wrap it up for today." Ginni got up from her armchair and stretched her tall form. Her neck hurt from the hours of leaning over;

repeatedly drawing sketches of designs; until she was certain, they were faultless. All that she had left to do was to get through the fashion show at the opening night of the luxury boutique, without any glitches. Ginni had seen the guest list and it read like the who's who of the Middle East. A dozen Sheikhas, ambassadors' wives and two female ministers as well as leading Middle Eastern personalities in the local art and fashion scenes had confirmed their attendance already. Seating them all at *'Al Jawahir'* premises without causing an international incident was going to be a logistical nightmare. Ginni was glad she was not in the shoes of Jewel's event organizer.

The city buzzed with the anticipation of the event, which was going to be the highlight of the social calendar. At parties and dinners throughout Dubai, people asked each other "Did you get an invitation to Jewel Al Gaafari's opening?"

She stood up and wandered to the window to look outside. Jumeirah Beach road was still bustling with life at this late hour. It was Thursday and the beginning of the weekend. The street was filled with cars and Dubaians on their way to some fun place or other.

Some were no doubt going to the many restaurants and coffee shops dotting the beachfront, many on their way to a night spent dancing at a nightclub of choice…still others to peruse the malls and catch a movie.

She thought of her own plans for that evening and a feeling of unease gripped her. She really did not feel like spending the evening alone. After whatever current warm body in her bed had left for the night, after she had dimmed the lights and after the city mellowed down to a hush, her memories crawled out of their hiding places. Like maggots that lay in wait for their chance, they showed up regularly, to horrify her over and over again. She did not like to be around when they did. Maybe she will drive over to her regular nightclub, have a few drinks in the bar, and who knows what other things might crawl out tonight. *Pah! Enough with the gloom* she told herself. *I deserve a treat after today's hard work.* A relieved smile flitted onto her lips. She knew exactly who to call, Fares. It had been too long since they met and she needed to something about it. Yes, Fares Dracolakis sounded like the man who could distract her from just about anything.

First, she needed a shot of something to get her into the mood. Something powerful enough to help her gets rid of the memories, to numb them up. Later when they rear their slimy heads again, she might need something stronger, but that will come later, much later in the night.

Then she picked up her silver mobile and dialed. "Fares, hi...you want to have some fun tonight?"

******

"*Namaste* uncle," Ginni greeted him ducking out of his way. An apprehensive look stood frozen on her small face.

He grunted drunkenly and went right past her into the tiny ramshackle abode they called a home.

"He is nasty your uncle," her friend Anjuli said in a matter- off- fact way, staring at the incredible mass of people parading in front of them.

The streets were always busy in this neighborhood packed with other decrepit and rickety mud brick dwellings, on the very outskirts of the city of Delhi. Garbage and dirty sewer water flowed in the streets, skinny dogs and cats lurked in the corners, and a customary fat rat raised its ugly head out of a hiding place.

A commotion of sort was gathering at the far end of the street. A group of men seemed to be fighting with each other. Ginni and Anjuli stood on tiptoes trying to see over the heads of the gathering crowd. It was a common sight. Poverty, unemployment, and alcohol brought out the worst in many of the men, and they found no release except to take it out on their wives and children, and often on each other, in street fights erupting over the slightest perceived offense.

"Oh good, they are not using weapons this time," Ginni, being taller, pronounced importantly to her shorter friend who struggled to see what was going on.

"That fat sweet-shop man is pushing someone. Oooh, here he goes... right in the mud...that's funny." Ginni continued to narrate excitedly as Anjuli pouted, envious that she could not see the fight.

"On the account of being a midget," Ginni teased her incessantly about being small.

Nothing much happened in terms of amusement during the long, boring school breaks. They had no cinema, or trips to the zoo or the park. Observing the eccentric and slightly insane neighbors was the girls' only distraction. They stayed away from the other kids in the street. They bullied Anjuli for being an orphan, and Ginni stuck by her friend unwaveringly, having to chase the ragtag misfits off with a stick each time.

******

Ginni listened to the sounds of the neighborhood slowly winding down for the night. She turned her face to the wall and pulled the thin blanket to her neck. It had been a long and eventful day for her. She was tired now and hoped that tonight she would be allowed to go to sleep, peacefully.

A sound outside her door, light footsteps, and she knew that peace would not come tonight. She continued to lie down, pretending to be asleep. The door creaked slightly. He opened it and slipped quickly inside. Even while drunk he was aware that he must be terribly cautious. He felt the enormity of the act he was committing, but did not care enough to stop. He was too far-gone. The copious amounts of the alcohol that he could not live without, have curbed any remorse he had.

She could already smell him, his breath, body, and clothes reeking of the revolting homebrew he drank every day. She wanted to jump up and run out of the room, never to come back, but she did not. He was close, sitting down next to her on her low wooden bed. He did not say anything but she could hear the breathing, that awful disgusting breathing, slow at first then…faster and faster. He pulled the blanket off her legs exposing them. Ginni knew not to fight him. She had tried it before. The less she moved the sooner it would be over. He continued to remove the blanket until she was completely uncovered, her thin form curled up ready to pounce in defense.

He was almost finished she could tell. She covered her ears with her hands to block out his awful sounds; she imagined she was outside with Anjuli throwing rocks into the puddles of rainwater…

After a while, Ginni realized her uncle had left. She was alone, and she slowly rolled down her nightdress and then pulled the threadbare covers up all the way to her chin. It was late and she had to wake up early. She was glad that at least now she could get to sleep. Tomorrow was the first day of school after their vacation and she looked forward to it so much. To escape this place, the insanity, the two damaged people with whom she shared the house.

She had to be strong and rested, she had to remain calm, because maybe tomorrow he father would finally send for her… maybe he had at last heard her prayers and was coming to take her with him, somewhere, anywhere, where no one would be able to hurt her.

Chapter 27

David

David faltered by the door of his office and looked around uneasily. It was late. He was sure most employees were already on their way home, or stuck in the horrendous evening traffic.

The office boy was in the kitchen, getting ready to wrap his day up as well. David nodded at the young Sri Lankan pleasantly.

"Good evening sir, have a nice weekend," the office boy was new and friendly.

"Thank you, same to you...er..." He could not recall the tea boys' name. David went back into his office making sure to lock the door behind him. He sat at his desk, enjoying the familiar feel of the soft leather under his tired muscles. A throbbing headache threatened to rip his head in half.

Jassim's sudden announcement that afternoon and the ensuing developments had sent shock waves through the firm. Events of catastrophic consequences to David had been set in motion. He had been waiting all day for the opportunity to sit unobserved in his office and go through some documents in his files.

Damning documents.

It was too late to regret it now. He riffled through the cabinets roughly, scattering the neatly organized papers. *What he had done was done with. He had to deal with the consequences.*

A sickening feeling in the pit of his stomach washed over him again and he felt beads of cold sweat on his forehead. *Jesus Christ what if they do find them? What if Jassim's anti fraud team found the documents that he has gone through great pains to keep hidden? After all, didn't a high-ranking Australian CEO go to prison last year over a similar case?* David could only guess, what careless oversight, which mislaid document had brought that CEO down.

He swept his brow with a shaky hand, his anxiety rising with every minute of the prolonged search. *Where did he put them? Did someone get their hands on the documents already? Was Jassim already aware of David's terrible disloyalty and laying a trap for him?* The tension had been building up in him all day and he feared that he would not be able to keep himself together.

It had all seemed so easy at first. The amount of money that had passed through his hands every day was unbelievable. He wanted to laugh at some of the incredible figures he was dealing with. He was astounded that he was being trusted with the care of all the company money. After a while, it seemed sinful that it should all belong to one person. Jassim had more money than he could ever need in his life. Even if he shared it with all his relatives, it would be enough to last them all through generations. They had investments in real estate throughout the world that added to billions of dirhams. The conglomerate invested in diverse projects from oil and gas to movies and transportation. The tentacles of the 'Al Gaafari Group' were many and far-reaching.

At first, he took only small amounts, a few thousand dirhams, which nobody was going to notice missing for years. The amount he took the first time was much less than what the company spent on their complimentary coffee and pastries every year. He surprised himself by how little remorse he felt over the incident, even though had always considered himself an honest, hardworking man.

What happened to him? He had hypothesized endlessly many times while sitting in his car, stuck in traffic for what seemed like the millionth time. Those hours he had spent in enforced confinement in his car with nothing to do except accept it and wait it out. Such times eventually served him well as an escape from the demands of his job and the deteriorating condition of his marriage.

During one such long trip home, David's thoughts wandered to the fact that if he lost his job with Al Gaafari Group he would have to go back to the cold and gloomy confines of an uptight English accounting practice. He was shocked that this distressed him more than he expected. He realized that he hated working in England with other boring middle-aged accountants, doing the same thing day after day, year after year in the cold and rainy world that was his home. A vehement surge of rebellion against such a development rose in his chest like a storm.

The idea of growing old in their monotonous suburb of London and always thinking of the glorious sunny days spent in Dubai and what could have been filled him with dread. Like many before him, David felt incurably cursed by Dubai's exotic charm, and the titillating sense of opportunity...doomed forever, because now every other place on the planet, even his dear England, somehow paled in comparison.

Of course, he would always loathe the heat and the humidity of the summer months. The dust storms and the traffic jams, the sometimes-incomprehensible rules of conduct in work situations, the fierce competitiveness, and cutthroat attitude in the workplace. However, the excitement...the pulsing energy and the intrigue... the opportunity, the beaches and the incredible jumble of humans and the stories that brought them all together in this city, those things he would sorely miss.

A knock on the door rattled him so bad he dropped the file he was holding in his hands. Then he opened the door cautiously.

"Sir I will be leaving now...you need anything sir?"

It was the office boy, probably wondering why David had locked himself in his office at this late hour. He looked at the clock on his desk. It was past nine already and he still could not find the bloody document. *Where had he put it? Maybe he should go home, take a shower, and think about it calmly.*

He would remember for sure once he was relaxed.

******

"David...are you all right?" Jane raised her eyebrows quizzically.

David seemed jumpier than usual, distracted. He was on his computer, still in his work clothes...typing fervently. She looked at him with aversion.

How did they drift apart so much? He was a different man, one that she felt little connection to.

What was going on with him lately? Jane thought irritably, flipping through the pages of Arabian Woman magazine. Her friend Jewel was featured in an article on Emirati women philanthropists. *What a beautiful woman*, Jane sighed while peering at the pictures taken of Jewel posing in her *Abaya* at the family desert retreat. The journalist went on to describe Jewel's lifestyle and mention that she was a busy mother of four, a community leader involved in numerous charity projects throughout the country.

Jane held the magazine up, "David, your boss's wife is in the magazine, look."

David muttered an incoherent reply barely glancing up from the screen. Jane felt irritation…incomprehension flood her like a swift wave.

"Exactly what is happening to you David?" she placed the magazine in her lap and sat up facing him stiffly. She had to get to the bottom of this. They had been skirting the issue for weeks. "David, can we talk dear?" she asked carefully."Could you please talk to me for a minute?"

He looked up then. His bloodshot eyes and a gaunt face shocked her.

He seemed to be weighing his options, but then turned the computer off and faced her, "Yes, yes of course we can talk. What would you like to talk about dear?"

Always so polite, always the consummate English gentleman, Jane thought to herself with a melancholy smile. She remembered how proper David had been when he courted her. Impeccable manners, even though endearingly stiff, but in all these years of marriage, he had never uttered a bad word, or insulted her.

She sat up in the sofa, got more comfortable. "Well for one, what's going on with you?" she blurted it out. He looked taken aback.

"You haven't been sleeping," she continued sternly. "I can hear you all night. Why…once you even called out, sounded like you were afraid of something David." Jane was getting more disturbed as she recalled the incident. She had watched terrified as David mumbled and trashed in bed, and then let out, what she could best describe as a…moan. Then suddenly, he stopped, making her think the next morning that she had imagined it.

"It's nothing dear, really," David said.

Jane glared at him. He has been so quiet lately she realized. She had been too busy with her life too notice, but it struck her now. She felt guilty.

"Are you positive you don't want to tell me David?" She asked him, in a kinder, softer voice this time. "Because I do know there is something worrying you." *Was it another woman?* She balked at the thought. *No David would never...but maybe.* After all, the city was notorious for splitting people up; divorce rates among expats were high. Jane looked at her husband closely. He looked tired, worried and like he needed a good rest. He did not look like a man having a hot and heavy affair with his secretary.

Jane tried again, "You would tell me if there was anything upsetting you won't you David?"

He craned his neck slowly, smiled tiredly, "Yes, of course I would Jane dear..." He placed his soft, warm hand on hers. "Don't worry I will be fine."

Chapter 28

Cora

The pain jolted Cora awake. It arrived unexpectedly, too early. It gripped her insides, as if a beast was on a malevolent rampage within her belly. She gnashed her teeth trying to keep quiet. She twisted in the bed trying to get up but slammed right back into the pillow in agony. The baby was coming and she was not ready for it. She never had been ready for it.

Whimpering like some captured animal, from the terrible spasm wracking her body she managed to sit up and then in between the contractions, she hobbled to the door of her room.

Peering outside at the darkened hallway of Girlie's flat Cora thanked God that her cousin was still away in Bangkok with her wealthy Kuwaiti boyfriend. How lucky she had been to find a place of refuge in her distant cousin's home. Cora's condition troubled Girlie but she allowed her to stay, remaining cordial but detached from the precise details of Cora's predicament. Cora preferred it stayed that way as well. She did not inform her cousin of the true reason she had left her job so unexpectedly, only saying that her employees had treated her badly and she wished to find other employment.

A vague air hung over the real motive and Girlie did not insist on an answer, turning a blind eye…preferring instead to concentrate on the pleasant aspects of her hectic life. Cora knew that Girlie had doubts, occasionally catching an odd look in her cousin's eye, and she knew that she would be expected to deal with her problem alone. In the meantime, Cora knew that her cousin looked forward to a hasty and quiet ending to her already prolonged stay.

The last few months had been slow and uneventful. Cora had kept a low profile and stayed in the room by herself whenever Girlie came home. Thankfully, she had hid her advancing pregnancy well. Like with Cora's first pregnancy her slight frame only showed a small bulge, cunningly covered by loose, slovenly outfits.

In any case, Girlie was usually away at work as a dancer at a nightclub called 'The Gypsy' or traveling throughout the region to entertain at parties and events. For the past week, she had taken off to Bangkok with a new 'Sugar Daddy'…the most recent in a procession of many.

Cora continued her slow and arduous walk towards the bathroom. The flat was dim, lit only by the verve of the street outside. The neighborhood had proven a lively one, she much preferred it to the coldness and isolation of the large villas in the upscale neighborhood where she used to work. Cheerful singing reached her ears from the Filipino karaoke bar across the street. It seemed surreal that life could be happily prancing along, oblivious to the ordeal she was going through.

Cora grabbed the door hinge to steady herself while yet another awful contraction ripped through her. She felt nauseous and cold. A film of cold sweat was causing the thin cotton nightgown to cling to her body. Inwardly she cursed at, everything.

The bathroom door was close now. The pain was merciless, unapologetic, and urgent, demanding swift action. Cora anticipated that she was going to have the baby alone. She had hoped to be out of Girlie's house by the time it came, but this baby was arriving on its own time. *So stubborn,* Cora mumbled to herself, her legs almost buckling from the effort of walking. *Why could it not die when I tried to abort it? Why is it clinging on, does it not know nobody wants it?*

Once in the bathroom she locked the door, laid some of Girlie's pink towels on the cold tiled floor, and lay down, bending awkwardly as she did so. There was enough light streaming through the glazed bathroom window so she did not turn on the light. This whole street lit up every night as if it was New Years Eve.

It all happened so quickly after that.

Those incessant wracking contractions, the pressure, and the excruciating, hot pain. If only Luca knew this was happening now. Her fuzzy brain tried to hold on to some wonderful memory of their time spent together. Some way to help her ease the pitiful position she was in now. She was pushing now…it was coming unaided…in a hurry to meet the world that did not want it, a mother that will not welcome it.

Cora bit her lip, hard, and tasted that metallic taste when the blood seeped from the cut. She was not worried about anything but getting this baby out of her agonized body, the body that the relentless child was surely going to rip apart any minute now.

Her breathing was coming short and fast but she managed to pull herself up on her elbows, and pushed again. She was grateful now for the merry singing voices wafting from the karaoke bar through the sleeping neighborhood. They covered up her muffled screams and sobs. Cora almost laughed aloud in her delirium.

She wanted to laugh at the idiocy that had led her to this horrible night. The sequence of events that had deluded her further into thinking she could have this fantasy life that she saw in Dubai. Maybe she could have the life that she had seen in the glossy pages of Zoya's weekly 'Hello 'and 'Ahlan' magazines.

She mocked herself now. How preposterous of her, how incredibly naive of her. How could she think that she would ever have a life akin to the life Luca and Parisa led in their impressive house by the beach? The life she so craved, complete with their fancy parties and their important, talented friends.

A life that had seemed within her reaches when she met Luca. Now look at her. Here she was.

A deplorable Filipino maid, an adulteress, fugitive from her sponsor, alone, on a bathroom floor giving birth to a child that no one wanted.

She did not think anymore. She just wanted to survive this.

She could feel the horrible pressure in her groin, and stretching her legs as far apart as she could, she pushed. Abruptly the baby's head pushed through, and swiftly, the little body followed. It slithered onto the pink towels, marking them red with her blood. Incredulous, Cora looked down. The pain had evaporated as suddenly as it had started. She knew that more was to come…the afterbirth. She quickly concentrated on the child. It was very small and completely quiet and she leant over to look at it in the diffused light of the small bathroom window.

It was a boy. He lay unmoving, still covered in blood and the glue like whitish discharge that had protected his small body all these past months. Then suddenly he let out a feeble cry, startling her.

She knew where the scissors were, knew what to do next. Her first child, Bobbi, was born at home in their island village and she had watched the island's sole midwife cut and tie the cord. Without further thought, she snipped across the engorged tie that bonded them together. She tied it off and stuck a towel between her legs to stop the blood and the water that were leaking out.

Slowly she knelt on her knees and continued to look at the baby. She looked at it for a long time. He slept, but she could see his chest rise and fall as he took small shallow breaths.

The contractions started again, breaking the spell, and the last remains of her pregnancy rushed out of her body, leaving no trace of this child.

She had made her decision.

Cora sprung into action. She wiped herself with the towel, and then got up, her legs shaking crazily. She steadied herself on the bathroom sink and then splashed some cold water on her face. Her eyes fell on her image in the mirror above the sink, and she recoiled from it in horror.

In the half-light, it looked foreign, unfamiliar to her, staring at her with the burning eyes of a mad woman. Cora tore her gaze away; her face was set in a rigid, expression, and she continued with her ghastly preparations.

A housedress she wore during the pregnancy to hide the growing bump, hung on a hook by the door and she put it on, first stripping the bloodied and sweaty nightgown. She is going to have to get rid of it as well, she thought to herself calmly. Quickly, before she wavered even more, she ran a comb through her hair and slipped her feet into some flip-flops.

Next, she picked up the still baby. She held it in the towel for a minute, unable to tear her eyes away from the scrawny body, the tiny hands, fingers and toes, the dark hair that was exactly like Luca's, and for a minute, she felt incapable to go through with it.

Someone sang 'Baby One More Time' at the bar. Abruptly, she swaddled the small body in the large pink towels. Once, twice, she rolled them around her son.

He was invisible now, resembling a large pink and red parcel. She looked around the bathroom for something else to put the package in. Wearily, she realized she would have to go to the kitchen and find something. Slowly she raised herself off the floor, wobbly on her legs, and hobbled to the kitchen. There she found an empty cardboard box with a water bottle company logo on it. She hobbled back to the bathroom picked up the bundle and pushed her package into it, closing the flaps over securely.

Then she hurried out of the bathroom, out of the flat and into the streets of Dubai to dispose of the body of her newborn child.

Chapter 29

Jassim

Jassim Al Gaafari was not accustomed to people denying him anything. His good looks, charm, and auspicious pedigree ensured that he was welcome by most and fawned over by many.

Liliana gave into Jassim's charms only after months of persistent and aggressive courting.

"Go and meet him for God's sake already." Vikki was fed up with the entire drama, the endless flower baskets, and chocolate boxes that she had to sign for on delivery to their flat. She was tired of Liliana's endless rants on why she should not agree to go out with one of the wealthiest most successful men in the Middle East.

"Listen you silly goose, no one is telling you to get involved, just have coffee with the man so he can leave us alone."

The moment Liliana had sat down with Jassim at a luxury hotel's private dining room and after the first few sips of her latte, she had regretted this decision. Because once in his proximity, once she smelled him, felt his hand on hers, once she had looked into his eyes, she was completely at his mercy. Her hands trembled slightly when he shook them on arrival, looking directly into her eyes, visibly happy to see her.

"I have been waiting for this moment for so long Liliana."

Her name rolled off his tongue slowly, deliberately, the sound of his distinctive voice having a disconcerting effect on her body. She giggled, and then regretted it, immediately. *What was wrong with her? He was a mortal, just like all the rest of them.*

His dark eyes had stared unflinchingly into her blue ones as they spoke. Well traveled and well educated Jassim's life sounded like a fairy tale compared to hers. She felt stupid and insignificant next to his accomplished, lavish life. *What could this man possibly want from her? She could guess the basic answer to that of course, but why her? Why pursue her all these months when he could have any woman in the city, maybe even, in the world?*

Why, when he was married to one of the most beautiful women she had seen. Once while skimming lazily through the pages of a glossy society magazine, Liliana had come face to face with Jewel Al Gaafari. The picture was from a charity event and Jewel looked radiant. *Why would Jassim be disloyal to woman like that?*

She had felt a torrent of guilty conscience wash over her as she pondered the woman's exquisitely chiseled face. *The man had four children for God's sake!* She knew she should not be involved in this kind of situation. Liliana wowed not to talk to him again. *She had no shortage of love struck suitors after all.*

Her resolve however, had melted away dangerously as the evening progressed. Jassim never implied anything inappropriate but she found herself watching him intently, his strong hands holding the coffee cup firmly, his thick salt and pepper hair visible under the perfectly white *Gotra...*

To her surprise, he left it at that for many more of their meetings. She started to feel that he valued her companionship, and she started to relax but alas, it had become impossible for her to stay away from him. Just as she had feared, it would. Liliana wished many times that she had never listened to Vikki.

"It's your fault you know." She would say to her impulsive friend jokingly.

Of course, it was not Vikki's fault. It was Liliana's fault, for not resisting. For not running away from him as far away, as possible the first time he had approached her.

One evening as she finished her dance and bowed, she sensed something. Oddly, she could feel his presence in the audience. She could not see him from the lights shining into her eyes and the crowd of people at the tables, but she instinctively felt that Jassim was watching her.

She walked to the changing room quietly; certain, that he would come to her tonight. He had been patient long enough and so had she.

In the dimness of the hallway, she saw him, standing still, and waiting. She imagined that she could smell him, knew that he was too far away. Her heart had accelerated suddenly, pounding in her ears, threatening to rupture into irreparable pieces. In a moment, she had made her choice. She hurried, no longer caring for rules and restrictions. She had tried her best to escape this inevitable ending, had failed miserably. In a sudden urgency to get to him, uncaring of the consequences, feeling as invincible as the mountains in Romania, she ran towards him. Her high heels clicked on the marble floor.

Liliana bounded into Jassim's arms to the sound of a stunned intake of breath from Habib, the only eyewitness to the scene.

The faithful bodyguard watched despondently, as they walked out through the back door, hand in hand, to Jassim's waiting car.

Chapter 30

Tara

"Girls please stop; mommy is trying to talk to daddy ok?"

Four brown eyes stared at her fearfully. Her voice must have scared them. Tara felt guilty. She needed to get a grip on herself. A smile crept to her face and she winked at the girls.

"Listen, you goofy heads if you go to bed right now and start on your books I promise to come and finish reading to you in a few minutes," she made a comical pleading face and the girls rolled on the floor clutching their stomachs, giggling in joy...relieved.

"Mommy is so funny but sometimes she gets scary," Miriyam whispered to her sister Aisha on their way to their bedroom.

"Yeah...she did it last time too," Aisha cuddled with her teddy and pulled the purple and pink bedspread up to her chin.

"Ok let's read...," Miriyam commanded her sister and the assortment of soft toys that lay out on the bed.

172

******

Tara stood in the doorway silently looking at her husband. *Where had that much-loved man had gone?* His zeal and passion for good that had attracted her years ago only scared her now.

Qays was on his laptop typing agitatedly. His form bent and tense, he was always tense. She was going to have to reach him again. She has to try for the girls' sake. She steeled herself for a confrontation, and walked into the living room.

"How is work?" she sat on the edge of the seat by his side. Only now, she noticed how haggard he looked, as if he had aged overnight. *Why hadn't she noticed this before?* Qays raised his head for only a second, looked at her, but then, abruptly returned to his tapping.

"Work is fine, busy…that's all." He ignored her again.

Tara pushed on unsure of where she intended to go with this even if he answered. Last month she had told Dr.Ghassan that she could not continue to see him anymore…could not keep up the lying anymore.

"I feel too guilty, and lately I have been afraid, terribly afraid," she told him one evening in his office, while the girls attended a birthday party.

He had looked at her silently, waiting. She admired that about him, his ability to wait for anything, even when he knew what it would be. That is why he sat in his usual armchair, hands poised in a triangle, perfectly steady. Only a shade of something akin to hurting in his green eyes, and then it too was gone.

"Are you sure?" he had asked slowly.

"Yes, I'm." She looked down, at the clean, antiseptic floor of his office. Tara remembered how much love she had found in this office. Then she raised her head, looked him in the eyes. Almost gave in, almost collapsed into his familiar comforting embrace. Her fear was stronger. She stayed in the chair.

What madness was this? She had to be firm because there was no way for them to continue, no way at all. It was wrong, damnable, perverted. She should just rip her scarf of her head, never to wear it again, screaming for all to see her duplicity. Admit that she was a hypocrite, a *zaniyah*, an adulteress. Ah, the guilt was like a knife in her side. Her eyes filled with tears. They came together with tears she thought, and now they are separating the same way.

"Please" she said softly. "Let me go".

He did. Tara had not seen or talked to him for an entire month. Each of those days, she had cried. Cried because she loved him, cried because she was a sinner, and cried because there was nothing she could do to change that.

Qays looked at her. He stopped typing and put the laptop aside. "What is it?" he asked cautiously.

"What do you mean?" feeling guilty already, the question made her nervous.

"You look different." His tired eyes roamed over her face, looking for something. She smelled his breath. It smelled of toothpaste.

"I'm tired," she said. "How are you?"

He paused, a look of dread in his previously weary eyes, "Just tired too."

"Had the meeting at Abu Salem's been cancelled tonight?"

"No, actually I felt too exhausted, so I didn't go." He looked away. He was lying too.

"So everything is fine then?" Tara shifted her position, turned around to look at him closely. He seemed troubled but at least they were having a conversation. He was not ranting and raving or lecturing. It surprised her.

"Well, yes, as I said, I have been overwhelmed with work." Another lie, she thought.

"There is talk of cutbacks and the entire city is in turmoil," he added.

That part was true. Up to that time distant, snickered at rumble of change, of financial distress, had bared its teeth in Dubai as well. The world was crashing down and taking the previously untouchable, golden city with it.

"Have you heard of the recent corruption charges at Al Gaafari Company?" he was curious.

Tara's surprise at his change in demeanor grew. "Yes, I heard from Jewel, we had lunch last week." Jewel had invited her and twenty other friends to a luncheon at her sprawling villa in Jumeirah. She had met the famous designer Ginni Karisma that afternoon. Tara had been uneasy at first by the talent at the gathering but had soon settled in and ended up having wonderful time. "Times have changed right?" she said sadly. Ghassan's face filled her mind.

Qays looked at her solemnly. His face was set as if carved from stone. "What would you do if you found out something about me you did not like?"

Tara's stomach did a somersault, and then rolled and heaved as it did the two times she has been on a boat. *What does he mean? What does he know?*

"Well, I would like to think we could share everything, and discuss everything." *What a good liar she had become, and what a fraud.* "Why do you ask this question?" Her voice sounded foreign to her ears.

He thought for what seemed ages, closing his eyes at one point as if to gain strength, "If you found out I had been unfaithful…"

Tara felt her hands go cold. She sat awkwardly, afraid to move, sure that he had found out about her unforgivable affair. Certain, that he was going to punish her for that.

He was still waiting for an answer and she managed, "What are you saying Qays?" Barely audible, her voice sounded like someone else's. Her gut still heaved. Slowly she licked her lips. Qays continued to stare at some indefinable object in the distance. He was silent.

Was he going to withdraw into his shell again…remain unexplainable as he always had been? Was he going to let her incriminate herself even more, and then strike his final blow? "What are you saying?" she repeated again, this time louder. She needed to find out what he meant. She thought he had forgotten about her, wanted nothing to do with her. He had created his own little fantasy world and so she had found one too. Anger grew in her chest, galloping alongside the fear, shoulder to shoulder. She might be a sinner but so was he. *Qays and his crazy lectures, fixated ideas, his apathy to her pain and loneliness. He was a sinner because of the way he had ignored them …no! …He was guilty of the callous way he had shut out his daughters for months at a time.*

"Remember when I told you once I wanted to die before I sinned too much?" he said. Tara sat alert, poised. "I have sinned Tara, I have sinned a lot." His words tumbled out suddenly.

She was not sure what it was that he was saying. *HE had sinned He was not talking about her.* She relaxed. Let out a breath.

Qays whispered, "I have been a bad husband, a bad father…I know."

One outrageous revelation after another, what has gotten into him today, she wondered. Qays spoke again, his voice trembling this time, "I need to let you know that I'm ashamed of what I have done. I hope that we can do something about it." He looked at her now, the gaze of a broken, shamed man.

Tara was stunned. The last hour had been nothing like what she had expected. It was like a roller coaster ride with Qays. One moment he seemed aloof, distant and cold and then suddenly he was pouring out more of himself than he had in years… apologizing. She needed time to think about what just happened. She sensed that something more serious was bothering her husband than what he had confessed. In all their years of marriage, she had never seen him this dejected, this apologetic.

She moved in the chair, met his eyes. A volcano of feelings felt like pouring out of her unruffled, composed countenance. "I appreciate you saying this Qays, I really do." A pause while she struggled what to say. "Let's talk about it again; okay…it's getting late now."

Qays nodded his head, relieved that it was over. He did feel fatigued. They rose and made their way to the stairs. Tara turned the lights off, checked the front door lock. In the dark stillness Qays called out softly from the landing, "Good night Tara".

Tara leaned on the wall, closed her eyes, "Good night Qays".

Chapter 31

Parisa

*T*he welcome January breeze pleasantly cooled Parisa's face through the open window of the limousine. She had spent an hour in a mad scramble to get ready for Jewel's high profile boutique opening night, and ended up sweating profusely under the thickly applied foundation. Now her expensive makeup threatened to slide right off her moist face.

Oh, whatever...it was Jewel's night anyway. Checking in the small compact mirror again, she sighed. *No one will pay attention to me.* Of course, she knew that was not entirely true. Parisa was a celebrity in her own right. She was a famous painter, wealthy widow and recently, the laughing stock of the town.

"You look beautiful mama," Zoya looked over at her and smiled.

They were in a limo, in the valet service lineup, waiting for their turn in a long motorcade. A couple of Chinese tourists took pictures of the gala event-taking place. Others too, ogled the hip, fabulously dressed guests that were arriving for the party, pointing at some familiar face from TV or the society magazines.

Parisa looked over at her daughter proudly. She had not realized that Zoya had grown into a young woman, was not a child anymore, until the unraveling, shocking events of the last week. For the hundredth time that evening, she brushed those thoughts aside, only for them to return stubbornly a few minutes later.

A simple white dress showed off Zoya's delicate shoulders and her curly hair, all one color now…dark brown. She had a tranquil smile on her dewy face and seemed as fragile as a young, budding flower. Parisa felt a pang of guilt for what she had put her daughter through this past couple of years.

No, I'm not going to let myself think about him now, she admonished herself, feeling queasy at the thought of Luca. To distract herself she turned her attention to the action on the street outside the tinted limo windows. A lively pedestrian crowd thronged the Jumeirah Beach Walk this evening.

Dozens of restaurants, coffee shops, and eclectic high-end boutiques lined the beachfront promenade, which nestled cozily at the feet of a swarm of towering skyscrapers. She loved to come here on the weekend with Zoya, for coffee and fresh croissants and enjoy the fresh air and festive atmosphere.

Today they were here to honor her good friend Jewel and all her hard work. She had already sent the painting ahead, to be unveiled at the party. She hoped Jewel would be as taken by it as she was.

Parisa felt a smile creep onto her face. They had been friends for many years. She remembered when Jewel's oldest child Nora and her Zoya attended the same kindergarten class at a private British school in Jumeirah. Those were the good days, before her husband had died, she thought wistfully. Memories of what was gone brought on a pensive mood.

"We are almost there mama," Zoya was excited and had almost glued her face to the window.

A mob of people congregated at the entrance to the well-lit boutique. *'Al Jawahir'* it said in shining letters over the front door. A dozen uniformed security men with earpieces walked around self importantly, not really doing anything at all. Parisa did not want to face all these people. She felt safe inside where they could not see her. Trembling slightly, she pulled her pashmina around her shoulders.

"Duset daram," I love you, Parisa whispered in her ear. Zoya grinned,

placed her small hand over her mother's. Finally, it was their turn to exit the car.

"Good evening madam." The valet smiled broadly, greeting them in a thick African accent and giving them an appreciative look over. They were magnificent. Mother and daughter, poised and confident, they held their head high, undaunted by the curious masses who awaited them ahead.

******

A mob of overzealous photographers accosted them immediately.

Two attractive Turkish girls in *Abayas,* models, hired as hostesses for the event, greeted them with a polite smile and led them towards the open doors of the festively decorated boutique. Jewel had spared no expense on this opening night. Top event coordinators had worked on all aspects of the party and the fashion show for months; finally producing what was to become the most talked about event in the country.

It seemed as if the moment they had stepped out of the car they were transported into another dimension. It seemed that they had landed in Hollywood.

"Mama, look," Zoya was laughing, happily pointing to a group of mime performers following them. Their white faces produced expressions that brought more squeals of delight from the arriving guests.

This way and that they turned, smiling widely, as the photographers called out to them to have their picture taken. A wide, red carpet had been laid out in front of the entrance, like the one at the Kodak Theater in Los Angeles on Oscar night. Another traffic jam, this one of human bodies ensued. The crowd moved at a snail's pace, in no particular hurry to enter the building. Rather, they were taking their time having their photos taken by the army of photographers vying for a shot, talking to reporters, and chatting. Some of these guests greeted Parisa with air kisses and hugged Zoya exclaiming how much she had grown. Everywhere, the smell of expensive perfume mingled with the smoke of Cuban cigars. No one asked her about Luca.

A Jordanian socialite strutted by on sky high Louboutins, all pouting collagen lips, tightened and botoxed face and masses of black hair extensions. She looked ravishing, and the photographers could not get enough of her.

"*Marhaba* Parisa, good to see you," she waved in their direction. Parisa smiled back, waved weakly. She had known the socialite for years, and she was friendly, sweet even, but Parisa could not be friends with her.

Something about the fake dead hair and frozen face simply freaked her out.

They were inside now and the two hostesses had disappeared, after offering them the glossy program for the evening.

Parisa needed a drink and moved towards the interior of the fabulous store. It resembled a magic fairyland…white and gold stars hung from the ceiling, twinkling discreetly, hundreds of white Calla lilies flown in for the occasion from Europe adorned the tables, and a famous local DJ spun some popular Arabic fusion music.

A giggling group of social butterflies stood in the center, constantly swinging their fake extensions that had been flawlessly highlighted, blow-dried, and then set in careful precision hours before. An immaculately turned out Pakistani beauty stood with this group, a haughty, pinched look on her face. Her unease was only apparent by the constant adjusting of her expensive, tight Cavalli evening gown. The Filipino wife of a well-known diamond merchant, fiddled with her glass of champagne, constantly looking around the room, seemingly in need of rescuing.

Manolo Blahniks and Jimmy Choos adorned their pedicured feet. Shamelessly expensive diamond, gold, and crystal bangles and rings the size of limes glittered on their wrists and freshly manicured hands.

The eager faces glistened with the effect of today's spa treatments, maybe even the gold facial where the face was slathered in powdered gold with the tantalizing promise of a gloriously youthful appearance. After the requisite collagen, the lips too, were assembled in a perfectly enhanced, glossy pout. Tanned, massaged, wrapped in seaweed, and scrubbed, then exfoliated with decadent concoctions made out of diamond dust, chocolate or caviar…these bodies glistened like those statues of ancient Greek goddesses, intimidating in their perfection. Parisa knew the kind.

Those socialites who would be present at the fashionable opening of even an envelope, those who desperately hoped to make it into the glossy pages of 'Hello' or 'Ahlan' magazine the next day.

The multitude of Dubai women who spent hours at the gym, sweating to Body Pump classes, getting lightheaded on the Power Plate machines and keeping the spa and beauty salon owners very busy and very rich.

Seemed like all some women did was hop around the city all year, from one designer shoe boutique opening or the unveiling of a 'must buy' jeans store to any other inane gatherings. Such events were always chockfull of expatriate women who had long ago forgotten the real reasons for moving to live in Dubai. Now they were in a hunt of the hottest, most lavish events and parties they could manage to get themselves invited to. This obsession with celebrity status, the quest for recognition took on bizarre proportions.

Everybody in Dubai yearned to be a 'Somebody'.

Parisa grabbed her longed for glass of champagne from a passing, haughty looking maître d' and went in search of Jewel. Her friend should be here somewhere. She saw Zoya in an animated conversation with a tall, young man. *Oh yes, Jake.* Of course, he would be here with his mother, Jane. Parisa liked the young man, who unlike his father had an amiable and easygoing manner. Zoya and Jake both attended the same expensive high school and recently had started 'dating'.

Parisa sighed at that thought. She knew her late husband would not have approved of this strange and modern concept. After all, he had been Iranian and even tough well educated, and well traveled; those old traditions had a way of cropping up when ones' daughter was in question. However, times had changed and Parisa and Zoya's relationship had deteriorated since Luca entered their life. Any objection voiced by her mother only seemed to prod Zoya further in that very direction. Since the events of last few weeks, Parisa had felt a renewed sense of hope in their bond. Another thing that comforted her was that Jake was her friend Jane's son and that in itself stacked points in his favor.

After a good ten minutes of mingling and admiring the interior decoration of the boutique, Parisa decided Jewel must be busy behind the scenes...getting the fashion show ready.

******

A week ago Parisa's world had come crashing down.

"Luca there are police officers at our door...they want to talk to you." Zoya had called out nervously from the door of their living room. She had faltered uncertainly, looking worried. Parisa looked up from her book. Luca was in the pool, by the edge, ready for another lap when he heard her.

He had lingered for a moment too long, his eyes hardening then mumbled slowly, "*Buena,* yes I will be there in a minute," and lifted himself out of the pool effortlessly, his muscles rippling in the morning sunshine.

Parisa remained seated; her book lay open in her lap, her body tensing as if ready for attack. A light fluttering in her stomach started to build up... *what was happening?* She felt sluggish...her body was stiff this morning since she had stayed up late again at her studio, painting.

What was going on…there are police…at her door?

Really, the worst reason for them being here was some sort of nasty traffic violation. However, she was sure that kind of violation would not require a couple of serious looking police officers to drive to their house and take her husband to the police station for 'questioning'. Usually polite and friendly, these two did not appear like the usual sort she had come across a few times, twice for traffic accidents, once when the maid absconded, and she had filed a report.

Those police officers who filed the forms seemed interested in her as a person and they chatted pleasantly throughout the encounter. They sympathized with the plight of duped sponsors whose house help jilted them after they had invested enormous sums of money to get them into the country, providing visas, air tickets and an exorbitant sum to the recruitment agency.

Luca got dressed while the two police officers waited at the door, "What is the reason for this, officer?" she had asked in as dignified a way as possible.

One of the men, avoiding her eyes and looking embarrassed said, "Sorry we cannot discuss the matter now…we need Mr. Finelli to come with us to the headquarters."

Parisa had followed Luca to the main gate to watch in disbelief as he went away meekly, without a remark, without any of his usually sassy attitude towards authority.

"I will be right there Luca." she assured him. "Don't worry… I will take care of it."

His head bowed, he looked at her and Zoya briefly and turned around, got into the back of the Land cruiser and was driven off.

Zoya came over and put her arm around her mother's shoulders. It suddenly got chilly as it only does in the desert, even while the sun is shining brightly.

"Mama, let's go inside…we will call the lawyer, we will talk to him and see what we can do. Come on," she had prodded her silent and shell-shocked mother gently on into the house.

Chapter 32

Jewel

"Jewel, Jewel!" Parisa finally let out a shout in a desperate effort to find her friend. The hectic atmosphere in the dressing room, the loud music, and the cacophony of voices made this attempt futile. Her friend however seemed to be busy elsewhere, Parisa just could not find her.

About a dozen models, young, tall and culturally diverse, were getting their final touch ups to their face and hair. A group of frantic makeup artists dressed in black hovered over them.

One tall, dark skinned man with a stud earring in his nose bent over a flaxen haired model, dabbing, brushing, and fussing. The girls sat facing improvised dressing tables. Eight hairstylists moved around busily, waving their combs and blow dryers like weapons, looking very self important while they too, fussed and tormented themselves over their creations.

While Parisa observed this scene with curiosity, she caught sight of Jewel, across the room, immersed in a conversation with a few nervously gesticulating people. Parisa moved towards Jewel trying to catch her friend's eye, and she waved again, fruitlessly. Sighing, she knew that she would have to battle it through this minefield of hysterical prima donnas and effeminate stylists with an attitude. Somehow working in the fashion industry gave them all license to be rude and self-absorbed...demanding a celebrity status just for powdering some models nose or blow-drying her hair.

By the look of things, everything seemed to be coming together, the fashion show was due to start soon, and despite the frenzy in the room Parisa was sure Jewel would pull it off perfectly. As she evaded dashing assistants carrying items of clothing, glasses of water, ringing mobile phones, she could hear a melody of lively sounds spoken in at least a dozen languages.

Four, Parisa spoke fluently herself...Persian, Arabic, English, and French, the other colorful spurts of vocabulary she could recognize from the many years of mingling with a culturally diverse group of friends.

She evaded a thickset woman giving orders in rapid German to her frazzled assistant. A tall Asian man argued with someone on the cell phone in Gujarati. Two skinny Polish models giggled over some gossip. Some self-important Colombian photographer strode impatiently through the room snapping photos and grumbling about the lighting.

However, the most flamboyant of this eclectic group of individuals was a short middle aged Frenchman dressed in a three-piece white suit with a red kerchief in the lapel pocket and apparently the one wielding the most power over the assembled group.

His nasal French rose over the other voices in haughty, exasperated tones. "....he hated it all, they were all morons, they are ruining his precious handiwork, Ms. Karisma would be livid with this unprofessionalism," and on and on, he ranted. The entire time he swaggered from model to model, peering at each from all sides, shoving his face into theirs to check the makeup and then wrinkling his nose in disapproval and wiping his brow with the red handkerchief, theatrically feigning distress.

The crew, obviously horrified by this little man, tried to stay out of his way, but he seemed oblivious to their displeasure and kept on, unrelenting in his little crusade of terror.

Parisa tore her eyes away from him and spotted that gorgeous model she had seen previously at another fashion event. Parisa could not forget a face and body that beautiful; in fact, she had asked the girl to model for her once. She tried to remember the name...

"Excuse me, do you remember me," the lovely, guttural voice said. The girl was a vision in one of Ginni Karisma's creations of flowing silk. She looked at Parisa inquisitively with those gorgeous violet eyes. *Oh how she would love to paint her...*

"Of course I remember you; you are not easy to forget," Parisa laughed and extended her arm. The young woman smiled shyly. Parisa eyed the graceful model with an appreciative artist's eye. *Her bone structure is extraordinary.*

Liliana turned to receive instructions from the petite designer who had followed behind her.

"See here...and here...pull that...okay...*merde!*' he exclaimed throwing his hands up in the air and lambasting his terrified assistant with rapid fire demands in French.

Liliana continued to wait patiently, until at last the Frenchman was satisfied. He waved to the henpecked assistant and they rushed off huffing, chasing after another model in dire need of their help. Liliana and Parisa looked at each other for a moment and then both let out a meaningful chuckle.

"Pierre is something isn't he?" Liliana was busy adjusting her long sleeves and tugging on the gorgeous two meters span wings that Pierre had adjusted to her back, just minutes before.

The angel wings complimented the fashion show theme 'Angels and Fairies in the desert'. This particular piece astounded Parisa. The wings Liliana had on were white and glittered with hundreds of crystals... shooting off millions of little sparks onto the girl's face. She seemed like a real angel, ethereal and delicate.

"You look gorgeous Liliana. I know you will do a great job out there," Parisa held her hand warmly.

"I really appreciate that Mrs.Finelli," Liliana smiled once more and joined the procession of other nervous and chattering models on their way to the ramp.

"Oh, thank God, there you are," the familiar voice came from behind and Parisa turned to see Jewel. They hugged tightly, kissed on the cheek and then Jewel looked into Parisa's eyes seriously.

"I'm so, so sorry about Luca, there is no way to express how bad I feel Parisa," for a long moment, she hugged her friend, who was hurting but was here nevertheless, to support Jewel.

Parisa nodded sadly, then forced a smile, "You have things to do...off you go, I will be right here and will talk to you later after the show."

Jewel blew her another kiss, and then hurried off after the fairies, angels, where the celebrity designer Ginni joined her.

Parisa saw the two women immediately enter into a heated discussion over some aspect of the show. Frayed nerves and tension were obvious on Jewel's face. Parisa knew that Jewel was going to do a great job but also knew that her friend constantly doubted herself.

In spite of the deceivingly charmed life, the many successes she achieved, yet Jewel still needed to prove herself to her family and peers, especially to her untrustworthy and controlling husband. Parisa sighed, *men*…she remembered her own cunning spouse. There was a sticker with her name on a seat somewhere and she started looking for it. It was in the first row and Jane's name was right next to hers.

Just as Parisa was about to sit down she glimpsed a handsome young Indian man talking to Jewel. Long, billowing curtains hid them from view but every now and then, the spinning fans would send a blast of air their way. The curtains parted slightly, flirtatiously. Parisa felt herself drawn to the sight. Then the man moved, turned towards her and she saw it was the driver…Raj. The one all the women had stared at when he appeared at their table to pick up Jewel. Parisa shuddered. She felt ashamed of the thoughts that had run through her head at the time, of her suspicions about Jewel and her driver. *How could she think that of her friend, about this decent woman and loving mother long known to suffer at the hands of her husband's callous treatment?*

Wait…what is this now? How bizarre, Parisa thought. Why was Jewel talking to her driver there behind the curtains? It just looked wrong. Surely, Jewel knew better. She was shrewd enough and knew not one to take chances with her reputation, Parisa wondered. The curtain moved again, tantalizingly, inviting her for a closer look. Parisa turned around, to see whether anyone else was watching. No one was. They were all busy making an entrance, finding their seats or chatting excitedly. The noise level was thunderous as the hall filled up with gorgeous people, their expensive perfume, and the sensation of something special about to happen.

Parisa could not take her eyes of the couple behind the curtain. She half stood, half hunched in order to see. Suddenly she felt ashamed of what she was doing, what she was thinking. *Jewel was talking to her driver, giving him instructions, why was she making it into something sinister… diabolical.* Shame filled her. Luca's conduct had affected her deeper than she thought. Not everyone had such lax values as her husband Luca she chastised herself.

She decided to sit down and stop spying, but as she looked one last time, she saw something that chilled her. Jewel had leaned into Raj, was speaking into his ear...a sight in itself so shocking to Parisa that she felt paralyzed. The slipping, sparkling *Sheila* obscured the look on her friend's face but Parisa saw her lips move determinedly, harshly. Raj listened, rooted to the spot. Even from this distance, she admired his features, his trim body. However, his expression moved her. On his face was a rapturous smile of pleasure, his lips half parted, his eyes closed, as he listened to Jewels' instructions. Yet none of these things chilled her to the bone as the realization that Jewel was handing Raj something as she talked.

It looked like a bag, funny shaped one, plastic and heavy, *probably just something to take to the car, quite ordinary.* However, Parisa knew she had witnessed something she should not have. Just as she knew now that her friend Jewel had a side previously unknown to her friends. Mystified and shaken she finally sat down. After a few minutes, she looked again, twisting to see over the seated crowd, but they were gone. Feeling wobbly, like a dreadful, insincere friend Parisa tried to gain her composure, to forget about the puzzling incident. She fanned herself with the program brochure, realizing that she was flushed and hot.

Slowly the lights dimmed and music that had been playing stopped, causing the milling crowds to hurry to their seat in anticipation. The audience was filled with Sheikhas and heiresses, local artists, and designers, businesswomen and ministers.

Right next to this esteemed group of well dressed and immaculately groomed women a famous Lebanese singer and an older Egyptian actor chatted amicably. Parisa knew many of them personally and the others she had seen gracing newspaper or magazine pages. All of a sudden, Jane slipped into the seat next to hers and smiled apologetically. They were supposed to meet earlier.

"David had a meltdown," Jane blinked her eyes as if that proclamation was enough to explain everything. "Sorry for being late dear," she settled comfortably into the velvet-cushioned chair and crossed her firm tanned legs. Parisa could not help but notice that all eyes in their proximity, male and female, admiringly settled on Jane's legs.

The show was apparently going to start as smoke rose from the floor and exotic Arabic inspired music flowed into the room.

The crowd turned expectantly towards the ramp. A surprised gasp went out from the audience as they saw a slender girl suspended above them. Liliana was gliding in the air, floating with the help of a high tech suspension system that sent her soaring and dipping above the audience, her magnificent white wings sparkling, the luminous gown billowing behind her. Her long locks shone as if sprinkled with gold dust and she held her hands clasped humbly together, looking down on them with goodwill.

The audience was stunned. Their thunderous applause erupted, feverish with undeniable approval. No one had witnessed a fashion show like this before.

"Did you know about this?" Jane had to lean over to yell into Parisa's ear over the music and the thrilled babble of the spectators.

"No, she didn't tell me." Parisa was smiling, deeply proud of Jewel and her visionary style. Ginni Karisma and her team had outdone themselves this time. The two women clapped ardently. The show continued when, yet another model, this time a sparkling green fairy, started walking towards them briskly.

"Incredible, what a show," Jane gushed enthusiastically. "How are you feeling?" She turned to look at Parisa, whispered the question in her ear. Parisa smiled and nodded, so and so. The women exchanged an understanding look. Jane knew about Luca. Everyone in Dubai knew what her husband had done. They all knew he had gotten the housemaid pregnant. The entire emirate was talking about it, discussing it behind the closed doors of their Majlis, their lavish salons.

For just a moment, she thought of telling Jane about the strange exchange between Jewel and her driver. Then the moment passed. She realized that she did not trust Jane. She could not trust anyone with these preposterous doubts about their closest friend.

Thunderous applause again roared in Parisa's ears and she suddenly felt exhausted from this showy, loud place. All she wanted was to go away somewhere and allow for the storm of gossip and shame to pass. Even her aunts in Iran had called asking about her, wanting to tell her, "We told you so", but they bit their tongues because it was not the right time yet. Parisa realized she would have to deal with everyone, eventually. Right now, she needed to think. She had to figure out a way to minimize the damage from Luca's terrible betrayal.

Chapter 33

Ameera

"*Yalla, Yalla….hala…*" The group of rambunctious young men crowded around her, calling out encouragement, lewd suggestions, and vulgar taunts aimed at her body.

Ameera had resigned herself to this. She had lost count of the number of parties she had danced at, the number of men that they had forced her to sleep with. This party bustled with young men of all ethnic backgrounds and all shades of color attended this party. They appeared well dressed, many of them driving expensive cars, which she had seen earlier when she arrived.

A couple of the boys, no older than twenty, clapped to the tune of music and her rhythmical hip shakes. Two or three more whispered to each other and giggled like shy schoolchildren, but continued ogling her anyway. She kept her eyes open. When she had started dancing a year ago, she had to close them, terrified of the audience.

She tried to remember when her eighteenth birthday had been. Seemed like a century ago that she had arrived in Dubai. It felt even longer since her parents' death, her life in the small house on a hill in Morocco. It felt like eons since she had seen her feisty sisters, her gullible grandma. Of course, she knew that it had only been a year ago. So much had happened during this time. She felt like she had lived a hundred different lives, many times over.

Wolf whistles, then someone pushed her and she was out of the room. It was her guard-dog, the disgusting driver. He handed her a cigarette and watched her light it. They were at the back of the large hillside villa, facing the dark silhouette of a mountain.

The villa was secluded, nestled in the crook of a rocky hillside, somewhere outside Dubai. The boy's parents used it during long weekends but tonight they were blissfully ignorant of what was transpiring in their gorgeous mountain residence. Tomorrow after the cleaning company had cleaned up all the disintegrated beer bottles, hundreds of stinking cigarette butts, leftover pizza and vomit, the chalet would once more shine and sparkle. Tonight's events must remain a secret, never to be divulged by those attending. Ameera would remain as always...a phantom. Her very existence denied, by no means mentioned, never acknowledged. The act itself denied vehemently because she was someone to be embarrassed off...disposed off. The young men and boys, who drank, smoked, uttered profanities, who treated her like the scum on their shoes, would go home to their comfortable rooms, their mothers' loving embraces, and their sisters' affectionate hugs.

The weather was cooler than in the city and Ameera shook uncontrollably in her skimpy, barely there outfit. Her teeth clattered in protest. This time she had a pink mini skirt and bustier on, something Kareema had dreamt up, complete with little tassels that jiggled when she danced. It was vulgar and slutty and Ameera hated it. There was no point in voicing her opinion though. All she would accomplish is some form of punishment from her 'jailers' as she had collectively started to call them. She did not want to humanize them by using their names, because they could not possibly be human.

"Kayf al hafley?" the man asked her, as usual. He served as her bodyguard as well, not that she had ever needed him. There was no point of contention with her customers. They were always satisfied and never argued over the payment. A number of the men became regular clients, coming for more.

Ameera usually preferred the parties, where little else was expected of her, other than to dance and look sexy.

"A bunch of spoilt rich kids," she blew smoke at him. "A surprise birthday party, for one of them." She turned to look at the hovering outline of the Hajjar Mountains in the moonlight. What a beautiful setting for a home, she thought. As they drove up early that evening, it had reminded her of the surroundings where she grew up, the crisp, dry mountain air, the rocky ground, hidden pools of chilled rainwater...

The cigarette burnt her fingers and she yelped and threw it to the ground. The driver laughed, cruelly, making no effort to ask if she was all right.

She gave him a smoldering look, and then said, "I want it now."

"Why now," he always played this game with her.

He loved to see her beg for it. She swallowed hard. "I want it ...now!" something in her eyes scared him this time, and without a word, he dug a small box out of the pocket of his *Jelbab*. She held out a trembling hand and he dropped two small white pills into it. Ameera immediately swallowed them, expertly with no liquid. A look of contentment came over her face and she opened her eyes to look at the 'driver'.

"Anta Kalb," she said matter of factly and turned to go back into the chalet. She had just called him a dog, and yet he just stood there and laughed. She could still hear his laughter when she walked into the small hallway at the back of the house. She really needed to use the bathroom before the next dance and she looked for it urgently. There it was. She went in and locked the door. A mirror hung above the sink and she checked her face in it. Some young, gaunt looking girl stared at her. Kareema had lined Ameera's sad eyes theatrically with heavy kohl and pink glitter; rouged her cheeks with hot pink blusher and her lips looked grotesque from the amount of lip-gloss.

I look like a clown. They have turned me into a hooker, and a clown, that's funny...a clown. She giggled at her hideous reflection. The pills had started doing their magic, she could tell. She felt much lighter, prettier, and more confident all of a sudden. A banging at the door startled her and she forgot why she was in the toilet. She needed to get out and dance...

She opened the door and three of them dragged her out rudely, one of them pulling her hair, the other one trying to grab her behind as she backed into the kitchen looking around for help.

It was the three shy boys. *What was wrong with them,* she wondered in her fogged up state of mind, *she was just about to go out and give them the best show of their lives...*

Ameera wobbled dangerously on her incredibly high, red platforms. She pressed her back against the wall. The boys had a plan it seemed because one of them starting ripping her bustier, and it came off easily, being just lightly tied at the back with a ribbon. She held the pieces to her chest, not letting go.

The oldest of the trio was filming her on his mobile and snickered now as the other two laughed and chattered excitedly to each other, ignoring her protests, her threats of calling the bodyguard. "Stop, please..." She begged. Her pleas did not mean anything. *She was a ghost, a nonentity. She was nobody's sister or daughter, nobody's friend, cousin. She meant nothing, valued nothing, like a boring used toy, which they used up and then threw on the already huge pile they owned.*

One of them grabbed her exposed breast and started gyrating crazily with his navel. "Wow, look at that," the other two laughed wildly, their excitement fever pitch now, and they were ready for anything, drunk on the illegally obtained beer and the view of her naked body.

Ameera started crying. Helplessness and loathing rose and fell in her like hot waves, finally engulfing her. Her slender, battered body twisted over like a crushed bloom in a futile attempt to hide...to vanish.

Suddenly there was a commotion...loud and angry voices. She could not see because she shut her eyes tightly, in order not to see their repulsive out of control faces, their driveling lips, and boyish malice. Her tormentors were arguing with another young boy. She forced herself to open her eyes. She had to see this. No one had ever come to her aide before.

An unbelievable scene played in front of her eyes. The three boys were in an intense argument with a young man, blonde and blue eyed, taller than the trio, and apparently very brave. He was also very foolish.

"You need to sod off man...is not your business," one of the sleaze balls kept repeating menacingly. He chewed a piece of gum rapidly, obviously quite disturbed by this development.

"Yeah man, we just having some fun, taking some pictures for later you know...we didn't hurt her," an attempt by the camera holder, looking like he wished to make a retreat and disappear. This was not what he had intended. Just a little fun at the expense of the girl, some nice nude pictures to show his other pals later, keep for whatever need might arise.

After all, what's all the fuss? She was just a hooker.

"Hey, dude who died and left you in charge?" Things were turning violent as the boy who had grabbed her now started jamming the blonde one with his finger repeatedly. He was shorter but stockier and had an air of entitlement about him. He kept pushing, shoving his finger into her savior's chest...

"I said leave the girl alone, she is here for the dancing only, you hear?" The blonde boy looked menacing enough, his fists clenched but down by his side, his jaw squared and lips tight in a stubborn line. Blue eyes darkened warningly under thick brows. It was obvious that he was not budging.

The music still played loudly in the back and male voices rang out. It sounded as if the rest of the party were unaware of the drama taking place under their very noses. Ameera still stood transfixed and somewhat unsteady from the pills she had taken. Nevertheless, she was also on the alert, incredibly curious about the outcome of her rescue...

"You British....just rubbish," the bossy one spat the words out. The three seemed unsure how to proceed without losing face. They were tired of the game and a tiny seed of anxiety had found its way through to their foggy minds, making them nervous of the possible repercussions.

They were not worried about the girl, just the nauseating possibility that if their peers found out of their sadistic tendencies, this might very well be the last party they would be invited to. The prospect of their friends ostracizing them from the group suddenly seemed more significant than getting it on with this girl.

"Akhh, who cares?" The camera holder waved his arm nonchalantly and turned to his partners. After a moment of subdued quarrelling among the trio, Ameera realized it was over. They walked away giving her dirty looks and still snickering, one of them indicating to his phone, as if to caution her that she was still on, he still had her.

"You take her, English boy....we are done anyway," their leader mocked. Swaggering conceitedly, unapologetic, they went back into the interior of the house, no doubt to join the party as if nothing had occurred. To them she was insignificant. A dancer, prostitute, and such girls deserved whatever they got.

She was easy prey.

Ameera's thighs were trembling, and she slowly started to slide to the floor. The shock of the attack had finally hit her full force. She collapsed into a drug and hunger induced heap onto the cold, expensive tile floor.

******

193

The sun woke her up. She was in a car, lying down on the back seat. Someone had covered her bare body with a denim jacket.

The car was moving fast. She stayed stock-still for a minute, trying to get her bearings and recall what happened last night. How did she end up here? She peeked at the driver.

A head full of curly blonde hair...slim shoulders. They belonged to the boy who saved her last night.

"Hey," she got up, still feeling dizzy, confused, but glad that it was he.

He half turned, keeping his eyes on the desert road. It looked like they were driving back to Dubai. In the distance, she saw a sign indicating the next turn into downtown.

"Hi, are you better?" he grinned shyly, "I got kind of worried, thought you might never wake up." Ameera had learned enough English to understand him. His accent was funny, alien to her ears. "Listen I'm going to drop you at the police station," he glanced at her again to check her reaction. She balked and withdrew into the seat. *He was taking her to the police*. She glanced around the deserted road in alarm. It was dawn and only an occasional semi truck thundered by, in disregard of the speed limit.

"No, no, don't be afraid." He looked more afraid than she was, she realized, annoyed at him all of a sudden. He continued to persuade her, talking fast, apparently still on an adrenalin rush from his adventurous night. "Listen, er, what is your name?"

She answered after a while, not sure what to do, "Ameera."

"Okay, Ameera...this is the plan. I will take you to the Deira station, tell them about the people keeping you to work for them ...okay." His blonde head bobbed up and down as he drove. Her head shot up, curious as to how he knew this.

"The boys were all talking, everyone knows. They are not naïve..." He smiled at her then, showing his perfect smile, some expensive Jumeirah dentists' work. She stared at his face visible in the rearview mirror. She could not believe her ears. *She could go and it would be all right?*

"What if they find out? What if they punish my family?" she spoke slowly, the English language still a minefield of danger for her. Her savior seemed to understand her perfectly and replied quickly.

"You will be fine I'm sure, the police will take care of that." She caught sight of his brow, creased in worry. Ameera pulled the jacket tighter around herself. It was cold and the heater was not on. She felt queasy, from sitting in the back in the speeding car and mostly from trepidation. She had no idea what might happen if she went to the police. *Would they believe her? On the other hand, would they put her in another kind of jail?* All of past year, she had been dreaming of escaping, and now that it was happening she felt paralyzed, not as ecstatic as she thought she would be. *How could she show her face in front of grandma, sisters, and her relatives?* After everything, she has been through, that simple innocent life seemed so far away. That innocent, pious Ameera light years different from the one, she had become.

She looked at herself. Torn, barely there trashy clothes, clung on her bruised, emaciated body. Her thighs and arms still glittered from the silly lotion she had to slather on every time she went out, and she rubbed at it, trying to get it off. Her bare feet were filthy and she could not find her shoes. She sneaked a peek into the rearview mirror quickly, and gasped. A tangle of disheveled hair stuck out on top of her head like some crazy bird's nest. Gone was the careful hairdo Kareema had spent half an hour arranging. Her makeup looked even scarier at the moment, after she had soaked it with tears and rubbed it with her hands, then slept in it.

"You will be fine, here," he saw her reflection and guessed her dilemma. He handed her some wet tissues and a bottle of water, then another smile over his shoulder. *Who was this person?* He seemed like some character out of a movie, heroic and incredibly mature for his age.

"This is my mother's car, she keeps tissues and water at hand all the time," he paused, rummaging for something on the seat next to him. She stole another peek over the passenger seat.

It was a woman's bag. Similar to those gym bags, that she had seen rich women carry with them to their expensive gyms. Like a magician, the boy produced a Nike t-shirt and leggings yoga outfit and some plastic flip-flops, a hairbrush, and then, triumphantly a biscuit. She looked at it.

It was a raisin and oatmeal power bar. She ate it in three bites, while he drove on silently, then she took off the filthy pink skirt and shredded bra, and thankfully put on his mothers' clothes. They were big; she must be a tall woman, Ameera thought, enjoying the feel of the soft cotton, the smell of another woman, a mother's scent on the t-shirt. Suddenly she felt a warm, contented feeling suffuse her…an enormous feeling of gratitude towards the boy.

She settled on the back seat hugging her knees and subtly observed her young hero while he concentrated on the road. They could see the Dubai skyline, the towering skyscrapers, and the pyramid like shaped tip of the

Raffles Hotel. He gripped the wheel with strong-bronzed arms. *He must play some sports* she mused; *he was out in the sun a lot. He was so young, not much older than I am, and rich.* Ameera looked closer at his profile. Fine stubble showed on his face, fair in color like the curls on his head framing his handsome features. For just an instant, she caught the sparkle of a stud earring in his ear.

"Can I ask your name"? She looked at him shyly.

He shot a look over his shoulder and said in his strange, English accent she loved. "My name is Jake...Jake Andrews," before turning right onto the exit ramp to Deira and the groggily waking city.

Chapter 34

David

"Come in David, sit down," Jassim pointed at the leather chair facing his massive glass topped desk. It was almost six in the evening, and David had been in complete misery since seven that morning, long hours that he had spent in morbid anticipation of this very moment.

The previous night was a sleepless one; its long lonely hours spent in self-loathing, recrimination, and finally fear. Jane had slept through his torture. At one point, he almost woke her up, in order to confess everything. When he turned over to wake her up, he had seen her peaceful beautiful face, the long lashes fluttering slightly in her sleep, the golden curls strewn on her silk pillow, and he could not do it.

She will be better off remaining in the dark about the full extent of it, he reasoned. I need her to be strong for Jake. Jane did not need to know... she could not do anything to help him anyway.

The course of their lives had been irretrievably set in that one moment when he had signed his name on that first fraudulent document. That deceptively simple action of scribbling the letters that made up his name had caused this avalanche of events, the coming ones much more grave than any they had experienced in their years together. He would not make excuses. He should have known better, he should have…It was too late for regrets. There was only time for action, probably only a sliver of hope for clemency. He faced his judge, with a calm face, tremulous spirit, and clammy palms.

He wore his best work suit, an Armani actually, and a silk blue tie. He had combed his salt and pepper hair smoothly over his forehead and he presented the aura of an important and successful man, a man who after all can be fallible, weak, and sometimes dreadfully stupid.

Jassim settled comfortably into the custom-built leather armchair, adjusted his white *Gotra* with misleading calm, and then focused his shining black eyes on David. Fire streamed out of their depths, and David could not bear to look away.

This must be what it feels for a rabbit when faced by a stalking wolf, or an antelope cornered by a ravenous and resolute tiger. Suddenly very calm, secure in the knowledge that Jane and Jake will be fine after a while. Undoubtedly, they will suffer and mourn but life will go on, and soon it will be just a tragic episode in their past.

Jassim will not have his revenge, he decided at that moment, because a thought so brilliant had just materialized in David's head that he knew it must have been simmering there all along. This thought must have been in the back of his feverish mind throughout those long terrified nights, the endless late hours at the office spent in frantic and obviously futile covering up of incriminating evidence. It must have burrowed its way in the weeks of ugly, swarming thoughts and ludicrous schemes for a way out.

There was only one way out of this mess.

"David, I think you know why I have called you here," Jassim had all right to be angry. No, he was much more than that, he was revolted, and David could see it on his face. His winged brows furrowed threateningly, and his eyes were dark pools of contempt, "you are aware that a team of auditors has been looking into our contract disputes with four other companies."

Yes, he was aware. He knew all about the contracts, the bribes, and the checks. He knew all that because he had been the one who signed the papers, deposited the checks, all twenty five million dirhams, in his alternate account in the Cayman Islands.

David could not help but notice how daunting Jassim was. How dignified and commanding he looked, like a king on a throne, in his corner office, flanked by floor to ceiling windows, with views of the Dubai Creek and beyond.

Jassim Al Gaafari was like a lion leading his pack. This company, just like this amazing office tower, with views to the new Dubai and the older Bur Dubai areas, faced the new world order, growth and progress. However its owner was always glancing over his shoulder at the old areas of the city, feeling the pull of the forefathers, staying devoted to the its past.

******

Jassim gave David a quizzical look, "…I think it is for the best interest of all that we deal with this matter quietly and if possible privately."

"David?" He asked sternly, in no mood for games, but concerned at the Englishman's lack of response, the disassociated look in his sad eyes and the ashen pallor on his usually ruddy face. He had expected a more penitent reaction from the man. After all, he was guilty of a serious crime. Jassim noticed how David's slick hair suddenly looked less shiny and the expensive designer suit hung limply on his slouched shoulders. He looked like a defeated man. Oddly, he also appeared composed, sincerely contrite as he faced Jassim.

Nevertheless, he continued, still keeping a stern eye on the apparently terrified accountant. Jassim hoped the David would not get ill right here. He disliked having to deal with people harshly, but the man had stolen millions from him! Controlling this company took more effort than any of his relatives could imagine. The constant stress and pressure to compete rendered him depleted at times, lately, more so than in previous years.

He could feel a deep sorrow in his very soul, seeping in, burrowing its way into his life deeper each day. An unpleasant, insistent feeling of jealousy followed him at all times.

Jassim knew the reason for his condition. Her name was Liliana. Thinking of her shot electric like vibrations up and down his body. He felt as if a highly powerful current had cruised through him.

When she had ended their relationship Jassim remained unconvinced, confident of his power to get her to come back to him. He was positive she would see the error of her ways, realize that she could not stay away from him. Liliana had remained firm though, despite his gallant attempts to win her back, the expensive gifts, and countless bouquets of flowers, unusual balloon arrangements, and persistent phone calls. To his disbelief none of his tactics worked. "Why are you doing this?" he had asked repeatedly.

She had looked at him sadly, "Because I can't do this anymore, it's not fair."

He laughed, confused. "Not fair to whom?"

"To all of us Jassim," Liliana said surprising him with her uncustomary, unyielding stance. There was no future with him. She might be a nightclub dancer, a poor working girl from Romania, might have made some bad choices when men when were concerned, but she was not a home wrecker. Moreover, she did not like him telling her what to do.

"It's not fair to you, to me, to your wife or your children," she lit a cigarette. Her hands were shaking.

Fine, so she wanted it all, he felt his mood shift. Fine, he would marry her, make her the second Mrs. Gaafari, and do whatever it takes, whatever she wanted. Her response to his proposition left him seething.

"I will never marry you Jassim."

He gasped, *how dare she?* Liliana held his face between her hands, looked into his eyes. She repeated, "I can never marry you Jassim, it can never be right for us." Then the final blow to his ego, a softly spoken, "You have to let me go."

At first, he had been desperate, and then, months later, when it was obvious she was serious and unrelenting, he became infuriated. Day after day, he paced back and forth in his office, debating his situation. He was tired of groveling and begging. It was not having an effect on Liliana anyway. He had tried all civilized means of persuasion. Another woman would have been ecstatic by all the attention.

About a month ago, he had a brilliant idea. He approached Iliya, a nightclub manager and a man known in certain influential circles for absolute reliability in matters of confidentiality. Jassim knew just the right people in the right places who could get him in touch. It was easy. Everyone knew everyone in Dubai. Like in the movie 'Six Degrees of Separation' where one needed only six people in order to connect to anyone else on the planet.

Jassim needed only two. Two phone calls and he had the information, the number and the appointment set up. After a half an hour clandestine meeting in the clubs' underground parking garage, a business deal came into being.

"What do you want me to do?" the reptilian looking man had asked him. Liliana worked for him. She was under a fixed contract, her residency in the country depended on her work in the club. Liliana would know to pay heed when Iliya spoke to her. She would be much more careful with her boss.

Jassim thought deeply for a moment, "Find out if she is meeting someone else, what she is up to." He gazed out of the tinted, darkened window of his Maybach. The garage was dark. Only a weak overhead neon light flickered. It cast a morbid shadow over Iliya's face, the garage, and the interior of the car. Jassim felt an unexpected sense of dread. *Perhaps this was not such a good idea. Has he truly sunk to this level of wretchedness, allowing a silly girl to lead him to such a pathetic move?* It unnerved him, this hesitation, so unlike his normal decisiveness.

Then just as quickly, the moment had passed and he turned to Iliya again. "I need you to make her come back, do something, anything, so she comes back." She left him no other alternative. He had to use cunning, underhanded means if needed. It was not the first time he had to resort to unscrupulous behavior to get his way. It was the first time however, that he was doing it for a woman. Iliya looked pleased, "Fine, no problem, I will take care of it." He did not mention payment for his services. Jassim could pay him back in other ways. It had not been difficult at all, Jassim thought while driving back home to his mansion in Jumeirah. Iliya was a sleaze ball, and he had hated shaking his hand, but he was the only person guaranteed to keep these kinds of arrangements entirely secret. It would be a complete scandal, not to mention illegal, if anyone ever found out that Jassim Al Gaafari had hired goons to follow and spy on his ex mistress... *However, wasn't there a famous saying that "All was fair in love and war?"* Jassim reasoned.

******

David blinked a few times. The lamp on Jassim's desk was too bright. He shook his head as if to clear it of something, and rose to stand up, cutting Jassim off. "Jassim," he begun, he spoke slowly. He was tired.

"I have stolen your money," he said matter of factly. "Millions of dirhams in fake contract deals, forged checks and signatures. I have infringed on every code of honorable conduct and have damaged this company's name forever." He paused to take a breath. He felt so exhausted. All he wanted to do is close his eyes and rest.

Jassim stared at him in disbelief. Slowly his face clouded with anger.

"Words cannot express how sorry I'm for what I did. I do not expect mercy or forgiveness from you....only that you do not punish Jane and

Jake for my crime. They do not know anything of what I did." His voice faltered for a second, catching in his throat. He cleared it and continued, "I did this terrible thing, mistakenly, stupidly, and believing that one day Jane and I can go off somewhere where no one will know us...and live happily ever after." He smiled sadly. Jassim continued to sit in his chair, motionless.

"I didn't know how I will explain the money to her; I did not care at the time. I just wanted it. I wanted to be my own man, not somebody's..." He took a breath, "....minion. I needed to enjoy life while I was still strong and healthy enough."

David started to turn as if ready to walk out of the office, but then because he had to say this, he turned around and looked fearlessly into the dark whirlpool of Jassim's' eyes.

"I wanted to be like you."

Chapter 35

Cora

The handsome young *Imam* knelt on the prayer rug and led his faithful worshippers in the final words of the *Esha* prayer.

*Al Salam Alaikum...*he spoke softly, reverently, nodding first to his right side then the left.

Zohour Khan and the congregation followed the *Imam's* lead and a chorus of voices repeated the famous greeting. Zohour lingered on his prayer mat even as others rose and rushed out of the mosque in pursuit of other, worldlier interests. Their required prayer quota for the day was over and they saw no reason to stay longer.

Zohour sat on the carpeted floor quietly, enjoying the peace and security he felt whenever in a mosque. He watched as other men passed by. A father with his two young sons, all three dressed in flowing white *Kandooras* walked by and he smiled pleasantly at Zohour. A pleasant whiff of *Oud* reached his nostrils.

A very old Afghani shopkeeper was the only one still praying…dutifully offering the extra two voluntary verses of prayer. His beard was snow white and rested on his chest. He looked like Zohour's father back in Pakistan.

A dignified looking Sudanese police officer in a freshly washed and pressed uniform walked by, deep in thought. Zohour gave *Salaams* to all his Muslim brothers respectfully, kindly nodding and smiling at everyone. It was finally time for him to leave as well.

He still had a good few hours until his shift ended and then he could catch the first deluge of moviegoers, as they charged for the line of taxis waiting patiently at various cinema venues.

He looked for his slippers among the sea of shoes, sneakers and plastic flip-flops discarded hastily at the entrance to the prayer hall. There were a few expensive leather slippers arrogantly jostling for place among that mass. Zohour spotted his worn out black pair and slipped them on, looking around the quickly emptying parking lot. It was a small and modest mosque in the energetic hub of the city.

Cool air welcomed him when he stepped outside and Zohour tightened the belt of his beige raincoat. Underneath he was wearing the light cotton *shalwar* pants and a traditional Pakistani shirt, *kames.*

He sighed when he remembered how far he had parked his taxi. After he had finally dropped a bickering American couple close to a traditional Indian restaurant, he had then decided to perform his evening prayers at the local mosque. He was familiar with most of the city, especially Bur Dubai, being one of the oldest in Dubai.

Frustrated with the lack of available parking places in proximity to the mosque he had parked a good three blocks away, in a darkened stretch of road. As he walked, he calculated his oldest sons impending university fees. His son Abdulla was attending a good university and one day *Inshallah*, God willing, he will become a great accountant, much better educated than his taxi driver father ever was.

A few people passed him on the way. It was getting colder in the evening and many did not venture out as much as they used to when the weather was balmy. They preferred to spend time in the malls, cinemas, or restaurants that thrive in profusion all over the city.

He could see his taxi in the light of the overhead street light, and relieved at its proximity started to cross a deserted patch of land that was ready for construction, but abandoned just now. He saw the twinkling inviting lights of the 'Filipino Karaoke Club' shining on the other side of the street oblivious as to what kind of place that could possibly be. He shook his head in bewilderment at some people's frivolity.

Suddenly he heard a sound, a hum. He stopped, stunned. He could not believe his ears. Turning around in a circle, he looked for where it was coming from, the sound of a baby crying, very low, and frail. Still he was sure he had heard it.

Very close to where he stood, were two large steel 'Dubai Municipality' standard issue trash bins. He strained to hear but there was no doubt at all, the sound of a baby crying was coming from one of those containers...

Hundreds of thoughts were rushing through his mind as he sprung into action with agility, surprising for a man his age. He approached the bins, listening again. There it was...that whimpering again. He clambered on some discarded boxes left by the bin and looked inside. It was dark and smelly and he could not see anything. Then again, the baby whimpered, this time louder as if pointing Zohour to its location. It was in the other bin!

He was fast and determined now. The street was still deserted and for a moment, Zohour worried what a passerby would think if they spotted a bearded elderly Asian man in a raincoat riffling through the garbage. Then he relaxed. Nothing probably, it was a common sight these days throughout the city; hard on their luck men searching through other peoples trash, passersby averting their embarrassed eyes. Zohour was hanging suspended half in the steel bin and half out.

The baby was quiet as he tried to adjust his eyes to the shadows inside. Thankfully the bin was not very full, but smelled horribly nevertheless.

A car was approaching and before it passed him, it lit up enough of the interior so he could see. He picked up the trash bags one by one and wiggled them. He was at a loss as to how to find the baby unless it helped him out by making a sound again. All the trash looked the same...big black plastic bags mostly...but then he saw a flash of something pink. He stretched out and pulled the pink thing closer. It was a piece of cloth stuck between the lids of a small cardboard box. A blue water bottle on the front proclaimed its freshness. He could see well now, an approaching car illuminating the horror of what he was doing.

Only the ribbed, soft edge of the material was showing but it was enough reason for him to haul it out. The box was light. Zohour laid it on the ground, sweating profusely despite the cold.

He was feverish with his discovery. He did not think, just ripped the cover revealing a roll of pink towel inside. His eyes bulged, his pulse raced, terror gripped him, as he had no choice but to unravel this horrifying package. He unwrapped it quickly...still no sound, no movement. In a second, it was in front of him. He could take his eyes away, feeling the ground sway, and his insides lurching up. He tasted the remnants of his dinner in his mouth.

Bismillah Rahmanu Rahim...he whispered in total shock, in absolute denial, yet sure, that it was indeed a very tiny baby that lay in front of him on the bloodied pink towels.

Bile caught in his throat; he wanted to cough but instead let out a moan. A peculiar void enveloped him, the buildings threatening to close in on his hunched, thin, body. He was oblivious of the approaching car, the door opening, the same serious Sudanese police officer from the mosque questioning him. Zohour remained crouched on the ground with his discovery, unable to speak or stand up.

The police officer was on the radio now, making calls, shouting for the ambulance, all hell was breaking loose, but Zohour knew it was too late. They were all too late.

******

Cora was shivering from the cold that had infused her body since the birth. Back in the cursed flat again, alone and bleeding she thought of Luca. Even at this moment, she still loved him. She remembered his kindness, how he cared about her family back in the Philippines, giving her extra money to send for them.

She took a sip of water from the plastic bottle by her bedside and pulled the covers tighter around her fever-wracked body. She did not dare think of the baby. It was dead. *What would she do with a baby? How could she go back to her husband with another man's child in her arms?*

Tepid liquid seeped between her legs, soaking the heavy pad she had shoved between her thighs. She could feel her blood soaking through her clothes and then it is flowing onto the bed, flooding the mattress too, but she had no energy or willpower to do anything about it. She lay in this hot and bloody puddle of shame and sorrow and hoped that she would die.

******

Girlie slammed the door of her boyfriend's car with force and stomped up the steps of her apartment building in a huff. How dare he? How dare he talk to her as if she was some cheap bimbo...like those trashy girls he ogles every time they pass them downtown, those streetwalkers, shamelessly, suggestively pouting their lips and deliberately swinging their hips, openly trying to attract the scores of men passing by in their flashy cars?

Girlie was petite. Barely four and half feet tall, she staggered on impossibly high orange sandals into the building and fumed in the elevator all the way up to her flat. She unlocked the door and kicked it shut with a bang. Then she remembered her cousin Cora was supposed to be here too, and felt a pang of guilt at making a ruckus. She did not want Cora to know she was having problems with her man.

"Hey Cora!" she looked into the little kitchen and living room, found them empty. Still in her heels, she threw her Prada handbag on the armchair and proceeded to get a bottle of water from the kitchen. As she took big gulps from the bottle, still inwardly cursing men…she saw what looked like something spilled by the trash can. Something about that stain bothered her. She drew closer and bent to look at it. *Jesus!* It was blood… dark brown and dry now, but unmistakably blood.

She rushed to her bedroom and finding it empty went into the small study that served as a guest room and where Cora slept on a folding metal bed. The curtains were drawn, the room dim and clammy. A strange smell assaulted her nostrils as soon as she stepped in. There was no circulation in the room. The windows were closed and the aircon off.

"Cora?" Girlies's own voice sounded alien to her, the petrified question sticking in her throat as she spoke. She approached the bed and with each step, the smell got stronger, metallic, and recognizable. Girlie wanted to call someone, but knew that she had to see for herself first. A form lay under the covers on the bed. In the dim evening light she saw it move, breathing, barely.

"Cora, are you all right?" she bent over the bed and moved the blankets to see the face.

A ghost like Cora lay in the bed. Curled up like a baby, her face white as powder, her lips bluish, her expression set in a painful frown. She looked dead. Girlie pulled the blanket further down and she saw it then.

The pool of drying blood that her cousin lay in…so much of it, Girlie could not understand how a small person like Cora could have so much blood in her petite body. She felt a strong urge to vomit, and turned opened the window…a cold draft rushed in and moved the drapes gently. She felt better immediately. She had to call the ambulance, someone…

Jesus, what happened to her? She should have never let Cora stay here, Girlie thought as she dialed the number for the ambulance. She was trembling, from fear, realizing just how much trouble this could mean for her. There was no way out of this disaster, except right through it.

"Yes, please send an ambulance immediately...my friend," her voice faltered as she bit her lip. "She is bleeding...yes...the address...can you hurry up. I think she is dying."

Chapter 36

Liliana

*L*iliana unlocked the door to her apartment, went in, and kicked it shut behind her. She flicked on the light and slipped her ten-cm stiletto sandals off. Her feet ached after all those hours spent on the catwalk and later at the after-party. She did not drink much, just a glass of champagne because she never drank when working, yet she felt slightly lightheaded.

Oh yes, I need food! She had not eaten all day.

There were two reasons for that...one that she was too nervous to eat while working on a modeling job and two, going hungry for a few days helped tone her tummy and keep her nimble on her feet.

"Vikki, hallo I'm home..." *Strange,* she wondered, *I thought Vikki would be home by now...oh of course, she was spending the weekend with Adam and his daughters.* She recalled Vikki talking about Adam taking his daughters on a special weekend at the Atlantis Hotel resort. This must be the week it was happening.

She was happy for Vikki. Liliana opened the fridge and checked inside. Wrinkling her nose at the contents, it was empty. She had not been grocery shopping for more than a week, and Vikki ate with Adam at his condominium in the Marina daily so she never bought anything either.

It seemed that Vikki was hardly ever at home lately. Iliya had kept them all busy, rehearsing for a new show that the club would unveil during Valentine's Day celebrations. It was going to be a good act really. She lit a cigarette, and grabbed a packet of crackers from the cupboard. Finding some canned green olives and hummus paste, delighted at her discovered bounty, she sat at the little kitchen table and proceeded to assemble her modest dinner.

The CD player was on the table and, she turned the radio on, her favorite DJ was live on air…playing some great R&B classics.

The little apartment filled with the thud of the familiar tune and lifted her spirits immediately. Liliana did her best wiggle and shake…*I never could resist music* she thought to herself, and look *what that has gotten me!*

This is not so bad, she thought as she sang along with a fantastic tune by 'Akon'.

"Shut up Liliana, you can't sing," she told herself with a giggle. She was glad she did the show in spite of her reservations after finding out it was Jewel Al Gaafari's boutique collection. When she had agreed to the job, her agent had only told her it was modeling for the famous Ginni Karisma.

"Vikki guess whose clothes I'm going to be modeling?" she had asked her friend. Vikki was painting her toenails purple, leaning over her tiny body on the couch.

"You know that Indian designer who is all over the papers, she was even at the Gypsy once, remember her?" Liliana winked.

"Oooh yes, I remember her, she is that wild one…love her style though," Vikki raised her legs up in the air, admiring her handiwork. "Too bad we can't afford to wear any of her designs."

Liliana laughed. "Who knows, maybe one day baby, one day soon."

It was impossible to pull out of the show once she had found out she would be in the same room with Jewel, maybe even have to talk to her, face her. Vikki had laughed at her concerns.

"Don't be a silly goose, she doesn't know who you are," she rolled her eyes. "It will be over in a few hours and no one will be the wiser." Vikki was right of course. Liliana could not pull out of the show now, at the last moment, the agent would have been furious and blacklisted her.

Thankfully, in the bustle of the boutique's opening, the craziness of it all, she had been able to avoid Jewel. They only met briefly as Liliana was walking onto the ramp. Jewel had looked at her with those amazing green eyes, and nodded. Liliana was sure that the woman could not have known of her affair with Jassim. She had nodded back and smiled. One day maybe Liliana could forgive herself for what she had done. The microwave beeped… the frozen pita bread was hot now, ready to eat. Her dinner was complete; but she took a long draw from her cigarette and turned to look out of the window. The view never ceased to amaze her. Particularly at night, the city came ablaze with millions of megawatts of electric power. Lights that shimmered…enticed and tempted…it looked as if Dubai was celebrating Christmas every night of the year.

She went out, leaned on the cement balcony, searching the street and promenade below with her eyes. There was an alluring world at her feet tonight and she determined that from tomorrow she would grab that world with both hands. She really was ready to move on from Jassim. It was the right thing to do…the decent thing. Her mobile rang…its high-pitched ringtone rudely bringing her back to reality.

"Hey, girl…it's me." Vikki sounded happy.

"Hey, Vic, where are you?" Liliana was glad to hear her friends' voice. She sat at the table nibbling on the zesty tasting green olives while she caught up with Vikki.

A vase brimming with fresh red roses stared at her from across the room. How did they get here? She walked over to the counter where their cleaner must have placed the bouquet earlier today. Liliana had failed to notice it when she came in.

"So how is it going? How are the girls? What are you guys doing at Atlantis…?" She continued to talk as she searched for a card amongst the blood colored blooms.

"He asked me to marry him Lila," Vikki said excitedly, stopping Liliana midsentence. It took Liliana a moment to take in what her friend was saying, and then she shrieked into the phone.

"Oh my God…Oh my God Vikki…this is so fantastic…my dear friend I'm so happy for you," they were both laughing and crying, and talking at the same time. Liliana sat back down, taken aback by this news.

"How and when?" she was rooted to her spot on the chair, forgetting the roses, her hunger, everything.

"Well, he proposed today while we were watching the girls in the pool…he just looked at me and said, I really want to marry you …I love you Vikki," Vikki was crying softly into her phone making funny little gulping sounds.

Liliana's heart flooded with tenderness for her friend, her eyes filling with tears of joy. "Oh you silly girl...why are you crying?" she spoke soothingly. "Vikki he loves you, just be happy...you deserve it girl."

Vikki giggled...unable to stop crying at the same time. She snorted. Both of them broke out in laughter. "Just make sure Adam never hears that snort before he walks down the aisle," Liliana teased. They paused, silent for a minute, each contemplating the enormity of what was happening. She gazed at her cold dinner with indifference.

Vikki was moving on. Liliana was overjoyed for her friend...but saddened by the news too. She was going to be all alone now. She will miss her endearing Aussie friend, her optimism, spunky attitude and the soul-to-soul chats. She knew their separation will not be immediate, but over time they will drift apart each pulled by her heart in a different direction. Things would never be the same again.

The breakfast together in their little kitchen, the all night partying and their dancing. She will miss everything about Vikki.

"Listen Lila...I have got to go...Adam is waiting for me...I will see you in the morning, maybe we can have lunch or something if your schedule is free and we can talk, okay?"

"Yes of course sweetie, just call me anytime...I'm home tomorrow not working at all."

"All right then, I will see you tomorrow, good night Lila..."

"Good night to you Vikki, Er... Mrs. Adam," they both shrieked like two twelve year olds at that.

Vikki paused for a second unwilling to hung up yet. "And Lila," she paused, swallowing hard. "I want you to know how much I love you...you have been my sister, my best friend. Thank you." Vikki's voice choked up again and Liliana decided it was time to let her go.

She said firmly, "I love you too you silly, you are my sister too, *Yalla*, come on, go to Adam go."

After her conversation with Vikki, Lila sat quietly at the table for a long time, staring at the roses. The card was from Jassim. A lone tear rolled down her cheek as she read it. In his firm handwriting he had written, "*Lila, I love you, Te iubesc. Just come back to me.*" That was all. He had finally learned how to say them in Romanian. She cried. This was the first time he had done it.

She wanted to believe him so badly, she wanted a happy ending...the

Arab prince and the castle and ever after. However, it was not to be. She did not feel hungry anymore.

Slowly, she went outside again and lit another cigarette…she craved the fresh, zesty smelling air tonight. It was a cool night and she shivered slightly, wrapping her slim arms around herself. She was still wearing the slinky black cocktail dress and now, it failed to offer her comfort against the wind. Up on this floor, it was always windy but tonight even more so. Winter has arrived. *Oh, I cannot wait for the rain to come…*

A wave of hope and enthusiasm washed over her. She inhaled the fresh ocean air deeply…it smelled of fish. A sea of stars shimmered off the mirror like Gulf waters…beckoning.

The doorbell rang, just as she was finishing the cigarette, unnerving her. Taking one last look at the luminous sea below she closed the doors and hurried to answer the doorbell.

*Seriously, what a night…*she grumbled to herself as she went to peek through the spy hole at the late visitor.

It was Lazar. What did he want at this hour?

Iliya must have sent him because of something critical, otherwise; he would have just called as he usually did when he needed her. Suddenly she was terrified that something had happened to one of the other girls and Lazar was coming to tell her personally. Lazar never made house calls. She fumbled with the key to the door. Her pulse hammered away in her neck. The words spurted out of her before she even let him in…

"What is it Lazar? What happened? Is everything OK?"

She stopped talking. A sudden sense of peril inundated her.

Something was not right. Lazar walked in slowly, closing the door behind him, and then turning to look at her with his colorless eyes. He did not speak yet just looked at her as if deciding about something. He was wearing his standard black leather jacket and jeans.

Lazar was definitely not famous for his sense of fashion or good hygiene. Decades of smoking had yellowed his teeth, and rendered his breath foul smelling. His razor straight flaxen hair, once thick, was thin and matted to his head. He boasted that he took no interest whatsoever in his external appearance, holding all those who did so, in contempt. Lazar saw himself as the last and true, Siberian male.

Liliana moved away from him, towards the kitchen, slowly.

Her senses kicked into overdrive. She was acutely aware of his every move from the corner of her eye. In fact, she could feel that prickly feeling at the back of her neck, could sense threat in the very atmosphere of the room.

She had no idea why he was here but she instinctively felt menace in his very presence. Her thoughts raced feverishly, trying to recall the few times she had talked to him. *Had she somehow rebuked him, offended him?*

Typically, the girls had stayed away from him at the club. Thankfully, they had not been in much contact with Iliya's henchman, as he kept to his own shadowy corners, smoking his foul cigarettes…lurking, always observing. His job was to interfere when needed, otherwise to stay behind the scenes. Iliya liked to project a clean, refined atmosphere to his patrons, and for this reason, the pale Siberian remained for the most part tucked away well out of sight.

This arrangement seemed to suit Lazar just fine. He always claimed he preferred that others stay out of his way and he out of theirs.

Isuse Christoase, she was alone with him at this time of the night. Why doesn't he say something? She made her way towards the glass cabinet. "Do you want something to drink Lazar? She asked him politely, reaching for the glass, buying time…

Lazar did not respond to her so obviously insincere comment. He was far too cunning for her. Sure, she feared him, but it did not occur to her that he might physically harm her. After all, he worked for Iliya and was supposed to look out for his interests. He was like a guard dog. They too, supposedly, posed no threat to their owners.

She was getting angry at his attitude. Whatever it was he needed to leave and let her know in the morning. Liliana took a deep breath and turned around to tell him so, but at that moment, Lazar lunged for her, grabbing her by the waist and clamping his other hand over her mouth quickly. She let out a muffled scream, too shocked to react at first but then her survival instinct kicked in. His hand was suffocating her, and it smelled foul, like something evil. She bit it anyway. "Oh," was his only reaction. He continued to grapple with her trying to pin her arms behind her to render her immobile. She brought up her knee swiftly, kicking the dumbfounded man in his groin with all her strength. Lazar doubled over, clutching himself and swearing, his pale face turning angry red, threatening to burst.

Liliana kicked him again in his stomach as he knelt, doubled over on her living room floor. She tried to get over him and to the front door, out of the flat, but he grabbed her hand as she passed him. His face was still red but his breathing slowed down. Through clenched teeth, he managed to swear at her threateningly, "You bloody Romanian *karova*. Listen… one minute."

He is calling her a cow, a bloody cow. Liliana gasped in fury, in pain. She could not believe this was happening.

Her wrist burnt from his vice like grip. He was incredibly strong and very angry. Liliana was not planning to wait for him again; he had already surprised her once. She twisted and kicked but he was faster this time and strong as an ox. He got up swiftly, grunting slightly as he did from the pain she had inflicted on him.

Then in one fast motion, he pushed her forcefully into the armchair. He yelled Russian profanities in rapid succession…

"What do you want Lazar? What!" terrified and trembling she screamed at him. This did not make sense. *Was he going to rape her?* His mobile phone rang. It startled them both, and they froze. They glared at each other angrily like two boxers in the ring, weighing their opponent.

Not taking his eyes off her face, he answered calmly, "Alo?"

Liliana looked around as her assailant continued to listen to the mysterious caller on the other end. On some level of consciousness, Liliana was aware that he was dangerous but she could not have anticipated this. Lazar blocked the exit of the flat, there was no way out.

Suddenly, she let out a blood-curling scream. Springing out of the chair, she dashed across the living room like a mad woman into the kitchen. She flung the balcony door open. She was going to go on the balcony and scream for help. Her palms slipped on the handle. They were damp.

He was behind her within seconds. In his clumsiness, he knocked into the counter sending the vase with the roses crashing to the floor. The glass exploded like a bomb into a million glowing pieces. Delicate crimson petals scattered all over the kitchen floor. It was inevitable that he would reach her right away. The balcony was a dead end. Confused and terrified, Liliana had trapped herself. There was nowhere else to go.

Lazar was as mad as hell. His breathing came in short, angry bursts. The unfathomable colorless eyes were indifferent as he looked at her tear stained face. Her exquisitely beautiful face, one that had stopped men in their tracks in the streets of Dubai had no effect on him.

Liliana tried to speak, to ask him why in the name of God was he doing this, but no words came out of her mouth. She half crouched on the floor of the balcony as Lazar towered over her. A surreal feeling of peace flooded her body *Doamne fereste…Oh my God, he is going to kill me*, went through her head, with certainty.

Before she had time to react, before she could ask for an explanation, or plead for her life, Liliana watched in numb horror as he leaned over her and grabbed a handful of her black hair. Then he yanked it. He swung it viciously once...then again...into the concrete wall. Liliana let out a soft, childish cry.

******

A strange sound reached her killer's ears. It sounded like someone had cracked his or her knuckles. He looked down at the silent girl. She was not moving. She had stopped struggling. A bundle of her hair was still in his hand and he stared at it as if seeing it for the first time, as if he had just woken from a depraved trance. *What beautiful gypsy hair,* he thought for a moment. There was something sticky on the hair. He looked at his hands.

It was blood. He could see it clearly in the radiance of the moon. The moon was so close he felt he could touch it if he only stretched his arm. He thought it looked forbiddingly down on the scene...angry with him. As if to confirm that, a rumble awoke in the sky, low at first ...then stronger, more volatile...and then, a majestic sword of lightening shot through the sky, then another, and another. The heavens were raging too and they roared their displeasure with at him in their full magnificent glory. The sky opened up sending the much-awaited winter rain to replenish the parched ground, the eager souls. Lazar let go of Liliana's wet hair, turned and looked out over the balcony.

His icy eyes took in the pleased twinkling lights over Dubai, the glistening sea ahead and then finally down, by his feet on the cold floor, the beautiful and lifeless body of Liliana the Romanian dancer.

Chapter 37

Lazar

Lazar looked around carefully before getting into his white Toyota and driving off quickly.

How did this night go so wrong? What is he going to tell Iliya? Moreover, his worst fear, how are they going to tell Jassim that his great love is dead?

He lit cigarette after cigarette on the way to the club. The streets were calm now…it was almost dawn…almost time for the *muezzins* call for prayer. The sudden downpour had abated, already turning into a light drizzle.

Soon the streets will start filling with construction workers waiting for their buses to take them to the soaring skyscrapers, where they will spend the next fourteen hours, high up in the sky, building yet another amazing structure in the shifting sands of the desert.

His head clamored with a whirlwind of conflicting, irrational thoughts, and ideas. One moment he felt no remorse for what he had done, the next, grief so strong gripped his chest that he thought he might not survive.

She had provoked him; he argued with himself. All he wanted was to talk to her, to get her to go back to Jassim. That is what Iliya had sent him to do. He never intended to kill her, never, but...that slut she hit him... he could not believe it.

After all this time of being there and watching over her, protecting her from the sleaze who wanted a piece of her every day, following her day and night, making sure she was home safely after work. This is how she repaid him. The look of contempt on Liliana's face when she opened the door and saw him was enough to send Lazar into a rage. Why could she not look at me the way she looked at Jassim?

Oh yes he had seen them, spied on them numerous times when they were sneaking around in their intimate moments. That animal Jassim, with his money and his women and fine ways, he should be dead right now. He was the reason she is dead. He had ordered Iliya to spy on her, to scare her and report to him. He is the one who went crazy jealous when she left him.

Jassim had her constantly followed, asking Iliya to keep her under twenty four hour surveillance. A few times, she had almost figured it out, bumping into Lazar while he waited for her in the garage after work.

Lazar thought back to the day Liliana had stared at the darkened windows of the Toyota, startled and confused, while he filled his eyes with her for a long moment, safe in the anonymity of the car, unable to look away from her terrified violet eyes.

The Toyota was a vehicle Lazar only used for his odd jobs, the illicit errands Iliya sent him on. He stashed it away in a rented garage far from the nightclub. No one knew he drove that car except Iliya.

Lazar failed to see an oncoming car at the roundabout and, as if he had woken from a trance, blinked in shock at the sleepy driver, the irritable, piercing sound of a horn.

He thought of Liliana laying out on that balcony, the rain soaking her body, the blood trickling in streams from her head...He thought of the flowers scattered on the floor, of her long hair, the way her body felt when he grabbed her, the image of her dancing all those times while he watched, mesmerized from the shadows.

He choked up. A horrible sound escaped his lips. His large, calloused hands gripped the steering wheel tightly, but he could not see the road because his eyes overflowed with a burning torrent of tears.

Lazar drove through the streets of Dubai, half-blind and crazy from grief while in the distance the first ray of the winter sun burst into the sky painting it a dozen gorgeous shades of red.

Chapter 38

Qays

Qays was sitting in his car outside the towering apartment complex. The rain was starting to ebb and small drops of water sprayed his face through his open window. He did not feel them. The car engine and lights were off and he sat like that for a long time, very still, not doing anything at all. He took no notice of the rain.

He was thinking of his wife Tara. He wondered what she would do if she knew. If she knew what he had been doing, what he had been dreaming about.

If *anyone* knew, that he was skulking around in a dark parking lot, following an immoral girl to her home. Then waiting in his car, not sure for exactly what to happen, consumed with a thousand conflicting feelings, torn in a thousand pieces by his lust infused body.

He remembered the first time he had seen her. It was in an advertisement for a dance show…a small photograph in a local newspaper. A group of attractive European looking girls stood around in a circle on what looked like the stage of a nightclub. Dressed in long evening dresses and those strange long gloves, the women appeared to gaze challengingly at the camera.

He had stopped turning the pages of the newspaper and brought the photo closer to his face. He saw the women well…the photo was good, the exposure clear.

A pair of violet eyes looked at the camera seriously. Qays remained awestruck by those eyes, by that angelic face.

Who was this girl? He felt overcome by a feeling of desire so strong he felt dizzy for a moment. Then a sudden fierce curiosity to know who she was gripped him overwhelmingly.

Over the course of the next few months, he tracked her down. He spent countless hours on his laptop perusing the websites advertising the show that she was a part off, feverishly searching for any personal information about her. He even entered that pit of snakes, that lair of sin, that nightclub, just to see her.

Her dance routine left him more spellbound, more under her spell and even more filled with self-loathing and shame.

His trips to the mosque grew more urgent; he spent more time within the shelter of its walls. There, in the safety of its shadows, he performed many extra *raqaas*, praying fanatically for release from this vile affliction.

The meetings he had previously attended so diligently became a burden, because he could not face the good men who attended them. Their plans for a peace rally across the Middle East, the hopes of opening channels to interfaith dialogue and bringing people of all religions together. The project brother Abu Salem had funded through his charity foundation, an ingenious, novel way to show the world that not every Muslim was a fanatic, a zealot.

"The Middle East is where we should start, my brothers," he would say repeatedly.

"We are a blessed mixture of religions from ancient times…look at Jordan, Syria, Lebanon…Sudan, Egypt. There are Christians, Coptics, Druze, and Muslims who have lived in peace all over the Middle East." The men would always listen intently to brother Salem's wise words.

"The communication and dialogue had always been open among us Arabs. We have to start with something. Anything is better than blame and violence. Then we need to talk with the people from the West as well."

"*Walla*," he had laughed, "Just look at where we live brothers…what more tolerance do you need?" His charismatic face had screwed up in a smile, and the rest of the congregated brothers laughed too, comforted by the message of hope he gave them.

Qays believed in this message with every cell in his body. He had dedicated himself zealously to this cause, in organizing the march, his money for donations, and his time, not spent with his family. He knew that his secret cravings for another woman, cancelled all the good that he did. He was a hypocrite of the worst kind. He could not sit with these faithful, loyal men and claim to be one of them. Somehow, along the way he had gotten lost.

He could not look his wife and his little girls in the face anymore. He had failed them miserably. Lied to his beautiful little girls...to that good woman, Tara, who stood in silence, and looked at him with her reproaching brown eyes, each time he withdrew to his own make-believe world.

The appearance of the same blonde man he had seen at the nightclub interrupted Qays from his reverie. The large, strange looking man had an unsettling effect on Qays then and it happened again now. The man was exiting hurriedly, the very building Qays was watching. The man stopped and looked around quickly before getting into his white Toyota and driving off.

Qays felt disorientated by this development. He was not aware of Liliana's...because that was her name...involvement with this man. Obviously, he had been visiting Liliana at this late hour, for reasons, which Qays did not want to envision.

Jealousy inundated him, his body and soul like a tidal wave. Trembling from the force of this awful unbearable feeling, he started the car and drove off. He was going to pray the *'Fajr'* at the mosque and ask Allah for forgiveness. He would beg him for understanding, for he has never strayed from the path of straight and narrow, never in his life engaged in sinful and unlawful relations. Tara was the only woman he had been intimate with in his life.

Now he had ruined it all. *What was he thinking*? Of course, this girl saw men all the time. He was aware of the permissive conduct of most Westerners. After all, he had lived in America for so long. Throughout that time, he had kept himself pure, untainted by their beliefs, their modern morals. What an outrageous thing he had done. He wanted to bang his head against something.

He remembered a conversation with Tara, a long time ago, when they were both other people. They were sitting on a bench, in the student lounge…

"What is your biggest fear?" she had asked him in her straightforward way, so different from his.

"What do you mean?" he squinted trying to understand.

"I mean, what is it that you fear most in this life, and the one after." Her kind eyes stayed on his face.

No one had ever asked him this question. He did not want to answer it. Tara waited, focused on his face, patient, and he had to.

"I fear sinning the most." He stared at his hands, played with his nails…"I wish to die soon, before I sin too much," he looked at her, quizzically. Then, when she smiled, and her eyes creased in the corners, he knew she got it. He felt safe.

Now after all these years, he had permitted his one incursion, the only indiscretion into a fantasy world, enough power to disgrace him and his lifelong dedication to his faith. He would never forgive himself. He could only hope that his wife would forgive him.

He could hear the call of the prayer, its haunting resonance coming from a dozen minarets…This is what it would sound like if the sky could sing, Qays thought gripping the wheel, careening madly on the wet street.

True believers were on their way to the prayer already, he saw. That unique group of pious, Allah fearing men, the kind he used to belong to, Qays thought gloomily.

He stopped at that very first mosque that met him on his way home. He screeched to a halt in the front of the gate, not bothering to park his car, a frantic urgency in him to reach the refuge inside its walls.

He performed his ablutions quickly, splashing the cold water over his face, feet, and hands hastily and then joined the lines of men for prayer. He faced his creator in fear this time.

Qays felt slightly crazy and terribly tired as he started to recite the first words of the prayer. His cheeks were still wet, he realized, stunned. He touched his face, tasted the wet liquid with his tongue…it was salty. He started his plea zealously, overcome with emotion.

*I truly have gone astray; I have strayed so irreversibly…*he whispered, his tongue tripping over the words in his rush for absolution. *"How can you ever forgive me these shameful deeds"*, a drop landed on his hand, and he realized he was crying.

"*I'm only your slave. A sinful servant…give me the courage, a chance to do right*"…his voice broke. "*I know you are merciful.*"

Qays paused, suddenly overcome and sobbing uncontrollably. A storm made out of months of pent up emotions, came bubbling fort, released.

"*Can you forgive this miserable, wretched man…?* He drew a dismal picture huddled on the floor, tears rolling down his face, tears that he did not bother to hide, "*Can you keep me on the path of the straight and the narrow?*" he asked, repeatedly.

Chapter 39

Vikki

*V*ikki could feel the exhaustion seep from her limbs as she hauled her heavy Burberry weekend bag into the hallway. She was surprised that the door was unlocked; *Liliana must be down the hall, throwing the trash.*

To make sure she called out cheerily, "Heya…stranger," and then whistled softly, their regular greeting, the sound piercing the silence of the apartment. The balcony door must be open, she figured, because a draft of fresh sea air had rustled the pages of a newspaper, as it lay scattered across the floor. She took off her leather jacket wearily and hung it on the hook by the door.

She made her way into the flat, marveling at the clear sky visible through the windows. The rain had cleaned the city from the sand and grime, at least for a while. It took her a minute to take in the disarray in the living room, the overturned chair. Slowly her eyes moved to the beautiful, limp flowers strewn on the floor. Vikki inhaled sharply, confused for a second. She looked around… alarmed. A definite feeling of apprehension gripped her insides, a realization that something was horribly wrong…

Her instinct pulled her towards the open balcony door. A ghastly squeal escaped from her mouth. Liliana was lying on the floor, her long legs bent at an awkward angle. Her dress had crunched up her thighs, exposing her underwear. Her head fell sideways, like that of some damaged marionette, touching her chest. Long, wet tendrils obscured her face. The floor was still damp from last nights' rain and she stepped onto the balcony.

Vikki tripped, overcome, and then collapsed on the cold tile next to her friend. Very gently, she adjusted Lila's head, slowly, tenderly smoothing the blood-caked hair from her face. Liliana's violet eyes were open, staring up in wonderment, straight at Vikki. She cradled the slim, beautiful girl in her arms; bringing Liliana's body to her own, feeling her friends cold skin. She rocked her gently, like a child.

Then she screamed and screamed and screamed.

******

"The police are here Vikki," Adam wrapped her in his hug. Vikki leaned into him, tried to block out the image that was now burned, seared into her memory forever…*her friend, her beautiful Liliana, dead.*

Adam had arrived within minutes, because he had been waiting for her in his car downstairs. She had come home to get some of her belongings and to see Liliana before going back…to stay with Adam at his villa. Adam had kept his wits about himself, called the police, and called their neighbor, Amrou from the flat below. He had called Iliya and then he had held her in his arms until the tormented sobs stopped. He had comforted her until she became conscious again, because the sight of Liliana's dead body had created a hole into which she had slid, headlong, like Alice in wonderland, deeper and deeper, possibly never to return, never to see the light of day again.

"Shhh…shhhh…my love, *habibti,"* Adam said repeatedly. The security men from the building had come up too. The police were milling around the apartment, in their dark green uniforms, some in black, looking grim. Vikki looked up from where she had buried her puffy face into Adam's chest.

A police officer was talking to Adam, "Is she all right? Should we get her some medical help?" he asked. A sympathetic look creased his young face. Adam nodded, but did not speak. He was overwhelmed too. Amrou was across the room, they were interrogating him. He had a look of complete and utter disbelief on his face. *How could this happen? How does a friend, a lovely young woman get killed in her own house, why?*

These are the questions going through everyone's head, as they took prints, looked for fingerprints, collected evidence, and photographed Liliana's body. Then they covered it, put it on a stretcher, and carried it to the street below, among the gaping, horrified crowd which had gathered around the medical examiner's vehicle.

"Miss Vikki, can you tell me why anyone would do this to your friend?" the sympathetic officer had a notepad in his hand.

Vikki looked at him for a very long time. You could almost see the wheels in her head turning, thinking what to say and what not to say.

"Is there anything you think would be useful for us to know, something that could help us catch her killer?" he asked again. She looked at Adam, questioningly.

"Tell him Vikki, just tell him what you think," he placed his hand on hers reassuringly.

Vikki cleared her throat. It was dry, hoarse from her screaming when she spoke. "Liliana was seeing a man…and she ended the relationship. He had threatened her". She paused, clasped her hands, unable to go on.

"Who is this man?" the officer had bent down, writing in his notebook.

Vikki said the name. The officer looked up. "This is the name of a very influential man, a respected family man," he said. "Are you sure this is the person your friend was involved with. Could there not have been someone else?"

Vikki stared at him. *What is he saying that I am lying, that Liliana was a prostitute?*

The police officer spoke again, considerately this time, "What I meant was do you have proof of this? Could you provide evidence if needed?"

Vikki stood up, walked briskly to where her bag lay on the couch. For a few minutes, she riffled through its contents and then came back with a small black object in her hand. It was a camera. The officer stared. Adam just waited. Soundlessly Vikki handed the camera to the officer. He took it, hesitant at first, but then proceeded to push the buttons, his face darkening with each new slide. Photos of Liliana and Jassim having dinner, photos of the trip the four of them had taken on Jassim's yacht. Liliana, striking in a white bikini, her black hair blown back by the warm wind of the Gulf, stared at the camera confidently. There were photos of tender moments between Liliana and Jassim, on the beach in the Maldives, in Bangkok, in Spain, all stored in her camera. Vikki had borrowed Liliana's over the weekend; hers had suddenly given out.

The officer avoided her eyes, "I will have to keep this, for evidence, you understand?" Vikki nodded. The officer handed the camera to the technician who put it in a plastic bag.

"Thank you, we will need it in the future, I will be in touch." He picked up his notebook, thanked them, and left to join his colleagues. They spoke to each other in Arabic in hushed voices, looking over at Vikki and Adam frequently. Adam shifted closer to Vikki, who had not moved from her place on the sofa. She sat there silently with a look on her face that he could not figure out. Her tears had dried out, anger had replaced shock, and she looked ready for a fight. "I know it's that maniac Jassim," she said. Adam leaned closer because she was whispering the words.

"I could feel it in my gut,"…she looked into his eyes pleadingly. "He was never going to let her go."

Adam lifted a finger warningly to his lips, "Don't say that Vikki, you can't be sure."

"Who then?" she mocked him. "Who would have reason to kill her?" she shot back. "No Adam, not with all that was going on in her life recently. He had threatened her for God's sake…" A sob crawled up her throat again; she tried to swallow it back, push it back down…

Adam sighed, he was tired. "Just don't say stuff like that for now Vikki, you have to be careful." He looked at the police officers. They were leaving, the apartment was not as crowded.

"What are you saying Adam, just let it be?" Vikki was angry. "Let him get away with it?"

"I'm saying let's just go home, you are in no position to make judgments now *habibti*. And remember we have to go into the police station later."

Grudgingly, she agreed. The police had asked them all to come in to give their statements. She knew Adam was right. She was stumbling, wounded…her friend dead, left to die on the balcony like some cheap piece of trash. She needed to think and plan.

Liliana had no one in the city who would truly mourn her. Nobody to make sure her killer got the punishment he or she deserved. Vikki planned to change that.

Chapter 40

Jane

Jane was listening attentively to the priest. Jake was here, right next to her. That was all that mattered. She heard him sigh heavily, smell his breath, orange, from the juice he had for breakfast. He fiddled, uncomfortable in his black suit and tie. It was a predictably rainy, murky February afternoon and they were at a cemetery in a small village in Cornwall…David's village.

Their family was here too, some of David's friends, not many, and certainly none from Dubai. Jane adjusted her leather gloves, stroked the rim of her black hat. She felt silly all dressed up like this. It was the end of the ceremony and she was glad for it.

"Ashes to ashes dust to dust…" the priest was almost finished with the service. They had known the vicar for years. He was a sweet man and she was thankful that he had helped with all the arrangements when she could not think, had no idea where to start.

The famous words she had heard innumerable times throughout her life. This time however, each word tore into her deeper and deeper, until she feared they would shred her to pieces, until she could not bear them anymore. Breathing deeply, Jane glanced at her beautiful son again. She kept looking at his profile, marveling at his courage and strength in the face of something so awful. She tried to concentrate on the service.

Very slowly they lowered the coffin into the wet ground... some woman was crying, Jane could not recognize her...she looked like David's only aunt, but she cannot be sure since it has been decades since they last met. The rain was hammering down like mad. It tried to chase them off into some warm dry room, but there was nowhere to go, and they have to finish this.

She put her arm around Jake's shoulders, pulled him closer. He was quiet, her only man, bravely poised and grown almost overnight. She watched his grim face tenderly.

It was hard to lose your father at any age, but he was so young, he needed David so much. She felt tears sting her eyes, and brushed them away. The vicar went on with the service, disregarding the pouring rain, and Jane thought back to the events that have led her family here. Two were alive, one dead.

It had all gone so bad, so quickly. One day they had been a seemingly ordinary family, but within a few years, it had all changed. They had all changed...in some ways to the point that there was no turning back, no second chances.

Who could have guessed David would do this? What had happened to her sweet, kind husband? She repeatedly went over their last year of life in Dubai, mercilessly, spitefully, looking for clues, blaming herself for not seeing any.

The uncomfortable truth was that she had not noticed David's' quiet, downhill spiral because she had been busy living her own fantasy. The fantasy of who was wealthier, younger looking, better dressed, and invited to a more extravagant party. Those perfect, sweetly twinkling lights of Dubai had blinded her. Shameful but true. She saw it all now...clearly. She saw David leave Jassim's office that fateful evening. Saw him take the elevator to the nineteenth floor roof and step of the edge.

He had landed in the street below, falling for twenty-three floors, almost unrecognizable to her when she had to identify the body, except for his wedding ring and a whitish scar on his torso from an old motorbike accident. *How does she tell her son this?* How does she go about telling her son his father was gone, and he could not even say goodbye.

The ceremony was finished, the casket with David's shattered body lowered deep into the ground, and someone was urging her to scatter some soil onto it. She looked around baffled. The earth was dark and soggy, and there is nothing to scatter. Finally, she bent and picked up a chunk of wet, sloppy soil in her gloved hand, unable to sprinkle it over the grave because it was sticky, stubborn. The ball of mud slid slowly into the grave from her palm leaving her glove stained, damp.

The small group of relatives loitered around making small talk, not sure what to do, desperately wishing to leave this sad wet scene. They were all embarrassed for her and Jake. They thought she was as well, and each politely avoided any questions relevant to her husband's illegal activities in Dubai. Her sister was here and she approached her, hugging her tightly. "Are you okay?" she peered at Jane, then at Jake, concern in her kind eyes.

"Yes, we're okay," Jane smiled, holding her sisters' hand in hers. They walked together towards the group of mourners, huddled together under dripping umbrellas.

Jane kissed many cheeks, and shook many gloved hands extended to her in sympathy. These were good people, their loved ones, yet she remained unmoved by their expressions of grief and pity. She had enveloped herself in a hard, unbreakable shell, just in case someone tried to break in. She had to guard herself, because she knew what they were thinking. "Just imagine...all the way to Dubai and this is how he ended up."

Another would say in hushed whispers, "I heard she spent thousands on her cosmetic surgery procedures...she spent so much..."

"I couldn't believe it when I heard....David of all people."

"That quiet, kind man...what drove him to this?"

"I heard rumors...It was much more than just the money, he was drinking too."

Then the final inevitable conclusion, "Well, this is what happens to Englishmen who live above their means...who become infatuated with that lifestyle *over there.*"

The last couple of words almost spat out in contempt because to these simple men and women it made perfect sense that Dubai was to blame for David's untimely and tragic ending. Jane had a lot to do with it...with her ostentatious lifestyle of decadence and superficiality...but Dubai... that city was just as guilty as if it had pushed poor, delusional David right off that roof. After all, it had a reputation off seducing the gullible and spitting them out mercilessly once their time was up, or once they fell for her charms. Dubai was like an Arabian femme fatale, mysterious and tempting, always on the prowl, they said, for those in search of adventure, but once she got them in her cloying, intoxicating hug, she would not let go.

The priest was saying something to Jake, holding her son's cold hands in his wrinkled old ones…whispering words of encouragement. Jake bowed his head, his blond locks dripping from the splattering rain. He seemed to be listening attentively, yet she could see he was not. His skin was ghostly pale and he appeared years older than eighteen did.

"What are your plans Jake?" the vicar was saying, "Are you going to start University then this year?" his eyes peered with concern through the downpour.

"Yes, I'm…at the London School of Economics," Jake answered, slowly.

The vicar saw Jane. "I was just going to congratulate Jake on the university news, how brilliant," he placed his hand on Jake's arm. "I know your father would be proud of you my dear boy". He was right of course. David would have been delighted with this news.

Jane nodded, "Thank you, we appreciate everything you have done for us," she shook the old vicar's hand. "We will be in touch, yes of course."

Then Jane put her hand around her son's elbow and led him away, politely, but firmly. She did not turn back, and she did not let him do so either. Jane knew David's desperate last act of love, had saved them all. He had pulled her from the brink. He had finally gotten them out. She saw his sacrifice, his total commitment to her and Jake. She owed him.

Determinedly she led the way for them both towards the car. They walked through the wind. It whipped their faces mercilessly, unforgiving. Jane welcomed the pain, relished it. For too long she had been numbing herself from the pain. They passed under the tree branches, which were groaning and straining from the force of natures wrath, threatening to come crashing down. They hurried through the small lakes of water, jumping over them, eager to get out of the storm and out of the cemetery, eager to escape the sad, prying eyes.

Jane held her son tightly, not letting go, and he followed, peacefully, trusting, that she will see them through to the end, regardless of what came their way.

Chapter 41

Ginni

*A*njuli is smiling her biggest smile. Ginni can see her vividly. For once, *Anjuli is wearing a lovely orange and pink dress, proudly displaying its ruffles and layers, and then she gives it a quick spin.*

She cocks her head to the side inquisitively, her dark braids making their way down her chest like two thick skipping ropes. Her small hands spread out in a gesture of welcome, waiting for Ginni patiently.

Ginni is writhing, pushing the images away, the silk sheet slipping of her naked body to the floor.

No Anjuli, no, she tries to call out, tries to scream but nothing comes out, and she is terrified that she will fail her little friend as she had done for the last twenty years. She has turned into a pillar of salt, unable to move or speak even while terror so malevolent grips her, threatening to consume her even while she watches helplessly.

Anjuli is still smiling, "Come Ginni, come on ladki, what is wrong with you today?" she giggles and runs her hands over the new dress. It is Diwali and they are going to the festival. A festive mood prevails even in theirs, the poorest of neighborhoods.

Anjuli holds a bunch of vibrant yellow flowers in her hands and she motions for Ginni to take them, to hurry, they will miss all the fun. Flowers of all colors, jostling, cheerful people, and wandering animals fill the streets. Anjuli is ahead, making way through the throng of bodies, happy for once. Her new dress is excellent and she twirls, the skirt bursting out around her like a rounded firecracker, sending her into giggles of joy.

There is a commotion behind her and Anjuli finally hears it, starts to turn around, curious. A man is standing behind her. He is wearing a grey coat, but it looks bulky to her, and Ginni holds her breath and still no words come out of her cursed throat. Anjuli has a smile on her dimpled face, she looks up at him in anticipation….What is he hiding under that coat.

Suddenly, people are running around bumping into each other, petrified, and desperately trying to avoid the man in the turban, the man in the bulging coat.

Ginni is watching him fixedly.

She has witnessed this scene dozens of times in her life, relived it repeatedly, and still it refuses to leave her, it refuses to become any less horrific.

The man in the grey coat is shouting ominously. He wants justice; he is angry, he hates these people. Ginni does not understand what he is saying, but it is apparent to her that he is evil and mad, because his black eyes are glistening sickeningly like two dark pebbles from hell.

The festive atmosphere of the marketplace of a few moments ago transforms as mayhem ensues. Mothers and fathers are pulling their little ones, trying to outrun what is coming, left and right, because everyone wants to live.

Shrieks and pleas of horror rise as they attempt to escape their already sealed fate...The man closes his eyes slowly, he looks completely calm, his face is devoid of anger at the moment. Then he presses his thumb to the detonator.

It all happens within seconds. Ginni can see Anjuli's eyes in those moments before the blast rips her small body to shreds. She sees her little friend, the pretty dress, and the shiny, oiled braids. Then she is gone.

Tears had soaked the expensive Ralph Lauren pillowcases she slept on. Ginni was wide-awake. She rubbed her wet face into the silk material. She was angry, at the recurring dream, angry with herself for not being able to forget, angry with Anjuli for not turning around sooner…she let moments pass, laid quietly. She waited hopefully, for forgiveness, because she had failed to warn her friend. However, it did not come today either.

She turned over in bed realizing there was someone next to her. Her eyes fell on the handsome face of Fares Dracolakis. It had been many months since they met at the Burj Al Arab party, but she had known this was inevitable the minute she had seen him. Some perverse part of her wanted to acquire, to conquer everything intriguing that crossed her path.

She continued to watch him, as he snored softly, sprawled over most of the king size bed in all of his six foot glory. She rested her head on her hand and with squinted eyes further investigated this man in her bed.

Many had been here, most for only one night, some for a few weeks. Occasionally she would allow someone she thought might be special to stay longer, but predictably, less than a month later she would grow dissatisfied with him. Relentlessly, as the years went by, she continued her search for that elusive perfect man. Only he could fill that aching, gnawing hollowness in her chest...the odd and indescribable feeling of loss, of despair, which she dragged around with her day after day.

Maybe he would be the one to douse the burning rage in her soul, the angry fire. There was a man out there like that, she could feel him. In the meantime, she had yet another show, another design, for yet another very important and very fashionable lady of Dubai.

Ginni gave Fares a dismissive look and standing up abruptly, not bothering to cover up, headed to the shower, nude. She had to face another day, and her eccentric teammates. A permissive smile crossed her lips as she turned the hot shower on full blast. Pierre, Mercy...what a quirky and amazing group of individuals they were. They were the family she never had, she realized suddenly.

The shower finished, she slathered body butter on her hot skin, pulled on her bra and panties, and walked back into the room. It was still early, and Fares had not stirred yet. She dressed in jeans and a silver tank top, her own design. She dabbed lip-gloss and mascara on, then fluffed her hair with her fingers.

Grabbing her enormous Prada handbag, her mobile, and car keys, she then stepped into her scarlet Louboutins. She steeled herself at the unappetizing idea of facing the malicious gossipy hordes of her fellow spoilt Dubaians.

Then she opened the door of her upstairs apartment and stepped out into the sunny hallway ready to face the day.

Chapter 42

Raj

"Anything living finds it physically painful to be outside in this crazy humidity, man. This is why for six months out of the year these people stay indoors, hiding out in the chilly air of their expensive cooling systems." Zachariah had his eyes glued to the dark street in front of them. They glimmered in the dull light of the half moon, reminding Raj of a nocturnal creature. The African was chewing on a toothpick in his casual, relaxed manner, which irked Raj. Even at times of extreme stress Zachariah seemed not to worry, eternally nonchalant.

"There is another side to it though. For about five months, starting in November and ending in March the weather becomes cooler, it rains, sometimes it even hails, and on a few occasions, it has snowed in the mountains of the desert!"

Raj listened, captivated as always by Zachariah's stories. He marveled at the man's' insight into the hidden world of the city. *Where did he learn all this stuff? He was like a walking fact list of information.*

Zachariah chuckled, apparently amused by the antics of his fellow Dubaians. "After long months of abstinence they came out of their dim, cool homes, dubious of the pleasant transformation of the weather, cautiously at first, blinking their eyes in the daylight, like stiff prisoners released from a dungeon."

Raj let out a sigh. This was turning into a long wait. He scratched himself. Zachariah went on, unfazed. "They came out exhilarated…to jog, take walks, push babies in strollers, play with their kids in parks, fly kites, surf, play tennis and polo. They drove sand buggies, went dune bashing, sand skiing, rode camels and horses, camped in the '*wadis*' and just generally become silly, carefree and adventuresome."

He slobbered on his toothpick; he was not finished with his tirade. "Concerts, circuses, parades and marathons, excite the entire country. Did you see them? Dubai resembles a carnival. Colorful flags and banners adorned the malls and streets, funfairs, musicals, art shows, and exhibitions". Raj had learned that his friend's favorite word in the English language was 'crazy', and then learned to live with it. The African lit his fifth cigarette.

They have been skulking around for an hour now, and Raj was getting nervous. This was his first sale and he was full of doubts.

Zachariah showed no hint of worry. He dragged on a cigarette deeply, continuing, proud of his apparently infinite supply of information about the city. He rubbed his chin contemplatively, "I tell you…it's crazy, man".

Raj was familiar with the faces on those glossy pages, the well-photographed socialites, jetsetters, or those who were simply clingers on. Yes, he agreed, everybody is afraid of the boiling summer months, desperately hoping for the cooler days and nights to linger, before the muggy heat descends upon them, so they wait, uneasily, as the mercury steadily rises upward.

A mass exodus ensued very soon after the high temperature begins and as soon as schools close for summer breaks. He had witnessed it himself this year. Families leave for cooler climes in droves. The city seemed deserted, sad somehow without its many younger residents.

"Then on the other hand, inhabitants of those same colder places, hungry for sunshine, rushing over to the desert to barbeque themselves on the beaches and ski inside shopping malls!" The two men both laughed at these frolics of the affluent set.

For some reason it made perfect sense to all parties involved…but to a keen and impartial observer, the yearly event must seem akin to a hysterically madcap game of musical chairs, Raj thought to himself.

"I see a car," Zachariah leaned front in the seat of his beat up Suzuki. Raj followed suit and strained to see who it was. The car stopped a few feet away, turned the headlights off, and a man stepped out. Zachariah opened the door as well and scrambled out, greeting, talking rapidly.

"Yes, I got it all, it's in the back," he turned around, nodding to Raj. Raj knew what to do; Zachariah had been coaching him for weeks. He went to the back, and produced a large cardboard box out of the trunk. He looked around nervously before carrying it to the front and handing it over to the swarthy young man talking to Zachariah. The man ignored Raj focusing on the box.

"How much this time?" he asked reaching to open the lid, peeking inside.

Zachariah boasted, "Five bottles of Scotch, five of red wine and three of good Russian vodka, man." Raj backed up, standing apart, still worried.

"Fine, but next time try to get more of the good stuff ok?" the man said, then laughed, and his face transformed. Visibly relieved, Zachariah laughed too, looking over his shoulder at Raj. He winked, as if to say, see I told you it would be fine. I told you everybody these days bootlegs. Raj exhaled, realizing how scared he actually had been this whole time. When Zachariah had approached him with the scheme, he had rejected him flat out. Many months had passed since then and his original reaction changed. It became acceptable because like a hungry worm, the idea, found a domicile in his head, enticing him to do something about it.

The possibility of making more money was just impossible to ignore. He agreed on this drop off as a onetime thing, just to see… to consider. Zachariah had slapped him on the shoulder and bellowed his deep boisterous laugh in pleasure at the news. He had been in dire need of an associate. Someone to help, someone to watch his back in case things went wrong. With Raj near, he felt more in control, safer.

"So what did you think?" Zachariah was in a great mood. They were driving back to the house. It was late, and they were tired. However, Raj was thinking of madam. He was thinking of what she would say about his activities tonight. He shifted uncomfortably in the seat. The mere thought of her stirred things inside him, things he had no business feeling. He stole a furtive glance at Zachariah. The man would lose it if he even mentioned the subject.

"I think it was okay," he already felt regretful about the episode.

Zachariah guffawed, "So how about some more of that, ha?" He shoved Raj in the ribs, laughing all the time, "More *mulla,* more money, baby?"

He is strung out, high on something, Raj thought. "Zachariah you really should not drink and drive," he admonished his unruly friend. He resented Zachariah's dismissive treatment sometimes. *What did Zachariah know of him...? What if Zachariah knew of the incredible things he had done. Would he be laughing at him then?*

Would he be astonished at the things Raj was capable off?

The Nigerian gaped at Raj open mouthed. Then he shrieked, almost choking in his amusement. "Raj...Raj, sometimes you kill me man, look at you." He waved his arm, "Sounding like a proper little gentleman all of a sudden. What's gotten into you man?" he continued laughing, driving haphazardly, and talking about their next heist.

Raj tuned him out. He was tired and fed up with it all. It seemed that whatever he did he could never get to the other side of the proverbial fence. That place that he had been dreaming off ever since he stepped on this desert soil. He realized that he would always remain a poor driver from Rajasthan. He might make some money if he continued bootlegging with Zachariah, but he will always stay on the wrong side. His life story, his fate, his destiny had been sealed by the very place of his birth. He had been doomed from the moment of his conception.

Chapter 43

Ameera

$\mathcal{T}$he rickety, bronchial taxi climbed through the narrow, bumpy streets. It waddled and sputtered, heaved and groaned whenever the driver shifted gears. The drive was precarious...nerve wracking because it seemed as if the taxi would die out any moment, sending its passengers spiraling into the depths of the valley below.

Ameera shifted in the back seat, mindful of the approaching pothole. The taxi regained its balance again. The driver lit his umpteenth cigarette and they plodded on, as if oblivious to all its shortcomings. He seemed unperturbed by his vehicle's agony, blowing smoke languidly, occasionally stealing a look into the rearview mirror at her. Ameera was aware of those glances and ignored him. Her attention was on the outside, the dusty mountains rising above the busy city below. She was glad to leave it all behind, the noise and congestion, the hectic airport from which she had hailed this taxi.

Hours earlier, she had been in a plane, flying away from Dubai, astonished at the speed with which her life had unraveled. Shell shocked, as if she had been asleep all this time, as if she had come from a parallel reality. One moment she was dancing half-naked in front of a horde of drunks, who then attacked her, and the next thing she knew a kind stranger had whisked her away...magically it seemed. It sounded almost too good to be true. It certainly took hours of explaining to the skeptical police officers.

"Here, take this money, it's yours," Jake had pushed crumpled bills into her clenched hand. "Take them, do not give them to the police, do you understand?" he had looked around the empty street. It was dawn and the streets were still deserted, save for the occasional truck on its way to deliver fruit or some other fresh produce to the supermarkets. He had parked further down from the police station, which she could see clearly, lit by a thousand bulbs, like an icon of security.

"Thank you," she had said quietly, with downcast eyes. She did not want him to see her eyes because they were ready to burst with a yearlong supply of tears. Her carefully construed dam was about to burst wide open, letting out a flood of emotions. Her fake indifference, her false mask of mocking bravado, was dissolving under Jake's kind eyes.

"You are very welcome," he smiled, nodded his head. "You have to go now, Ok?" he asked, a bit loudly, making sure she understood him. "Tell them what happened, they will help you, I'm positive," kindly, encouraging. Ameera had placed her hand on his softly.

"*Allah egzeek kheir,*" *May Allah bestow goodness on you...*she had told her young blonde rescuer, for surely *Allah* had sent her this man in a boy's body as her savior angel. Ameera understood. All her prayers for help had been answered. They had heard her pleas for help. Her mother and father had made sure of that.

She opened the door of the car and stepped out into the fresh morning air. She stopped for a moment, inhaled deeply, the sweet smell of freedom. *Was it possible? Could she really be free...or could this be a cruel prank played by Kareema? A way to play with her emotions, break her, to laugh at her when she realized that it was all a setup.* She looked around fearfully, expecting Kareema to appear behind her, grab her roughly and laugh her vulgar, repulsive laugh. However, nothing happened.

The street remained silent, except for the revving of Jake's car as he drove off. He raised his hand in a wave and she waved back. Slowly, she had started walking into the police station.

The taxi jerked, and she lurched against the front seat. She was home, and thankfully these horrific events behind her. The street was narrowing and did not climb any more. Ameera recognized her neighborhood, knew the house should be just around the corner. Her heart pumped happily, but her hands shook from fear. *How will she face them all? After all this time of being away, after everything she had done.* The memory of the sins she had committed haunted her. She found no comfort in the fact that she had been enslaved, drugged, abused, and blackmailed into performing those sinful acts. Maybe time will help her forgive herself. Maybe time will help her forget.

Her mind drifted again to the events of past few months. "Ameera, they caught them," the large police officer had been proudly jubilant. She was smiling, her large, round face stretched in kindness.

"All of them?" Ameera had asked, afraid to call them by their names. That might bring them into her life again. Saying them aloud made her afraid, to the point where she had to look over her shoulder, expecting Kareema to be standing there, that sly, cunning smile on her face. *"Did you think you could just walk out on me?"* she would say, mocking her.

"Yes, all of them," the police officer smiled again. "They were terrified, denied everything, but then the driver confessed." She handed Ameera a packet of biscuits.

"Will they all go to prison?" Ameera took the packet warily.

The woman nodded. "Yes for a very long time, *ma tkhafi,* don't be afraid."

"Here eat this, you look like *mout,* death."Ameera ripped the plastic and gladly chewed on the sweet snack. They had given her dinner and tea a few hours ago but she was still famished. This was her second day in the women's prison. The police had interrogated, questioned, poked, and probed her here. A gynecologist examined her. A psychiatrist and a sociologist examined her. She told them all the truth and they had no choice but to eventually believe her.

They treated her, stuck her with IV fluids, various shots for malnutrition, her bruises were dressed. They tested for AIDS, hepatitis and tuberculosis. After that, they left her alone. In the quiet of the clean, stark examination room at the prison, she had fallen asleep peacefully, for the first time in a year.

"Moroccan embassy representatives have been notified," the large police officer had finally told her, and will be taking her away with them soon, buying her the plane ticket that will take her home.

Ameera realized they had reached the house. "Stop here," she told the driver. They were in front of the house. The taxi coughed up a black cloud of smoke and then fell quiet.

"Here we are," the cab driver was smiling proudly, apparently taking credit for the steep drive. She extended a wad of notes to him. He had an almost imperceptible twinkle in his eye, attempting a sneaky half look over her figure. It made her shudder in revolt. All men made her shudder. She got out of the cab, relieved when it disappeared around the corner. She was glad the constant peeking at her in the rearview mirror and the driver's intrusive questions were over.

Ameera turned towards the short door of her house. It was quiet. The children, who had filled the streets all day, playing in the dust, were gone, probably called inside for their evening meal. The smell of fried pastries and the mountain air mingled together. Soon it will be time for the evening prayer. Ameera picked up her duffel bag and walked the few remaining steps to the door. The embassy representative…a small, soft man had given it to her. It contained a few hygienic products and a couple of boxes of chocolates for her sisters.

She rapped on the door softly. A million tumultuous things were going through her head, like a whirlwind, no…like a nightmare. She did not know if she should be here at all. Maybe this was a mistake. Her heart yearned to go inside, hug Raya and Samar, and grandma Balqis. It yearned so much that it squeezed itself into a tiny little corner of her chest, hiding, because it was afraid of this love, this yearning.

Suddenly the door opened. In the soft dusk light, she saw a small girl. Her hair was frizzy and wild, her face deeply tanned. It was Raya. The sisters stared at each other for a moment, each shocked at the sight of the other.

Then, Ameera's chest exploded in a jubilant shout of her sisters' name and she bent down, hugging the small, thin body to hers, and sobbed.

Chapter 44

Parisa

"Hey, mom we are landing." Zoya was shaking her from an uncomfortable slumber. She looked around, confused, and slowly realized they were on a plane. Yes, she could remember now. A twinge, and ache, stung her memory; she wished she could have stayed asleep for a much longer time.

"Look out the window mommy," Zoya had her face pressed against the first class windowpane. She was visibly excited. After all, it was not every day that a girl moves to New York. Parisa knew how lucky she was. So fortunate she found out what Luca had done. Not all women are that lucky she thought. Many remained clueless for decades, only to discover the truth when it was long overdue. At times they found out when faced by the husband's illegitimate child or children...sometimes even at his funeral. Then, it was too late. At least she stumbled upon the extent of

Luca's deceit before it was too late for her. However, it had been too late for one innocent party in this elaborate deception.

The police had taken Luca in for questioning that day at the pool. She had felt a twinge of suspicion at the time, a sliver of dread slide under her skin, like an itch she could not scratch, but she had blocked it out.

She had dressed hastily, got into her car after reassuring Zoya that she would be all right, just some nonsense about speeding tickets, and then she had raced to the police station. The officers who took him said he would be at the main station in Deira.

"Don't worry Parisa, it's probably just his driving, you know how he is," Jane had told her over the phone. "Do you want me to go with you?"

"No, its fine really, I'm sure you are right," was Parisa's brave answer. She had called Jane to cancel their plans for that evening. They were going to watch a touring production of a Shakespeare play at the Madinat Theatre and have a late dinner afterwards at one of the restaurants facing the canal. The two women shared the same interests in arts and theatre, and attended gallery exhibitions, plays and concerts together on many occasions. Zoya's and Jack's infatuation had blossomed between them further, drawing the women closer, and binding them into a sisterhood of worry.

"All right then, I'm off, will talk to you after I figure out what happened," Parisa said and hung up. She knew where the police station was. She had gone there to report the runaway maid, Cora.

The station looked, as before, well attended to, clean, and efficient. Male and female police officers in new uniforms went about their business in a confident, efficient manner. One of them, a man, took her to see Luca. The expression on his bearded face was indifferent as he ushered her into the inner sanctum of the station. The further inside he led her, the more concerned she became, *all this for a speeding ticket?*

"Champagne madam?" the friendly steward was holding out a golden glass of perfect beverage. A celebratory drink she thought. "Yes, thank you very much," Parisa took the drink, it was refreshing, just what she needed. Zoya was putting some make up on, getting ready for their adventure in New York. New York University had accepted her and she was ecstatic about starting in September. Parisa smiled at her daughter's young, eager profile. This was good, she thought. It feels right; I can feel it in my bones. *Moving to New York is the first right thing I have done since Babek died.*

******

"I'm sorry madam, the news is not pleasant," the short, efficient officer said to her as she sat down in his office. He was the proud, bustling kind. Parisa felt a tremor, a shadow pass across the room. "Yes, please tell me. Why has my husband been arrested?" she had her bag in her lap and she grabbed the handle.

The officer cleared his throat, "Well, your husband is involved in a case concerning the death of a newborn baby. He is also accused of having an illicit affair with your maid Cora, an act which then led to the death of this baby."

There he had said it. It was done. It was right in the room with her now, the ugly, monstrous truth. In all her worst scenarios, whenever she had doubted Luca, none of them had come even close to the truth.

Sometimes, Parisa had worried Luca might be cheating on her. She feared that she was too old for him, not attractive enough maybe. Angry at herself for being suspicious of his motives, that he might be using her for her contacts, or her friends. She thought she knew another Luca, a different Luca from the one the officer was talking about.

"Where is my husband now?' Her head held high, dignified as always, even though the room moved around her and her palms dripped sweat. She doubled over, hugging her stomach where a massive dagger had lodged itself.

"He was detained, until he can get a lawyer," the officer was kind. "Madam I recognize that you are in shock. I feel bad that it happened to someone like you." He nodded amicably. "Your husband's charges are very serious and complicated. A baby died due to his actions. We do not take this lightly."

Parisa stared ahead. Slowly she asked, "What will his sentence be, do you know?"

"It's hard to tell, depends on many factors, but since he has confessed already." The officer shrugged.

Parisa jerked her head up, startled. Luca had confessed already. He must have realized straight away when they took him from the house. That is why he looked so sad...*Luca, why, why...*

The police officer continued, "I'm sorry to have to tell you this madam, there is no other way." He looked uncomfortable yet solemn and plunged ahead with the thing that had apparently been bothering him from the beginning. "I have to ask you a question?" he coughed, shuffled some papers. Parisa just stared at him. "Did you have any idea about this? I mean did you have any reason to suspect of your husband's affair with the maid? After all she was right in the house with you," his face piqued with attention.

Parisa smiled at him, "I don't blame you for this question officer, it's a good question." Her voice trembled, "But I have to answer a firm...no." She looked him in the eyes. "I had no idea my husband was sleeping with our much younger, simple maid in our own house, probably in our own bed. I had no idea that they were having a child together. I also did not know that this child died because of these two selfish, callous people," she started to cry, inconsolably. An image of Zoya as a baby filled her mind and she felt a overwhelming sadness. "How stupid of me, you must think, not to know any of this?" She sobbed. The officer handed her some tissues.

Parisa's voice sounded alien to her ears when she spoke, "I loved him you know. I suspected, but I loved him." Her eyes clouded over, like someone had shut the door enveloping it in darkness. "I can't believe he did this in my home, with my daughter right there," she blew her nose into the tissue. The idea that she had put Zoya in harms' way...had ignored her daughter's warnings crushed her even more. So much pain, so much regret she felt right now.

******

"Mom, we have to get ready, it's almost time," Zoya was near, smiling, poking her shoulder. Parisa grasped her daughter, drew her into her arms, over the hand rest. Zoya yelped in surprise, and then giggled.

Parisa kissed her cheeks, her eyes her hair... *"Duset daram* my love," she said. There were tears of apology in her eyes.

Zoya understood. "Mom it's all right, really, its fine. Just forget it okay?" She smiled, pulled out of the embrace. "You really should put some make up on, you look like crap," she teased. Parisa laughed and rubbed her eyes. Yes, she would wash her face and put on some make up. Tomorrow they awake in a new home, in a new city. One that was even more famous and vibrant than the one they left behind. She got up and made her way to the bathroom.

******

"Do you want to see you husband?" the officer rubbed his chin. He seemed tired. He must have many more cases to deal with. Her answer must have shocked him because his eyes widened as he sat up in his chair.

"No" Parisa says, "No I do not wish to see him, ever again." She stood up.

"But madam what about a lawyer, other legal matters...who will do that…you are his wife." The officer was clearly surprised by this turn of events. He must have been expecting vengeance or some other emotion from her.

Parisa was at the door, ready to leave the gawking officer. She turned around and smiled at him. Her eyes were still wet; she was not done with mourning. That will come later, much later. "Thank you so much for you kindness," she whispered.

The man lowered his head, nodding. "It is terrible, just terrible; I have heard of your art, you are such a good woman. Your late husband was well known and respected in this town. Too bad, that this Italian did not turn out the same."

"Thank you for your kind words," Parisa replied. "Just send everything to Mr. Finelli's lawyer, he will deal with it all," with that she left, closing the door softly behind her.

******

The plane was landing and they were ready, mother, and daughter as always. The sky was clear, the clouds low and wispy. She could already see the rising spires of the New York skyline. She held Zoya's small hand in hers, squeezed hard. They were on their way. To something better, she knew. Dubai and Luca were behind for now.

However, one day, maybe out of curiosity they would return. Just for a while. Just to see. They would walk down Jumeirah Beach promenade, mingling with the new faces, the old ones already gone, moved away to their next destination. They might visit the mall, buy some things, and meet those friends who remain in the city. They would laugh and talk of their new life in America, of Parisa's exhibits and of Zoya's upcoming graduation, her engagement to Jack. Yes, Jack would be there too, and Jane. All four would visit together this city of memories, a city that they still loved. They might stand still at the place where Jake's father took his own life…silently, each saying a prayer. Parisa would probably drive by the jail where Luca still spent his days. She would feel his presence through the thick walls and feel his anguish. Nevertheless, she would go on.

During the visit, they would talk of their friend Jewel, the strange and bizarre case of her husbands' mistress. They might hear news of Jewel but not attempt to see her, to contact her. In their hearts, there was a thump, a quiver when they thought of their friend. In their subconscious they knew, they knew what she had done. Oh, they felt it in their very blood. They accepted her voiceless message that they would never see her again, and sadly realized that they did not wish to do so either.

Then, when they have had their fill of this city of their dreams and pain, the city that beckoned, only then, would they be able to leave forever.

Chapter 45

Tara

Tara was sitting in the living room quietly. The girls were upstairs, playing school. It was almost time for bed, yet she sat, unmoving. She was waiting for Qays to come home from the police station where he has been for the last three days. She was waiting to welcome him home. Three days ago, her cell phone had rung while she was grocery shopping at Spinney's.

"Tara, it's me," he said. She immediately felt that something was wrong. He went on without waiting for her answer.

"I'm at the police station, the criminal investigation section, can you come?" She felt calm. Complete calm. Finally, it had happened. The long months of dread, the elusiveness of his behavior, the strangeness, might finally be over. She wanted to know, was possessed with a need to know. *What was it? What did he do?* After asking for instructions about the location, she had rushed to the station. It was downtown. A couple of bored officers took her identity card, checked her personal information before asking her to wait in a small office. The minutes seemed like hours. Finally, the door opened and Qays walked in. She expected him to be wearing handcuffs, but he was not.

"Are you okay?" she had asked first. He looked awful. His beard and hair were bushy and uncombed, his eyes even duller, sunken, his entire face sagging. He looked ten years older that when she saw him that morning. He stared at his hands on the table between them. They both remained like that for a long time, like two people on the precipice of a maelstrom. She did not ask him any questions. Finally, he spoke in a voice that sounded like that of an old, broken man.

"I have sinned." Then he told her…everything. He told her in a bitter, emotionless voice about the picture, the girl, his visits to the nightclub and the hours he spent stalking her. He told her about Abu Salem and how he had failed the brothers in his group and how he had failed his faith, his family, her.

He told her that the more he felt attracted to the vice out in the world the more strict and fixated he become at home. Always worried that someone will find out what a fake he was, he tried harder to be pious, to rid himself of the poison cursing through his body like a virus. Tara listened with downcast eyes and relief in her heart.

"Why are they keeping you here then?" she asked when he was finished.

"The girl I'm telling you about, her name is Liliana," he paused, composed himself. "She has been killed, she is dead," the haunted look in his eyes again. *Did he love her?* She wondered, sympathetically. She knew how it felt to lose a love.

"Someone saw me, sitting in the car for hours, he took my number," Qays rubbed his eyes "They think I killed her".

Tara closed her eyes, said a silent prayer of thanks. "I believe you Qays. I know you did not, cannot do something like that," she smiled sadly…

Oh, if he knew what she had done? Would he still feel guilty? Would he still punish himself so?

She forced a smile to her frozen face. The relief was instant. The guilt would hover over her very existence like a sword until the day she exhaled her last breath. No amount of prayer or supplication will atone for what she had done; she knew that with a fierce certainty. She was also certain that she had been lucky, extremely lucky. She could not wait to go home and hug the girls. *Maybe she will take them out, buy them fast food even, and let them eat all the chocolate their little hearts desired. She felt the need to celebrate.*

Chapter 46

Cora

Cora looked out of the small window facing the women's jail courtyard. It was summer again, and the cooling systems were not good here. She felt hot.

She took out a folded photograph from her prison issue outfit. She unfolded it slowly, lovingly, and stared at the little boy laughing back at her. My baby, my *anak,* he has grown so much. A proud smile falters on her gaunt face. Mama must be feeding him her famous noodles and shrimp soup. A light shadow of a smile crossed her face. I cannot wait to see him... five more years. She comforted herself with this thought. She had no choice but to comfort herself, to find some goal in her long, humiliating wait.

She stiffened as another memory enters her already slipping mind. It is the memory of her other little boy, of a bloody pink towel, of searing pain. She remembered the gruesome hallucinations, which her overheated brain had created to punish her; all too clearly, and they still refuse to allow her peace.

Oh yes, unfortunately she had recuperated from the staph infection that almost took her life. The courts were unsympathetic to a mother who had killed her own baby, and sentenced her to five years in the Dubai women's prison, after which they will deport her from the country. Like a leper.

She accepted this; in fact, she deserved worse. She wished Girlie had left her to die that day. Destiny brought Girlie home early.

Other prisoners talked to her. She did not care; she never talked to anyone. Still staring out of the window, she noticed a tiny bird. *Look at it flap its tiny wings, mahal ko, my love...*

She knew it was the bird of paradise. Gorgeous multihued colors caress Cora's eyes; she smiled delighted...what a lovely name that is. Lovely... lovely, little bird, look at its little wings flapping cheerfully, its colors.... *Dios*, Jesus.

How beautiful and free he was she thought, straining to see more of its beauty, but wait... it was gone away again, forever. She pressed her thin face to the glass but could not see anymore, for it had flown away, free to do as it wished.

Cora felt so excruciatingly sad; her heart felt like it would explode from this sorrow, it was too much and she knew she would not be able to stand it. She felt like she might have lost her sanity already. Her hot, incessant tears flowed unrestrained down her face, soon soaking the top of the uniform.

She just could not bear that the little bird had left her and gone forever.

Chapter 47

Jassim

"Is everything okay?" Jewel asked her husband with concern. He looked drained as he walked into the house. His usually self-assured stride was gone, replaced with the hesitant one of a worried, sad man.

"*Mafi shay*, there is nothing," he did not sound convincing and she hurried to his side. The sun was just dipping behind the Burj Al Arab. Jewel could see it through the large window of their family room...the breathtaking sight almost stopped her in her tracks, but she remembered her duty and continued towards him.

"Jassim, what happened, what's wrong?" she knelt next to him on the pillows, and her long hair scattered over his white *Kandoora*, covering it like the wings of a falcon, her highlights shimmering like liquid gold in the sunset sun.

Jassim placed a hand on her head, "It's nothing Jewel, don't worry, normal trouble at work," he sighed heavily. His long eyelashes fluttered, casting trembling shadows over his face.

"Ever since David killed himself, the company has been in turmoil. I'm losing faith in myself. I fear that I will not be able to handle it," he said slowly.

Jewel listened carefully. *Yes, how sad for Jane what happened to David, and how terribly stupid of him. What will become of Jake now, after such a terrible tragedy?* She made a mental note to call them in England as soon her own concerns had settled.

"Where are the children, I have missed them," Jassim said, then closed his eyes. She noticed the streaks of grey in his hair, the fine lines around his expressive eyes. He was different, forever changed she knew.

******

Earlier that day, Jassim had received a phone call from the police chief asking him to come in for some questions. Jassim assumed it had to do with David's case, the embezzlement and suicide case. He walked into the office of the chief smiling, confident, and secure. In the past Jassim and the chief had always been able to reach an understanding on sensitive matters. There was the case of the girlfriend, whom needed a residency permit and that disgruntled and loud employee…little favors here and there. The kind of treatment Jassim expected from his friends in powerful places. It was only to be expected.

After the pleasantries were over the chief cleared his throat and asked Jassim, "Did you know a woman called Liliana?"

Jassim froze. "Yes I did." *The chief had said did you know in the past tense….*He tried to gather his wits feverishly, deducting, anticipating the next curve ball.

"Excuse me for asking but how did you know her," the chief had been his classmate in secondary school.

"She was a model at one of the parties I sponsored, and later we met through similar events," Jassim clasped his hands together and leaned forward. "What is the reason for these questions…did something happen to Liliana?" he asked.

The sound of the air conditioner in the room, the beep of a car, shrieking tires…even a cooing pigeon on the windowsill…he could hear them all. His senses were suddenly sharpened, intense and poised for anything.

Except for these words, "Yes, something happened to her… she is dead."

The chief watched carefully for reaction, "murdered in her apartment this morning...at *Fajr*."

Where was I at dawn? Jassim thought. A feeling of surrealism descended on him. Yes, he was sleeping in his bed with his wife... safe, clueless, wicked...

It took incredible willpower of him but he controlled his emotions, appearing slightly surprised, shocked even by the news. He did not look like his heart was cut into a million infinitesimal pieces, or as if he was being torn apart limb by limb...slowly, excruciatingly. *What in hell had happened?*

However, the chief was not done; he had more surprises in store, "We have arrested a couple of individuals and are interrogating them right now. They are suspects in her murder."

"I don't understand chief, why am I here?" Jassim asked.

"You are here because one of these suspects claims you hired him to threaten the victim, maybe even hurt her..." the chief was business like now. He was the law.

Another stab in the guts, an extra betrayal, it seemed the entire world was conspiring against him. The shocking embezzlement and the treachery from his own accountant and now... *He should not have trusted that Russian.*

"That is a lie of course, how can you believe such things about me?" he said indignantly. He tried to stand up, to demonstrate how insulted he was.

The chief was not having it. "Listen Jassim, sit down please, *ajlis,*" his voice was firm. He would not play Jassim's games. He knew him well; after all, they went to school together.

"What are you accusing me of?" Jassim was offended again. He was Al Gaafari.

"Of conspiracy to inflict bodily harm, kidnapping, conspiring to obstruct justice, inciting violence..."

"Stop...enough," Jassim raised his hand. He appeared exhausted. "What do you want from me?"

The chief leaned back into his leather chair, "Nothing."

"Nothing!" Jassim's winged brows form a perfect double arc as they shoot up in disbelief.

"Yes, absolutely nothing, unless you choose to tell us the truth of course," the chief had a smirk on his face. Jassim knew the man was enjoying himself.

"I told you already, I don't know anything about a conspiracy," Jassim shouted. Two officers entered the room, with a stern look on their faces. The chief assured them that he was fine. They left the room but shot an annoyed look of warning at Jassim.

"Listen, the truth is that I have to arrest you for these allegations. We are talking about murder here Jassim. This is a serious issue, not the same I'm afraid, as you had previously. There is nothing anyone can do about that, not even you." The chief did not try to hide his pleasure at saying this.

It seemed that this time even his friends had abandoned him. Jassim stared in disbelief. *Jail…They wanted to put him in jail. Were they serious?*

"Where is your proof?" he demanded.

"We have photos of you and Liliana in intimate positions…many photos."

"Fine, so what, I had an affair with her…I had affairs with many women. Is that reason for me to go to jail?"

"We also have proof that you have schemed to have her followed and have given instructions to Iliya Tarasov, a man of shady background, well known to us, to use any means necessary to get Liliana to come back to you."

"That does not mean I killed her."

"Yes but you conspired with those who did. If you had not gotten them involved, she would still be alive today. You sent sadistic criminals after her, what did you think was going to happen? Did you think they would ask her nicely? You knew the kind of people you were dealing with.

Chapter 48

Vikki

"So what happened? Who killed Liliana?" Vikki asked the chief. The interview with Jassim had taken place in this same room a week earlier. They had arrested him officially a few days later. Lazar and Iliya were standing trial within the next week. The arrogant Russian had screamed in protest throughout the interrogation while Lazar sat by his side, mute and unmoving. Liliana's murder had caused an outrage in public opinion, headlines screaming it daily from local newspapers. The high profile individuals involved in the case created a frenzy of interest, of speculation.

The chief crossed his hands on the table, "Well, after forensic evidence that we found on the scene of the crime, the testimony of the security guard and Lazars' own confession it appears that Lazar had killed your friend. We are almost positive about this now." He took a sip from a glass of water.

Vikki had her own glass and she drained half of it. It was time to get out of this town, she thought. She needed a break, to sort things out. She planned to travel to Romania with Liliana's' body as soon as all the formalities were finished she told the chief. "When can I take her?" Vikki could not believe she was saying these words. She wanted to get out of this room and never come back.

"Probably tomorrow afternoon, at the latest," the chief assured her. "I should not be telling you this of course, but since you are Liliana's' only family here, I will tell you." The chief continued in a conspiratorial tone, "We had another suspect for a while. Yes, an obsessed fan of Liliana's who had been stalking her for almost a year." Vikki remained unmoved. He cleared his throat, "The suspect drove the same kind of car spotted at the crime scene by your neighbor Amrou."

The chief looked sympathetically at the crushed girl. "Turned out the suspect was harmless, a married man, a religious man. It took me entirely by surprise. He did not fit the profile." He clasped his hands. "Well, this city is full of strange characters, as I'm sure you have found out for yourself."

The entire city seemed to have been in love with her best friend. How sad, how utterly sad that she had to be gone so early in her life. She did not deserve to die like this. Vikki felt tears welling up in her throat, her eyes, *my poor, sweet Lila…unlucky angel.*

After she left the chief, Vikki drove to the nightclub. Liliana's murder and subsequently Iliya and Lazar's arrest, had thrown everything into a series of cataclysmic events that had affected each person involved. The Gypsy nightclub had been closed indefinitely. The police had taken Habib in for questioning. They did the same with the dancers. The shell-shocked cast of the show scattered like shells on a beach, each in a different direction.

Now, most of them hid away, unsure about their future. They had no job, no visa to stay on in the country. They all mourned Liliana; her horrifying death had been too close to home for some girls. They questioned their own fragile way of life. Most inconsolable of all was Habib. He had remained stone faced, frozen as a mountain throughout the events. He broke down at the end, when it was time to say goodbye to Vikki. He had placed his large head on her shoulder and sobbed like a child. She could imagine the torturous thoughts going on in his mind. The crushing weight of guilt he would always feel for not being able to protect his friend. Vikki looked at him sadly, hugged him, knowing how much he had loved Liliana. There was nothing else to do.

She collected the few trinkets that remained in the dressing room. It was empty. The girls had taken their respective possessions already. All trace of them erased, as if they all had been visions, as if it all had never happened.

Vikki's eyes drifted to Liliana's dressing table. She looked at the items scattered in a hurry. The long black hair still entwined in the comb, the pair of earrings she had given Liliana for her last birthday…an antique compact mirror from their weekend trip to Oman. Vikki touched the picture frame, stared into the faces smiling back from it. They had taken this picture when they first came to Dubai and moved in together.

Two girls were hugging each other, smiling widely at the camera, one blonde, the other raven-haired. The background of the turquoise colored sea behind them. They were standing on the balcony of their flat, the same balcony where Liliana had been so brutally snatched from the world. *They had so many plans then, so many dreams, hopes.* Vikki took the picture out of the frame placed it gently in her bag. She left the other items, as they were… the earrings, the comb, the mirror, painful mementos of a past life. Then she turned off the light, shut the door, and left the vacant, sad club behind.

Chapter 49

Liliana

What no one knew is that there was another visitor to Liliana's apartment that rainy night. He had let himself in easily; minutes after Lazar had run out like a demented man. The door was unlocked, slightly ajar. He had come prepared though, and in case the door posed a problem, had all the tools necessary to get inside the apartment. The police never knew about him, because they had their man. They had the killer, after all he had confessed to the crime.

The second man had stepped in cautiously, silently, into the flat, and then closed the door. All was silent inside but outside in the stirring city, the call for prayer rang out from all sides, unnerving him. He forced himself to go on, as planned, as promised. *It had to be done*, she said…

Stealthily, he had peered into the bedroom and finding it empty continued to the living room, where he found signs of commotion. He stood there not certain of what to do. *Where was she?*

He looked in the bathroom. It was empty too...He checked the other bedroom as well with no sign of the girl. He found himself staring at the red roses on the floor, the fragile shreds of glass scattered like a carpet of ice. He felt a nudge, something like a rebellion in his chest for the first time that night. Some voice from the past that he could not recall any more telling him to be careful. Suddenly he was unsure that he wanted to go through with anything at all. Then the allure, the promise of her lips, her body, stirred in his belly a fury of passion like a roaring, thundering, living thing.

He was on the balcony; he did not remember making it there, over the glass pieces and torn flowers. He was already looking down at the dead girl. She looked sad, he thought to himself. He waited for a rush of pity, horror, anything...nothing stirred inside him. Well, his job seemed to have been done for him. Apparently, the girl had other enemies who had beat him to it. He almost laughed.

Then she moved her fingers...slowly at first, then faster. Her leg twitched, terrifying him. He jumped away from her grisly form.

*No, no, no what is this...this was not good...*He better do something fast or she will wake up and catch him here and then he will have to deal with it. He looked around frantically. The cushions on the kitchen chair. He took one and placed it over the girl's face, quickly. He did not think about what he was doing, because he had been coached...guided step-by-step through it all. He was going through with the plan despite the peculiarity of the circumstances he had found at the flat. His body tingled with the rousing promise of his payment, the prize he will collect for keeping his side of the bargain. His eyes wandered over the bloodied, twisted body as he held the pillow while the girl on the floor struggled, fighting for her life for the second time that night. All he could see was a tattoo on her shoulder, and it occurred to him what a lovely butterfly it was, but how terribly sad it looked right now.

Chapter 50

Jewel

*M*any had wondered in the past few months about the beautiful, long-suffering wife of Jassim Al Gaafari. The devoted mother, the philanthropist, trendsetter, successful businesswoman. Many titles crowned her lovely head.

Throughout the trial, she had remained silent. Dignified, as always, she appeared above those mere mortals and their theories, tucked away in her white and gold mansion from prying, but sympathetic eyes. Many felt pity for the deceived, naïve spouse of such an arrogant and belligerent man. They felt like they already knew her from the numerous profiles in newspapers and media about her life.

"The poor girl, her mother had died when she was a child." Impeccably coiffed homemakers gushed while having their weekly lunches.

"Unbelievable, what some men think they are entitled too," another shook her head while twisting her body into an impossible curve during a

Pilates class. All across the city, they talked. In coffee shops and restaurants, they gossiped. In offices and in the salons they speculated. Dubai held a collective breath, waiting, as a lover does for his beloved, for Jewel to emerge.

The news of the half-American beauty and her tragic story spread across Asia, Europe, and America. The women of the world felt her pain. They proclaimed feminist support, blaming all men, for the unfairness. Concerned aunties, cousins, and friends descended on Jewel's home demanding she cry, rage or complain. She did no such thing. Rather, she remained unwaveringly calm throughout the entire circus and then closed the doors to all, claiming that all the frenzy was affecting the children. Slowly, the public became bored with the waiting. The case was closed, the guilty parties in jail, justice served.

Faced with a tedious wait regarding this case, the media turned their attention elsewhere. Jewel's tactic had worked. Her lack of drama and refusal to feed the media frenzy with additional information had forced everyone to abandon her…finally, thankfully. She went about her business quietly, taking care of the children, following up on the boutique and waiting. She was alone. Most of her friends took affront with her constant evasions, unreturned phone calls, what they considered ill-mannered and cold behavior.

Jewel did not need them. She did not need their questions, their insincere sympathy. Two of her best friends had to leave the country, one because of a similar betrayal, the other due to a death. She missed Parisa and Jane. Yet, she was glad they were not here, because they would have insisted on answers, they would have remained hovering over her, with their occasionally cloying concern, their motherly affection suffocating her at times. Under Parisa's burning gaze, Jewel would squirm. Her friends would realize what she had done. She did not need that. It was better for her to be alone, safe in the knowledge that only she knew the complete truth about the murder of a Romanian dancer.

******

"Raj come in …it's all right, sit," she waved her arm, pointing to the soft armchair across from her. Raj remained standing, looking slightly dumbfounded. When Viola had asked him to come to madam's quarters he had refused at first, suspicious. Then at Zachariah's insistence, he gathered his wits about him and entered the previously forbidden section in the house.

It was quiet here. Scented candles burnt, sending off a familiar aroma into his nostrils, Magnolia. Raj did not look at her directly, afraid that if he did he might do something, something that he wanted to every day, every minute even when she was not with him.

After the first time he had held her hand in his, looked into her inviting, kohl-lined eyes, smelled her intoxicating breath on his face, ever since that day he had wanted more. His body mocked him nightly, and he tossed and turned, feverish, half-mad with yearning. He tried to cure himself of her. Oh, how hard he tried.

He had followed Zachariah on his visits to a certain flat, where girls offered their services. Raj vented his fury there, angry that none of them was she. That he could not have his untouchable, perfect goddess...his Madam. For months, she had tortured him this way, by the tenderness of her voice, the private, special look she cast in his direction when they were alone. No words passed between them, making it even more unbearable. At first, he could not believe she was flirting with him.

He was incredulous, ecstatic. Was this his glimpse of the much dreamt of 'other side'? Was this his ticket out? Was the poor boy from Rajasthan finally going to make it in life? Will his be a happy ending? His uncle's warning rang in his head once. He pushed it out of his mind, too young, too passionate, and too curious to care.

Over the past months as their trips to the supermarket, the tailor, the boutique became more frequent so did their silent flirtation. As she exited the car, and while he held the door for her, she would silently brush his arm with her sleeve. Occasionally, she would look directly into his eyes while he drove, then avert them, while he stared in the rearview mirror as she shifted in her seat.

One day, after they had driven along a quiet street on the outskirts of the city, something astounding happened. It was as if his fantasies had come true, except he could not trust his eyes and pinched his thigh to make sure it was real.

Slowly, carefully, Jewel had opened the buttons of her *Abaya*, one by one...the sight of her long red nails on the black silk making Raj gasp in anticipation. He tried his best to keep his eyes on the road, to keep the car straight. Mercifully, it was a quiet street...deserted. The windows were tinted a deep black for privacy. No one could see her. She knew that. Deeply buried into the soft leather seat, hidden behind the dark glass, undetectable to the outside, Jewel continued.

Unhurriedly, she had pulled the *Abaya* of her shoulders, shrugged it off. Then, while his eyes protruded out of his head in astonishment, she let the veil slide of her hair. Raj gasped; swallowed hard, almost hit the brakes. She could have been reading his mind all those months he had fantasized about her in the dark of his room.

Fear kept him driving. The sight of her hair fascinated him. Finally, his bulging eyes filled with the veiled treasure she previously had denied him. Masses of golden hair bounced, touching her bare shoulders. Gently, they brushed, caressed the flimsy camisole she wore. She glanced at him in the mirror, held his gaze. The music was on as usual…Lionel Richie and his love songs.

Except that day Raj could not get enough of the music, because she was moving to it. Subtly, she moved her body to the beat. The sight of her bare arms, shoulders and the outline of her breasts almost drove him insane. He wanted to stop the car right there, then get into the back, and take her on the seat in the middle of the day, in the middle of the road, in the middle of the city and then happily burn in hell for it.

Black shadows danced across his eyes, and he gripped the wheel, forgot to breathe. His excitement was unbearable, begging for a release.

The song ended. He focused on her again and saw that she was dressed and delicately putting on her veil again. She kept her eyes off the mirror, kept them on the passing rows of trees, the upcoming intersection, but never looked at him.

Shaken to the core of his being, the cells in his body throbbing from desire, Raj had barely made it to his room. There he burned for hours, making himself crazy, replaying the incident repeatedly in his head. The next day and the next…it continued.

The silent seduction.

He grew to expect it, curious how she would surprise him next. *Did he really think this was all there was to it?*

Later, about a month before her boutique opening night, he was driving her to the boutique. She needed to do some more work tonight, she said. He smiled, fixed his cap on his head, and drove dutifully. She was quiet on the way there, as they drove through the dark drive-up to the delivery door of the building. It appeared that no one was there tonight.

She got out and simply said, "Come with me."

His blood thundered through his veins at a million miles per second. He felt lightheaded with a weird and wonderful terror.

Was this it…was it really going to happen?

He locked the door, looking around the small, empty parking area nervously. Jassim was out of town he knew, but still he felt the fear. He walked in behind her. She led the way to the back of the hallway. There was a room there; it seemed to be a sitting room. Soft furniture, a thick carpet, large potted plants. He saw them but did not, because he was looking at her now. Silently, wordlessly, boldly, Jewel undressed. Raj froze.

Her *Abaya, Sheila*, and the long black dress she wore all piled up next to her on the floor. Only her underwear and her high heels remained. She shook her hair, allowing it to rest on her back, glistening in the sliver of moon- light that entered through the blinds. It was quite dark because she had not turned the light on, but he could see her outline. He could see enough.

She came towards him, held his hand in hers, and then ran her fingers through his hair. "I have wanted to do this for a long time," she finally said. She smiled. Raj forgot about the fear, the reckoning, and the risk. All he saw, all he wanted was Jewel, and right in that room, she let him. After the dry parched season, after the agony of wanting her touch, he finally got his reward for being patient.

After that night, it had been easy. Sometimes they played games in the car while he drove, other times they went to the boutique. One month after this perfect, trancelike happiness started, she said to him while he was undressing her, "Raj, do you love me?" Raj mumbled a reply, his hands, and his five senses too busy. "Raj...!" her shriek startled him and he stopped. "Do you love me?" she asked adamantly, again.

He did not hesitate. "Of course I love you, you are a goddess to me... don't you know already," he continued to kiss her face, her neck.

"I need you to do something for me Raj," she moved away, held her shirt against her bare chest. She looked annoyed.

"What is the matter, did I make you angry?" he looked desperate.

"No, it's not you...it's my husband," she said. The moon lit her face and the sight of it distressed him. It was the face of a stranger. Her lips were set in an angry line; her lovely eyes seemed those of another woman, a bitter, dangerous woman.

Raj felt an icy hand pass across his arm, "What happened with him?" Raj tried never to think of his employer. The thought of him put him in a jealous rage. He hated each moment Jewel had to spend with her husband.

Jewel told him. How Jassim had cheated on her all these years, boldly, even with her best friend. The way he controlled her, patronized her. How he only grudgingly agreed to her business venture after years of waiting for his consent. She told Raj, of her husband's numerous expectations of her in their marital bed, to which she had to acquiescence, even though aware of his affairs. Jewel looked into her young lover's eyes, burning him with her luminous gaze. Surprisingly, he saw determination and endless pain in those emerald green eyes.

Then, Jassim had committed the final, ultimate treachery. He had a long lasting affair with a young dancer that had reached intolerable proportions.

"I heard him tell her he would marry her, begged her to marry him," Jewel put her head on his chest, covered in black hair. She traced her long nails over them, gently. Her voice was that of a broken, unhappy woman. Raj felt his chest expand with a new feeling. He felt…defensive. He wanted to protect his goddess.

That night Jewel and Raj talked for hours. For some inexplicable reason they were not worried. They planned, schemed, promised and then they came together again in an embrace more passionate than ever before. It was as if Raj was pledging his allegiance to her, as if she was sealing her promise to him. "If you kill her, I will be yours forever."

Raj felt an uncontrolled shiver glide across his skin, like the chilly scales of a cobra he had touched once. From that night forward, she stopped going with Raj to their hide out. She avoided his eyes, his looks, even the secret rides in the car.

He cornered her one-day agitated, worried. "Why are you ignoring me?" he begged. Jewel told him they would talk, later. That afternoon she called him to her quarters. He stood in front of her like a student, grief-stricken, groveling for her attention, ready to do anything to win her favor again.

"I want you to trust that it is better this way," she said kindly, "I need to concentrate on the opening night and you need to concentrate on what we talked about." She looked uneasy for a second. Her eyes clouded with a shadow. It faltered, and then vanished.

"But I told you I would do it…didn't I?" Raj wailed.

"I know, and I believe you…but if we are together all the time you won't be able to think properly," Jewel lowered her gaze, touched the hem of her silk robe. With his eyes, he followed her long fingers, the intricate henna design twisting itself around her hands. She was right of course. He had to think, and he could not do that if all that was on his mind was his pleasure.

Opening night came sooner that he thought. It was the night he would keep his promise to his woman…to free her of her husband forever.

At the party Jewel gave him a bag with money, and some tools for opening the door. She was too busy with the show and therefore unable to give it to him in the privacy of her Bentley she explained. She said she had found the tools through an online site and had them delivered to her private post office box.

Raj found it incredibly easy to kill. *The dancer was half-dead anyway,* he reasoned. He left unobserved, and threw the unused tools and the small pillow away. Nobody would find them in the limitless hidden corners of the desert. He sent the money to his mother, so she could get his sisters married. He had done it! Finally, he was a man of ambition, a man of action.

Epilogue

The sun is rising on a new day in a magnificent city. Its majestic, cloud-reaching towers seem to ascend out of the sand like a mirage…a hallucination. It is another scorching hot, muggy day in the desert. Even the birds, the ants, and the flies of the city have gone into hiding. Come evening they will venture out, but not until then.

The sounds of young voices and peals of laughter escape from the gold and white mansion. These are the happy sounds of children getting ready for first day of school. They come out, all four of them, the boys tall and handsome like their father, the girls willowy and sweet like their mother. Jewel is beside them, pulling on her veil, getting them into the car. Raj is behind the wheel, looking handsome in his new uniform. They smile at each other. She looks at her children, fondly. She is so proud of them. She would do anything for them. They were her life, her one true love, the reason she existed, the reason she could breathe each day.

Was that not why she did what she did? She did it for the children, did she not?

What was she supposed to do... allow their father to leave them for one of his many lovers?

Cause them such immense anguish, such disappointment... for what? For a no one, a simple mountain girl with a few good dance moves. No, she could never accept that as the way to live. This was for the best. No one needed to know. Everything would go on as before.

Their father will soon be home. He will explain his one-year absence by saying that he was falsely incriminated. Jewel will back him up all the way. It will not matter what the wagging, malicious tongues of the city alleged. In front of the children, they will stand together. Once more, be the Gaafari.

As for Raj, he could never talk. He was so fiercely mixed up that no matter what he did or said he would be in enormous trouble. He had violated all the rules, all the codes of conduct. All he could do is pray that this realization comes to him later, much later. So that he does not realize how she had used him. Right now, he still thinks he got the girl. He still thinks he has a chance.

She will allow him this illusion, but for a brief time. Then when the time is right and he has outdone his purpose, she will let him go...gently. Probably send him off with a wad of dirhams and gold bangles for his mother. He will protest, but after she tells him the truth, he will leave the city gladly. He will thank heavens for escaping unscathed, unpunished. He might even feel regret about what he had done.

Jewel feels no remorse for him. She had paid a high price for his cooperation.

After all, why should she? He was just a driver.

LaVergne, TN USA
24 February 2011
217814LV00002B/63/P